The Fiery Visitation

The Fiery Awakening Series

Book 1

Mick & Kelley Jordan

Printed in the United States of America

First Printing, 2019

ISBN 978-0-9600425-1-7 - Amazon

Two Rivers Ministries Publishing
PBM 46
12400-3 Wake Union Church Road
Wake Forest, NC 27587

www.TwoRiversMinistries.com

This is a work of fiction. Names, characters, businesses, places, events, locales, and incidents are either the products of the author's imagination or used in a fictitious manner. Any resemblance to actual persons, living or dead, or actual events is purely coincidental.

Unless otherwise stated, Scripture quotations come from the ESV® Bible (The Holy Bible, English Standard Version®) copyright © 2001 by Crossway, a publishing ministry of Good News Publishers.

Dedication

Thank you, intercessors, for your tireless
courage to stand in the gap—unseen, in secret,
on your knees, where the Father sees and hears.

Thank you, Anne, for making
this book possible.

"I have come to ignite a fire on the earth,
and how I wish it were already kindled!"
(*Berean Study Bible*, Luke 12:49)

1

It Is Time

A vast column from the unquenchable inferno cut through utter darkness, rising like a massive, solar flare. Greedily fueling itself with souls, the crackling, licking flames twisted and danced with a will of their own, desiring only to profane Heaven. Caustic smoke swirled around the pillar consuming yet never destroying the flesh of the damned. These remained imprisoned in the foreboding darkness of eternal judgment and unending death.

At the heavily fortified entrance to Heaven, the fire seemed to taunt the angelic guards whose mission was to restrain the hellish blaze. Ashes carrying the blasphemies of the condemned twirled around in hundreds of tiny whirlpools, maneuvering as if to slip in unnoticed.

The flame foretold Lucifer's arrival at the Gate of Accountability. He had been called to present himself before the Father, Son and Holy Spirit. The accuser snarled and taunted the righteous guards who had once been his brothers in serving the Most High. He knew well that these faithful servants had rejected his rebellion from its inception. Even so, each time he was summoned to give account before the throne, he predictably practiced a futile scheme to turn the loyal guards' eyes away from the Creator.

Escorted by his ex-brothers, Lucifer approached the throne which he had attempted to rise above. Now, he who was once beloved of God was accursed. He bowed, lauding the truths of God even against his will as it is written, *At the name of Jesus every knee will bow, in Heaven and on earth and under the earth, and every tongue confess that Jesus Christ is Lord, to the glory of God the Father.* "In the Lord alone are righteousness and strength. Jesus the Christ is the slain and risen Lamb who takes away the sin of the world."

"From where have you come?" asked the Son.

"From going to and fro on the earth, and from walking up and down on it."

"What have you to say?"

"Have you considered Your Church? She is like the Israelites who rejected Yahweh, turning to false gods of fleshly desires. She is easily deceived, worshipping an imagined redeemer distant from Your Truth. She follows a more palatable savior, one who demands no repentance, one commanding no obedience, one who never judges and preaches a gospel void of hell." He dared laugh even before the Almighty's throne. "Are you powerless to stop me, Most Holy One? You gave man free will. Have you not noticed that your beloved creation freely chooses me?"

The accuser had ended his case against the Son's Betrothed. He bowed again, and the two guardian angels escorted him to the gate from which he had entered. Lucifer again mocked his former friends, then rode the accursed flaming tornado, disappearing into the blackness.

Outside the gates of gold, the flame burned on, coiling around itself like a gargantuan serpent, flicking its tongue in search of ways to blaspheme the Creator. Embers floated outward from the spiraling blaze, carrying the anguished cries of lost souls: "Whyyyyyy?"

The sound, emanating from the blaze, went unheard by the inhabitants of Heaven, but not unnoticed by the Holy Three—the Father, His Son Jesus, and the Holy Spirit. "Let Us go to the gate and see for Ourselves the source of this commotion."

"Lord Jesus, why are we condemned to this fearsome place?" one called out when he saw the Godhead peering into the blaze. "Have we not prophesied in Your name, cast out demons in Your name, and done many wonders in Your name? Are we not Christians who went to church and praised You? Why have you sent us to the abyss of torment?"

Their cries pierced the Savior's heart—once again—grieving the Father and Spirit equally. The Holy Three wept for those who had rejected salvation while still living on the earth, thus forever forfeiting their rightful inheritance. Jesus lowered His head, still weeping as He spoke. "If you truly were Mine, you would have believed in Me, confessing your sins, turning from them, and accepting Me as Lord of your life. You would have kept My commandments."

At these words of purest truth, uttered with such tenderness, the fire heaved back and forth, causing the little embers to appear as multitudes of people, thrashing about on the tumultuous waves of an angry sea. Anguished voices called out again: "But we trusted in our church and its leaders to teach us truth. We believed what they taught us. The fault should not rest upon us."

Jesus gazed intently into the fire for a long moment before

responding. "Did We not send you the Holy Spirit to lead you into all truth, guiding you to study the Word for yourselves? Instead, you created another jesus—not of Truth, but of man's fabrication. Each of you had access to the Word of God, leaving you without excuse. If you had read My Word from beginning to end, you would have known Me and you would not have been deceived by the evil one, Lucifer himself."

A horrifying scream erupted from the flames, sending shock waves throughout the Kingdom. "Noooo ...." begged the voices. "It's not fair! We didn't know!"

Jesus' command was firm ... and final. "I have already spoken that I never knew you. Depart from Me, you who practice sin through rebellion, doing what is right in your own eyes. You lack the covering of My worthiness and My blamelessness."

The glowing embers immediately obeyed, retreating into the whirling blaze until the day they would plead their case once again at the Great White Throne Judgment. With broken hearts, the Three returned to their honored places on the mountain of God—the Father upon His throne, the Son to His right, and the Spirit burning as the Fire of Heaven in their midst.

The Son was solemn as He addressed a vital issue. "Many leaders have deceived My Bride, the Church, with half-truths and lies. In their greed, they have exploited her with false teaching. And she is not entirely blameless. Having itching ears, she has pursued teachers to suit her own passions. She lives in the false security of a counterfeit godliness, and by her behavior, denies the power of true godliness." He paused, then leaned in to whisper, "Father, let Us awaken My Bride."

The Father's face radiated a flash of pure light, its illumination cascading throughout the entirety of His creation. The shaking eruption of Holy Fire alerted the Council of Heaven that a great intervention into mankind's heart was imminent. The host of angels set apart for this day also recognized they would soon be dispatched to engage in focused battle with their former brothers—beloved comrades who had betrayed the Holy One to pledge their allegiance to Lucifer.

The Father joyfully commanded, "It is time!"

At His decree, flashes of lightning, and rumblings and peals of thunder came from the throne. Seven mighty angels blasted their trumpets of proclamation—beautiful music of God's heart that resonated within each heavenly citizen. As the familiar call to war sounded, the Host of Heaven fell in line, eager to serve their part in the Master's plan.

The Father's words broadcast throughout Heaven. "The Final Awakening commences. My Son's Bride must be made ready for the wedding feast that is being prepared in the Great Assembly Hall.

"Lucifer and the fallen ones have worked feverishly to remove the seed of My Son's Truth as evidenced by the Bride's carnality. Few remain surrendered to Him, truly loving and revering His name. I declare My Son will find faith upon the earth as We will arouse the Bride from her stupor and chasten her willful disobedience to revive her first love."

Worshipping angels extolled the greatness of the Ruler of the Universe. Messenger and healing angels stood at the ready, awaiting their missions. As warrior angels drew their swords in unison, the multitudes of weapons sliding against their sheaths resounded, invoking intense reverence and worship throughout the Kingdom. The Host had been appointed to battle, yet again, as the Light of the World waged war to give His Betrothed one more chance to free herself from the choking grip of Lucifer's darkness.

Soon, the final Great Deception of that serpent of old, the devil, would come upon the world with multitudes succumbing to its treacherous hold. Yet in the outpouring of His lovingkindness, a gift of immeasurable mercy would be laid open to those presently held as prisoners under Lucifer's beguiling seductions. Salvation had come from the heart of God from the beginning—even at Adam and Eve's rebellion in the garden—yet in these last days, His unfathomable love would unquestionably give the Bride opportunity to make herself ready.

The Son gazed upon the Father who *is* Pure and Holy Love. "Yes, Father, My Betrothed has played the harlot in following lying shepherds, blind teachers leading the blind into the belly of hell. Her numbers will be few unless We intervene to save her from her willful waywardness."

Nodding, the Father agreed. "Let Us send the Fire of Heaven to pierce mankind with conviction, judging the thoughts and intentions of their hearts. Those We have prepared and preserved for the work of the Final Awakening will be called out, for We have not forgotten Our promises."

Then the Father placed His hands on His beloved Son's shoulders, reflecting upon one faithful servant of another era. My Son, We gave Our promise to Joseph while he was young and unprepared. Before he could fulfill his mission, by Our design, he bore the humiliation of slavery and was thrown into the King's prison—not for any violation of the laws of either God or man—but for his obedience to keep Our commandments and believe Our promises. His ankles were bound with fetters; his neck, bruised with iron. We tested Joseph's character—much was at stake. He endured until the fullness of time and the fulfillment of the dream, and, indeed, We found him faithful, shunning the entrapments of Lucifer's lies."

"Father," began the Son, "Your purposes are flawless and executed in perfect wisdom. Man cannot understand Our ways, yet every proclamation of Your throne releases Your love and majesty.

What man may see as hardship, ruin and even death presents as life in Your Kingdom. Father, I intercede on behalf of My Bride that she would understand Our Kingdom principles. O, Father, release the Fire of Heaven so she will learn to embrace Our ways."

"It is time!" declared the Father again with exuberance. "The Final Awakening begins, for Our mercy is extended to man before the time of great tribulation."

"Two believers living now upon the earth have been tested under Our watchful eye as the kindling for the Fire of Heaven," the Son interjected. "They have been prepared through brokenness and have waited for the dream as Joseph waited. The Church would not choose them, for there is nothing in their outward appearance to suggest leadership on such a scale, but they have been tested beyond their own strength and have held fast to the promises. Faith built upon the strong foundation of death to self can prepare any saint to fulfill his heavenly mission. Let Us release them from their fetters."

"Yes," said the Father. "We have collected the tears of these saints and now their tears will become a river of blessing. The long season of preparation was necessary, for little do they understand what will rest upon their shoulders. Without that painful preparation, they would not be able to endure the barrage of fiery arrows that will be aimed at them by the enemy."

Jesus stepped away from His throne to review the myriad of angels who had been prepared for this very hour. He spoke as a general to his troops, walking amongst them. "My faithful and loyal servants, do not be discouraged at the hardness of man's heart. See man through your Father's eyes of love.

"The multitudes have allied themselves with the adversary—whether knowingly or unknowingly. They are Lucifer's, held captive by rulers, authorities and powers of an evil world, blinded by darkness and unable to know Light. Their hearts are void of My Spirit."

Each angel stood as a ready soldier, zealously committing his full allegiance to the King. The Lord's Glory reflecting from the angelic faces manifested above them as brilliant rays of a rainbow.

"The Fire of Heaven will visit man's world in great measure and the Fear of the Lord will be released. Those with tender hearts will fear Me and see their true state of darkness and surrender to the Light. However, there will be many who refuse the Light as they are determined to remain in the blackness they worship.

"As much as you desire for them to know Truth, you cannot make them choose rightly; it is each one's decision. Rejoice over the ones attentive to My call. Embrace them, for these will be counted as fellow servants, worthy to live in My Kingdom forever."

The Host of Heaven shouted "O, Light of the World, Advocate of the Bride, and Great High Priest who reigns victoriously at the right hand of the Father, Your will be done on earth as it is in Heaven. We, your loyal servants, pledge to faithfully execute Your commands. Let the battle begin and let the Fire of Heaven go forth as You have spoken. Amen and amen."

When the last syllable of the last amen sounded, the Son vanished from their sight to share the good news with two others.

2

Where It All Began

Day was done—one more twenty-four-hour cycle he had managed to survive. Another box marked off on the mental calendar Gregor Wallace kept, tracking time until the day of his release. The focus of his hope had become freedom from this world. He wasn't suicidal, not even depressed. He was just tired, worn out, ready to go home. Oh, not his address on Cedar Road, where he and Jean had finally landed after years of Abrahamic wandering. But Home—to the heart of his Lord and King, Jesus Christ.

Click. The light off, he slipped in between the sheets, leaned over, kissed his wife good night, plumped his pillow and sank his head into its fluffiness. The only sound was the white noise machine and an occasional snort from Jean. The lack of distracting stimuli magnified the intensity of the war in his mind.

Lying beside his wife of nearly forty years, Gregor was wide awake. While Jean slept, memories rolled across the screen of his mind in rapid succession. That moment in prayer when, as a zealous twenty-five-year-old, he had prayed for a double portion of the Holy Spirit—much like Elisha had asked Elijah, that great prophet of old. He mulled over his prophetic vision of the Last Days, in which the Lord had revealed Gregor's part in preparing the way. Then … the long years of waiting, suffering, testing ….

He had to admit, he was the kind of guy who was either all in or all out. If he was going to follow Jesus, it had to be with all his heart, soul, mind and strength. His life had to count for something in God's kingdom. But when he'd prayed that youthful prayer, he hadn't considered the cost; didn't know there *was* a cost. All he knew for sure was that, more than anything else in life, he desired to be near the heart of God.

He hadn't known that the answer to his prayer would start him on a long and arduous journey, traveled by few. There was no briefing or pregame huddle that laid out the plan for dying to self and becoming more like Christ. No prior warning for what was coming. Only trials and tests, one after the other. Deeper into his training, the flood of difficulties became more intense, sometimes all but engulfing him. And this long wait. He had anticipated a season of preparation, but not a *lifetime*. More than thirty years into it, he was still waiting.

Gregor shifted a little in the bed, careful not to disturb Jean. Probing his conscience, he realized that he was guilty of no known sin. He harbored no hidden wrongdoing to invite the enemy's attacks, yet a steady stream of challenges plagued his life. Like Joseph of Old Testament times, and without cause, he was strategically hurled into a prison of sorts.

Gregor knew that his prison was not of this world. No jail cell nor bars. No beatings, leaving visible bruises. Nothing that could be seen with the human eye. In fact, the apparent ease of his American life made him feel guilty. Brothers and sisters in Christ throughout the world suffered horrendous atrocities far beyond his experience.

He felt uncomfortable even acknowledging his pain, but the intensity could not be ignored. His pain was real and hard to endure.

In a moment of sweet intimacy, Jesus had reassured him: *I work where each person is—both geographically and spiritually. You are here in this country and not living somewhere across the world. I AM perfecting you in perseverance and patience. And ... I AM preventing you from a future sin.*

Preventing you from a future sin. At first, this had been a perplexing statement, but he got it. Gregor had lived long enough by now to watch the fall of many mighty men and women of God, deceived by power and pride to invite entrapments outside of His will. He watched as people, who in their early love for God had taken His commandments seriously—as a matter of life and death—plummet into realms of unimaginable darkness. Continually ignoring the promptings of the Holy Spirit, these mighty leaders had fallen, taking innocent people with them.

Knowing that he was not immune to the enemy's campaigns of destruction, Gregor had prayed that he would never presume God's power could ever be manipulated by man. *Yes, Lord, do whatever it takes to prevent me from a future sin. Rid me of any desire that would destroy what you would do through me.* So, Gregor had continued to quietly submit to the sculpting of his character through the testing of his faith.

It was a radical faith. He and Jean had been asked to undertake things that seemed too difficult—or downright peculiar—for others to accept. God's requests were unsettling, to say the least. But the two of them had always feared the consequences of disobedience more than doing the thing He asked of them.

The Lord's first out-of-the-box command was to sell their house, pack up their belongings and three small kids, and drive to a destination that only He knew. Two cars with the trunks filled with a few clothes, toys, money and a guitar headed down the highway. Gregor recalled how they went from hotel to hotel, trusting God completely and filled with joy and expectancy.

The fact that they had no income and no place to live didn't matter. They had God and the assurance of His presence guiding them. Certain they were on the cusp of something amazing, they weathered this test, ready for whatever was next.

Then it happened. In the very midst of complete submission, the sweet voice they had trusted suddenly turned silent. *Lord,* Gregor groaned silently, *where did You go during that time? Did we do something to cause Your withdrawal?*

Flinching, he recalled those days in those cramped hotel rooms. Where to pray with three sleeping kids? The bathroom. Jean would sit on the edge of the tub, playing the guitar softly, while the toilet became Gregor's chair. They literally cried for direction and the comfort of His presence. Silence.

Gregor remembered the sickening grief that seized them. Had the Lover of their souls abandoned them, leaving them at the altar of their sacrifice? They felt jilted, like a broken betrothal. Everything was so terribly wrong. The joy of life fled, and now they merely went through the motions.

Man! These memories were excruciating, and rather than wake Jean, Gregor eased out of bed and sought the comfort of a tall glass of milk from the fridge. At the kitchen table, he buried his head in his hands, still revisiting the painful past.

For the sake of the children, they had attempted life in the "normal" lane—church attendance, corporate prayer, fellowship— but it all seemed so forced, so artificial. They were ruined for average Christianity. God had given the two of them a promise, and nothing less than that promise was good enough.

To make matters worse, they didn't understand God's plan, and He offered no explanation. Even though they both earnestly sought Him for answers, they were forced to settle into status quo Christianity. Having experienced the deep, only to be limited to the shallow was frustrating. They needed His life-giving breath, but that breath was not found in church—at least, not this one.

They were the anomaly that did not testify of the "abundant blessings" message preached from the pulpit. No one understood, nor did they want to understand. Church was exasperating, not for being misunderstood, but because the life of the Word of God was missing. It was easier and more enriching to just stay home, so they stopped attending. No one noticed. The family was invisible now.

Sighing deeply, Gregor rose, rinsed out his glass at the sink, and shuffled back to the bedroom, stumbling over a shoe on the way. He heard Jean cough, then moan again. *Nuts! I woke her! She doesn't need another sleepless night! He* didn't need that, either.

"Sorry, hon," he said, reaching for the light switch on the bedside table lamp. In the dim glow, her face looked pale and drawn. Through the years, he had seen it like this hundreds of times—a combination of multiple illnesses, often requiring months in bed.

"I wasn't asleep anyway." Her voice quivered.

"What is it tonight?"

"Neuropathy. Prickliness, burning, muscle cramping—the works. I pray ... but God seems a million miles away," she said through tears.

He hurried to the freezer to retrieve some ice packs, ignoring the twinge in his back. These persistent physical ailments attacking both of them, compounded by the emotional stress of their unorthodox lifestyle, had further depleted their strength ... but not their faith, although he knew Jean often questioned the process, sometimes spiraling into depression.

She propped herself up on the pillows, a bit of color returning to her cheeks. Despite the lateness of the hour, she seemed ready to talk. "Did you hear what our old friend, Jeff, said about us today at the bagel shop?"

"Umm ... no. What?"

"That we must have committed some horrible sin for God to punish us like this—always sick ... financially strapped ... moving from place to place like ... like gypsies ...." Her voice trailed off before adding in a subdued tone, "I feel like a leper. Even our closest friends have cut us off—like our troubles are somehow contagious."

Gregor nodded. He, too, had felt the hammer blows of pain, loneliness and failure as these chiseled away the flesh, forming in both of them a more accurate image of Christ. And perhaps just as importantly, in His generous mercy and lovingkindness, God's foreknowledge was helping them avoid a potential disastrous iniquity.

"I know. Character-building sometimes hurts, doesn't it? Jesus never said that following Him would be easy. In fact, He promised just the opposite." Gregor sighed, then switched off the light and crawled back into bed, pulling Jean's head onto his shoulder. "Try to get some sleep, hon. Tomorrow is another day, so let's find something fun to do, OK?"

She nestled against him, soon purring in the first stages of much-needed rest.

But once Jean was sufficiently out, the prison walls pressed in again as he lay in the dim room, staring at what seemed like endless, empty space. The anguish of the harsh prison years once again launched his flesh into conflict with the Spirit. It was a battle staying strong. Agreeing with the jeering voices of evil was not an option, yet the ugliness of the remaining self in him lusted to surrender to the enemy's barrage of taunting thoughts.

If God was with you, bad things wouldn't keep happening, so better brace yourself for the next blow. God doesn't love you as much as he loves others. It's His fault your family is suffering, so you have a right to be angry. Face it; you're just not good enough. You are an enormous disappointment to God. You're a loser. You failed your family and God. How could He ever use you?

Gregor closed his eyes, trying to block the lies. He recognized that the originator of those black judgments was goading him to succumb. Yes, there were tears along the way, but no surrender, at least not yet. Resistance took every bit of strength he could muster. He did his best to send the accusations back to darkness from whence they came.

In desperation, he prayed silently: *O Lord, I know you see my scarred soul. I am so worn out from one battle after another. Where is the promised season of rest and refreshing? You told me to live by what I know to be true and not what I feel, but the battle is so intense, I ache to feel You ....*

Fiery darts pierced his thoughts again. *Have I failed the Lord? Have I sinned against God and disqualified myself? Have I lost the spiritual inheritance promised for my children?*

He searched the years for reasons, but surrendered, knowing that the Lord would not reveal any. He clung to the truth that God is love and that God would work the afflictions for good. He reminded himself that the Lord ordered his steps while holding him up in loving hands. He was exhausted, yes, but resolute to stay the course.

Tears welled up in his closed eyes and dripped onto the pillow. He lovingly touched his wife's hand and pleaded, yet again, for God to heal her broken spirit and body.

Remove this dark heaviness from our souls. How long, O Lord, until You show Yourself strong on our behalf? When will we see the promise ....

Slowly, Gregor's mind drifted from prayer to the quiet refuge of sleep. Sleep, when it came, was the only escape from the pain in his body as well as in the most secret places of his soul. Sleep was the one state of mind where sorrow retreated for a few hours.

This night played out year after year. But tonight would be different.

3

Meet With Me

Gregor, arise.

At this unexpected sound in the middle of the night, Gregor was jolted awake. Was he hearing things ... or was he only dreaming that a voice was whispering his name?

It had been quite a while since the call to awaken for prayer had come. In the early years of zealous love, intimately connecting with God came easily, and distinguishing His voice seemed effortless. But time, the long season of trials, and Heaven's stone silence had banished Gregor and Jean to an existence of blind faith.

The flame might have flickered, but it was far from dead. In the early years before the refining process, there had been late-night gatherings in the living room with others who yearned for a close relationship with Jesus. Worship, praise and prayer flowed freely. The small group of Jesus-seekers grew stronger in their relationship with Him and more confident in hearing Him speak through the precious presence of the Holy Spirit.

Their living room became Heaven's classroom. The Holy Spirit taught the principles of the Kingdom of Heaven's authority over the kingdom of Lucifer's world and the constant spiritual battle between the two realms. Bondages holding Gregor and Jean from moving deeper into God's Kingdom were broken. They learned how to fight Lucifer through prayer and deliverance from darkness's influence.

Fully awake now, Gregor recalled the evening when a young man came to the prayer group at the invitation of another member. Gregor and Jean had reluctantly welcomed a glassy-eyed, greasy-haired twenty-something with the lingering smell of marijuana on his ratty clothing. His name was Kyle.

It was obvious that Kyle was a recreational drug user and did not know Jesus, but as he continued to come to their gathering, week after week, they learned that he had been sexually abused as a child and had been involved in the occult—a tough case, for sure. Gregor and Jean were not hopeful, but God had a plan giving them a foretaste of what was to come.

He had set the others free from various bondages, so it was only natural that they should pray the same for Kyle. Every week that passed, he seemed less tied to his old world. He wanted what Jesus had to offer and, over a three-month period, God delivered him from the desire for drugs and the effects of his sordid past.

Kyle's ravenous hunger for the written Word and the Person of the Word drove him to pray and study the Scriptures while careful to listen to the Holy Spirit for interpretation. He dreamed dreams and saw visions. His understanding of the Word surpassed educated seminarians, and when he shared with the group what God revealed to him, they eagerly listened to his life-giving insights. The smelly, mindless drug user was now teaching the prayer group!

The boy's dramatic transformation right before their eyes, together with prophetic words and songs that had begun to come forth in their meetings, seemed to portend the promise of the Final Awakening of souls. New hope rose as the Holy Spirit equipped the group to counter Lucifer's attacks as the battle heated up.

Gregor, arise. Come pray, called the voice again.

Many times before, Gregor's heart had quickened at the possibility that he was hearing the Lord speak, but it was only his desperate desire that Jesus' presence had returned. *I'm tired,* he argued with himself. *I've been through this drill many times before, getting out of bed for nothing. It's likely not God anyway.* Dejectedly, he pulled up the covers and rolled over, shutting out the voice.

Come meet with Me. This time the tone was insistent, brooking no delay.

A twinge of hope pulled on his heart. He replayed the message in his mind over and over. Only four little words—*Come. Meet. With. Me.* But they rang with power and authority, like the command of a high-ranking military officer who expects instant obedience. W*hat if it is God and I refuse His invitation?*

Just as Gregor quit debating with himself, he felt a Presence that had been absent for a very long time. It was a warm radiating Presence, deserving of all reverence, saturating him with love, forgiveness, and son-ship. The heavenly sensation grew stronger—so strong he expected to see the Lord standing at his bedside at any moment. But when he opened his eyes, there was only the shadowy outline of a window.

At last, the magnetic force of the Presence compelled him to leave the warmth of his bed. He pushed aside the covers and swung his legs around until his feet touched the floor.

No need to turn on a light. He had walked this dark hallway many times before when sleep escaped him. Even memorized the steps to take to avoid the squeaky spots in the wood floor—a technique he had developed so as not to wake Jean. Left side, five steps; cross over to right side, three steps; stay in the middle until you reach the carpeted living room.

Gregor never fully understood why the nighttime prayer had been instituted. Maybe a dimly lit room prevented his attention from wandering to the things that needed to be fixed around the house—broken plaster where a picture used to hang or a crayon mural that needed to be painted over. Maybe the tranquility while others were asleep made it easier to still his mind and listen to God's voice. Regardless, he coveted these late-night meetings with his Lord. But years ago, without warning and without a given reason, the familiar routine suddenly stopped.

When he got to the living room it was cold and dark. Doubt rushed in, and he felt stupid for believing that God had really called him out of bed to meet with Him. *Here we go again.* He slumped onto the couch and sighed.

Had it been his imagination all along? Yet the Presence and the light were real. Maybe God was just letting Gregor know He was still around. Maybe it was just a morale-booster before the hammer fell again.

Just as he was about to go back to bed, Gregor heard, *Get down on your knees and pray as you did in your younger years.* The voice seemed gentler somehow, sympathetic to his struggle.

He hesitated to obey. He couldn't remember the last time he'd prayed in that position. Too painful. He knew if he went to his knees, his previous surgeries would remind him in the morning.

Trust Me, said the voice, anticipating Gregor's protest before he could speak it aloud.

Gingerly, Gregor knelt between the couch and the coffee table. As he bowed his head in reverence, the atmosphere in the room changed. Once again, he felt bathed in the warmth of love, forgiveness and adoption. A brilliant light radiated from the center of the room.

For so long, he had feared that his fiery passion to run after God had cooled, that a part of him had died. In fact, it felt that his earlier intimacy with God belonged to someone else—maybe someone he had read about—but certainly not to him. At the start of his journey to love Jesus with all his heart, the Lord had given him the vision of a returning to God wholeheartedly before the time of tribulation. In the vision, Gregor experienced His holiness. He knew this radiating light to be the holiness of God.

At first, the purity of the light was so terrifying, Gregor felt he might die. It didn't matter that he had experienced this holiness once before. Now, as the remaining strength in his body left him, he fell to the floor, paralyzed.

A hand touched his right shoulder. In that instant, power charged his body like a current of electricity. Gregor wept as God's love filled him and the Holy Spirit swept through him like a strong wind, giving his hollow frame substance. This was not his imagination; this was very real. Had he survived the long season of preparation? Was this the promised commissioning that was spoken to him thirty years ago?

The powerful, yet sweet voice of Jesus spoke once more, His words creating strength where before there was none. *Gregor, arise. You have claimed your citizenship in heaven, and now I will show you things of the heavenly places. I have called many, but some willfully rejected the sifting. Others succumbed to the seduction of the evil one's schemes.*

I placed My chosen messengers of Heaven's Awakening in a prison of My own design, testing and refining them through the baptism of fire just as I prepared Joseph long ago where, in prison, self was sifted and slain. Death to self is a gruesome thing. I take no pleasure in it, but I do take pleasure in the fruit it bears. You have borne much fruit. The long, difficult road was a necessary preparation to accomplish My Father's will through you. Awaken souls to My love before the evil one is released to fully rule over the earth in fulfillment of the prophecies.

Gregor was still on his knees, bending low, when Jesus reached down and placed His hand on Gregor's head. One touch filled his body with youthful energy. A fiery intensity coursed through his inner being, and a strange feeling came over him. It was the absence of pain in both body and soul! Thoughts of being too old and broken to serve the Lord vanished. He was hungry, eager to listen and learn at his Master's feet.

Gregor was still facing the floor when he opened his eyes. There he saw Jesus' feet beneath a glowing white robe. The Savior's skin shone like the reflection of mirror-like, burnished bronze. Gregor dared to look upward. A golden sash girded Jesus' waist and above that, His hair of the purest white, rippling to His shoulders. But His eyes ... those fiery eyes!

No words passed between them. Yet with a single glance, Jesus commanded Gregor to look at Him. In that moment, His eyes communicated every attribute of God. In turn, Jesus searched Gregor's eyes, reading his heart. Knowing that nothing was hidden from his Lord, Gregor dropped his head, ashamed to have Jesus look upon his past failures and brokenness.

With one hand, Jesus gently tilted Gregor's chin to meet his gaze. As their eyes locked, a revelation of Jesus' heart overwhelmed Gregor. He felt His Savior's pain as an infinite number of heart cries rose from the earth. He experienced Jesus' grief as billions of tears fell to the ground, each tear collected and individually experienced in His own heart. The pain was so intense, so unbearable, Gregor's body crumpled as if melting in anguish. Jesus reached out with a strong arm, steadying him as Gregor looked away.

For the first time, he understood that in all the years of pain, Jesus had felt each pulsating beat and had wept with him. If there had been any other way, Jesus would have chosen it. The pain was necessary. Great Love had allowed the pain and suffering to do its deep work in Gregor's heart.

He dared not ask Jesus why He had allowed the afflictions in his life and that of his entire family. Yet, the fleeting glimpse into the joy of sharing in Jesus' sufferings was the beginning of understanding, something previously incomprehensible. Suffering had brought Gregor's heart into the same bloodline of Christ as if the life blood of the guiltless, slain Lamb pumped through his veins!

He realized, at last, that he had never been alone or forgotten. Jesus was present in every step of the journey, bearing the pain *with* him. No, there was no price too great; if anything, Gregor hadn't paid enough.

There was a master plan at work, and now he was about to see the fruit of his devotion to the One he loved the most.

4

Vision Of The Cities

Suddenly, Gregor was vaulted out of time and space and into the spiritual realm where past, present and future merged. Mere words were powerless to express the scene that met his eyes. A rush of events, moving beyond the constraints of time, unfolded in sequence before him.

He watched the worship of the Heavenly Host, gaining in volume and strength as a thundering voice spoke all things, seen and unseen, into existence. The sounds of singing and shouts of joy resonated as the Builder set the cornerstone of the universe. It was good, very good.

Gregor felt the love of the Godhead as They scooped up the dust of the earth and formed man into Their own image. One eternal breath, and he experienced the same exhilarating warmth of life that filled Adam's lungs. The intimate, inescapable love of God for the first man also breathed new life into Gregor.

With dreadful bewilderment, he observed as the highest of created beings cast off perfect beauty and wisdom. Believing that he could be equal to or perhaps greater than God, this magnificent creature discarded his role as the most powerful cherub who led all of Heaven in worship. Never before had pride or lies entered this exalted realm; sin was birthed in his heart to raise its ugly head on earth forever. Not only that, but this same angel robed himself with such dazzling seduction that he persuaded a third of the Heavenly Host to serve under him in his defiant kingdom.

The measure of this grievous sin could not be tolerated nor forgiven. Neither mercy nor restoration would be extended. Thunder spoke. The rebellious cherub and a third of his rebel brothers were cast out of Heaven forever.

At their expulsion, no trace of God's Glory remained on their countenance. Instead, the fallen angels—now to be known as Lucifer and his minions—reflected ultimate ugliness and unrighteousness. Unrecognizable in their new state of hideous evil, every foul thing, every perverted act and every wicked thought darted from their eyes. Hatred spewed from their mouths, corrupting the atmosphere with a powerful stench. Revenge filled their beings. Profound loathing for the Creator fueled their mission to destroy all that was holy and loved by God.

Jesus directed Gregor to look beyond the horizon. He leaned in, squinting in order to see more clearly. The scene before him—what he soon realized to be the final battle of all time—was powerful, rattling his insides and shaking him to the very core of his being. Led by the archangel Michael, the Heavenly Host, whose numbers seemed infinite, waged war with the powers, principalities and kingdoms of darkness.

Propelled into the midst of the battle, flashes of light popped all around Gregor from different directions—one here, another there, some near, some distant.

A great opening unfolded in the sky, revealing One on a white horse. His name is Faithful and True, The Word of God, Jesus.

He wore a white robe dipped in His own Blood. An army dressed in white linen accompanied Him, so many in number, they looked like voluminous clouds. Out of The Word of God came a sharp sword, slaying all His enemies.

Oddly, beautiful praises and worship rang out as the army declared the truth of their Commander. The battle gleamed with such brilliance and color that Gregor was spellbound. As the Heavenly Host and the Saints warred against the evil one, he heard an inexpressible loveliness of sound and witnessed what was almost tangible love. He marveled at the contradiction that holy war against evil could actually be strikingly beautiful.

Jesus sensed Gregor's confusion and explained, *Love for Me opens the door for worship to flow. As worship flows, power and strength are released. The greater the love for Me, the greater the power grows. In true worship, the Heavenly Host and the Saints gain sufficient strength to overtake the enemy.*

Jesus redirected Gregor's gaze away from the horizon. *What do you see in the valley to your left?*

Turning, Gregor saw that the expansive valley was covered in a canopy made of a dark gooey substance, oozing and undulating with evil creatures. The mass hovered over a city, blocking all light. Long tentacles extended down into the city, feeling its way to its next target. The putrid stench of decay mixed with sulfur burned Gregor's lungs. He covered his face, choking as he gasped for air.

Jesus instructed him to look again.

The sticky goo tormented the people's minds and singed their souls, compelling them to engage in all sorts of evil thoughts and actions. Every citizen of the city was affected by the goo as they were infused with all imaginable and unimaginable forms of wickedness—violence, sexual immorality, witchcraft, hatred, rage, greedy self-gratification, addictions, envy, strife, confusion, and every deception of the evil one.

Thick goo covered the people's eyes and ears making them blind and deaf to Truth. Securing themselves with long claws, the evil creature's bit off chunks of flesh, preventing life from filling the hollow human forms. People hunched over under the weight of the parasites as they sucked the life out of their host. Continually reaching into the great canopy of darkness, the vile beings grabbed more of their kind, adding to the lost souls' burdens.

Some people carried the creatures willingly and sought after more, reveling in the goo, playing in it like children. Others were covered in the sticky substance because of some evil perpetrated against them. Hurts and abuses opened doors for it to enter the deepest parts of youthful souls.

Unaware of their own blindness and deafness to Truth, the victims succumbed to lies, gradually conforming to the very essence of evil. Those who searched for freedom trudged through the city, looking in the wrong places for the only One capable of opening their eyes and ears and removing the mire. The place was void of anything good. No hint of God's presence could be found.

Gregor felt ill and thought he would vomit, not only from the stench, but from grief. He wanted to shout a warning blast to break through the blackness, wanted to pick off the blinding and deafening glop so the people could see their true state. *Open your eyes! Open your ears! Don't listen to the lies!*

He lunged forward, but Jesus restrained him. *Hard hearts prefer darkness over light, Gregor. They love the praises of men and seek the worship of self; thus, they are given over to a spirit of deception. Putting self above God is the same lure that drew Lucifer away. Yet, I am longsuffering, desiring that not one should perish, that all should come to repentance.*

Each person has a choice to make—whether he will put self to death daily and follow Me, or search out fleshly pleasure of darkness. When the seed of self dies, it causes the seed of My Spirit to yield a rich harvest. Unless one gives his life away to Me, My Spirit will not rise up in him with power.

"Lord, how then can any be saved?" Gregor asked, feeling a sudden sorrow.

I will send messengers to snatch souls from the mire, but because darkness tries to extinguish light, the messengers will be killed as if for sport. When faithful children are martyred, lovers of evil will congratulate one another, believing they have rightfully removed narrow-minded people who prevent their wicked agenda. Despite this, some will believe.

Gregor's heart sank at the news that those sent would die in their effort to save even those who sought to kill them. But he sensed that, while Jesus also bore that burden, He could see beyond the circumstance of the moment, knowing that nothing in the earthly life really mattered other than belonging to Him and doing His will.

Vile and perverse spirits will rule because the Restrainer will not be present in the evil cities. Man justifies his wicked flesh and his defilement of that which is pure, deceiving himself that he can escape the judgment of his wrongdoing. In his rebellion against what is holy, he doesn't realize that he has already judged himself.

Chaos and unspeakable evil will rule the cities devoted to darkness, because continued sin summons even more vile spirits. My sheep, those who love Me and have given their lives to Me, will dwell safely in cities of My life. The goats, those who have rejected My gift of salvation, will dwell in cities of darkness.

Look again into the valley.

Gregor saw multitudes of people emerging from caves where they had been hidden away in safety. Where the Light of Heaven shone, the cave dwellers now stood, bathed in the brightness of Truth.

Those in the caves are the many faithful believers whom I have preserved and prepared as laborers for the Final Awakening, Jesus explained. *These laborers willingly entered the furnace of affliction so that their hearts could be made pure and able to carry a great measure of the Fire of Heaven.*

I want you to explain to the laborers that I did not leave Elijah alone, and I have not left them alone. Confusion and grief would steal the promises given to them many years ago, but through you, I will woo them back. To the victorious, I will reveal the hidden manna of My Word.

At Jesus' last words, Gregor saw that they were now high above a city, connected to Heaven with the pure light of Truth. The light was like a highway of holiness and repentance.

What do you see?

The landscape was indescribably gorgeous. Everything grew to perfection with a particular pleasantness that filled Gregor's soul with joy and peace. Unlike the stench of the city of darkness, the city of light emitted a distinctive fragrance, which could only be described as abundant life in the love and goodness of God. Gregor breathed in deeply this time.

Aware of Lucifer's tactics and empowered by the Holy Spirit to effectively battle such invasions, the people in the city of light lived in true freedom in the Fear of the Lord. They communed with God in the Spirit of Truth and worship without interference from dark powers of hell. They served one another in the pure love of their Savior.

The people lived with an attitude of reverence and repentance, aspiring not only to know the Word but to live the Word without compromise. Unlike the city of darkness where people heaped up sin upon sin, the citizens of the city of light immediately obeyed the promptings of the Holy Spirit, laying down every disobedient thought or act before the Lord. God was ever faithful to exchange the sin for His righteousness and forgiveness as manifested by the pure brightness of their garments.

Many will be spared the long process you have endured. Instead, they will be transformed by abiding in My presence, Jesus assured Gregor.

In an instant the two were overlooking the entire earth. From their vantage point, the earth resembled a giant ball, hanging in the darkness of space, yet seemingly, close enough to touch.

What do you see?

"I see the earth with two kinds of cities scattered about," Gregor replied. "Some, illuminated by a flaming light, and some, covered in complete darkness."

Jesus nodded. *Yes. I will gather people from all nations. The cities of light are like silos where the farmer temporarily stores his harvest until he takes it to market. In the silo cities, believers will grow in godly character and love for Me, preparing them for the persecution to come. When darkness demands their worship, they will refuse at the cost of their lives.*

Gregor's heart lurched at the thought of believers dying as martyrs, possibly tortured for their faith.

Do not fear for them, Gregor. I will bestow great honor on those who refuse to bend a knee to Lucifer. They, as well as you, will count it a privilege to die for My name's sake. When blood flows from the bodies of the martyrs, a new song is released from Heaven, and the great cloud of witnesses worships with overwhelming joy.

Any man, woman or child who surrenders his life to Me, whether or not he dies a martyr's death, stands as an eternal testimony of My truth, ripping power from Lucifer. I AM the Way, the Truth and the Life. The deceiver hates the truth that through death in Me comes life.

Go now with the Fire of Heaven and gather laborers.

With that, Jesus withdrew into the light, and the living room grew dark once again. The light may have left the room, but it burned—white-hot—in Gregor's heart. He sat for a time, trying to grasp the enormity of what had just transpired.

Before going back to bed, he went to the darkened bathroom. On his way out, he happened to glance over at the mirror and was startled to see a strange reflection.

"What's that?" he said under his breath. He leaned in, brow furrowed, thrusting his face closer to the mirror. Two small circles of white fire stared back at him. He jerked his head around to see where the weird glowing image was coming from. Nothing behind him.

Again, he leaned forward, and, like a slap against the back of his head, he knew. He was looking at *his own image!* The white glow was radiating from his eyes!

The Fire of Heaven burning inside Gregor had produced a revolutionary transformation, erasing the pain and loneliness of prison. The glory of the Kingdom now shone in a visible display, confirming to him that the Final Awakening was at hand ... and that he, indeed, would play a significant role.

5

Crisis Call

Jean sat down at the kitchen table and began her morning ritual—counting out her pills for the day: two blue and green capsules, three white capsules, one yellow gel cap, two pink tablets, six of these, two of those .... This pill addressed that problem, but caused unpleasant side effects, requiring another pill to counteract it. Those little daily pill containers from the drugstore were too small. She needed a bucket! What kind of existence was this?

Hmmm ... and what was Gregor up to? He had been in the bathroom when she got up and he'd been ... *singing*, of all things! Hadn't heard that sound in ages. As far as she was concerned, there wasn't anything worth singing about. Her whole life had been one round after another of sickness and pain. Wasted. She did what she could when she felt well enough, but the physical trials limited her.

"Goood morning!" Gregor called cheerily as he entered the kitchen with an unusual spring in his step. He poured himself a cup of coffee and one for her.

She shot him a skeptical glance. He was already dressed—and at this hour of the day! "What's so good about it?"

He set their cups on the table and leaned over for her inspection. "Notice anything?"

Jean gasped and dropped the bottle of pills she was holding. "Your eyes!" Gregor steadied her as she peered into his face. "They're white ... like white fire! What happened to you?"

For the next hour, Gregor filled her in on his surreal experience of the night before. "Hon, God has great things ahead and we need to be ready."

She listened, feeling a slight surge of hope. But what about all those times they had gotten their hopes up for nothing? Still, Gregor did seem ... different.

He paused, his countenance growing a bit more somber. "The battle between darkness and light can only heat up as the end nears. So, for believers, there will be a price to pay." He recalled the Lord's prophetic word to him, then decided against sharing the whole story with Jean at the moment. His slight frown gave way to a wide grin. "Whatever it is, it will be worth it."

She took a deep breath and picked up her empty cup, ready for a refill. "Maybe after thirty years of waiting, it's finally time to taste the first morsel of the promises." She sighed, daring to believe that God might still have a divine plan for her life, too.

* * *

In a hospital room at St. Vincent, Dan and Barb Taylor waited at the bedside of their only son, Jason. The victim of a head-on collision three days earlier, he had been crushed in the wreckage and was now brain dead and on life support. Today, the Taylors had to make a decision—one that no parent should ever have to make.

Barb sat in a chair near the bed, holding Jason's hand and talking softly as if he could hear her. She opened a drawer of the bedside table, took out the Gideon Bible and read Jason's favorite stories as she had when he was a little boy.

Nearby, standing at the window overlooking the hospital parking lot, Dan was growing increasingly agitated. He never had understood Barb. How she could act so calm when their only child was dying was beyond him!

Dan's gut was twisted with confusion and spasms of pain. Only dimly aware of the beeping monitors and the rhythmic clicks and heaves of the ventilator that was keeping his son's body alive, all he could hear was the doctor's voice on a never-ending loop, Y*our son has no brain activity and cannot exist without life support.*

Dan wanted to switch places with Jason, not for noble reasons, but out of pure selfishness. Death had to be better than this hell. No more fishing, golfing, renovating, talking or laughing, ever. His beloved son was a living corpse. His brain refused to command his body to function. But ... removing life support was so permanent, so final. Yet facts were facts. And Jason was, for all intents and purposes, dead.

Turning from the window, Dan's gaze met Barb's, and he nodded. It was time to sign the papers to pull the plug. Today was the day to say goodbye forever.

The doctors assured the Taylors their son would pass quickly once life support was removed. Few survived more than a few minutes. *Small comfort,* thought Dan.

Hours after the plug was pulled, however, Jason lay in limbo between life and death. Parts of him were alive and other parts were not. The doctors were surprised he had not passed away immediately, but still offered no hope for survival.

Barb joined Dan at the hospital window where he had stationed himself throughout the ordeal. The night had morphed into morning, and it looked like he was watching the sun rise. Barb knew differently.

She knew Dan was reliving life with their only child, much like watching a movie.

She grabbed his arm and lovingly squeezed it close to her body. They stood quietly for a while longer. "Call the man," she said softly.

He turned, looked at her and made a face. "Nah, it's too crazy," he countered. "It was just a dream—a stupid dream! Didn't mean anything.

"Please, we have nothing to lose. It's Jason—our son. Please, Dan," pleaded Barb.

"How can I call him? I don't even know who he is."

"You have a name and you saw a face. Search the Internet. Look on social media."

Dan drew in a deep breath, raised his eyebrows and let it out slowly. "OK, guess it wouldn't hurt to try," he conceded.

They both entered the man's name into their phones and began the search. Finding this stranger seemed statistically impossible. A name and a face with no phone number, no address, not even a target country. "Hmph!" Dan grunted. "There's a greater possibility of winning the lottery!"

Choosing not to respond, Barb prayed a silent prayer, *Lord, help us find the man in the dream.* Every so often, she turned her phone to show him a picture, only to hear a *nope-that's-not-him* grumble from Dan.

After scouring the Internet for only thirty minutes, Dan blurted out in disbelief, "No way! No freaking way!"

Barb looked up. "Let me see, let me see."

He pointed to the information that had shown up on his phone. "That's the man! That's the guy in the dream!" Dan plopped down in the chair near Jason's bed.

Studying the picture, Barb thought, *So that's the man ....* From the address, she saw that he lived nearby!

"Ok, I need some air," Dan puffed. "This is weirding me out."

Telling the charge nurse where they would be—in case there was any change in Jason's condition—they headed out of the hospital, stopping at a vending machine to get a couple of Cokes. Pssssss. Dan popped his can open and took a big gulp. They headed toward Barb's car parked in the hospital lot.

Dan leaned against the door and rubbed his eyes. "Let me call a guy at work. He'll get the phone number for me."

Moments later, Dan had what he needed.

"Just give him a quick call," urged Barb.

Dan had made many difficult phone calls in his lifetime, but this one topped them all. He entered the number into his cell phone and waited. Part of him desperately hoped the man would answer, while another part of him desperately hoped the man would not.

* * *

Jean had listened intently while Gregor recalled the Visitation. Careful to omit no detail, he'd given a play-by-play account so she could experience it, too. She had walked every step of their long journey, suffering the effects of the prison along with him. He was not about to leave her behind now that hope was dawning on the horizon.

Just then, Gregor's cell phone rang. It was an unfamiliar number. "Hello?"

"May I speak to Gregor Wallace?" From the slight quaver in the voice, the caller was obviously nervous.

"Yes? What's this about?"

"My name is Dan Taylor. You don't know me … and I know this is going to sound crazy, so please don't hang up." There was a long pause … "Umm … yeah, uh …"

Gregor sensed this might have something to do with last night. "Try me, I'm a little crazy myself right now."

"OK, I'll get right to it. I saw you in a dream. Jesus told me that you and your wife would pray for my son. He was involved in a terrible auto accident three days ago. He's brain dead." Dan's voice broke on a sob. "He ... Jason ... is our only child."

Another pause ... "He's off life support and the doctors told us Jason should have died by now ... but he's still alive ... barely. I know this must sound like I'm some kind of nut job. Heck, I'm not even a Christian! I don't really believe in visions and dreams and all that stuff. All I know is what I saw and heard. My wife insisted I call you. I searched social media, recognized your picture and got your info."

"Of course, we'll pray, but I can't guarantee ...." Gregor caught himself speaking like the old Gregor. Things were different now. "Where is your son?"

"He's at St. Vincent Hospital."

Time became nonexistent. There was no past, present, or future. Only brokenness and heartache. A bolt of lightning and an immediate booming thunder jolted Dan back to reality. Instantaneously, heavy drops pelted him. He and Barb jumped into the car to escape the downpour.

"Dan, hello, are you still there?"

"Uh, yeah, yeah, I'm still here."

"We can meet you at St. Vincent in forty-five minutes. Since you know what I look like, you'll have to introduce yourself."

"Ok then, see you in forty-five," Dan replied, thinking. *This is too weird to be true!*

Gregor ended the call and turned to Jean, a puzzled expression on his face. "You are not going to believe this. Some guy named Dan, who says he isn't even a Christian, said Jesus came to him in a dream last night. He saw us praying for his son in the hospital and healing him. Anyway, we're supposed to meet him and his wife at St. Vincent Hospital in forty-five minutes."

Jean jumped up from the table. "Give me a few minutes to brush my teeth and throw on some clothes. You drive. I'll put my makeup on in the car. I'll be honest. I'm fighting all the past failures we've ever had. When was the last time someone was actually healed when we prayed for them? Sometimes they got worse ...." Jean's voice trailed off as she ran down the hall to the bedroom. Gregor heard a muffled shout, "Oh, Jesus, give us faith!"

By the time she reached the bedroom, she realized that her back wasn't hurting! Her joints no longer ached! The tingling and pain in her feet and hands were gone! Her soul felt whole and intimately connected to God. She ran back to the kitchen, grabbed Gregor, and spun him around.

Seeing her, he cupped her face in his hands and looked closely. "Jean! Your eyes! They're glowing! White fire!"

They held each other, Jean burying her head in his shoulder, sobbing with relief and joy. For moments, they stood locked in an embrace, trying to absorb all that was taking place. The desolation of the past thirty years was swept away in a moment.

Gregor and Jean left the house and hurried to the hospital, a little anxious about what lay ahead, yet eager to see what God had up His sleeve. On their way into the lobby, Gregor whispered to Jean, "Oh, I forgot to tell you, the boy is brain dead."

Jean rolled her eyes, giving him a sharp nudge with her elbow. "Thanks a lot," she murmured. "I needed that right now."

Inside, Gregor spotted a handsome couple, scanning faces as visitors entered the hospital lobby. The man appeared to be in his fifties. He was fit, tall, good-looking with wavy, dark hair and a hint of gray at the temples. He reminded Gregor of Cary Grant or Gregory Peck—polished, handsome and confident. He was dressed in jeans, a plaid, untucked collared shirt with the sleeves rolled up to his elbows and brown leather sneakers. His eyes were a little puffy— from crying? But this was a hospital, after all. That could be anybody.

Clinging to the man's arm was an attractive woman, her auburn hair cut to a sassy chin length with bangs swooping over the left side of her face. She was wearing sunglasses and could have been mistaken for a movie star. She, too, was dressed casually in jeans, collared shirt, scarf, and boots. On her, the look was classy. Even from across the room, Gregor and Jean could not help noticing the sizeable diamond ring on her finger as she pushed her bangs out of her eyes.

"Hey, maybe that's your guy and his wife," whispered Jean, nodding in their direction.

"Not sure. I'll send a text and they can find us." *In the lobby by the big potted tree,* he messaged.

In seconds, he noticed that the man they had observed was checking his cell phone and looking up to scope out the potted palm. He then grabbed the woman's hand and headed toward Gregor and Jean. Where was that absolute confidence he had had during the Visitation?

"I'm Dan and this is my wife, Barb," he said, stretching out his hand to shake Gregor's.

After introductions were made, Dan apologized. "I'm sorry for making you rush over here, but I'm afraid it's too late. Jason was officially pronounced dead just a few minutes ago. They've already moved his body." Tears rolled down the tanned face. Praying wouldn't matter now; Jason was dead.

Dan had given up, but Barb was resolute, determined to follow through on Dan's dream. She struggled to shut out the sound of the nurse's voice telling her that her son was dead and that they needed to make arrangements for a funeral home to pick up his body as soon as possible. Instead, she listened intently for the voice of the Holy Spirit. *Believe.*

Dan looked down at the floor, his voice choked. "Jason's body is in the morgue." He looked up again, questioning. "What happened? I was almost ready to believe that Jesus was going to heal him." He shook his head, running his fingers through his hair. "This is all very confusing. In the dream, you prayed, but I don't know what happened after that. Maybe if I had called you sooner .... " He covered his face with his hands. Maybe it was *his* fault that Jason was lying on a cold, metal table in a refrigerated cubby of the hospital basement.

All four stood in silence, feeling his grief.

Barb lifted her sunglasses and rested them on top of her head. "Well, *I'm* not quitting on my son—not ever. I know Jesus raised people from the dead before, and I believe Jesus can raise Jason now."

Again, they waited. Gregor felt that they were on the edge of a towering cliff. Should they play it safe ... or should they jump?

He broke the long pause. "Dan, nothing is impossible with the Lord. Jesus sent us here for a reason. We have nothing to lose, right?"

"Do *you* believe Jesus can raise Jason from the dead?" Jean asked Dan softly, hardly believing these words were coming out of her mouth.

Dan didn't answer right away. Then he nodded uncertainly. The word was barely audible .... "Yes."

6

Resurrection

Barb broke Dan's blank stare with an unexpectedly passionate declaration. "I believe Jesus can do *anything,* even raise the dead. Jason gave his life to Jesus, and if my son's time with us is over, I will release him. But I don't believe it is his time. I can't explain it, but something deep within my spirit is telling me to believe."

No one said a word as the two couples worked their way down to the morgue. Taking the initiative, Dan opened the door to the office, where a receptionist was seated behind a desk. He'd made it a practice to notice name tags and call people by their first names; it was a helpful tool in his profession. The habit kicked in—even on this dreadful day.

Scanning the ID badge pinned to the jacket of the morgue attendant, Dan read the name and approached the desk. "Susie, we're here to see my son's body. Taylor, Jason."

She consulted a ledger, made a note, then led the way to an inner area with refrigerated cubbies. The cavernous room was stark and cold. Footsteps echoed against the hard-tiled floors and walls. A rotten, sweet smell mixed with the odor of cleaning chemicals nearly gagged Jean. Rows of stainless-steel doors, stacked three high, lined a wall where the bodies of the deceased awaited autopsy or identification. The attendant drew out the slab, making a nerve-grating sound of metal against metal. Jason's body was completely covered with a white sheet.

Hesitantly, Barb pulled back the sheet. Tears rained down her cheeks as she took in her only child's mangled form—now all shades of gray, black, blue and yellow. One look told her that this boy she had loved for so long was no longer there. His cheeks were as cold as death.

Gregor stood on one side of the slab and Jean on the other. They looked at each other, communicating wordlessly. *What are we doing?* Gregor nodded slightly, indicating that they should begin. Taking a deep breath, they both laid their hands on Jason's lifeless body.

"Lord Jesus," Gregor prayed, "You are the Author of life. Today, let Your name be glorified. Holy Spirit, we ask that You come and fill Jason's body with the breath of life from Heaven. Defeat death so the world will know there is only one true God." He paused, silently seeking the power that could only come from the One who had risen from the grave two thousand years before. He took in a breath, then declared, his voice rising in volume and intensity. "In Jesus' name, I command Jason to come forth from death to life."

Susie, the morgue attendant, had seen this before. Crazy religious nuts trying to bring back a loved one from the dead. *It never works and it won't work this time,* she thought. She rolled her eyes, let out a huff of disgust and began to clean up some things on a table in the corner.

Almost immediately, the clammy coldness of the morgue began to moderate. Indescribable peace flowed into the room, brushing against their skin gently at first, then circling them like a warm breeze, growing stronger and stronger. It was belief—the intimate agreement of the Holy Spirit, with their own hearts. Their tears of sorrow dried, the cutting blow of Jason's death swept away. All four intently examined his bruised and distorted face for signs of life.

Susie swiveled her head around to see what was going on over there. The atmosphere of the morgue had never felt like this after a prayer to raise the dead.

Jean leaned in for a better look. Abruptly, Jason's eyes opened wide. She jumped back with an adrenaline rush. Could it really be true—an answer to their fervent prayer for a kid they didn't even know?

As they watched, his skin morphed from the pallor of death to a peachy flesh color. He gasped, sucking in air, and coughed a couple times. He seemed confused for a few seconds, then shifted his body a bit and pushed himself up, moving as if to stretch sore muscles. Loud popping sounds filled the room as Jason's broken bones snapped into place.

When Susie collapsed in a heap on the floor, Jean rushed over to make sure she was all right and helped her to a chair.

Dan was trembling violently, his knees, weak. He, too, hurried to a chair before he was the next man down. Barb squealed, leaned over, and grabbed Jason by the neck, hugging him tightly.

With his face buried in Barb's shoulder, Jason's muffled voice broke the tension. "Mom, let go of me! I can't breathe!"

Barb released her hold immediately, backing away, but still gazing at him as if to assure herself that her son was truly back with them. "Oh, honey, I'm just so happy to see you like this ... instead ...."

Jason turned to Gregor who hadn't moved since his "dead" body had opened his eyes. Gregor gaped in total astonishment.

"I know who you are," said Jason as he focused on Gregor. "I saw you in Heaven talking with Jesus. He told me that you would come here and pray for me."

Turning to address his dad, Jason saw that Dan's fingers were wrapped around the arms of the chair so forcefully, his knuckles were white, matching his face.

"Dad, when I was in Heaven, I saw you leading many influential people to Jesus. Big plans for you," Jason stated matter-of-factly, unfazed by his own resurrection.

Dan was still too much in shock to speak. He slowly lifted himself from the chair and walked a few steps to the table where Jason still sat, covered only in a white sheet from the waist down. He reached for Jason's hand ... and Jason responded, stretching out his own hand. When their fingers touched, an electrical shock instantly coursed through Dan's body, throwing him back into the chair.

"What just happened?" Barb wanted to know.

"Ow! Holy ...!" Dan caught himself. Barb didn't like it when he swore. He shook his hands and arms while walking around as he tried to shake off the tingling sensation. "I was nearly electrocuted!" he exclaimed.

Curious, Jason looked at his hands, flipping them from palm side to back side. *What the heck was that?* "Hey, all I know is I felt a power shoot out of my body."

"What do you mean?" Barb questioned as she, too, reached for Jason's hand. She had barely touched his finger before she was jolted the same as Dan. Electricity shot up through her finger, hitting her crazy bone, causing her to jerk back. "Ow! What's going on?"

It's happening! It's really happening! Gregor's lower jaw slowly met his upper jaw, curving into a broad grin. "A gift of God's power is pouring through Jason's body," he explained to the group huddled around the young man. Susie, sitting across the room, still looked dazed.

"You were in Heaven, really in Heaven with Jesus! What did He say to you? What was it like?" asked Barb, wanting to hear every detail.

Jason swung his legs around and dangled them over the edge of the table, adjusting the sheet to stay covered. "Hmmm ... well, I'll try since it's gonna be hard to describe the colors, sounds and smells of Heaven—almost impossible, I'd say. I just know I had no pain, discomfort, worry or fear. Jesus told me that my purpose had not been fulfilled. I had to go back with the Fire of Heaven in me to be a witness of His love to my generation." He paused, cleared his throat, and added, "Pretty tall order ...."

Barb wanted to fire questions at Jason, but forced herself to be quiet so he could continue.

"Jesus pointed to a man sitting under a huge tree by a river; it was the Tree of Life, and it was you, Gregor, sitting under that tree. He said he had to show you what was about to happen, because you are one of several appointed leaders of the Final Awakening. Jesus left, then an angel named Storis took over."

Dan could hardly take in Jason's words. He was overwhelmed with the fact that his son was alive now, talking to him about Jesus, angels and Heaven, of all things! Dumbstruck with the idea that it was all real.

"Before I knew it, I was looking at the Fire of the Spirit of God. It was pure and glowed white-hot, like molten steel, with the aura of a rainbow around it," he grasped for the words, "like light shining through an emerald. The Fire swirled around and in and out of itself. I was afraid. I was sure if I touched it, I would be a dead man. All I could do was fall on my face.

"Then Storis touched me, stood me on my feet and told me to walk into the Fire. Well, believe me, I was almost paralyzed. I was so afraid I couldn't take a step. Storis gave me a reassuring look, nudged me, and said, 'It is our Lord's will.' So, I took a step forward, and the towering Fire just sucked me right into its center. It circled all around me, went right through me. It swirled inside of me like I was hollow. It felt like every ungodly thing in me was burned up. I know it's hard to believe, but it was like God and I were ... one. In the midst of that Fire, I was sinless. Awesome ... amazing ... indescribable ...."

Jason's excitement wouldn't allow him to sit any longer. He grabbed the sheet, secured it around his waist and hopped off the table. He dramatically moved his arms, mimicking the Fire's height and shape, trying to demonstrate what it was like.

"Then Storis joined me in the midst of the Fire and said, 'The Fire of Heaven is the seven Spirits of God that burn continually before the throne day and night—the Spirit of the Lord, Fear of the Lord, Wisdom, Knowledge, Understanding, Counsel, Might. You are able to stand in the midst of the Fire, because you are sealed to Him in the Book of Life through the Blood of the Lamb. The Fear of the Lord is the beginning of wisdom, and knowledge of the Holy One is understanding. God's people do not understand worshiping in Spirit and Truth in the Fear of the Lord.' Huh, can't believe I remembered all that," Jason marveled.

"Storis and I were still standing in the middle of the Fire when he said, 'The Spirit of the Lord was released at Pentecost when the Church was birthed. The Awakening will be marked by the Fear of the Lord which will convict the world that they have rejected the Father's Christ. They will know there is no other name in Heaven, on earth or below the earth that can save man, but the name of Jesus. Every knee will bow when the Spirit of the Fear of the Lord is present in their midst. Even so, some will still reject.'"

By this time, Jean had pulled out a small notebook and pencil from her purse to make some notes of Jason's encounter. She didn't want to forget any important detail.

"Then Jesus came into the Fire with us after He had talked to Gregor. He said, 'When the man under the tree lays hands on you, you will go back to your earthly body. I have appointed you to free the captives of this generation from the oppressor. All authority has been granted you in My name as the Holy Spirit leads you. You will not be perfect as you are now, standing in the midst of the Fire of Heaven. All I ask is that you be faithful and do as the Spirit asks. It is time you return.'

"I told him I didn't want to go back." Jason looked over at Barb. "Sorry Mom, I love you, but nothing here compares to Heaven. That's when I heard Gregor's voice calling me back to my body. I opened my eyes ... and here I am."

With that, Jason suddenly realized that underneath his hospital "toga," he was naked, with a tag dangling from his left big toe.

7

Media Frenzy

Early the next morning, before Jean was out of bed, her phone rang.

"Jean, this is Barb Taylor. Reporters and photographers are camped in my front yard. There's already an article online with pictures of Jason's X-rays and death certificate. It includes quotes from anonymous hospital staff. What should we do?" Barb was monitoring the activity outside from behind a living room drapery she had pulled to one side.

"Please don't identify me or Gregor in any way," Jean urged. "We're not trying to create a following for ourselves. Just tell the truth: Jesus healed Jason."

"Understood … but this is going to be a big story because of Dan's position on the Hill. Apparently, news of Jason's accident was broadcast almost as soon as it happened. That morning in the morgue … well, we knew it would eventually get out. The morgue attendant could have called a TV station, or it's possible a reporter has a contact on the hospital staff. Whatever the source, it's a madhouse in my yard. If it weren't for the police barricading the front door, I think reporters would stampede and break it down!"

Jean was silent as she took in this new information. "What do you mean by 'Dan's position on the Hill'?"

"He's been in the news so often lately, I assumed you knew when we met at the hospital. He's Chair of the Senate Intelligence Committee."

Jean was stunned. "Dan is *that* Dan—Senator Dan Taylor?"

She felt stupid for not knowing. She and Gregor had stopped following the news lately; it was just too discouraging. How could both of them have missed what now seemed such an obvious fact?

Realizing the seriousness of this latest turn of events, the two believing women prayed together over the phone, asking for God's guidance. Shortly, they felt the Holy Spirit instructing the Taylors to speak the truth boldly. Not to worry about what to say; the Spirit would give them the words at the proper time.

"Jean, I'm nervous. Is there any way we could meet soon, like *tonight?*" Barb felt that if she—a believer for years—was floundering, her husband—a newbie Christian—must be drowning. And what exactly was Jason supposed to do with the Fire of Heaven?

"Yeah, anytime is fine. As far as I know, we have no plans." While she spoke with Barb, Jean had turned on the TV and was watching the craziness outside the Taylors' home. "What about the media following you? Won't that be a problem?"

"Hmmm … yes, of course. I'll text when we're done addressing the press."

"Great! I'll look for it." Jean said. *Wait till I tell Gregor who Dan is!* she thought. *There's a much bigger plan here for the Taylors than just getting their son back.*

* * *

When Barb's 911 call to Jean ended, she gathered three Bibles and set them on a small table near the back door leading to the garage. Then she joined Jason and Dan who stood peering out at the commotion. Jason thought it a bit comical. Dan knew Jason's resurrection altered everything, especially his own purpose in D.C.

Barb reported the details of the phone call, including their prayer, then added, "Remember, when you talk with the reporters, don't think of what you're to say. The Holy Spirit will speak for you."

The mood was somber as the three held hands and prayed. Nothing would ever be the same. At that moment, the Spirit's presence came again as a slight breeze, warm and reassuring, but within seconds, they could hardly stay upright as a mighty, swirling wind toppled lamps and lofted some papers on a coffee table into the air.

Despite the grim scenario, Jason grinned. "Gotta warn you. This is just a hint of what's coming. Once you open that door and talk about somebody being raised from the dead, all the winds of hell will come against us. But on the bright side, we have the winds of Heaven at our backs to resist the evil. Don't worry. God's got this!"

Barb and Dan gazed at their son in awe. Was this the same Jason they had brought up as a little boy? Suddenly he seemed light years older than twenty-seven ... and wiser.

The winds subsided, the curtains settled back in place and the papers floated to the floor. Fresh strength and power filled them, they were ready to introduce the world to the Kingdom of God. The great gathering of souls was launched.

Dan opened the front door and they stepped outside into the bright sunlight.

This wasn't the first time the Taylors had spoken to large media groups. Barb's diplomacy had complemented Dan's no-nonsense legal smarts more than once in his political career. Crews turned to focus their cameras on the family as reporters pressed in tightly.

"I want to thank you all for coming here today and trashing our lawn and our neighbor's lawn." Barb's casual comment was calculated to ease the tension.

The reporters chuckled, but regardless of the joke, it was true. It wasn't unusual for media to destroy flowers, fences, bushes and entire lawns when ferreting out a big story. And this one—the resurrection story—was *big* and had hit hard and fast. There were at least fifteen news crews, some with their big trucks and elevated satellite hook-ups pointing to the sky.

All the driveways near the Taylor house were blocked, and no crew was about to move now that the Taylor family had appeared. Curious neighbors looked on at a distance—from behind the safety of a window—or ventured out on front porches or lawns. One was bold enough to walk over and join the herd of reporters.

Dan took another step forward—Senator Dan Taylor, North Carolina, Republican, Chairman of the U.S. Senate Select Committee on Intelligence, whose son had just been resurrected from the dead. He had a momentary twinge of doubt. What mayhem the press would likely create out of this unusual event. As a senator with high-level security clearance and respected leadership, he was comfortable speaking about matters critical to national security: cyber threats, terror threats, economic and energy threats, globally organized crime threats, space weapons, biotechnology, artificial intelligence. Speaking about the supernatural workings of God, however, was completely out of his wheelhouse. But with little time for second thoughts, he called upon his newfound faith in Jesus, simply praying one word: *Help!*

The sight that met his eyes was a full-blown circus, complete with the media clown parade. In the midst of the chaos, a sense of peace and boldness of purpose surprised him. Yet, this was probably the single most significant mission he had ever undertaken—to deliver what might be a final warning to the leadership in Congress, in addition to the executive and judicial branches. Washington was not going to embrace God's message. No question about it. In fact, just forty-eight hours ago, he himself might have been one to oppose God's directive.

He figured his detractors would not sit still for this, but Dan didn't care. He knew the hard message had to be given, and he was willing to risk his political future. For now, he just had to report about Jason and then trust God for anything more.

After one last surveillance of the bedlam around him, he was ready to speak: "Of course, you already know my son, Jason, suffered severe, life-threatening injuries in a car collision. A distracted driver hit Jason's car head on, crushing him in the wreckage. At the hospital, he was declared brain dead and put on life support. We were told that there was no hope for survival, and life support would only delay the inevitable. After removing life support, he was officially declared dead around 8:00 a.m. yesterday. A death certificate was issued, and his body was taken to the hospital morgue. The doctors told us that Jason should have died at the scene of the accident. It is, therefore, incontestably a divine miracle that he is alive and stands before you today."

As Jason moved into view, there were a few gasps as some of even the hard-bitten reporters reacted in a spontaneous response.

"No medical intervention saved my son. Jesus and Jesus alone revived him. There is no other explanation. I was there when we prayed over his lifeless, mangled body. I heard his fractured bones snap back into perfect alignment. I was there when death fled and life rushed in, filling his lungs with the breath of Heaven. Anyone who knows me will tell you that I am not a religious man, but that's all changed. I've seen the power of God work in front of my own eyes, and I cannot deny Jesus ...."

He paused and cleared his throat. "To those who have lost all hope, I say hope again. To those who do not believe in Jesus, I say believe. If you serve Jesus, you are a citizen of Heaven, but if you reject the Savior, you serve Lucifer and are conscripted into hell. I tell you: The Kingdom of God has come in power; therefore, choose wisely."

With that last statement, the crowd went ballistic, angrily shouting defamatory remarks. "Lunatic!" "Liar!" "Religious nut!" "You're insane, unfit for office, a threat to national security!" The message to the nation burned in Dan. He was determined to finish what the Holy Spirit directed him to say, continuing with warnings for the nation. The words flowed effortlessly as the Spirit spoke. Dan felt God's pleasure in his obedience as he stood in truth against the angry mob.

At that, Jason moved past his dad. Immediately, the throngs of reporters rushed in, falling over each other to push their microphones in front of his face. Police pushed back, giving the Taylors some room. Dan put his arm around Barb, and they stood close behind Jason.

Reporters swarmed him, shouting questions, speaking over one another: "Jason, were you really dead?" "What did you experience when you died?"

He studied the ground for a few seconds, composing his thoughts. After a deep sigh, he lifted his head and began to speak. "You ask me if I was dead."

As soon as the first words left his mouth, the Fire of Heaven shot out, penetrating people and electronics. News crew gear popped with a sudden burst of power. All the noisy reporters were stilled, their voices silenced.

Carrie Summers, a WNN News correspondent, hurriedly scanned the scene to make sense of what was happening. Unbelievable! Camera's shooting sparks with the smell of melting components.

Loud cracking sounds and flashes of light jutting from satellite feeds. Was it a lightning strike?

Carrie felt her knees buckle as strength left her body. Before she could speak a word, she was on the ground, along with everyone else. Her brain said, "Move!" But her body wouldn't cooperate. Still cognizant, she could hear other reporters grunting as they made attempts to get up, but with no success. Voices remained silent except for an occasional groan. The media mob seemed glued to the ground.

Jason turned quickly to make sure his mom and dad were all right. Barb smiled as if to say, *We're fine. Just say what you're supposed to say.* Dan gave a fatherly nod of agreement. "Go ahead, son."

As reporters and their crews lay prostrate on the ground, Jason continued to talk. "Yes, I was dead. I was in Heaven with Jesus, but He sent me back with a message for you: Lucifer, the dark leader of all evil, commands fallen angels warring against mankind. Going forward from this day, you will see Lucifer's kingdom of evil increase in power while at the same time, the Kingdom of God will also increase in power. Sitting on the fence is not an option. When we die—and death will come for all of us, sooner or later—Heaven or hell is the destination we face. Whose kingdom will you choose? What you decide in this life—right now, maybe today—will determine where you will spend all of eternity. You may never get a second chance."

So many thoughts raced through Carrie's mind as she lay there in the Taylors' front yard. *What's really happening? Is Dan Taylor, respected senator, a newly converted religious fanatic? Why? Was the resurrection legit?*

Carrie knew a little about Jesus from Vacation Bible School as a child; every summer her neighbor had invited her to the week-long church-sponsored event. She had listened to the stories and memorized Bible verses for one reason only—to get the snacks, play the games and do the crafts. It never progressed beyond that. She certainly did not consider herself a follower of Jesus or even remotely religious.

Carrie was young, but her tenacious resolve in getting to the bottom of a story moved her to a top position at WNN. As lead reporter covering the Senate, she knew the integrity of Dan Taylor's work. *This will kill his career, but why would the senator create such a dramatic hoax?* Her investigative nature insisted on searching out the truth until she found it. *I want an exclusive interview with Jason Taylor.*

After Jason's last statement, the Taylor family turned to go inside. Barb paused to slip porch pillows under the two police officers' heads, still lying on the concrete front porch. Taking advantage of this pause in the activity, the three retreated to the family room in the back of their house.

Jason was still a little wobbly from the power surging through his body. "Whoa! What was that?" He slumped onto the couch.

"Well, son, that might be our new normal," his mom replied.

"When you talked to Jean earlier, did you set a time to get together?" Jason asked as he experimented with a lamp, turning it on and off with the lingering power in his hands. He felt an immediate reprimand from the Holy Spirit. *My power is not a toy, and I will not tolerate man's manipulation of it.* At that, Jason immediately sat up straight and dropped his hands into his lap.

Dan looked over at Barb. "And what about the media herd? If we drive away, they'll follow."

"I have a plan," said Barb with her characteristic confidence and a twinkle in her eye.

8

The Rescuer

"Quickly!" Barb urged. Dan and Jason followed her to the back door. "Our only hope of getting away unseen is to leave while everyone outside is still on the ground. Grab a Bible on the table and follow me."

"Where're we sneaking off to?" Jason wanted to know.

Dan wasn't surprised that Barb had planned an escape ahead of time. He had always been drawn to her resourcefulness. Her quiet faith and strength had seen them through more than one dark valley.

The three slipped through the back gate and skulked through the neighbors' yards, hoping not to be noticed. A couple of blocks away, they jumped into an older mini-van, parked at a corner—Barb in the passenger's seat, Dan and Jason in the back.

"Hey, it's Gregor!" said Jason, noting the driver of the van.

Gregor, new at skulking, had had the foresight to smear some mud on the license plate to obscure the numbers. Maybe that would make it more difficult to identify them. Every car that drove behind them for more than two blocks felt like a threat. One had followed for nearly two miles. At their destination, Gregor purposefully passed by his house, testing the potentially adversarial vehicle. It drove on.

Circling back around to his street, he was relieved to find no other vehicles in sight. He drove up the driveway and into the garage. The minute they were inside, Jean met them and hit the button to lower the door before the passengers could be seen exiting the car.

"Do you think anyone noticed that you left your house?" Jean asked Barb.

"I don't think so. I left the TV news on and some lights on timers so it would look like we're home. Reporters were still stuck when we left, but who knows how long that will last."

The inviting aroma of homemade cinnamon rolls and breakfast casserole filled the house. "Hungry?" Jean asked, pouring coffee into mugs while Gregor filled some glasses with ice cold orange juice, served on the kitchen island. The mid-morning brunch was a welcome diversion from the harrowing events of the past few hours.

"I could use a little vodka in my drink," Dan whispered to Jason.

They filled their plates and carried them, along with their drinks, to cozy spots in the den.

Once they were settled, Jason asked Gregor, "What's really going on? Can you explain any of this? It's all so bizarre."

Gregor leaned forward to answer the question. "We live in extraordinary times as the final chapter of man comes to a close. You momentarily experienced the Holy Spirit's power—without measure. But Jesus is just as passionate about rescuing all those heading into the depths of hell.

"At the end of the age, all those without Jesus' seal will be cast into the lake of fire. In a vision of hell, I once saw multitudes of people walking in an orderly procession on a smooth, wide road. Thousands, recently deceased, flowed into the back of the continuous line, funneling them to pass between two massive pillars. They had no clue what waited for them on the other side. Some were laughing and joking about being dead; others were crying and wanting to return to their families."

Dan felt an adrenaline rush and his heart rate increase like he had just missed the worst accident of his life by nanometers. A mere twenty-six hours ago, he would have been among those marching toward hell's gate.

"Next, I was taken to a high point above the front of the line." The finality of the people's horrible fate made Gregor's voice crack as he continued, "Angels escorted people to the gates of hell. Once past the pillars, the level of torment correlated to the level of their own evil acts while alive. Their sins on earth were heaped upon them and relived over and over forever. Many cursed the name of Jesus, while others begged for mercy, but no mercy was granted. No second chance to choose differently was offered. Jesus showed them He had personally chased after them. He revealed how they had continually rejected His gift of knowing Him. Indescribable anguish filled their entire being at the realization that they had rejected God's truth, actually condemning *themselves* to hell forever with no hope of escape."

At that, Dan was visibly shaken. His head was down, covered by one hand, and his body quivered. Barb reached over to put her hand on his.

Gregor cleared his throat again, "Nothing can change for those already in hell, but if you're still breathing on this earth, you have a chance to escape that horrific sentence. The end of the age is here, and billions of souls are at stake. Jesus is moving mightily to make the message known, but He won't force people to believe. Each person has to choose for himself."

He sat back in his chair and stared out into space for the next few seconds, recalling how he had felt when he looked into Jesus' eyes, brimming with tears as He wept for the lost. Gregor teared up again at the precious memory. "Listen, Jason, I don't know why He chose you or why He chose me, but He did. Put that question out of your mind forever. His ways and thoughts are way above our ability to comprehend.

"Understand that when He gives you His Spirit without measure, the Fire of Heaven's power burns in you, through you and to the people God wants to touch. Always be mindful you do not direct this power, only Jesus does. When this happens, the world will oppose you, but no power of darkness can stand against His will. His Kingdom is coming and His will, will be done. Trust me."

"Uh ... yeah ... I learned that lesson this afternoon," Jason interjected. "The Fire is not a toy, and God *definitely* doesn't want His children playing with it."

"Absolutely," Gregor responded. "The powers of darkness are seeking to destroy you. If Lucifer can't stop you, he will try to push you to the left or right of God's appointed plan, causing you to crash and burn ... whoops ... sorry, Jason, no pun intended. If that doesn't work to get you off target, the evil one will lead you far beyond. This is particularly sneaky of Lucifer because pushing past the goal gives you the illusion of doing the right thing."

Jason responded, "You mean like hyper-grace?"

"Exactly!" Gregor sat up straight. "Grace has been stretched past its original design. The hyper-grace lie is eternally catastrophic. Followers of this doctrine ignore the mandate to abide in Christ by following His commandments as He clearly said we must if we love Him. They think that since we are under the covenant of grace and not the Mosaic Law, it lowers the standard. You've seen it—the attitude that Christians are forgiven anyway, so adherence to what they see as inflexible rules is irrelevant. Wrong. The new covenant of grace actually *raises* the standards. For example, the Law says, 'Thou shalt not murder,' but Jesus said that even if you're angry with a brother, you are subject to judgment. The Law says, 'Thou shalt not commit adultery,' but Jesus said if you look lustfully at a woman, you have already committed adultery. The Law was to discipline the body, but the new covenant takes it deeper to discipline the mind and heart."

Gregor paused, setting his plate on the coffee table before continuing. "Lucifer did a great job of selling people on the idea that we have the freedom to sin at will without any consequences because Jesus forgives everything. But that's just not true. The Word says that if believers live in deliberate sin, no sacrifice for sin remains, only fearful expectation of judgment. Lucifer twists just enough truth around grace to give folks a false sense of security. Yes, Jesus forgives our sins, but the Bible is clear that godly sorrow and repentance must precede forgiveness and only those who do the Father's will enter Heaven."

"Yeah … some guys I know are always trying to convince me that it doesn't matter if they sleep with their girlfriends, watch porn, talk trash about other people, and pilfer things from work—stuff like that," Jason interjected. "They claim their actions aren't hurting anyone, so they justify sin saying it's all covered under grace anyway."

"Understand, every sin we commit has consequences," Gregor commented. "Ignoring the prompts of the Holy Spirit to repent makes you hard-hearted. You quit listening and fall deeper into more sin."

When Gregor paused to take a sip of coffee, Jean jumped in. "Years ago, I had a dream. I saw a road with a canopy of fire over it—like an arch stretching from one side to the other. If I stayed in the center of the road, the fire couldn't hurt me, but if I moved closer to the shoulder of the road, I could feel the heat. The evil one is the fire over the road, always luring us to come closer to the flames. You obviously get burned with blatant, easily distinguishable sins like murder, theft and adultery. But just as easily, if more subtly, you can definitely be scorched with sins like presumption, pride and selfishness.

"We need to check our thoughts and actions against His Word daily, even hourly, if necessary, especially now with His Spirit released in greater measure. King David in the Bible was scorched and scarred when he went after Lucifer's dangling carrot, Bathsheba. He let lies take hold in his heart, causing lust and self-importance to quench his passion to obey."

She stood to gather some plates but then sat again, adding, "The more God has given you, the greater the accountability. There is no room for prideful blunders. This is serious business. Leaders especially will want this power. Don't assume. Always ask. The Fear of the Lord will keep us from deception. Remember, obedience to God is not a burden; it is a gift of protection."

There was absolute silence as everyone processed all that had been said. The calming, holy breeze moved through the room, making its way around each soul. In the quietness, Gregor was flooded with the Lord's presence as he had been during the Visitation. One second he was sitting in his recliner; the next, he was standing before Jesus and Storis in Heaven.

Jesus spoke softly, placing one hand on Gregor's shoulder. "Gregor, I am assigning Storis to help you execute My plans by providing protection for a short time. Impart the Fire to Daniel and Barbara."

Gregor didn't know if he was traveling to Heaven in the body or out of the body. He was here, then there, then back here. He breathed deeply. His directive was to impart the Fire of Heaven to those appointed by Jesus. Today, Dan and Barb were the appointees.

9

News Flash

The next morning, Jean woke up feeling more energetic than she had in years. Her hair, however, hadn't benefited from the healing, the familiar one-sided morning Mohawk having defied even the power of Heaven! Anxious to see the media's take on what was happening, she ate her bowl of cereal in front of the TV.

"This is a WNN News Update," stated the anchor as the program graphics scrolled across the screen. "Welcome to *D.C. Today*. I'm Shane Sanders. Let's go right to Carrie Summers, who broke this bizarre story yesterday. Carrie, what can you tell us about Senator Dan Taylor and his son, Jason?"

"Gregor, come in here!" Jean hollered. "The Taylors are on the news!"

Gregor hurried to the living room and sat next to Jean, their attention riveted on the screen.

"Shane, two days ago, reports of Jason Taylor, son of Senator Dan Taylor of North Carolina, being raised from the dead came from sources at St. Vincent Hospital," replied the attractive reporter. "As word of Jason's resurrection spread, news agencies flocked to the

Taylors' Bethesda home, filling the street with multiple media outlets including television, Internet, radio and print.

"The scene was chaotic—nothing unusual for a breaking news story, of course. However, as Jason Taylor began to speak, unexplained events occurred, surprising everyone. Due to an undetermined electrical interference, some camera footage was lost, but all audio was salvaged. To add yet another twist to this story, Senator Taylor concluded his statement about his son's medical condition by giving an incredible fire-and-brimstone warning to America. We go to a clip of the scene …."

Images played across the television screen showing clamoring reporters stretching microphones to catch any word from the subjects in question, satellite trucks lining the street, curious neighbors craning their necks, and police controlling the crowd. Suddenly, the video focused on the porch where the Taylors were standing. The senator's speech sounded innocuous enough to the casual listener. But those paying attention heard the sitting senator recall the absurd story of his son's resurrection.

To top it off, Senator Taylor, in a tone reminiscent of Moses standing before Pharaoh, warned the nation of God's coming judgment. Between questions, reporters shouted insults and slanderous remarks as they pushed against police, vying for a better position: "Senator, what psychotic medications are you on?" "Does insanity run in your family?" Then, in a slightly soberer approach, someone asked, "Why would a loving God bring judgment?"

Here the video broke off. Carrie's mind went blank as she recalled how she felt that day—confused, conflicted, and strangely convicted. She was terrified to admit she'd experienced something other-worldly. She didn't want to be looked upon as a weirdo as the country would surely view the senator.

Fighting to maintain her composure, she stalled. "I would like to finish the entire audio portion of the segment before returning to the senator's … uh … unusual proclamation. When Senator Taylor finished, his son, Jason, spoke. After the electrical storm, we could hear Jason, but we were unable to move or speak. It was very unsettling … even mystical …." *Oops! Why did that word come out of my mouth?* she wondered as a wave of nausea rolled across her stomach.

Carrie was known for the integrity of her reporting, so when she suggested what happened might be something supernatural, Shane was curious. "Wait, are you telling me it was some kind of spiritual phenomenon?"

Oh, crap! With so many other things to comment on, why did Shane have to zoom in on that one word, mystical?

Even in the most heated of interviews, Carrie was rarely nervous, but this time, she feared her anxiety was beginning to show. "Taking into consideration the religious content, yes, it seems possible," she observed with reluctance. "Lightning strikes have been ruled out. There were no earthquakes or magnetic disturbances. The military stated there were no training exercises or tests of military apparatus of any kind near D.C. If it was not a natural phenomenon, then what's left but the supernatural? I have no other way to explain it."

"I'd like to hear more about that," Shane insisted, "but right now I want you to recap the last part of the senator's message."

Carrie's eyes teared up a little and her upper lip quivered as she prepared to speak. She cleared her throat, giving herself a stern internal lecture: *Buck up, Carrie! This is no time to break down!* "As you heard, the senator warned America of judgments from Heaven." Her heart pounded uncomfortably. *Keep your head in the game and just report the facts, girl.*

Referring to her notes, she reported the highlights of Dan's message: "Senator Taylor said he was like the biblical prophet Jonah, warning Nineveh to repent and spare themselves judgment, and urged America to do the same. He begged the people of this nation to open their hearts to God's message of grace and love."

Shane interrupted, announcing a commercial break as he looked into the camera, "Fascinating story, Carrie. We'll return with more after this." Once off camera, he laughed. "Taylor has lost his mind!" In a mocking gesture, he spun one index finger near his temple just before the director signaled the end of the insurance company commercial.

On camera again, Carrie didn't let Shane throw her off balance and continued with Dan's second point. "Senator Taylor stated that America is realizing the fruit of tolerating and embracing depraved behavior. Violent crime is set to explode, with an unimaginable rise in random killings. Terror activities with high levels of death and destruction will cause panic, leaving America susceptible to even more savage attacks."

Faint snickering from the director and crew was annoying. They hadn't lain face down in the grass for hours as she had. No, there was something much deeper going on here than a lunatic's rantings. What she had experienced was real, making her all the more determined to get the whole story.

Despite the rude distraction, she continued with her report. "The senator's message also stated that corruption will rule the business and banking communities like never before in the history of the country. Our economy will collapse shortly unless we, and I quote, 'repent from our sinfulness in rejecting Jesus and His commandments.' End quote. The occult, drugs and perversion will overtake our children, eventually collapsing communities. In contrast, places where biblical principles are lived out will be spared these judgments. He concluded by saying that God has given America a choice, so we should choose wisely." *Whew! Glad that segment's over!*

"Wow, Carrie! *Lucifer, hell, eternal torment!* Don't quite know how to follow that. Thank you for that in-depth report." Shane turned his gaze directly to the camera with a profoundly doubtful expression on his face. "Is Senator Taylor suffering from a mental disorder? Is the senator unfit for office? Is there any truth in the resurrection claim? If not, why would the Taylor family concoct such an elaborate hoax? Coming up next, a focused panel discussion about these topics with Dr. Ellen Morton, Ph.D., Divinity Professor at Frederick University, along with Pastor Heath Windsor from the Unitarian Fellowship Church in Washington, D.C."

Gregor turned off the TV and called Dan. "Did you see the WNN report on TV this morning?"

"Yes, and I'm already getting calls from my fellow senators. This has opened Pandora's Box, which probably means political suicide for me. According to some, I am literally insane and have kissed my political career goodbye. Racine Joyner, senator from crazy town, is already gathering support for expulsion proceedings. I might do the same if one of my colleagues stood on his front porch proclaiming imminent disaster sent by God. On the other hand, a few encouraged me to start a prayer movement on the Hill."

"So, what're you gonna do?" asked Gregor.

"Follow the Lord, even if it costs me my name, career and income. Media hasn't stopped hounding my office, even my personal cell number. I used to be glad when they wanted my attention—good for the polls, you know. Not so much now. I've already seen headlines like *Senator's Son's Resurrection Hoax, Jesus Freak Taylor, Senator's Gone Mad* and *Dan in the Frying Pan*. I think my political career *is* cooked unless God has a job for me here in D.C. There's already a cartoon on the Internet of me in a strait jacket, running around like Chicken Little." Dan laughed. "This is going to be a rough ride."

"Let me know what Jean and I can do," Gregor offered. "I know God will empower more people to stand in key positions. You won't be alone in this."

"Washington, D.C. is lean on God's righteousness; that's for sure," Dan observed. "Never was more aware than now. There are a few men and women of God in Congress. I've always admired their integrity and courage to stand for Christ, even though I wasn't a believer myself. But it will take an act of God to get the Hill to change its ways. Unfortunately, the god of most politicians is their own best interest."

* * *

One spirit of darkness was painfully aware of the Visitation. He was assigned to watch the pathetic creature, Gregor, and had expected this divine encounter for some time since the trials had been endured for years. No, the dark spirit was not looking forward to reporting to his leader that the Glory of the Lord had descended upon the man's house.

That night at the Wallaces' home, the radiance of the Holy One had shone as it does in the throne room, pushing him and all his cohorts far away. There were always other means of collecting detailed intelligence than direct observation. He was fully aware that he could only know what the Almighty allowed him to know. This time, though, a bit of noteworthy information *was* granted.

The resurrection of a man was certainly evidence enough to make a report to his leader. Others of these mortals had also noted the miraculous and busied themselves spreading the news of the Holy One's wonders, albeit not with truthful understanding. And then there was that warning to America. Something was brewing in Heaven—never good news for the powers of darkness.

This fallen angel assigned to watch the Wallaces hated the Father, Jesus and Holy Spirit more than he could express. He desired to strike the Nazarene like a python strikes its prey, piercing with strong fangs, then slowly squeezing out the breath of life. Impossible, he knew, but dreaming of it fueled his twisted hatred, making him feel better in a perverse sort of way. He could not directly strike the Nazarene, but he took evil pleasures in assaulting all those the Nazarene loves—His beloved creatures called man.

Too late, the spirit had realized he had made an eternal mistake in following Lucifer, the father of lies, the one who had conceived and birthed the first lie. Forever banned from God's glorious presence, this prince's only choice was to remain loyal to his deceptive leader. Report he would ... even at the cost of Lucifer's wrath.

10

Just In Time

Almost every afternoon, Gregor took a walk in his neighborhood. Since he worked from home, he needed to get out of the house and decompress from the day's stress. It was also a time to listen. While in the wilderness of God, most solitary walks were pretty quiet, but on a rare occasion, the Lord would speak to him. Gregor started out with expectation sincerely hoping that the silence had ended.

With a pocketful of dog treats, he passed the usual houses on the usual route. He had walked for a few minutes when he arrived at the little yellow house where Quinn, his playful, terrier dog-friend, was waiting for his treat. Quinn's owner was amazed at her dog's attraction to Gregor. The small terrier could smell Gregor coming a block away and would paw the door to be let out. Then Quinn patiently waited for Gregor at the end of the driveway, barked once, and wagged a friendly hello to say, *I'll take my treat now.*

Then, there was the big two-story under renovation by a young couple with two precocious little girls. The children usually had something interesting like a bug or a stone to show him and were determined to share the entire story behind their great find. This time,

Gregor stopped to admire an orange leaf displaying a green and yellow striped caterpillar.

While he was extolling the wonders of the girls' treasure, the Lord spoke to him. *Gregor, go ring the doorbell of the blue house with the white picket fence. A man named Tony Robertson has a gun in his mouth ready to kill himself. I have appointed him as a laborer.*

Gregor sensed the urgency and sprinted to the house described. When he was younger, he easily ran ten miles in his daily training regimen. In fact, he had recorded the fastest time in the state, earning him a full college scholarship for cross country and track. But his running career abruptly ended with knee injuries.

Funny, he thought, *my knees don't hurt today! I like this change.*

In no time, he was standing on the porch of the blue house with the white picket fence. His finger rested on the doorbell button, but he hesitated. Mysteriously, the doorbell rang! *What?!* He hadn't pushed that button! But someone did! Maybe it was Storis.

At that moment, Gregor heard determined footsteps approaching the door. No turning back now. A man peeked out a skinny, side window.

The door remained closed and a deep, voice boomed, "What do you want?"

"My name's Gregor. I'm a neighbor. Jesus sent me."

"Go away. I don't want to go to your Bible study, or church or buy anything you're sellin'!"

"He sent me to stop you from killing yourself."

At that, the door was flung open, but the face of the tall, muscular African-American man was contorted with barely concealed rage. Still, before he could say another word, his arm—seemingly acting independently—gestured for Gregor to come in.

Gregor obliged, somewhat reluctantly. This was no average-sized man hovering over him in the foyer. Although probably in his fifties,

Tony's massive, yet well-toned physique gave him the appearance of a man in his thirties. Those powerful hands could put a hammerlock on Gregor and crush him with ease.

Tony turned and walked into the living room. He sat down on one of the two dark blue couches facing each other, separated by a coffee table. Without invitation, Gregor followed at a discreet distance, taking a seat across from Tony.

As he caught his breath, Gregor took a moment to glance around the room, noticing the feminine flair. No doubt Tony's wife had done the decorating. If so, she had achieved a fresh, inviting feeling here. A slender white vase filled with handmade paper flowers adorned a baby grand piano in one corner. Paintings hanging on the walls spoke peace with their soothing colors and scenes.

"Listen, Tony, you don't know me, but the Lord knows you. You were seconds away from killing yourself. Matter of fact, just before I rang the doorbell, you had a loaded handgun in your mouth." Gregor moved a magazine on the coffee table to reveal the gun Tony had tried to hide. "You told God that if He didn't show Himself, you would pull the trigger. Am I right?"

"How-how did you know that?" Tony shot him an accusatory glance. "You some kind of cop or detective?"

"No. I know because I'm a follower of Jesus. Your wife, Andrea, was a believer and is with Him now. She cried herself to sleep at night, praying you would give your heart to Him. You treated Andrea badly ... even cheated on her. You want her to know that you did really love her, but she's gone now and there's no way to fix things." Gregor paused, waiting for a response.

"What?" Tony leaned back into the couch as if to escape. Then he bolted up and grabbed his head with both hands as he paced in front of the coffee table.

Gregor hoped Tony wouldn't punch him out. Storis was there to protect him ... right?

Suddenly, the man who resembled the model for a marble statue of Hercules stood with his face covered, sobbing, waves of anguish surging up from his gut. In his grief, he slumped over as he crashed back onto the cushioned seat, burying his face in the arm of the couch.

Gregor moved across to sit next to him, hoping to bring some small comfort. "Listen, Tony, you need to give your life to Jesus. Moments ago, you were willing to take your life. Now, are you willing to ask Him to save it ... because He is more than willing to grant a pardon if you truly repent?"

"Andrea's passing is so hard ... so hard. Can't get ... over it. Wish I had it to do over," cried Tony. The crushing reality of Andrea's death bore down on him once again. Every time he stepped into that house, the emotional reminders of her absence sucked him deeper into depression. Death seemed the only escape from the ravaging pain. "And there's no way I'll live long enough to make up for all the bad things I've done."

"It's possible for you to be reunited with your wife," Gregor assured him. "She's waiting for you once your assignment here is completed. Listen, Tony, you have a great opportunity to make up for all the wrongs. Jesus has appointed you to be a world-changer, leading many young people to live boldly for Christ. God wants to use you to spare a generation from eternal death and destruction."

"Huh! How could Jesus use *me?*" Tony retorted, turning to face him, tears streaking his cheeks. "I lied. I cheated on my wife. I mocked Him at every opportunity, and you're telling me that He wants to use me in some great way? That's a laugh! I can't be used by God. I've hurt so many people, especially the one I loved the most."

"Tony, you are exactly the type of person He wants. Many, like you, are chosen to bring people to Jesus before He returns. Time is winding down for mankind. We're living in the end of this age. Unimaginable judgment is coming, but with it comes a great movement of God's mercy." Gregor shifted gears and asked, "What kind of work do you do?"

"I chair the Philosophy Department at Frederick University. Yeah ... Tony Robertson, Ph.D., celebrated atheist." He swiped at his eyes and sat up straighter. "If you know so much ... do you know that I've torn apart many students in my classes who dared attempt a defense of the deity of Christ? I wrote a best-selling book laying out a strong case *against* Christianity—how they've caused wars and instilled intolerance and hate in society. No ... I'm not your man. I'm no good to God."

Huh ... yeah ... this is making sense, Gregor thought. He saw the beauty of Jesus' selection in Tony and laughed.

"My life has ended, man, and you laugh?" Tony growled, making no attempt to hide his anger.

"You are the ideal recruit. The generation Jesus is going after can't receive the message because of the messengers. Pat answers from religious, churchy types don't work with this crowd. You, on the other hand, will be a mystery, an enigma worth considering. Why would a highly educated atheist turn 180 degrees to become a dedicated follower of Jesus Christ? You are perfect, my friend!" Gregor gave Tony a brotherly slap on the back.

"What can one person do, especially someone like me?" Tony relaxed a bit, considering his options. Maybe there was something to what Gregor was saying.

He had to admit, though, that his lifelong disdain for religion made it difficult for him to take the Jesus card seriously. He had read the Bible and other religious writings, but only for the purpose of research arguing his position *against* God. He didn't understand the first thing about being a follower of Jesus. How could he defend something he had once hated?

Without warning, a bright light illuminated the room. Gregor was elated. Tony was baffled. What in the heck was going on here?! The room grew brighter and brighter until suddenly the two men were standing in Heaven.

Two figures approached them. One was the figure of a man, glowing with the same brilliant light that had shone in the living room. The other figure was obscured by the light radiating from the One in front. Tony wanted to look but knew instinctively that this One was too holy to behold. He dropped to his knees and cried again as his sin and shame overwhelmed him.

The shining One put his hands on Tony's shoulders and pulled him to his feet. "Tony, look into My eyes."

"I can't! I can't! I'm not worthy ... I've sinned ...." He ducked, blinded by the tears he could no longer hold back. "I cursed Your name and taught others to do the same."

"You *must* look at Me, Tony, and you *will.*"

Slowly, Tony lifted his head and looked into the eyes of the glowing figure before him. There was no condemnation in those eyes, only compassion, love, mercy and forgiveness. Tony beheld what was missing his entire life, unconditional love and acceptance.

"Tony, are you willing to accept Me as your Lord and Savior, and are you then willing to serve Me with your life?" asked Jesus.

"Yes, Lord, I will do anything you ask! I don't know how, but please teach me."

A flaming arrow whistled through the air, piercing Tony's ribs with a thud. He grabbed his chest, his shoulders folding inward, as the arrow's flame consumed his old heart.

He stood there—an empty shell. Jesus reached into His own chest and withdrew His hand. There in His palm rested a new heart. In one fluid move, He transplanted the heavenly heart into Tony's chest, and the heart began to beat, circulating the life blood of the Creator.

Jesus peered deeply into Tony's eyes, placing His hand over Tony's new heart. "I have created you a second time. Old things have passed away; behold, you are a new creation. All things have become new," Jesus spoke with tenderness, pleased with the work of His hands and Tony's surrender.

"From this day forward, you are a messenger of My truth and will lead many to a true relationship with Me. You will speak with great authority, and those listening will hear with understanding." He paused, holding Tony's gaze. "The gift I give comes at great cost. Many will try to silence you; some will threaten to kill you. Do not fear them. But I tell you this: At the appointed time, you will give your life for My name's sake."

Tony could hardly take in everything that had been spoken. He struggled to think; didn't want to think. He wanted only to stay in Jesus' cleansing presence, to feel His life, love, forgiveness and adoption.

"Through you, I will transform the faculty at Frederick University as you have been transformed," Jesus continued. "Your influence will stretch over America to other colleges. Whatever you ask in My name, My Father will hear and grant it to you."

Tony's face shone almost as bright as the sun. Never had he dreamed such love, joy and peace possible. Death for Jesus' sake didn't faze him now. He looked forward to the honor of that day. Undeserving of this second chance, he determined not to disappoint his Lord, but to run hard for Jesus and His Kingdom. The old Tony had died today. Not as the result of a bullet, but of a burning arrow of love.

With that, Jesus stepped to the side, revealing the person who had been standing behind Him. It was Andrea! Her face was young and beautiful, her eyes as blue as the deepest part of the ocean. Her radiance reminded Tony of their first meeting when her captivating smile had won his heart. Now, he knew that they would only be apart for a short season, and the two of them would enjoy the wonders of Heaven for eternity.

Andrea stepped closer, taking both of Tony's hands in hers. "My precious love, the Lord has answered my prayers for you beyond my wildest expectations. Seeing you here has made me love Jesus even more, if that were possible. He is Faithful and True. Once you fought against Him, but now you are among the privileged who freely offer their lives for His name. He told me about your special assignment. I am so pleased for you."

"Andrea ...." Tony struggled to find words. "Why did I trample on a fresh flower, something so tender and lovely? I was so cruel ...." His voice broke, and he could not go on.

Andrea saw his deep remorse and put her hand to his lips. "Throw away the rearview mirror. Do not live in the past; live in the present. It is not how you start this race, but how you finish. Finish strong and leave nothing on the table. Run for me, my love, but above all, run for Jesus."

Her touch was intoxicating. He closed his eyes, caressing her hand against his face. He didn't want to go back to his life, the college, that empty house. Nothing on earth was calling him. *I'll fail Jesus, just like I failed Andrea,* he thought. He desperately wanted to stay.

Andrea sensed the battle within him. "I see a great man of God, strong and faithful. We will have eternity together, but you must not focus on our love. Focus on Jesus' love for you and those who are lost. Tell them that time is short. Go ... fulfill your assignment."

As Tony was about to speak, he could feel himself being pulled away from her, away from this sacred place. He resisted with all that was in him. As hard as he tried, it was impossible to will himself to stay. Just as quickly as the two men had left Tony's living room, they were back on the blue couch.

Tony was still emotional about the gift of a second chance. His beautiful Andrea had forgiven him. Jesus, also, had forgiven him. Now, he would have to learn how to forgive himself. Perhaps this was the lesson he had to learn to bring the message to others. How would enemies of God and the lost generation forgive their past? Just like Tony himself, they would have to do it by faith.

Gregor waited while Tony processed the experience. After a few minutes, Tony lifted his head and looked to Gregor. They were brothers now, joined in a mission by a secret bond, their shared experience forging a new eternal relationship.

"Tony, I know you've already read the Bible from cover to cover as research for your book, but the Lord wants you to read the Bible again with a new heart and fresh eyes. Call me when you want to talk."

Gregor grabbed a pencil and a piece of paper from the coffee table, wrote down his phone number and put it into Tony's hand. With that, Gregor patted Tony's muscular forearm, got up and let himself out the front door.

Alone now, Tony reached into the drawer of an end table and pulled out a well-used Bible with hand-written notes on every page. It was Andrea's Bible. He began to read: *In the beginning, God created the heavens and the earth ....*

11

Secret Weapon

Jean was in the kitchen mixing a salad to go with her famed lasagna recipe for dinner when Gregor strolled in from his walk. For the past half-hour, he had been mulling over his extraordinary experience with Tony Robertson, the newest addition to the team. Tony Robertson, Ph.D.—ex-militant, God-hating atheist, transformed by the touch of Jesus into a true soldier of light! Inside, Gregor felt like jumping up and down like a little kid. *I might just do it,* he thought. Still, it wasn't the time to share with Jean. After dinner would be soon enough.

"Jean, have you ever been to Frederick University?" asked Gregor, heading for a plate of brownies she had set out to cool.

She raised her eyebrows in a silent question, *Dessert before dinner?* "I've driven by, but never walked the campus. Why?"

"Youuu ...," he began, drawing out the single syllable, "are going to teach at Frederick U." He took another bite of brownie and sat down at the table.

"Yeah, right," she said with more than a trace of sarcasm. "You know I'm no public speaker. The last time I spoke to a group, it was a Sunday school class of second-graders."

"I'm not joking," said Gregor. "You're going to answer faculty and student questions in a lecture hall." He popped the last bite of brownie into his mouth and licked his fingers.

Jean felt her heart skip a beat as she sat down across from him. "Really. What in the world would I have to say?"

"Simple. You'll explain how to have a close relationship with Jesus."

Jean drew in a deep breath and held it for a few seconds before exhaling audibly. If she knew the Fire of Heaven would burn while she taught, she wouldn't give it a second thought. When the Fire burned, the Spirit spoke. Done deal.

She felt a twinge of shame in not trusting Jesus completely and captured her doubt before it took hold. What if He let her flop as another character-building lesson? Another wave of embarrassment washed over her. Fear of man still occasionally haunted her—even after all these years.

They paused for a prayer over the food, then despite the tantalizing aroma of the dish before him, Gregor merely picked at it. Suddenly, he shot up from his chair and walked over to the window overlooking the darkening woods beyond their house. "Can this really be happening to us?" He paused, then turned to Jean. "I think I'm done with my job at Genomic's Software."

"Lord tell you so?" she asked softly.

"Not directly. I just have a sense that it's the thing to do."

"Not surprising." She sighed. "Nothing is normal anymore."

"Yeah, wish Jesus would just say, *Gregor, quit your job.*" He returned to the table and sat down. "Guess I'll wait to give my notice. We still need to put food on the table," he said, polishing off his lasagna. Then, with a puzzled expression on his face, he spoke what was on his heart. "I'll have to say that it's a mystery to me how this new life in the Kingdom is supposed to work."

Just when Gregor was about to tell Jean about Tony, he heard an incoming text on his cell and pulled it from his shirt pocket to note the caller. Snow Peterson! She was a trusted friend and intercessor who had prayed Gregor and Jean through some dark times. She knew very well the heartache of battling darkness. Cancer had tested her multiple times in her own body and, most recently, in her daughter's.

Snow was an experienced warrior of the Kingdom, skilled in pulling down strongholds of evil. Sometimes Gregor didn't exactly understand the depths of Snow's prayers, but he knew they were powerful and that God listened. Whenever the powers of darkness closed in and threatened to win some victory, Jesus prompted Snow to stand in the gap.

Saw you and Jean in vision ... what's going on ... call when you can, he read.

"Hey, a text just came in from Snow. I'm gonna call her," Gregor said as he headed to his office.

Three rings and Snow answered. "Hello, Gregor! So glad you called! Was hoping you would!"

"Have time to talk now?"

"Absolutely!" Before he could say another word, she jumped right in. "While I was praying the other day, I had a vision of you and Jean stepping off a huge cliff. Instead of falling, you were instantly lifted up into Heaven. Backpacks filled with heavy stones fell off your backs. Jean had a vile, hideous creature clinging to her spine. Michael, the archangel, dressed in swat gear, shot the creature with one bullet to the head, freeing her. It was glorious!" She paused momentarily, delighting in the recollection.

"Gregor, this may sound strange, but when I pray for you and Jean, I see you walking in the midst of a roaring fire. Not one of destruction, but a fire of power and love. Waves of it have been washing over me for days."

"Snow, as usual, you're always one step ahead of everyone. So much has happened, I don't know where to begin. If you have time, I'll fill you in." At her enthusiastic response, Gregor told her about the Visitation, the Taylor family and Dr. Tony Robertson.

"Gregor, my heart is leaping like a young girl! Wish my feet could follow!" She laughed her rich, contagious laugh. "I've prayed for this ever since we met at that little start-up church ten years ago. I know you felt empty when you prayed for me then, but because of your obedience, God has blessed me. I knew He was going to do something great! Oh, thank You, Jesus!" shouted Snow in her usual zeal for her Lord and Savior.

"Snow, I'm going to pray for you again. Sit down, OK?" Gregor instructed.

"Oh, I'm sitting, honey. My arthritis is acting up a little. But fire away and don't hold back. I want all that Jesus wants me to have. I have a short time left here before I am called to be with Him, and I want to run across the finish line, not crawl across. I want strength in these old legs!" Her hearty laugh rang out again.

Gregor could feel the power of the Lord surge within him. "Snow, in Jesus' name, I command you to see like an eagle, fight like a lion, and trust like a lamb. In the power of the Holy Spirit, may your prayers overthrow principalities, powers and kingdoms of darkness, hitting the target every time. I ask this in Jesus' name."

The sensation of electricity bolted through Snow's body, causing her to jump straight up out of the chair. She shouted a *Thank You, Jesus* before she lay prostrate in reverence of the holy presence. Gregor heard a thud as her phone dropped, but he knew she was all right from her shouts of praise and thanksgiving. She would call back later.

Tonight, another mighty force has been added to the team, Gregor thought with a sense of great gratitude. Empowered to enter into the highest levels of intercession, Snow would impart the same prayer authority to other faithful prayer warriors who had endured the long season of trials and tests. Over the years, Gregor knew that Snow had developed a network of intercessors across the country and, with this new boost of authority, she would simply mobilize these experienced fighters to prepare the way. She had always told him that intercessors were the spiritual air force, bombing the enemy and weakening his forces, making the way clear for the ground troops to advance.

Long claws and venomous fangs dig deeply into their enslaved victims, preventing them from hearing the message of freedom and seeing their true state of captivity. As their first mission, the intercessors would break the teeth and claws of deaf and blind spirits. Prayer would open the portal and, for the first time, Lucifer's victims would be able to hear and see with understanding that they must make a choice. In God's divine plan, the great harvest of souls was intimately connected to prayer initiated from His heart.

Gregor rejoined Jean in the kitchen and helped her load the dishwasher with the last of the dirty dishes. "Snow's on the team. She'll be key in building a strong prayer foundation."

With mounting excitement, Jean paced around the kitchen island as she felt years of deadness falling off her spirit. "You're absolutely right! The old way of prayer is out. No more fire hose approach, trying to hit anything and everything. We'll all have to be tuned into the Lord's will in every situation, hitting His mark dead center."

As Jean's faith rose, so did her voice. "Differing instruments, tuned and in sync—like an orchestra—will send the sound of Heaven to shake the powers of darkness. But that shaking will stir the hornets' nest. I can just see the angry demons going on the offensive and stinging those responsible. If we've heard the sound of Heaven, you know evil forces have heard it, too. So we can expect retaliatory attacks."

Attacks didn't matter. God was moving. Jubilation sprang up in Gregor and he couldn't contain it any longer. He did just what he'd thought about doing earlier. Like a child exploding with excitement, he jumped into the air, shouting, "Woo hoo!" Tony and Snow were on board, and now Jean, his best friend, his beloved wife.

He couldn't wait to bring her up to speed on all that had happened. Grabbing her hand, he led her into his office. They sat down in the two old wing-backed chairs, whose slipcovers didn't quite fit. He started telling his story, reliving the details of his walk—Quinn's treat, the little girls' caterpillar and then … what happened at the blue house with the white picket fence, followed by his talk with Snow Peterson.

Jean was overjoyed, marveling at how quickly God was moving. In the past, He had never seemed to be in any particular hurry. "You know, I might just jump up and shout, too! God is definitely doing something spectacular—and quickly!"

Gregor and Jean still had no definite blueprint, no plan of action, except to obey in the moment. No doubt they would encounter Lucifer's assaults in his attempts to keep souls tightly locked up for himself. He would not sit back and let this personal assault against his kingdom go unavenged. Would the Lord warn them of coming attacks? What would He permit Lucifer to do? How much depended on the harvesters? They did know that no advancements to take territory for the Kingdom of God ever ensued without first evicting the enemy. They prayed, seeking wisdom.

* * *

Storis stood between the two chairs, choosing to remain unseen. He also rejoiced in his Creator's work. He knew Gregor and Jean had conjectured correctly about Lucifer's counter blows. Darkness would not ignore the stirring and imparting of heavenly power. Yet even as a mighty, faithful messenger of the Holy One, the exact plan had not been revealed to him, either. He operated in the same manner as Gregor and Jean—simple obedience.

One thing Storis absolutely knew to be true was that the captive Bride would be set free from Lucifer's fetters by the power of God's love and truth. Gladness replaced his sorrow, knowing it impossible for Lucifer to thwart the Holy One's will. He looked to the glorious day of the great wedding feast. He rejoiced that at the Lord's direction, this new caliber of intercessors would disable strongholds, making way for foot soldiers to storm the gates of hell, then occupy and defend.

Storis also knew that the intercessors' second directive was to form a protective shield for the soldiers in this new call to battle. Jesus would not allow the birthing of the Final Awakening to be aborted. In time, human warriors would wield all the weapons of spiritual warfare, skillfully hitting the target each time.

The humans he had been assigned needed assistance, and he was prepared to fight on their behalf. For now, Storis would help them walk in the middle of the fiery road, avoiding a scorching from the enemy.

* * *

Jason was restless. He shuffled around his loft-style condo, briefly toying with the idea of cleaning his messy closet or getting rid of some moldy stuff in the fridge. And even the thought of doing something fun left him empty. He put on his shoes, shrugged into a jacket, and stood in front of the door, staring at the doorknob. But there was nowhere he really wanted to go.

Frustrated, he slumped down into a favorite overstuffed leather chair, grabbed the remote and turned on a recorded newscast. It appeared the whole world was coming apart at the seams. Reports of governments forfeiting their rights to foreigners, nuclear missile threats, Russian and Chinese cyber-attacks, the Deep State his father daily fought on the Hill, and impending collapse of the world economy scrolled across the screen.

The coverage of what happened on his parents' front porch came on next. He watched his dad give a statement about his son's resurrection and then issue a stern warning to the nation. Jason had never seen or heard his dad like this before, and observing him surrender his life to Jesus and boldly speak of God's love, power and judgment gave Jason an immense sense of relief. This was followed by his own statement—audible, but not visual, due to the supernatural power surge.

The talking heads' commentary was cruel. At first, the barbs directed at his family stung. *No, I'm not accepting this. I know the truth, and these people are agents of the enemy.* Slanderous statements about Jason and his parents were bad enough, but the way the self-righteous God-haters mocked the Almighty was intolerable. He fast-forwarded past the panel discussion.

Something in one of the segments drew his attention, although he didn't know exactly why or what. Rewind. Play. Rewind. Play. Over and over again, he studied the report. What was he looking for? Information? A person? *Hmmm,* he mused, zeroing in on the woman behind the anchor desk. *I remember that reporter.*

Still fidgety, yet focused on the TV, he did some jumping jacks and pushups, trying to alleviate his edginess. What was up? He was usually so calm and easy-going, but this feeling of confusion was out of character. He felt weird, like he had been told some classified intelligence from Heaven but couldn't remember what it was. "Jesus, what am I looking for in this video?" No answer. His restlessness grew unbearable. He headed out for a run. Maybe five miles would clear his mind and help him relax.

12

Prince Of Darkness

At the seat of evil's domain—the command post of heinous ventures—a vast cavern echoed with chaotic preparations for the quarterly state of the kingdom address. Here key ruling members of darkness had been summoned to assemble. At the head of a long table, a large throne was strategically placed to oversee the massive U-shaped cave. The throne was an attempt to replicate a former glory with jewels adorning intricate carvings of serpents and gargoyles, a caricature of hideous beauty. Sitting in this commanding position—at the very nerve center—was the high prince of darkness, Lucifer himself.

The chairs closest to the evil pontiff, although embellished, were a bit less stately in appearance and sat slightly lower than his throne, forcing everyone present to look up at him. Other tables, reserved for delegates of lesser importance, were situated near the outside walls of the cavern. This seating arrangement was calculated to demonstrate which of the evil horde was in Lucifer's good graces, determined by how well they had produced his mandatory outcomes. Thus, fierce competition kept the members distrustful of one another. No camaraderie existed among them. Yet, stolen glory was exactly the way Lucifer wanted it—indeed, the way he had sought to achieve it for himself.

A red-hot blaze, ignited by wickedness, burned before this throne, mimicking another high above; however, this fire bore no resemblance to the Fire of Heaven. At the center of the cavern, the foul-smelling blaze glowed as the antimatter of holiness. It brought death, not life. It radiated darkness, not light. It birthed deceit, not truth. It was cruel, not merciful. It reeked of hatred, not love.

Lucifer had no real majesty of his own, yet he had managed to establish himself as a god-like figure over his own kingdom with its own hierarchy—all in an effort to copy the structure of the Kingdom of God. Lucifer existed in a world of lies, even deceiving himself that he had power and magnificence. And he had duped many others, including the angels he had persuaded to follow him, exchanging the glories of Heaven for the false power and "privilege" of existing in the barrenness absent of the Almighty. Now, doomed for all eternity for their defiance of the Holy One, they awaited the final judgment to come.

This once mighty cherub of Heaven began the meeting with updates from the various princes who ruled the nations. Each ruling prince would be expected to stand to give a detailed report of his successes as well as failures. No prince would dare lie to the father of lies. The pontiff's network of moles reported regularly, keeping him apprised of all situations. This ensured that no misinformation affected his strategy to rule over every nation, eventually forcing their worship of him.

Evil must reign supreme, impeding God's Kingdom from stealing souls. Lucifer had no love for mankind. In his estimation, the only value of collecting souls in hell was to pierce God's heart at the loss of yet more beloved lambs.

The one thing Lucifer feared most was praying believers who understood and used their full authority in Jesus. Once he received the report of a kindling Fire of Heaven, in answer to the Saints' prayers, he immediately rallied all troops necessary to stamp it out. Otherwise, the nation birthing a starter fire might turn to the Nazarene, robbing Lucifer of power.

"Hmmm," he began, scanning the crowd. "Who will give the first report today? Prince of China, proceed."

The Prince of China wore a red silk robe, embroidered with dragons. Large protruding spikes on his back poked through the delicate fabric. He imagined that the robe gave him importance; it was, instead, a covering of corruption. He rose to his feet as he began, "O glorious king, most high god who rules the air and the earth. The true king of the dragons, the one who is full of deceit and hate …."

"Enough pleasantries," Lucifer said, waving off the disingenuous praise. He knew all his horde hated him as much as he hated them. "Just get on with your report. We will be here all day if each one of you proclaims all my magnificent qualities."

"Lord Lucifer, China continues to rule with intimidation and fear. The government, or should I say our dark forces, have nationalized Christianity, meaning the truth of the Holy Scriptures remains corrupted under the twisted lies of communism. A people of the Holy One's Christ cannot be ruled effectively by communist dogma for they are free indeed in the Nazarene and do not fear death. Therefore, we arrange for *true* Christians to be immediately marked by the government and targeted for persecution.

"I have convinced the leaders that true Christianity threatens social stability; thus, crushing the underground Church of true believers is imperative; in a sense, we are at war against these groups of Nazarene-followers. Gathering sites are torn down and heavy monetary fines are levied on those who defy the law regarding unsanctioned meetings. We sprinkle in the usual beatings, prison and death sentences among the punishments for defying the government in such matters. The communist church's mission is to force followers to submit to the whims of their leaders, who must be successful in denying their people Heavenly citizenship ...."

The Prince of China stopped abruptly when he noticed the look of dread on his cohorts' faces. Gasps and wincing whines echoed throughout the cavern at the prince's boldness in repeatedly using the offensive word *Christian*. All looked to Lucifer's reaction, because the dark leader usually hated the use of that term. Shockingly, he did nothing but smile and lean back in his ornate throne overlooking the Council.

Since the coining of the word, Lucifer had schemed to divest it of the essence of its meaning. It had, therefore, become largely inconsequential, presenting no relationship with commitment to the Nazarene. Now, it represented nothing more than a cultural reference to Western values or an exclusion of other religious affiliations. He could not be more thrilled at his success.

Beaming with pride, Lucifer signaled to the Prince of China. "Carry on, my prince. I like what I am hearing."

The prince continued, "And indubitably, spirits of Greed and Violence maintain the chasm between cruelty and compassion; there is no trace of benevolence in our select leaders. It is laughable, my dark lord, that the stupid world looks on blindly and with disinterest as China's leaders publicly pronounce that all their perpetrated evil is for the good of the country.

"The Internet is censored and tightly controlled, throughout the country, preventing truth from being known and preserving the veil which cuts off communication with outside believers. Many pastors are corralled on fabricated charges of possessing state secrets, cutting off the true 'meat of the Word,' as they say, to the aimless sheep of their flock. As you know, the Son of the Holy One calls Himself their Shepherd." With that, the Prince of China threw back his head and laughed.

Following his outburst, pure evil mocked the Nazarene's reference to Himself as a shepherd and His followers as sheep. One dark, prince bleated sheep noises while another licked his lips, joking of eating lamb chops, consuming them as evil consumes souls. Lucifer enjoyed the frivolity so much he moved the jokester to a table closer to his throne, sending the resident royal to the back of the cavern.

The Prince of China made a slight bow before proceeding. "I own Chairman Wu's soul via a pact promising him power until his death. If he remains useful to us, however, we will do our best to give him a long life. His partnership guarantees a stable and increasing resistance to faith in the Nazarene."

"Thank you, prince, for a fine and most productive report," stated Lucifer with a contorted smile of approval.

"Oh, but dark lord, there is more."

"Do tell," said Lucifer as he gestured to the Prince of China that he still held the floor.

"Proselytizing is forbidden and punishable under great cruelty at the hands of local leaders, using the neighbor-against-neighbor tactic. China asserts no clear definition of proselytizing, leaving wide latitude for arrests. Anyone can be arrested for the tiniest infraction at any time without any proof.

"Also, content of preaching is tightly regulated in the sanctioned Three Self Church. Forbidden topics include the deity of the Nazarene, His resurrection, His second coming, abortion and such. However, in their 'truth,' atheist-communists never go to hell as all good communists go to Heaven, my king." The prince paused with an evil grin. "Bibles are scarce, and to the Council's delight, Internet purchases of the Word have been banned."

Lucifer smirked basking the prince's success. Without the written Word to reveal the Person of the Word, more souls would remain his prisoners.

"If the creatures' thoughts are not held captive to the obedience of Christ, we of the darkness never lack opportunities to fill their minds for them. 'Idle minds are the devil's workshop.' Or so their saying goes." He laughed, knowing that God's foolish creatures speak these words flippantly, not realizing that they are declaring truth with serious consequences.

"China's economy grows stronger and moneys are funneled into war preparations. Soon the government will boast a military able to impose their will on any nation. Today, money is their weapon; tomorrow, bullets and bombs. View the great nation of China as the tip of your spear, my most excellent king, able to stop any nation from opposing your great plan."

With that, the prince knelt and kissed the gaudy, over-sized, pentagram ring on Lucifer's grotesque finger. The ring was black, absent of beauty—a fitting accessory to the wearer.

"Most excellent, my prince. Prince of Canada, relinquish your seat to the Prince of China. He has earned my trust and must be rewarded," declared Lucifer, reminding other council members that reward comes with results.

Lucifer's twisted smirk grew wider as he slowly rose from his throne. He let out a mighty roar and the fallen princes began to pound on the tables with their fists, chanting, *The Church is dead! Long live your kingdom of darkness! The Glory has departed.* Was it possible that the longed-for time of Ichabod over the Church had come?

Every evil being rose, shouting, *Who can stop the king of this world? Who can overcome his great princes? Let darkness rule over Light for ever and ever. Lucifer is lord.*

"Yes, I AM," Lucifer declared, in acceptance of their worship. "Thank you, my loyal servants. I have delivered to you the kingdoms of this world. Today we stand at the threshold of overthrowing Heaven, keeping our rule over earth. No more interference from the Nazarene and his meddling, holy angels. We declare our own commandments and will be worshiped as gods, because we are gods."

Every dark being that existed knew Lucifer's statements were lies. They had believed him once, landing them in the horrors of eternal, irredeemable condemnation. They were not gods and would never be gods as the Holy One is God, yet they reveled in their own lies and deceptions. However, restricted by the commands of the Almighty, they were unable to execute anything without His knowledge or outside the permissible latitude granted them.

The mighty Prince of Death bore the unholy image of his name. At first glance, he appeared to be wearing a white robe, but closer inspection revealed that he was covered in maggots, writhing as if devouring flesh. As he moved, disturbing the cloud of decay ever present about his person, the sickening smell of rotting tissue wafted throughout the cavern. Silence fell upon the room as he stood to speak. "Oh, great lord of darkness, I must ask a question. The Church in America has been the light opposing us for many years. Has her end come?"

Lucifer leaned forward, resting his chin on his hands, in deep thought. *If I can make China a communist-capitalist nation, why not make America a capitalist-communist nation. Such a subtle transition. Yes, that would do nicely to accelerate the destruction of the Church.*

He loathed America, that great modern nation of Nazarene-followers, for her missionary efforts throughout the world as much as he hated Israel. "Prince of America, report."

"Lord Lucifer, I have accelerated my plan. I rule the United States government. The strength of her pillars are shattered and civil war is about to erupt. The stupid creatures are tearing down every remembrance of their history in the Nazarene's statutes, such as removing the public display of the Ten Commandments from which their law originates. America is fragmented and fights within itself. The people want communism over democracy and censorship over free speech," stated the Prince of America.

The room broke out in applause and cheering that was heard throughout the dark kingdom. America was the most important target nation. If America fell, the other so-called Christian nations would also fall, giving darkness a broader footing over all nations upon the earth.

"May I continue, my lord?" asked the Prince of America.

Lucifer drew the Council's attention to the Prince of America again. "Take note and learn from this prince. America, is falling. Why, you ask? Because the followers of the Nazarene no longer pray—a great victory for us. The churches are pathetic, diluting the truth to make their members feel good about themselves ... all the way to hell." Lucifer let out an evil laugh, sounding more like a shriek.

"The Church is incapable of opposing your rule, O great Lucifer. Other religions grow faster than Christianity. I easily lead lambs to the slaughter," stated the Prince of America as the inhabitants of the dark cavern remained in awe of his authority over his region. "My lord, the Church has lost its voice and power; the Glory has departed."

Lucifer spoke with fierce anger. "Just as long as they do not pray and take up their authority in the Nazarene! Just as long as their eyes are not opened to Truth and they start going about the Holy One's business. Right now, workers for the harvest are few with little effect." His hand rose, and a sharp finger stretched out as if to pierce each being seated in the assembly. With a loud voice, he said clearly and distinctly, "You ... must ... defend ... my ... territory. Let there be no prayer!"

The Prince of America interjected news regarding prayer, saying, "Few pray in the Nazarene's power. My lord Lucifer, the shepherds would rather teach social issues than actually exhort the flock with the true Word.

"The creatures so highly value love, a great weakness if void of discernment, so we gladly provide—falsely, of course. Grace of the Holy One is perverted in much of the Church. The creatures sin all they want while no conviction comes upon them, as they are told there is no accounting for their actions since all sin is forgiven anyway by the God of love. They have come to believe that repentance is old-fashioned and outdated. Sin rules in the Church like never before!"

The whole assembly, except for their great leader, leapt from their seats, shouting and dancing on the tabletops. Lucifer raised his hand and again, at his gesture, quiet fell upon the room. "Continue, highly honored Prince of America."

"Per your command, my lord, I maintain the influence of Apathy over the shepherds causing them to leave their greatest weapon dormant. They, themselves, do not pray the will of the Nazarene; however, we do encourage them to pray amiss for things they imagine will make their pitiful ministries larger as if mere numbers were the goal and not true disciples. They build their own kingdoms and not the Nazarene's."

Lucifer chuckled thinking, *Yes, the spirit of Apathy—an astute strategy equating dispassionate, lukewarm hearts which the Nazarene detests.*

Seeing Lucifer's pleasure, the prince took a half bow. "Be assured, O, great leader, the Nicolaitan doctrine is thriving, that which the

Nazarene also hates. Large assemblies on Sunday leave members passively entertained with an empty drama on a stage. Mostly they are fed the milk of the Word—if even that—and the passivity prevents them from articulating the truth leaving them 'unskilled in the Word,' as they say. The Church is most definitely exploited by an unordained hierarchy in which the laity is ruled by men leading them into the doctrines of ... well ... your canons, great pontiff." The prince paused awaiting Lucifer's reaction to this news.

Murmurs of awe swept through the Council. Lucifer waved his hand motioning for the prince to continue.

"Speaking of your precepts, high pontiff, I have begun a campaign to pervert the gospel, indoctrinating the youngest of minds via a cartoon character. This 'holy man' is an inept jesus, ineffective in his mission and a failure to the Father."

Lucifer sat beaming at the prince's brilliant strategy to indoctrinate young minds. *I will claim this idea as my own,* Lucifer thought.

"Another bit of good news, my lord. Corruption fills the administration of such corporations called churches as selfish pastors take exorbitant salaries being more concerned with personal gain than souls," the Prince of America elaborated. "Skillfulness in warfare prayer is no longer taught, another one of my great triumphs. Leaders no longer believe the great powers of darkness exist or influence people, giving us much more freedom in our methodology of destruction. In their minds, we do not exist and the realm of darkness is recognized only by the ignorant and uniformed."

The Council cheered at the Prince of America's report marveling at the command of his territory. The prince held his hand to quiet the group. All present were once again focused on his words.

"And for the latest nail in the coffin, as you already know, the introduction of pornography via the Internet has brought most delightful results. We have found it most effective in targeting the shepherds. When they live in secret sin, they do not preach the consequences of sin to the flock. A great percentage of the shepherds are themselves addicted ... and as the shepherd goes, so goes the flock!

"My underlings keep them on a cycle of sin, remorse, sin, more remorse, but without ever committing to godly sorrow leading to true repentance. I give you my word, O great Lucifer, America is breathing her last and will be dead like Great Britain, France and Germany."

The Council of Darkness erupted with a thunderous standing ovation. The one nation that stood in Lucifer's way was quickly fading into obscurity. America's death left few obstacles to prevent the One World Government that Lucifer would eventually rule.

"Prince of America, take your reward near me," said Lucifer as he gestured toward a nearby chair. There was a shuffle and a mumbling among the evil horde as the Prince of America took his place next to Lucifer.

"Soon I will rule this planet openly," declared Lucifer as he stood to his feet. "The Nazarene will hear the screams of humanity suffering in hell and cursing His name, and I will look upon His defeat. I will make His death and resurrection meaningless. The Nazarene bought this world with His Blood; let us take back His selfless deed for humankind and make His most precious creation mine. I will triumphantly rule as lord of this world and you will be gods forever."

The Council shouted, *Hail, lord Lucifer, ruler of the heavens and earth, who is greater than the Nazarene!*

In the height of this twisted euphoria, the effects of a holy wind blew across the dark fire before Lucifer's throne, nearly extinguishing it. He felt a jabbing pain in his side, causing him to bend over and groan. Lacking omnipresence and omniscience, Lucifer depended on his keen senses and network of informers, but this time he needed no conjecture nor intelligence. He knew the source of his agony.

He called one of his most trusted spies, Datter, and whispered, "Trauma in my realm stabbed me just now. Go quickly and find the point of the Fire of Heaven on earth. I must know if the Final Awakening has been kindled."

Datter stood, attempting to make himself appear loyal and dutiful. Lies. He nodded that he understood, then vanished intent on his mission.

13

The Least Of These

Gregor started the day early with prayer, around 6:30 a.m. He knew the battle between good and evil would be won in the Spirit on his knees rather than in the flesh with his two hands. He prayed for wisdom.

Instead of battling demonic distractions as in those years in the prison of affliction, an immediate open Heaven revealed itself like a secure phone line. No interruptions, no distractions and no doubt clouded his mind this time. He experienced what he could have only imagined a few days ago. In this moment, he felt the clear mind of Christ filling his mind with pure and powerful prayer.

Within the last few days, he had seen Jesus face to face more than once, the Fire of Heaven in his eyes, had felt the power of God flow through him into Jason's dead body. Even after all this, Gregor's inadequacy to lead the Final Awakening hung like a giant sign an arm's length in front of his face. He was a child expected to build a nuclear power plant. He felt ill-equipped and way out of his league. "Lord, help me. I don't know what to do."

Jesus' reply was immediate. No waiting or wondering this time. *All you need to do, Gregor, is obey. If you want to grow in My Kingdom, you must mature as a child and not as an adult. A loving and trusting child will jump off a roof into his father's arms if the father asks him to do so. Now you must do the same. You must not depend upon what your human experience tells you is true. You must live by the Spirit. Your faith must be wholly dependent upon Me as a babe is dependent upon its mother.*

Withstanding the furnace of affliction has given you a place of enduring faith and trust so that you will not lean on your own understanding. Self died so that you may receive a greater measure of My Spirit. Blessed are those who recognize their poverty of spirit, for theirs is the Kingdom of Heaven. Unless you believe in your heart that you are impoverished and have nothing in your flesh of worth to give Me, you will not enter the Kingdom or have access to all it offers.

"Lord, I want to bring the full Kingdom, but …" Gregor began, halting ….

Before he could finish his thought, Jesus was quick to explain. *How much electrical current can flow through a doorbell wire? How much electrical current can flow through a larger transmission line? The gauge of the wire determines the amount of current able to travel through it. Love is the conduit of My power. When My love is great in you, great power flows through you.*

Listen carefully. Tonight, at nine o'clock, take Jason and go to the heart of the city to Baldwin Park. The Barrios gang leader, Carlos Ortega, cries out to Me. He seeks forgiveness for himself and healing for his brother. Go to him.

Gregor's heart jumped. The Barrios were notoriously savage guys. Gregor feared that if he and Jason went there, they might never come back. "Lord, they'll laugh at us and kill us for fun," he protested.

Carlos is a chosen instrument of Mine to carry My name to bands of thieves and murderers. I will give him a new heart and fill him with My Spirit. I have longed to pour My love into such as these and raise them as workers of the harvest. Carlos will be standing at the corner of the 300 block of North Fisher Street when you get there.

With that, the holy presence left the room and, before he could back out, Gregor called Jason. "Hey, buddy. Get ready. The Lord has an assignment for us. I'll pick you up tonight about 8:30, and we'll head to the city together."

Jason was itching to do something other than hang around his condo, patrolling his living room and taking an occasional run. Across the street a handful of reporters stood at the corner, possibly afraid to get blasted with a repeat performance of electrical fireworks.

Later that day at the appointed time, Jason sneaked out the back of his building and waited for Gregor a few blocks away.

OK, Lord, let's get this show on the road. I'll do anything You ask. That was the deal. Just don't let me mess it up, Jason prayed.

Gregor spotted Jason leaning against the corner of a building and pulled over. He opened the door to the front passenger side of Gregor's van, slid in and quickly closed the door.

"Where're we headed?"

"Baldwin Park."

Jason's eyes widened and one eyebrow shot up. "Wow! Big assignment right off the bat. No warm-ups before the big game, I guess ...." He paused, checking out the vehicle he was riding in. "Uh, no offense, Gregor, your van isn't a hot ticket, but in that part of town, it could get jacked unless Jesus told you your car is protected."

"No promises about the car. We *could* park and take a cab."

"Huh! No cabdrivers will venture into that part of town, even in the daytime," Jason replied "Let me check the bus schedule." He Googled the information on his cell phone. "There's a park and ride pick-up with a drop not too far from the corner where Carlos is supposed to be."

"Hey, let's take the bus. God was with the apostles, but they still got beaten up and thrown in jail. If I die, at least Jean can still have the car," Gregor joked.

He parked the van and the two men hopped on a bus headed toward Baldwin Park. After stepping off, they walked toward North Fisher Street, a well-defended Barrios area. The deeper they moved into gang territory, the more colorful graffiti and gang emblems they saw. Cars set up on blocks with missing tires was common. Brightly painted low riders lined the streets were various small groups of hooded young people were clustered together, smoking and drinking.

As Gregor and Jason rounded the final corner, they became aware that they were being watched. Jason noticed several young Latinos wearing red bandannas tied around their heads, lingering on the corner where Carlos was supposed to be waiting. A few others approached from behind, although they failed to get a good look in the semi-darkness.

One large, heavily-muscled guy locked onto them. He pulled his shirt to the side, revealing a gun tucked into his belt, thus announcing to Gregor and Jason that he was in charge. His message was clear: *Vamoose ... or else!*

As Gregor and Jason walked in their direction, the gang swaggered toward them as one strong and angry-looking unit. Gregor and Jason were sandwiched in between the large group and the few behind them. The big Latino guy got up in their face. "You got nerve comin' on our turf. You cops?"

Undaunted, Gregor stepped in a little closer. "Jesus sent me to speak to Carlos."

The spokesman pulled out his gun and pointed it at Gregor's head. "Whad'ya want with Carlos? You can speak to me—Mateo," said the young man, who seemed fully prepared to pull the trigger. "Look, *chicos*, one of those religious crazies comin' here to save us from our sins!" Mateo laughed as he stepped closer, touching the barrel of the gun to Gregor's forehead.

The entire group burst into laughter, making mocking gestures like crazed street preachers.

"Carlos ain't here," Mateo drawled, pressing the gun against Gregor's skin, "so get lost ... or get dead."

Before Gregor could respond, Mateo laughed again. "Your Jesus gonna save you from this?" he asked, waving his weapon in the air before lowering it to take point-blank aim. There were four sharp sounds, so close together they blended into one: *Bang, bang, bang, bang!*

Sure that Gregor was dead, Jason reactively ducked for cover, thinking he was next. Then he wondered why he even cared. He had already died once, had tasted of Heaven, and never wanted to return to earth.

Unfazed by the blasts, the other gang members stood in silence. After the four shots had been fired, they all heard the sound of clinking metal ... one ... two ... three ... four pieces dropped, one after another. The bullets hit the sidewalk, rolled toward Mateo and stopped, neatly lined up at the end of his right shoe. He looked down at the four bullets, fully intact, as if they had never been fired. Confused, he scooped them up in the palm of his hand and stared. He then glanced over at Gregor, fully expecting to find him on the sidewalk, bloodied and dead. Gregor was as surprised as Mateo.

"What the hell's goin' on?" demanded Mateo. "You should be dead, man!"

Storis instantly appeared—all twelve feet of him—reflecting the radiant glory of God. Mateo let out a blood-curdling scream and passed out. He would have hit the concrete pavement with the full force of his 230-pound frame had Storis not grabbed him and gently eased him to the ground.

The other gang members scattered, running at full speed, wetting themselves on the run. Only one man stayed behind, apparently too dazed to take off with the rest of them. Gregor watched the color drain from the man's face and his legs wobble.

"Grab him, Jason, before he hits the ground. This guy's Carlos. Let's get him to a safe place."

Jason agreed and hefted the man's legs. "Oomph! Do I have an angel around somewhere, too? I could use a little help. This guy's dead weight."

"I don't think angels appear unless absolutely necessary." Gregor puffed as they moved the man toward the city park across the street. "We'll talk more about this later, but for now, let's get out of here."

"Guess no more angelic intervention is scheduled," Jason muttered under his breath as they reached a park bench and hoisted Carlos onto it.

"Carlos, Carlos, wake up." Gregor gently shook him, hoping for a response. "I'm here to help you. Carlos, can you hear me?"

Carlos mumbled a few indistinct words.

"What's he saying?" Jason looked around, scouting for trouble.

"I think he's in shock. Don't blame him; I would be, too." Gregor laughed. "Hey, I think he's coming around."

"Who are you? Whad'ya want with me?" Carlos struggled to sit up.

"My name's Jason and this is Gregor. Jesus sent us in answer to your prayer."

"How-how did ya know?" Then getting a good look at Gregor, he gasped. "You're alive? But I saw Mateo shoot ya ... couldn't have missed!" He paused, fumbling for words. "And ... and I saw some kinda angel .... Nobody knew 'bout my prayin' ... not even my little bro, Diego. If the guys ever found out …." He ducked his head, trying to clear his mind.

Gently, kindly, Jason told him about his own experience—how Jesus had brought him back from the dead … a true miracle! "Guess I wouldn't have believed it myself if it hadn't happened to me," he confided.

Jason went on with his story while Gregor prayed silently. "And now Jesus has sent us here to tell you that He loves you, Carlos, and that what He did for me, He will do for you … He will set you free if you accept His love and turn from your sinful, dead-end life."

These two strangers had risked their lives to bring him this good news. Carlos understood that kind of loyalty. As leader of the Barrios, he required that same kind of dedication from his followers. It was then that he broke down, sobbing uncontrollably—the first time tears had poured down his cheeks since the tragic night his brother lost his legs. Suddenly, the steel casing around his heart fell away.

He looked into Gregor's eyes and saw the Fire of Heaven blazing brightly. The same Fire was in Jason's eyes. Carlos lay back on the bench, speechless at first. As he continued to stare at them, something was communicated to him without words.

His whole body began to quiver. "But … but I've done so many bad things. I've hurt people … even my brother. I've killed people."

At first, Jason and Gregor thought Carlos was talking to them. "Well, yeah, but Jesus can forgive you," Jason assured him.

"I'm not only a drug addict, I sell drugs to young kids to get 'em hooked, ya know, to keep my business goin'."

Jason took a breath to reply, but Gregor nudged him. "I don't think he's talking to us."

"Oh … right."

"I steal stuff from poor people. They needed that stuff. I didn't need it," Carlos said through his sobs of deep regret.

A few seconds of silence.

"I've killed little kids by accident ... and it's my fault Diego's legs are gone. It's all my fault," Carlos cried in agony. "I'm a bad person. You don't really know me." He continued to sob, shaking his head from side to side.

A few more seconds of silence.

"How can I be a Jesus-man? How can I do good for You? Don't deserve Your love and forgiveness ...."

Silence.

"I believe! Thank you for forgivin' my sorry carcass! Take over. You're in charge now. Do whatever You wanna do with me." With that, Carlos rolled off the bench and onto his knees.

Suddenly, Carlos felt a strange sensation. "Man, what's happenin'? I feel like a tornado's blowin' insida me and I'm 'bout to explode!"

Gregor held Carlos tightly. "The Holy Spirit is filling you with the message of grace and deliverance. Don't fight Him, Carlos, surrender to Him. Jesus is setting you free."

As soon as Carlos surrendered to the cleansing work of the Holy Spirit, he let out a long moaning bellow as evil chains shattered and the Holy Spirit flooded his soul, casting out the demons of bondage. Tears of joy now rolled down his cheeks, knowing that at last he had a loving Father, that Jesus was real and would never leave him, that he was safe.

Carlos was ready to pray for his little brother. The three men raced to an old, rundown apartment building with graffiti sprayed around the first level. Paint was peeling off the trim of the crumbling brick structures that looked like they should have been torn down twenty years ago. The sounds of TVs, music, voices and crying babies flowed from open windows.

Diego ignored his brother's entrance—his mind lost in a video game world. He had refused help of any kind for rehabilitation, even the fitting of prosthetic legs, and dropped out of school. Unable to keep up with the gang, he lived in his online fantasy life where his disability didn't matter.

"Hey, lil' bro." Carlos greeted his brother.

Diego finally looked up. "Hey, who're these two white guys? You cops?"

"Chill Diego, these guys ... *amigos*." Carlos squatted near Diego's wheelchair to look his brother in the eyes. "Bro, these guys are here to pray for you ... to be healed."

"Whad'ya talkin' 'bout, man? You tellin' me these two guys gonna grow me new legs?" Diego's tone mocked his older brother. "You got some bad stuff. Go away ... leave me alone." He turned away returning to his game.

Carlos nodded at his two new friends. Gregor and Jason got on their knees next to Diego and prayed. An intense, fiery glow covered the teen's body, most powerfully where limbs should have been. Awestruck, the four men watched Diego's legs grow and take shape.

* * *

It was around 2:00 a.m. when Gregor dropped Jason off at his apartment. *What a day*, thought Jason as he lay in bed, reflecting. As he closed his eyes to pray, a vision of Carrie Summers appeared before him. Her face, with its beautifully proportioned features, looked expressionless. Her bright green eyes stared out a window over the D.C. night skyline as if searching for an answer to a question she didn't even know to ask.

Jason was startled when he experienced the same weird feeling.

There was something he was supposed to know, but he couldn't figure out what it was.

He opened his eyes, hoping the vision would go away. But when he closed his eyes again, he could still see Carrie's sad expression like a wounded child labeled the odd outsider.

An explanation for the vision finally came, and he knew he was to meet with her. Too wound up from the miraculous, he couldn't sleep, so he got out of bed and stood at the window, watching the lights of moving traffic.

All Jason knew right now was that he was supposed to meet with Carrie Summers. But why? The media hadn't been very friendly so far. He grimaced at the thought of facing a reporter ... even one as lovely as Carrie.

14

A New Thing

Sunday morning. Light clouds misted the trees in the cool, fall air. Gregor was lost in thought, sipping a hot cocoa while observing a few deer making their way through the woods, stepping with silent precision on the blanket of pine needles. The leaves were just beginning to change color—some, orange; some, red. This was a favorite time of year. For Gregor and Jean, the beauty of the woods provided a peaceful mini-retreat.

Deer, squirrels, crows and bluebirds were the daytime players. Foxes, opossums, and raccoons took the stage at night. Other actors throughout the forest appeared as if awaiting their cue—snakes, turtles, and a variety of birds, along with an interesting array of insects and lizards. Gregor and Jean especially loved the bluebirds that nested in their special box during the summer. Despite the differences in their species, all the wildlife had, oddly enough, become friends.

The breathtaking beauty and sometimes quirky display of God's creation had distracted them from pain and disappointment during their prison years. The allure of glimpsing the creative mind of the

Godhead intrigued them. The woods had always been a gift and helped them cope.

In house slippers and robe, Jean padded in from the bedroom and, cocoa in hand, sat across from Gregor at the table overlooking the tranquil scene. "Penny for your thoughts," she said.

He let out a slow breath. "My mind is racing all over the map. So many thoughts about what's happened with the Taylors, Tony, and the Ortega boys. Didn't sleep. The Lord said this movement was something that has never been done before and not to compare it to past moves. We have no blueprint, no plan, no idea what to do." Gregor turned to regard her, a serious expression on his face. "We haven't gone to church for ten years now. Try tellin' a pastor that God told us not to go to church. How d'ya think that's gonna go over?"

"Yeah." She sighed. "Who's gonna believe that?"

"Over the past thirty-plus years, all the pastors we talked with thought we were a little too far out for their comfort. They don't really want undesirables like drug addicts, prostitutes or the homeless attending. Those types just suck up resources and tarnish the aesthetics. Church leaders talk about revival, but according to many of them, true revival only happens within the walls of *their* church. The institutional Church is in danger of imploding—already a heap of dust and fragments. Too many so-called truths." Gregor let out another big sigh of frustration.

Jean listened with a blank stare as she looked out onto the serene woods. The crow family swooped down, feasting on the boiled eggs she had put out for them. Her heart agreed with Gregor. It had always been exasperating, knowing things should be different—that His body should not be fragmented but one—but with no power to make it happen. It had to be an act of God, not another organizational or denominational program.

"How will the Church ever come together in agreement?" Gregor continued. "If you mention sin and the 'archaic' practice of confessing and repenting, you're labeled a Puritan legalist. Nope, money is too important. Gotta keep those tithing seats filled." He paused in his rant. "Besides, where're we going to get enough harvesters?"

Gregor's mood suddenly changed, and he turned to Jean, his voice now tinged with excitement. "Can you imagine some of these gang members walking into a church today? Wait until you meet Carlos. He's kind of scary-looking in his skin of tattoos. These new harvesters are going to seem pretty rough around the edges, but radical conversions demand radical methods of discipleship. Grandma's sweet Sunday school ain't gonna cut it."

"Well, Jesus brought us this far. He'll tell us what to do," Jean sought to encourage him, then shrugged. "Our life's never been normal anyway, so why should we expect the rest of it to be normal? We have to relax and let Him do what He's going to do."

As Gregor and Jean prayed, the light of Heaven flooded the room as it had during the first night's Visitation and at Tony's house. To their amazement, Jesus walked out from the light and sat in one of the kitchen chairs. He looked much different from before. The pure white hair, those fiery eyes and the glowing skin like burnished bronze were temporarily veiled for Gregor and Jean's sake. Even so, an intense reverence filled their hearts. It was extremely humbling, and they bowed before Him.

Come. Talk with Me, Jesus invited. Then his tone immediately changed. He spoke intently. *Do not think in the old mindset. I AM doing a new thing in the Final Awakening.*

I will protect the birth of the Awakening, but soon I will lift some restraint from Lucifer. Expect resistance from the world and the Church at his hand. Do not despair. I AM always in control; nothing escapes My notice. The ministering spirits of Heaven and those whom

I choose on earth will work arm in arm with great power, easily countering the attacks of the enemy. Sadly, some of My own will oppose My works, believing they do My will. Some will say the acts I perform through you are of Lucifer.

The Church ignorantly accepts the blatant schemes of darkness and, in some cases, seeks the depths of demonic doctrines. The whole of My Word recorded in Scripture is falsely seen as optional—the earliest Words merely children's stories.

Jesus paused, sorrowed over lost lambs who had wandered away from his protection.

They have forgotten that sin creates a chasm between them and Me. Friendship with the world is hostility toward Me, for the world is evil and I AM holy. I will intervene with a firm hand. Would a loving father permit his children to play in a dangerous environment and not care what happened to them? No, he would not. He would do all within his power to teach his children to avoid such places, even to the point of repeated discipline. It is for the children's own good and the father's love for them that he intervenes.

As My people Israel were stiff-necked, so too, is the Church. Because of her hard heart, she will not be the main conduit of the Awakening. Infighting and mistrust divide and prevent the Body from working as one. Some elevate knowledge above loving Me. Others twist the truth of the Scriptures to wrap around their man-made doctrines. They appear to be ever learning, but are unable to come to the knowledge of the truth.

The Church is as Eli, who willfully permitted the sins of his sons, Hophni and Phineas, honoring them above Me by allowing them to defile My priesthood with adultery and theft. I have sent messengers warning My Church, but just as Eli did not heed My messenger, neither do the leaders of My Church heed Me. They tolerate sin in the flock, because they tolerate and excuse their own sin. I hate sin, and I died to remove the mark of sin, not embrace it.

Suddenly, the features of their beloved Lord were overshadowed by the great grief of His heart as He considered the fate of those who continually refused to accept all that He desired to offer them.

Ignoring the call to repentance opens the portal of hell into My sanctuaries. Secret sin invites more evil, more compromise, and more twisted meaning of Scripture. Their godliness is false and of this world, but when My righteousness is removed, My power is also removed. Practices of the evil one are intermingled in worship as My people lack discernment, attributing Lucifer's work to the work of the Holy Spirit. Once again, Ichabod is written over the sanctuary of My people; My Glory has departed.

Do not take the message of the Final Awakening to the Church for she will reject your mission. I will deal with her separately as I expose her sins. You and the others will be like Paul preaching to the Gentiles.

The River of Life from Heaven will split into two rivers. One river is the established Church. The other river is the new movement of the Fire of Heaven for this harvest of mercy. The second river is required until the first river surrenders to Me. At the Church's surrender—which will be at the close of the Awakening—the two rivers will merge and flow as one again.

Jesus' tone changed from that of an instructor to the stern voice of a prophet forewarning them of imminent chastisements from the brethren.

I warn you now: Expect attacks through the Church at Lucifer's hand. My own people persecuted and killed Me; know they will do the same to you and all others who flow outside the Church river. Remember, the real enemy is the evil one.

I will draw those who do not fit into the Church mindset to Myself in the first sweep of the harvesting sickle. They will be the leaders of this move. I have placed many like you in key cities in every nation. As leader over the first harvest of workers, your goal is to replace yourself as others rise up. You will not lead this movement at its conclusion, but your influence and foundation will establish it.

A servant does not know what his master plans to do. I have told you these things beforehand; thus, I no longer call you servants, I call you My friends. You did not choose Me, but I appointed you and prepared you so that your fruit will multiply.

At that, Jesus returned to the light and, gradually, the light faded away. If one could be both ecstatic and sober at the same time, this described the state in which Gregor and Jean found themselves. For some time, they could not speak, did not move as they absorbed the mind-numbing fact that Jesus Christ, the Son of the Living God, had sat with them at their kitchen table.

15
The Cycle And The Clock

"I don't think I'll ever get used to that," said Jean. Gregor's mind was somewhere else, and he didn't acknowledge her comment. "You know, sitting at the table with Jesus!" she reminded him.

"Yeah," replied Gregor, reflecting on what the Savior had told them. "I think I'm gonna go work on that old desk for a while." He headed out to the garage.

For years, Gregor and Jean had refurbished old furniture and renovated old houses. They had moved over eleven times, mostly to keep a job. Each house was in worse condition than the last. They had a sense of accomplishment and satisfaction in transforming old broken-down things into something beautiful. Jean was the one with artistic flair, and Gregor could fix or build almost anything. It was an outlet the Lord provided to keep them busy and their minds off their problems. In many ways, it foreshadowed their calling. Broken, forgotten furniture and houses would be replaced by broken and forgotten people.

A cloud of sawdust hovered around Gregor as his phone lit up. Caller ID revealed: Tony Robertson. Gregor quickly shed work gloves, dust mask and earplugs to answer. "Hey, how's it goin'?"

"I read the Bible through as you suggested, then went back and re-read the New Testament. Do you have some time to talk?"

Wow, he's a fast reader! We really need his smarts on the team, thought Gregor.

Tony's new passion for more of God, aided by his intellectual abilities, enabled him to blaze through the Bible. In addition, he was fresh, reading the Word of God without the tainted vision of denominational doctrines driven deeply into him. Talking with Tony would be a great break from sanding down the desk.

A few minutes later, Gregor skipped up the steps of the little blue house with the white picket fence and sat down on the cushioned wicker swing. The red maple trees in the front yard provided the perfect shade and were stunning this time of year.

Tony opened the front door and greeted Gregor with a big smile and an even bigger hug. "Hey, Gregor, thanks for coming." Tony had brought out two spiced ciders, handed one to Gregor, then sat in the chair opposite the porch swing. "If Andrea could see me now, discussing the Bible with you, she would be dancing. She often read her Bible and prayed on that swing. I know she really wanted me to be there with her, talking about God ...."

His voice trailed off as he teared up. He took a sip of cider, then cleared his throat. "Well ... you know, I was of the mindset that if it made her feel good, then I had no issues with it as long as I wasn't required to do the same. Never thought it would be me wanting to talk about the Bible in a positive way." He shook his head in amazement.

Gregor could not help observing that Tony seemed a completely different person—nothing like he was at their first meeting. He genuinely wanted to learn more about the Word of God for himself and not just to tear it apart, researching another book criticizing Christianity. Tony's heart still ached for his wife, but Gregor could tell there was joy floating around in that big, burly body and he was embracing all of it. In some ways, Gregor could see himself in Tony. Just like Gregor, once Tony decided to be in, he was all in. No doubting, no compromise, full speed ahead.

Tony fired questions as Gregor sat back, waiting for the Holy Spirit to reveal the answers to him. "OK, let me start with something general in nature. Why do people miss what God is doing? For example, with so much symbolism and foreshadowing of the Messiah, why did the Jews fail to see that Jesus is Messiah?"

Gregor was surprised to hear this from Tony. A Messianic Jew had pointed out the significance of certain prophetic Scriptures in the Old Testament, but Gregor had never noticed them on his own. He realized that during the Awakening, those young in their faith would be given unique insights. God would accelerate their knowledge and understanding as He had with Kyle, the young man from the early years of living-room Jesus-seekers.

"Great question. The Jews' understanding of the Messiah came solely from the Old Testament, of course, since the New Testament had not been written at that time. The Old Testament gives images of the Messiah as both a Lamb and a Lion. The prophecies of His first coming were fulfilled, just not in the way the Jews expected.

"Messiah came first as the perfect sacrificial Lamb of God, atoning for mankind's sin and making a way to restore relationship with the Almighty. At the end of the age, Jesus will return as the Lion of Judah to take his Bride—the authentic Church—to live with Him and finally judge the world. The Jews wanted the Lion first, but got the Lamb instead. Same mistake will happen; only this time, the Lamb will be expected and the Lion will come.

"Based on their understanding of Scripture, the influential Jews of the day wanted a powerful leader to overthrow the Roman occupiers and set up the Kingdom of God on earth. The existing religious establishment wanted to co-rule with the Messiah, believing their duty would be to enforce the Mosaic Law and the other hundreds of traditions invented by man." Gregor paused to take a few more sips of cider.

"Jesus' harshest words were always directed at religious leaders," he said. "He exposed the evil in their hearts, void of mercy, grace and love. Indeed, they loved their traditions more than God. When He confronted the Jewish leaders with truth, they wanted to kill Him! Prophets were imprisoned, tortured, rejected and killed by ruling religious leaders. Same thing will happen again."

"So, messengers of the Awakening will be persecuted like the prophets in the Old Testament?" Tony asked, furrowing his brow as he considered this hard truth.

"Well, yeah, because the Awakening won't fit into established religion's paradigm." Gregor explained.

"Jewish leaders studied Scripture, so why didn't they see it?" Tony wanted to know, setting his empty mug on a small table nearby.

"Hard hearts. Listening to God lost its importance; fruitless tradition became supreme. The Old Testament is full of God pleading with His people to have tender hearts toward Him, so it wasn't a new concept for the leaders of Jesus' day. That's why He rebuked them for hypocrisy and hard hearts. We tune into God through His Word and prayer. Hearts get hard when they stop listening. Much of church prayer—if it exists at all—is a Jesus-To-Do List. Rarely have I come across those who will first ask what they *should* pray. In my experience, most churches don't really *want* to hear from God because He tends to upset the status quo."

Tony nodded as he thought about what Gregor said. "Makes sense. How can you know someone unless there's communication, speaking *and* listening?"

Gregor leaned back setting the swing in motion. "Unfortunately, Tony, there's a lot of bad teaching out there—fluff to make people

118

feel good about themselves—modern psychology or New Age practices as doctrine. If pastors taught exactly what the Bible says about sin, the pew-sitters would vote with their money and their feet to support another church that will pardon their unbiblical lifestyle."

Tony sat back in his chair, pondering these concepts—traditions without heartfelt significance, meaningless and sometimes dangerous "fluff." That's one of the very things that had kept Tony from going to church with Andrea. The pat answers, the same ritual service over and over again—so predictable, even robotic. Cold, sterile, fake. If God existed, Tony wanted a deep, intimate relationship with the living God, not a club made up of "members" who had no clue as to what was really important in the heart of their Creator.

Tony had observed churchgoing coworkers and students act and speak a certain way on Sunday, but when Monday rolled around, they transformed into someone else. He often heard them speaking Christian lingo while haughtily looking down on others with gossip and back-stabbing. He pictured their cloud of pompous self-righteousness like the dirty cloud surrounding Pigpen in Charlie Brown—a cloud of hypocrisy, leaving a foul odor and a bad taste in his mouth. It really grated on Tony's nerves.

The numerous denominations bothered Tony, too. The Bible talks about *the* Body of Christ, not *many* bodies. Obviously, Christians couldn't get along among themselves. So why bother? Why should he be a part of something so dysfunctional and fractured?

"Gregor, where's the real stuff of Christianity, the stuff I read in the Bible?" Tony asked in all seriousness, leaning forward and resting his elbows on his knees. "Healing, deliverance, unbending faith, and true, intimate relationship with God Almighty?"

"A lot of the Church's idea of success is focused on growth, numbers and notoriety," Gregor began. "In the Kingdom of God, success is measured by nurturing Christ-like character through obedience, and obedience doesn't mean things always go smoothly. Many times, the fruit of submission is suffering. Few American churches will preach *that* message today. According to the gospel of prosperity, suffering and hardships are for losers. Actually, the real blessing is with those who suffer, yet worship Jesus with a pure and joyful heart."

Tony leaned back into the chair taking a moment to think.

"Hey, do you remember the woman who gave two coins at the temple?" Gregor asked interrupting the silence. "The disciples didn't notice her, but Jesus did and pointed her out. Rich people dropping money into the temple treasury probably sounded like dumping a bucket of coins into one of those coin counters at the grocery store. The poor widow dropped in two, small copper coins. *Clink, clink.*

"But what she gave was more valuable than what all the others gave. They gave out of their abundance; she gave out of her need. Ask yourself, did her two coins help the temple operate its daily ministries? Not really, but in the Kingdom of God, her small, sacrificial gift attracted the notice of the Son of God. It wasn't the amount that was given, but the desire of her heart to give God everything. He measures by His Kingdom standards, not by man's." Gregor stopped to allow Tony to digest the truth of what he was saying.

Tony was beginning to understand that many principles of God's Kingdom are opposite of how the world views things—like *dying* to have *life.*

"A few days back, I heard the Lord say, *You must learn to mature as a child and not as an adult,*" Gregor shared. "When we were first born, we needed our parents for everything in order to live. Over time, we grew more independent until we no longer needed them. In the Kingdom of God, it's the exact opposite. When we are born again into

His Kingdom, we start out very independent, but over time, we must become totally dependent on Him. Deeper faith leads to deeper trust." Tony's facial expression registered that he understood. *Aha* .... Jesus, in all humility and submission, always pointed the way to His Father. The gospel was simple and refreshing: Love God and serve Him through obedience.

"Hey, Mr. Ph.D., as you study the Bible, why don't you create a study guide?" Gregor suggested. "You're gonna need it when you teach others. No better place to come from than a young scholar like yourself."

"Young in Christ, yes. But young in body? No way!" Tony laughed, rising to give Gregor another hug before the two men parted.

* * *

That night, Jesus appeared to Gregor in a dream. He took Gregor to a large hill. On top of the hill sat a bicycle resting upside down on the handlebars and seat. The rear wheel turned, but never gained traction against the air, remaining in place in spite of its furious spinning.

Jesus explained, *Today, the ministry of the Church looks like an inverted bicycle. The axle at the wheel's center is the pastoral leadership, and the spokes are the people. Nothing reaches the spokes unless it first passes through the axle. In many cases, the axle (pastoral leadership) controls everything that goes to the spokes (the people). The bicycle wheel cannot turn unless power is transferred from the axle to the spokes and then to the tire.*

In the current church model, nothing happens unless it originates with leadership, and leadership often questions or even denies something a member of the congregation might feel led to do through

My Spirit. Pastors are shepherds of their flocks, not CEOs of companies. A true shepherd knows every bleat of His sheep—whether a cry of distress, a pang of hunger, or simply the need to be affirmed— and walks among them.

In truth, as My servant Paul admonished in the Book of Hebrews, all should be shepherds by now, leading and discipling others. There is too much passivity in the structure of the current church model. Too many of My followers desire to use their gift(s) but are often stifled by leadership."

He turned to observe the bicycle again. *The wheel has inverted itself. Do you see how it spins fruitlessly? The time of this model is finished.*

Suddenly, the scene shifted and Gregor saw a group of people looking at a table clock. The face of the clock opened, revealing the inner workings—gears, cogs and springs. All parts interlocked, working as one to keep time.

Fascinated by the gears, people moved closer to examine them. When a person touched a gear, he disappeared into the clock, becoming a cog. As more people disappeared into the clock, it grew in size until it towered over them like London's Big Ben.

The Final Awakening is like this mechanical clock, Jesus pointed out. *A cog, on a gear represents a person. A gear is a specific gift such as mercy, healing, or prophecy. Just as interlocking cogs on moving gears enable the clock to keep time, the Holy Spirit will dovetail the people, enabling them to use their varied gifts to advance My Kingdom.*

I will raise up ministry centers to train, equip and send workers for the Final Awakening. The centers will operate like the clock in that the leadership is not the center of the movement. No more passive participants. In the clock model, all believers will take up their call, working the fields ripe for harvest .... His voice trailed off as He faded from view.

Gregor awoke the next morning, puzzling over the bizarre dream. An upside-down bicycle? A clock? The Lord certainly used interesting props to get his point across!

16

Senate Prayer Breakfast

Senator Daniel Taylor walked into the Senate Prayer Breakfast for the first time in his career. Barb had encouraged him to go for years, but he'd dismissed her suggestion, thinking his peers who attended this silly event were either looking to broker a deal behind a cloak of religion or were misled into believing that prayer could really change things.

Senator Amy Sanders from Tennessee had personally invited Dan to the prayer time. She had met with him in his office after the news of Jason's resurrection broke. Amy was one of the few who believed Dan's account and cheered his warning to America, adding that it was long overdue.

Amy had also let him know that the breakfast was usually a small group of around fifteen senators. At the last minute, she had texted Dan the location of the room. When he walked in, he double-checked to make sure he hadn't read the text wrong. Instead of fifteen people, there were three hundred, filling every space in the room. Even if every senator attended, there would only be one hundred. Who were all these people and why were they at the Senate Prayer Breakfast?

People stared as he moved through the crowded room. He felt that there was a big sign, labeled "FREAK," hanging over his head. The entire Hill had heard about the resurrection and his warning to America. He frantically looked around to find a seat. Sitting would be less conspicuous than standing.

Amy spotted Dan and waved him over to her table. He headed in her direction, relieved that he could finally sit and have the support of an empathetic colleague. As he approached her, he realized there were no more seats at her table or any other table, for that matter.

Amy whispered into Dan's ear and his face turned ashen. He looked at Amy and then around the whole room. Dan had gravely misunderstood her invitation. Distracted at the time, he had agreed to attend. He had *not* agreed to be the keynote speaker.

OK, here we go, Lord. Do your thing, he thought.

He quickly texted Barb, Jason and the Wallaces to pray for him. He turned to walk toward the podium, praying like crazy. He slowly made his way up to the front, trying to give himself time to hear from the Lord.

On the way, something definitely changed. The Fire of Heaven burned in his heart, pumping the desire to speak Jesus' mind. With every beat of his heart and every step he took, the message pulsated stronger and stronger, consuming any previous hesitancy. In fact, he now felt he would explode if he did not speak.

He didn't know yet what to say, but the Spirit did. He was ready to hear what the Lord would say through him. Dan got out of the way and let the Lord step forward. Ignoring the mixture of applause and sneers, he turned around to speak with a big smile.

"My colleagues and friends, thank you for coming today to pray for our nation. By the size of the crowd, I assume your interest has something to do with my son's death and resurrection. There is no backtracking or getting around the truth. Jason was pronounced dead."

Perfect silence hovered over the room with every ear tuned on Dan's words, so much so that plates full of food sat neglected. He could hear himself breathing and his heart beating. Each person anticipated their own desired outcome. Some hoped that God would do a work this morning, while others hoped to flatten crazy Dan Taylor and be rid of him, once and for all.

Dan took a deep breath before beginning to speak. "I want to set the record straight. At the time my son was pronounced dead, I was not a follower of Jesus Christ. I thought religion was for weak people who needed something to believe in during the hard times in their lives. Belief in God wasn't anything real, only an imaginary crutch propping up fragile fortitude, a coping mechanism. I did not need a crutch.

"As my son lay dying in the critical care unit of the hospital, I had a most unusual dream. I dreamed of a man I did not know nor had ever seen. In the dream, the man laid his hands on Jason and cried out to Jesus to breathe life back into our son. I saw Jason get out of his death bed and walk to me, saying it was time to believe. At that instant, the dream ended. It seemed so very real, and one word would not leave me, the word *believe*."

Dan continued with the story of Jason's resurrection. He spoke of his personal struggle in watching his only child lying there lifeless, kept alive only by noisy machines. He explained how he found the man in the dream. He told the story of how this man prayed for Jason in the morgue, including details of Susie, the morgue attendant, and that Jason's dead, ashen body sat up, filled with vibrant life again.

"In short, I witnessed my son rise from the dead. Few in the history of man have had the awe-inspiring privilege of watching the genuinely miraculous hand of God. All I can say is that Jesus brought my son back to life. Now, I know you're all curious about the mysterious man in the dream—the man who prayed. He wants no attention drawn to himself, so his identity will remain unknown. My focus is on the One who can heal and raise the dead, Jesus Christ alone," said Dan. "And now, I, too, believe and have committed my life to serving Him."

There were some tears of sympathy as he concluded, with some huffing and guffawing at the wild improbability of his story. Dan scanned the room, searching for something he sensed he should notice. He saw nothing other than people staring back at him. Then he felt a fearful presence beside him. When he mustered enough courage to look, he slowly turned to see who or what was there. Immediately, his eyes were opened to another world, almost knocking him off his feet.

There was Storis, the faithful angel, standing directly to Dan's right, shining brightly in the reflection of God's Glory. Storis directed Dan's attention to the company of angels positioned in various places around the room, shining in the same light as Storis. A glittering sword dangled from a golden waistband wrapped around each of the angels' long white linen robes. The swords held the power of the Word.

In contrast, dark and grotesque beings lurked in the more secluded sections of the large meeting room, trying to avoid the angels, although the light was inescapable. The demon beings cringed in pain at the brilliance of the light of God, but they were under orders from their dark leader to complete a mission, so they stayed. Some boldly stood out in the open next to the people who hated the name of Jesus and wanted Dan expelled from his Senate seat. The evil beings whispered into the people's ears, goading them and heightening their already agitated state. Storis nodded to Dan, silently directing him to continue.

Dan spoke up with confidence. "Jesus has a message for this nation. First, repent, putting away all idols. I'm not talking about statues you bow down to. I'm talking about the obsessions we have erected in our own hearts like the love of money, power, knowledge, fame, entertainment, lust, and greed—whatever puts your will above the will of Jesus. We must surrender our lives to Him."

A few hecklers tried to shout Dan down. An angel under Storis's direction silenced the goading demons, stopping the hecklers' insults.

"Second, seek first God's governance in our lives and live according to His commandments. If this nation repents, God promises to provide for believers in the coming days of chaos. We, as a nation, must love Him with all our hearts, all our strength and all our minds. God will judge this nation, because America has left Him. He judges for the purpose of bringing us back to the safety of His ordered structure for life," Dan spoke clearly, powerfully, without searching for words as the Spirit spoke through him. "Jesus' commandments are for our protection and blessing. They are not harsh rules, denying us pleasure.

"You are eternal beings, whether you believe God exists or not. Just because you don't accept the truth doesn't make it any less true. When you die, you will still eternally exist—either in absolute peace and love in Heaven with Jesus or in absolute torment and hatred in hell with Lucifer."

The demon beings made strange noises, sneering at Dan when he spoke the truth of the two eternal destinations. The conflict between evil and good was staring him in the face. Passion for truth loaded his words with authority. "Make no mistake about this, my fellow Senators and guests, we live in the last days. Know that we fight against a real enemy. Our enemy has flooded the earth with twisted, perverted lies that have sadly been accepted and actually celebrated by those who call themselves Christians," Dan cried out, his voice reflecting the surety of his words.

The familiar movement of heavenly air brushed against Dan's face. The air swirled around his body, gracefully radiating as light with fiery tips like scalpels, powered by the Fire of Heaven. The podium curtains swayed back and forth. As the air rushed by, tablecloths flapped, toppling dishes and glassware onto the floor.

Blades with tails of light swooped speedily, penetrating hardened hearts, searching secret thoughts and motives. Dan heard some people sobbing for mercy as the Sword of the Spirit separated truth from lies. Some wailed, burying their faces in the floor. Naked in the Spirit, they attempted to cover themselves to camouflage harbored sin now splayed open, fully exposed. The revelation of their corruption caused them to shake with grief. All in the room were laid bare to the Holy Spirit's searching blade, with no escape.

Dan wasn't quite sure what to do as he watched what appeared to be pandemonium, but he knew all was ordered and completely under the control of the Holy Spirit. He noticed some very key and influential Capitol Hill kingpins quaking in their chairs, their eyes boring through him with hatred. Their militant abhorrence grew as the dark beings next to them spoke into their ears again. Those captive to the demons silently cursed Dan. *The power of hell will consume you, Dan Taylor, and all those who try to follow the Nazarene! You will not escape Lucifer's wrath!*

A little confused as to why the demonic beings did not flee at the powerful presence of the Holy Spirit, Dan turned to Storis, puzzled. Storis assured Dan it was part of Jesus' plan.

Dan looked back at the assembled group with the Fire of Heaven shining in his eyes. The Fire then bolted from his eyes as multiple strikes of lightning, piercing the evil beings and scalding them, leaving behind a smoldering sulfur smell. At Dan's command, every dark being fled from the room as the truth and light of God consumed their evil lies.

The people glaring at Dan—those who violently rejected the true and living God—fell backward as if someone had forcefully pushed them. Like marionette puppets with no control over their bodies, they were then lifted and placed on their knees.

The forceful juxtaposition of their bodies in disagreement with their hearts fueled their hatred and anger. Dan could hear them vowing never to give up their planned control of the government. The fight for the nation's soul was just beginning. The line was drawn that day … and Dan was called to lead the fight.

* * *

The lightning strikes of the Fire of Heaven proved too much to withstand. Datter and Gorfius, Lucifer's messengers, were forced to flee, recoiling in pain.

"My eyes, my eyes!" cried Gorfius.

A familiar demon swept past them, followed by another and another. Crowds of demons left the meeting room in great fear and trembling. Datter attempted to stop some of them to get a report, but they were terrified, determined to get out of there.

"This is bad, very bad," said Datter worried about the moment he would have to report this to his leader. "The Glorious One's power is here."

Gorfius groaned, rubbing his eyes.

Datter smacked Gorfius on the back of the head. "My eyes burn, too. Quit complaining."

The two fallen angels hobbled to a darker corner of the building.

"I hate this assignment!" Gorfius shouted as he marched around in a circle. "We have no control over when or where the Glorious One's power appears, but Lucifer always acts as if it's our fault."

Datter slumped in a heap against the wall. "We need to wait until the Fire of Heaven leaves to gather our strength. I have not seen a manifestation like this since Pentecost. Storis standing there reflecting the Glory of the Glorious One ... ugh! Such agony!" He winced. "This must be critically strategic to the Nazarene's plan to have such great guardians present. Yes, critical."

He rubbed his gnarly chin, pondering his next move. "This is big, very big indeed. Vigilance and preparedness, Gorfius, is in order. No more bumbling around. You can be sure that Lucifer will not let this slide. The leader will be in a rampage. The intensity of the battle increases, yes greatly increases."

"How will we tell Lucifer about the Glorious One's light and avoid his wrath?" whined Gorfius as he continued to walk around in circles, rubbing his hands together, worried about what punishment awaited.

"No matter how you look at it, Gorfius, we lose," stated Datter as he stood to his feet. "We always lose. Heaven will destroy us ... or lord Lucifer will." With that, a strategy occurred to him, and he abruptly hurled his body against Gorfius with the intent of causing visible damage.

Gorfius returned the blow with even greater force. The two creatures fought like alley cats until enough wounds had been inflicted to be convincing. Returning with this report of the presence of Jesus' light would be painful unless it appeared they had fought against it. Perhaps, with war wounds, Lucifer might lessen their punishment. Sufficiently tattered, they took off for the cavern to give their report to their master.

17

The Reporters

Jason sat down to eat a perfectly iron skillet-seared beef fillet, baked potato and garden salad. *A thing of beauty*, he thought, eying his plate with satisfaction while taking in the wafting aroma. Bzzzz. His cell phone rang.

To preserve some privacy, he had changed his number to avoid harassing calls about his resurrection. He didn't recognize the number on the caller ID and wondered who it could be since only seven people had the new number. *Maybe it's Carlos on a stolen phone*, he mused. *Have to talk to the boys about that.* If it was important, whoever was calling would leave a message. He took the first bite of steak when the Spirit prompted him to answer.

He pushed the accept button and then the speaker button. "Hello?" he said trying to quietly finish chewing.

"Jason, this is Carrie Summers from WNN News. Do you have a moment?"

Jason choked, coughing a few times. He was speechless, frozen with one hand holding a fork and the other a steak knife. *This is weird,* he thought. *I was supposed to call her. Hey, how did she get this number?* Words didn't make it out of his mouth.

"Jason, are you still there? Hello? Can you hear me?"

"Sure, yeah, I can hear you. What do you want?" He grimaced. Knife and fork went down. He stood, picked up the phone and paced as he listened.

Although people had often commented on his good looks—like his father—he'd always felt awkward around women. With the addition of a very attractive woman to the equation, Jason felt completely out of his element. Panic hit him as he realized he wasn't going to make any kind of favorable impression. *But what did that matter anyway? She's just a reporter.*

He couldn't figure out why it was so hard for him to talk to young, attractive, single women. As Director of IT for one of the largest area banks, speaking was never much of a problem. He loved his work and was an expert in his field. Presenting on any IT matter to any group, even high C-level executives, was easy for him. Jason knew more about information technology than anyone in the room and he knew it. He especially loved pitching his proposed projects to corporate executives. He never once felt intimidated or at a loss for words. Why now? Especially to this woman he's never really met and didn't especially like.

"I was hoping you had some free time to talk with me," explained Carrie.

Since the Lord told him to meet with her, he didn't press the issue of how she had obtained his phone number. "I am unemployed, with plenty of time. I guess you can imagine what they thought of me when they saw your report on TV."

"Sorry to hear you lost your job. You have to admit, what happened at your parent's home is, well, most unusual. I assume your employer feared you might fry all the building's computer systems. So, what are you going to do?" asked Carrie.

"This may sound a little cliché, but trust God. Don't have much of a choice anyway."

"I guess not. I want to tell America your story. Will you give me an interview?"

There was a pause. "Uh ... OK." Jason reluctantly agreed only in obedience to the Lord's command. "But no cameras."

"I was really hoping to get your story on camera." Carrie's voice exposed her disappointment.

"No cameras, no recordings, just you, me, paper and pencil."

"OK ... I'll agree to your conditions. Perhaps a casual lunch?" Carrie suggested with a hint of pleading in her voice. "My treat, of course." The compulsion to meet with Jason had been gnawing at her. If he wanted to meet underwater, she probably would have agreed as the desire to satisfy that yearning to get the story was strong.

"Sure, how about tomorrow at Pat's Deli, corner of 15th and K Street? Let's say 11:30? And this might sound a little cloak and dagger, but it would be nice if no one recognized you. I don't want the attention."

"Yes, that's perfect." Carrie was elated she got her foot in the door. "It's a date ... uh ...I mean it's not a real date. I mean, I agree on the date, place and time."

Carrie's face felt hot and flushed. *Good thing it's just a phone call,* she thought. "I'll wear something generic to blend in, not decked out for the WNN News camera. Should I wear a trench coat for a disguise?" she joked letting out a little giggle and immediately felt stupid like a middle school student. Whew! She couldn't hang up quickly enough.

* * *

Datter and Gorfius entered Lucifer's throne room with great trepidation. No matter how they reported the appearance of the Holy One's presence, the dark leader would be enraged. The masquerade of self-inflicted wounds was their only hope of escaping his wrath.

"Oh, mighty Lucifer, we bring you news. As you see, Gorfius and I have engaged in a mighty battle against the holy angels of the Nazarene, yes, a mighty battle," stated Datter with the most courage he could collect.

Lucifer tapped his fingers against the arm of his throne as he studied Datter's and Gorfius's wounds for a moment. He slowly rose then circled the two minions inspecting the gashes. Datter and Gorfius trembled in fear, keeping their eyes focused downward. With undetected motion, Lucifer struck both fallen angels with the end of his scepter. One moment Datter and Gorfius stood, then instantaneously, they were on the ground groveling at their leader's feet.

"Liars!" snarled Lucifer in a guttural tone. "You fools! You dare attempt to trick me, the deceiver? There is no remnant of Glory emanating from your injuries." His impatience grew stronger. "Give me the report, you human brained idiots," he bellowed in disgust.

Datter and Gorfius stood to their feet smoothing over their wounds.

"Oh, mighty and great king, ruler of earth, we report about a happening in Washington, D. C. The man, Taylor, performed a unique miracle walking in the power of the Nazarene." Gorfius rasped.

"Out with it! Withhold no tidbit of information. Remember, you are expendable."

"Lord Lucifer, the Fire of Heaven burned in the man as fully as it did in the Nazarene. This man, Taylor, has a son who was raised from the dead in whom the Fire of Heaven also burns. There is another man and his mate in whom the starter firebrand was originated," blurted Datter. "Yes, a firebrand."

Lucifer snapped his fingers several times in a row and asked, "Names, names, what are their names?"

"Gregor and Jean Wallace, people of no importance, my lord," Gorfius immediately offered.

"Do not tell me they are of no importance! The Fire of Heaven burns in them, and they have multiplied the Fire in others. That makes them important, you buffoons!" Lucifer howled.

"The Presence was so mighty, my lord, that even Prince Brakus was unable to engage in battle. Every dark being was scattered. There was no time to draw not even one sword." Gorfius bowed low cringing in anticipation of another strike from the scepter.

Just as Gorfius finished his report, Prince Brakus hurriedly entered.

"Well, nice of you to join us Brakus," Lucifer said sarcastically. "Have you come to tell me of your great victory?" Lucifer pulled a chair out from the table. "Sit, please, do tell."

Brakus feared Lucifer's punishment. He would have rather stood for better footing for a quick escape, but he sat as ordered. "Lord Lucifer, no prince of darkness had warning. None were prepared for what happened when the man, Taylor, spoke. I have not seen power like this since ..." he hesitated to mention the day "... since the Spirit of God was given to dwell in the hearts of man, Pentecost, my lord."

"Did I not order you to fill people's minds with hatred and corruption?" asked Lucifer as his voice grew louder. "Did I not order you to own the halls of the United States government? You assured me earlier of your confidence in victory." Lucifer stood behind Brakus, his hot breath felt on the fallen prince's neck. "Why then did you get run over at a pitiful prayer breakfast?"

Lucifer looked at Datter and Gorfius who were edging their way to the door and ordered them to stop and stay. Brakus sat, his eyes downcast, avoiding eye contact with the dreadful leader. "Continue, speak," commanded Lucifer as he pressed the scepter against an oozing gash on the prince's throat.

"I have worked to manipulate the prayer gathering for years now and have made it ecumenical and powerless. The Nazarene's name was not spoken anymore. In the past, the man, Taylor, turned his nose up at the followers of the Nazarene, so there was no impending danger. Per your command, I strategically positioned your servants about the room speaking lies to the attendees. Every dark messenger was astonished when the man stood and spoke with the Nazarene's authority and the Fire of Heaven proceeded out of him throwing humans to the floor causing some to …" Prince Brakus paused again afraid to speak the word.

"Well, well, causing some to what?" Lucifer pressed the scepter more forcefully against Brakus's throat causing droplets from the wound to fall onto the table.

"Causing some to … *repent*, my great leader."

With that Lucifer went into a rage. "Repent, repent, repent! The word is an abomination to me. Do not speak it in my presence!" He struck Brakus across the face for saying it aloud. "Why did you not stop them?"

Brakus continued, fearing yet another stinging blow. "I did try, my lord. The faithful angel, Storis, prevented me. He came upon me in great strength, threw me to the ground putting the sword of Truth upon my throat."

Lucifer was stunned and sat in disbelief. He had almost destroyed America from within. He had not calculated a divine intervention of this magnitude at this time. *What is the Nazarene doing?* he wondered. *Why send Storis, who watched over the earthly birth of the Nazarene, to an insignificant gathering such as the prayer breakfast?* "Get out, you idiots! Quench the Fire of Heaven by getting them off target through pain or self-importance—whatever method does not matter to me! Just turn them away from the Nazarene. Leave, now!" commanded Lucifer.

Alone, Lucifer paced back and forth in his queer copy of a throne room void of any heavenly influence. Murals depicting his great victories were painted on the stone walls. Eve's disobedience, Israel's idolatry, rejection of the Nazarene's gift and the growing, deeper deception in the Church were his favored ones. And now the latest painting—a comical jesus, stupid and incompetent. Each picture reminded him of his progress in destroying man, but every believed lie—no matter how small—was counted as a victory.

Lucifer spun around facing the wall behind him. There hung the picture he prized the most. It portrayed him as a little devil with horns, a pitchfork, a red stretch suit and pointed tail. An image far from depicting his former glory or even his strength as a fallen one.

The perfect cherub who had walked in the midst of the fiery stones on the Holy One's mountain is portrayed as a cartoon character, he thought. The image made him laugh. Lucifer had stealthily convinced the world he was an insignificant, feeble creature that one could flick away with a finger and a thumb. *Believe this, or better yet, do not believe at all.*

His best work was done under the cloak of invisibility. If he does not exist; there is no evil. If there is no evil; there is no hell. If there is no hell; there is no need for a savior. If there is no need for a savior; humans have no need to follow the Nazarene.

It didn't matter what god man worshiped, just as long as it was not the Nazarene. Let the multitudes worship the slew of Hindu gods, Buddha, Allah, science, atheism or a tree for that matter. Stupid humans worship something even if they claim they have no god. The pathway didn't matter to Lucifer. He delighted whether they followed him with or without full consent just as long as they belonged to him in the end.

Lucifer wanted revenge for his eviction from Heaven. He had never known anything but God's love, His Glory and the created perfection given to him by the Creator. All was lost now because of his rebellion. He knew the Godhead's deep unwavering love for Their prized creation, man, and that the only way to exact pain to Their heart was to destroy humankind—now his consuming mission.

He manipulated man through misery, working to place blame on God for pain and suffering, pressing the flesh to control the heart. He had convinced Esau to sell his birthright for a bowl of stew, exchanging the gift of God for temporal satisfaction of the flesh—a prominent memorial among the murals. Man was granted heirship to the Kingdom through the Son, but the schemer's plan had convinced multitudes to walk away from the eternal gift to seek worthless pleasures. Thus was a true and tried tactic to collect names for his book of the damned.

To the powers of darkness, adding a name to Lucifer's book was the greatest achievement and glory a fallen one could attain. With every name added, they grew in boldness and depth of evil schemes, working to take as many souls as possible with them in their condemnation. Being cast into the lake of fire was quickly approaching. A driving passion of destruction fueled every wicked, perverse heart. Time was short and they were bound by oath to make the Godhead pay a price for the judgment the fallen ones had brought upon their own heads.

Lucifer looked up and raised his clinched fist to Heaven as evil brewed beyond the imagination of angel or man. Only the Father, Son and Spirit knew the depths of darkness there in Lucifer's heart. He desired to have audience with God, but had not yet been summoned since the last time he accused the Church of infidelity. Lucifer had already been denied the small band of believers empowered with the Fire of Heaven, at least for now.

"Man belongs to me. I will convince more to reject you, Nazarene. I teach them to become like a god and fulfill the desires of their perverse and wicked hearts by making self king. You have said it Yourself: *'The heart is deceitful above all things, and desperately sick; who can understand it?'*

"I incite them to hate, kill and destroy and feel the same pleasure as I do when they crush another soul for their own personal benefit. I blind them to Your love and salvation. I persuade Your beloved man creatures that You are archaic and irrelevant with Your commandments denying them pleasure. You may have created man, but I will own man's heart leading multitudes to destruction!" His voice grew louder and darker. He would continue to fight the Host of Heaven, his former brothers. He gnashed his teeth, shook one fist in rage and overturned the conference table crashing it against the wall.

"You are a fool intervening on man's behalf with the Fire of Heaven when most of Your beloved humans have profaned Your name. Those creatures are not worthy of Your redemption. You freely give atonement for the dirty, imbecilic creatures incapable of appreciating Your Glory, yet You deny *me* redemption, the one who walked in the midst of Your Glory!" Lucifer shouted with boiling contempt. "I will exact my revenge. Their souls belong to me. Do You hear me, Nazarene? You invade my kingdom, I will invade Yours. Let us intensify the battle!"

18

Undercover Operatives

No news agency covered the prayer breakfast, but the gossip of the three hundred attendees shot throughout D.C. like a smoldering missile. There was no hiding anymore. The Taylor family was either the darling hope of America or the plague of religious conservatism that needed eradicating.

Dan did have a few sympathetic friends among the alphabet soup of agencies who passed on the word that he was under surveillance via the Deep State. The hidden government had made the false assumption that Dan's front-porch performance equated fatal humiliation, plunging him in a downward spiral right back to North Carolina. That didn't happen as hoped, and now the Deep State had a situation on their hands that needed eyes.

Soon, Gregor, Jean and Tony would be on the government watch list as well. Once the Deep State discovered Jason's friendship with Carlos and Diego, they would also be surveilled. The team needed to keep plans confidential for a short time until part of the Lord's blueprint had been completed. The Taylors' cars were the only ones identified as *to be watched*, so the rest of the team didn't bother with secrecy.

Keeping travel patterns covert was tricky, though, but they'd managed so far with the Lord's help. Sticking to the original plan, the Taylors made sure they were not followed, drove into the Wallaces' garage, after which Jean quickly closed the door.

Jason parked his car a block behind the Wallaces' and proceeded to cut through a neighbor's backyard to the rear kitchen door. As a kid, he would have bubbled over with excitement about the covert nature of his arrival—people with super powers, an evil underground government spying on the good guys, teleporting to an unknown world and battles in Heaven between good and evil spirits was the stuff of a sci-fi hero movie.

However, with the Holy Spirit's warning not to *toy* with His power, Jason took it seriously. He had died, gone to Heaven, talked to Jesus face to face, stood in the midst of the Fire of Heaven and felt the power of God flow through his body. *Serious, yes, but it's still pretty stinkin' awesome!* he thought. He knocked on the back door. Gregor was expecting him.

"Carlos and Diego should be here shortly. So, who else is coming?" asked Jason as he greeted Gregor.

"A neighbor, Tony Robertson. He's a professor at Frederick."

"Tony Robertson … yeah, I saw his cardboard image in a bookstore window advertising his book as a New York Times bestseller. A friend at Frederick said it was a very convincing argument against Christ. I heard it's required reading in one of the classes," Jason said as he eyed the food laid out on the island.

As Gregor and Jason were talking, the front door bell rang. "Hey, Tony, come on in." The two men gave each other a big man-hug, then cuffed each other on the shoulder. Gregor made the proper introductions and mentioned that Jason had been raised from the dead.

Tony's eyebrows lifted in interest. "Wow ... really?" He recalled times he had argued with students for claiming Jesus was deity and that accounts of resurrections were delusions of the feeble-minded. *How foolish I was,* he thought.

Just then, a loud rumbling caught everyone's attention and they huddled at the front window. The sound was generated by a thrush muffler from a multi-colored Monte Carlo lowrider. After several grumbling revs and a few low bounces, it pulled into the Wallaces' driveway.

A lowrider driving through this manicured Bethesda neighborhood was clearly an out-of-the-norm experience for all, including Carlos and Diego. Jean rushed out the front door to welcome them, letting the neighbors know these were invited guests.

"Hi, I'm Jean Wallace. I'm so glad to meet you two," Jean said as she looped one arm into Carlos's and her other arm into Diego's. The boys were surprised at her greeting, but it was genuine and welcoming, so the three walked up to the front door, arm in arm. "Come in and meet the others," invited Jean with a smile.

Carlos and Diego had never wanted anything to do with people like the Taylors or the Wallaces. White middle-agers in the high-end suburbs were never part of their world—unless targeted for burglary. Jean's warm embrace took the edge off their hesitancy. Christ's love surprisingly overcame them in this moment of acceptance. The tough gang members stood on the front porch, tears rolling off their cheeks, which made Jean cry, too.

The three held an embrace as Jean whispered, "I want you to know that we're all equal in Jesus' eyes. We're called to serve one another, so don't feel embarrassed or afraid to speak."

They released each other, wiping away tears.

"I'm sure tonight will be the beginning of a great adventure for all of us. Are ya hungry?" asked Jean.

The two boys smiled and nodded. They felt clean, like they'd had a good scrubbing, washing off the filth of their former life. They had experienced a mysterious metamorphosis, changing them from thieves and murderers to ambassadors for Jesus.

Everyone loaded their plates with food, ready to enjoy a meal together. Each one in this eclectic group was so very different from the other. Some, well-known; some, invisible. Some, educated; some, drop-outs. Some, long-time followers of Jesus; some, newly introduced to Him. Some, hardened criminals; some, who had never had a parking ticket. A miscellaneous handful of strangers transformed into a family by the power and love of their heavenly Father and the forgiveness made possible by the Blood of Christ.

They took turns telling their stories of God's intervention in their lives, each one with his own unique miracle. They listened, asked questions, laughed and cried together. By the end of the meal, they realized this night would be etched in the innermost part of their hearts. To them, it felt like Jesus was gathering disciples out of the world for the first time. It was a celebration of beginnings.

"Once things really get going, where will we meet?" Barb asked. "We can't equip an army of workers in the Wallaces' living room."

"Man, I have the right place for us—an abandoned warehouse in my neighborhood!" Carlos excitedly proposed.

"We need a place that big?" Tony asked, frowning.

Gregor grinned. "Yep, for what Jesus has planned, we need a big space."

Jason, proud of his first recruits, jumped in. "I can meet with you guys to scout it out." Jason and Carlos gave each other a special handshake no one else recognized except Diego.

The two brothers' faces immediately lit up the room. They shared how the Holy Spirit was working in the Barrios members who had witnessed the bullets—aimed point-blank at Gregor's head—falling intact at Mateo's feet.

"The Barrios fights the good fight of faith now," Carlos proudly stated, incorporating part of his first memorized Bible verse. "Our red bandannas use' to stand for the blood of our enemies. Now, they stand for the Blood of Jesus."

"Awesome, man. I love it!" Jason declared, with more handshakes between Carlos, Diego and himself.

The group bowed their heads, praying with thankful hearts, trusting that Jesus would equip them to do the job. A lovely aroma filled the air like the freshness of spring after a cool morning rain. Then, a pure quietness surpassing all understanding began as a point in the center of the room, radiating outward like a starburst.

Gentle tides of the Holy Spirit's whispers rose high, flowing through their souls like waves of the ocean, washing away more of the world each time the water receded. The cleansing waters flowed through their minds, working its way into the secret places, searching out motives of the inward man. Ocean waves transformed to the more serene waters of soft ripples rolling over river rocks, finally settling in their spirits as perfect love.

Love manifested itself as a point of light where the point of peace had originated. The group looked deeper into the intensely bright light, searching for something eternally valuable—the Pearl of Great Price, perfect communion with God through the Savior.

They were completely surrounded by the pure light—no shadow of darkness—that obliterated every argument and every presumption against the knowledge of the Holy One. They stepped deeply into its center, unable to see anything but the sacredness of Jesus' Blood covering their sinful failures. Overtaken by Heaven's radiance, their beings rested, subdued, in agreement with the mind of Christ.

From the glowing brightness, Jesus' familiar voice spoke, *Step forward.*

Even amidst the peacefulness of His presence, the inability to sense up from down challenged their bodies to take that first step, not knowing where they might land. The divine call urged them to trust. One step, two steps, three steps out of the light. Suddenly, there He was, waiting under the Tree of Life on the banks of the River of Life.

Adjusting to the crispness of Heaven's beauty, it seemed they could see in more than three dimensions. Every blade of grass stood perfectly at attention, clothed in brilliant greens. Trees displayed His artistry with exquisitely designed flowers and succulent fruits, hanging from their branches—like a painting in dazzling color. Everything vibrated with His life, and the small band of believers absorbed every wave of it. They felt so alive in Heaven that life on earth seemed like death.

Jesus motioned, inviting them to come near. "Come, sit."

Each team member acknowledged the invitation, sitting to form a semi-circle. Tony, it seemed, could not sit still. Effortlessly, he sat, then stood; sat, then stood, bouncing as if on a trampoline.

In response to the curious looks of the others, Tony explained, "Forgive me, but I haven't been able to do this for years without pain!"

Jesus smiled, then chuckled quietly. Soon the chuckle grew into a big belly laugh. Now everyone was laughing, enjoying the freedom with which this gentle giant could sit down and quickly pop up again, like a Jack in the Box.

When the laughter subsided, Jesus said, "I reveal only what is necessary. I will not be able to answer your questions now, but know we will have eternity together, and understanding will be imparted then."

Gregor noticed Storis leaning against the Tree. He was spirit with the likeness of man. His long, white hair rested on his strong shoulders. A large, golden sword engraved TRUTH hung from his waist, requiring no effort on the angel's part, for the Lord's truth is not burdensome.

Storis was magnificent by human standards, flawless in appearance and faithfulness. Yet, standing near Jesus, Storis appeared average. Jesus' beauty was different from the angel's. The essence of all Jesus' holiness and love made Him exceedingly beautiful, far beyond any physical attribute.

He began to speak, and all leaned forward to catch every word. "I reveal My plans to My prophets first; therefore, before they manifest on earth, I am announcing them to you.

"You know the Scriptures that instruct new wine needs new wineskins. Of course, this is because the old wineskin bursts as the fermenting wine creates gas; therefore, new wine must be put into new wineskins that are able to stretch. I will not pour out My Spirit into an old, weakened vessel, losing both the wine and the wineskin. The old vessel of the current church model cannot contain the new wine of the Final Awakening, similar to the Old Covenant's inability to contain the New Covenant. However, the Final Awakening is not a new covenant. It is merely an open window of mercy before the times of great troubles."

Jesus stood, pointing to a brilliant city in the distance. "Come."

Immediately, there was brightness all around and in the midst of the brightness was the appearance of a narrow, open door. Jesus stood in the doorway and said, "I AM the Door. No one comes to the Father except by entering through Me."

His appearance was as the Firstborn Lamb, slain and risen to life. Guarding the door on each side were two creatures, about twenty feet tall, so that no soul was able to pass through unless he had applied the Blood of the Lamb to his heart.

The living creatures radiated the brightness of Truth, like the shining city. Pristine wings covered their bodies, which glowed red-orange like a hot coal. When they stretched out their wings to bow in reverence to the Lamb, a rushing wind nearly bowled over the onlookers. With loud voices declaring their devotion, they called out, "Holy, holy, holy, is the Risen Lamb, who was and is and is to come!"

The words held the power of Truth, and the Fear of the Lord rushed out as a potent force knocking the team to the pure golden floor, smooth and clear like glass. Jesus touched each person, filling them with His strength and enabling them to stand.

His appearance changed again as they passed through another door. He no longer resembled the man they had spoken with under the Tree of Life nor the Slain and Risen Lamb. Now, the Son of God emanated pure light, brighter than the sun. His eyes were a fiery white-hot blaze like that of molten metal, His hair as white as the purest snow, and his skin like polished bronze with an aura of golden amber.

In the courtyard, all sorts of ministering creatures and angels of Heaven moved about. Some uniquely designed servants baffled the group, and what purpose they served was not revealed.

The group passed beyond the large space through yet another door where there, in the midst of crackling lightning, rumbling thunder and loud voices, was One seated on a throne, high and lifted up. Reaching to the height of the throne, burned an eternal flame that was never kindled but always existed, exists and will exist. It is the Fire of Heaven, which is the seven Spirits of the Lord, a manifestation of His complete nature.

Jesus sternly warned, "The moon is bright in the night sky, but the moon's light is only a reflection of the sun. The moon generates no light of its own. Once, Lucifer stood before the throne, reflecting Our Glory as the moon is to the sun.

"Remain alert, for the adversary lies in wait to devour with his greatest weapon, deception. All the holy angels of Heaven saw the Glory of the Lord you see now and even more that you do not see. If Lucifer's lying persuasions caused a third of the holy angels to rebel against Us, how much more should you beware? Cast out pride and thoughts of receiving honor for Our works before they take root. We are jealous for Our Glory and will share it with no one. I have told you."

The presence of the Almighty and the serious warning made it difficult to stand. The Spirit brought to mind the truth that Herod was eaten by worms because he did not give glory to God. He indulged in greed for recognition that belonged to the Lord, a sin worthy of death. They fell on their faces, earnestly pleading for the Father to grant them the Fear of the Lord to prevent them from such a grave sin. Jesus touched them once again, standing them on their feet.

"Do not allow self to rise from the grave; instead, be master over it. Depend upon prayer and fasting as you depend upon air to breathe. When you ask, I will generously give wisdom, preventing you from disastrous presumptions.

"Remember what I have shown you when hardships and persecution come. Rejoice that you are counted in the Final Awakening of souls before the days of great tribulation when it will be more difficult to break from the world and believe. Remember ... I have warned you ...."

19

Table For Two

Jason had never had a dream, a vision or heard God's voice before becoming a conduit for the Fire of Heaven. Recent events had flipped the definition of life. Nothing on earth now carried its previous significance.

Jason had been a committed follower of Jesus from an early age and took his relationship with the Lord seriously. As a deep thinker, he often sat alone for long periods, pondering questions that the average person wouldn't give a passing thought. He was thinking now. Considering the Final Awakening, his purpose and God's expectation of him as a sent messenger.

It was already 10:30 in the morning when Jason's alarm buzzed. His sleep had been restless. The serious warning of last night's Visitation to Heaven played over and over in his mind, making it hard to shut his brain down.

He looked at the time. "Oh, man! I have to meet that reporter in an hour! *Please God, don't let me say or do anything I'm not supposed to. I don't want to mess things up*, Jason prayed on his way to the shower at a dead run.

Thoughts whirled in circles. *How am I supposed to mix the two kingdoms together in normal, everyday life? Or is there such a thing as "normal" for me anymore?*

He didn't understand why he felt nervous about meeting a reporter. It was just a business thing. He figured it was probably just all that was going on right now, making him uneasy with life in general.

* * *

Carrie was running late. She knew she'd taken on more responsibility at work than she should. But she'd always had a hard time saying no. Whatever her boss asked of her—skip a meal, work extra hours—she'd always done it. No complaints.

And why? she'd often asked herself. OK, so she was an overachiever who felt she had to prove herself every day. On the outside, she appeared to have it all together—young, go-getter, reasonably attractive, confident, but … well … that was just a mask she'd learned to put on when the occasion called for it, along with her lip gloss.

She leaned toward the mirror to check her makeup. Her lip was twitching. *Pull yourself together, Carrie. This is just another interview.* Behind that mask of competence and professionalism was a heart desperate to find her lifetime companion. Work kept her mind off finding him and that was fine with her. At age twenty-eight, she'd come to terms with the fact that she might never get married. So what? Lots of girls were single these days. Good thing she liked her job … loved it really. Didn't she?

* * *

As Jason waited for Carrie, he looked around the deli. Usual routine. Regular customers. The owner, Pat, was behind the counter making his *Voted Best in D.C.* Reuben sandwiches. Ordinary felt good for a change. Maybe today would be a routine, regular, ordinary day.

Turning toward the door, he spotted Carrie entering the deli. She was wearing workout gear under a zip-up sweatshirt, her hair pulled back in a simple ponytail. He was relieved that she had honored his request not to come dressed as a glamorous news reporter. He'd give her that.

Searching the skimpy crowd—a little too early for the lunchtime diners—it was easy to find Jason sitting by the dessert display. Their eyes met and suddenly Carrie felt flushed and hoped he didn't notice. She was nervous, but knew of no reason why she should be. She struggled between getting the story that could take her career to the next level and her undefinable attraction toward Jason. She had never even met him before, so logically there should be no feelings whatsoever. He was a story only—the mysterious dead man risen to life again. That's probably what intrigued her. Yeah. Had to be.

"Jason, thanks so much for meeting with me today. I promised I would be on my best behavior, no camera crew or recordings. I just have my notepad and my Bic pen." Carrie waved her pad of paper and the pen in the air to prove it.

When Jason's eyes met Carrie's, he froze. It startled him when he saw her again as he had seen her in the vision—the rejected little girl, struggling to fit in. God had revealed to him her inability to find friendship. Jason was mystified by this detail, because she seemed smart, attractive, successful.

A few seconds lapsed with no acknowledgment from Jason other than a blank stare. "Jason?" Carrie firmly repeated to get his attention.

"Sorry, I have a lot on my mind lately. Guess we'd better order something before the lunch crowd comes in. Do you like Reubens? Best in D.C."

"Great! I love Reubens, but never actually made it to this deli. It'll be my treat." Carrie looked at the dessert display behind Jason. "Does this choice of seating have special meaning for you?" she joked.

Jason looked behind him to find shelves filled with delectable desserts. Lemon meringue pie stacked five inches high, German chocolate cake with three huge layers and the cherry pie, just waiting for that scoop of homemade vanilla ice cream.

"Huh, yeah, I guess it does. When I order the sandwiches, I'll tell Pat that we'll have two orders of cherry pie with a scoop of vanilla ice cream," Jason said, pointing to the scrumptious pie in the case. "Oh, that is if you like cherry pie?"

"Yeah, that's fine. I like cherries." Carrie smiled.

She didn't take Jason for the dessert kind of guy. He was very fit. The resemblance to his father was remarkable. Jason looked like pictures she had seen of his father as a freshmen senator, sporting the same dark wavy hair and handsome features. But she wondered what lay behind the good looks, other than the obvious story—dead man walking.

"I've been coming here for about three years," Jason began, just to make conversation. "My old job was a few blocks down the street. It was the highlight of my day to break off for an hour and eat here," he commented uneasily, still unsure of her angle.

Since it was her treat, Carrie insisted on placing the order. She made her way to the front counter and gave the order to Pat—two famous Reubens and two slices of warmed cherry pie with a scoop of ice cream. Pat looked over at Jason and smiled a *you done good, boy* at him. Even in a sweatshirt, Carrie was striking.

"If you haven't talked with any other news agencies, I would love to have the exclusive on your story," Carrie stated when she returned to the table.

"I haven't talked with anyone else yet. Give me some time to pray on that one, and I'll let you know."

Great, he hasn't talked to any other reporters yet, she thought. "Fair enough. So, Jason, tell me more about yourself." She cocked her head, pen in hand, eager to hear.

"I can assure you I am no one special. As you know, my dad has been a sitting senator for a long time. When I was growing up, he was in D.C. a lot, but when he was back home, we'd go bike riding, hiking, fishing, shoot baskets—guy stuff. He eventually bought a second house in D.C. so we could spend more time as a family. Even though we had the two houses, I pretty much grew up in North Carolina.

"I was homeschooled for a while so I could travel to D.C. without juggling an inflexible school schedule. I know people think homeschooled kids are weird, but that isn't always the case," Jason said as he realized that at this moment, he probably seemed pretty strange to Carrie. Seemed odd, even to him. He was a dead man raised to life. And that wasn't all. Now he had fiery power shooting out of his body!

"Well, strike that last statement." He chuckled. "Anyway, went to college in North Carolina, graduated and got a job. Eventually ended up here in D.C., working for National Star Bank, heading up their corporate IT department as department head of cyber security. It was a good job, paid enough to buy a condo.

"My life was pretty uneventful until the wreck. Some clown t-boned my car while texting to one of his friends. An SUV versus a sports car. Obviously, my car lost the battle."

This was more like it. This was what she had come for—the

story that could catapult her to journalistic stardom. "Did you know you were … dead?"

"Not sure. Maybe … I don't know. I never stopped existing, I just existed differently. I could hear people talking, monitors beeping and I think my mom crying. Then I heard the beeping monitors make that annoying flat-line noise—EEEEEE. At that point, I was drifting above my body. I could see and hear everything perfectly. I looked at my body in the bed and realized how badly I was injured from the accident. I felt fine and wondered why Mom and Dad were so upset."

"Did you see a bright light, a tunnel?" Curious—now, for her own sake, not just for the story—she leaned toward him.

Jason stopped for a moment to think. "No, there was no tunnel or bright light experience for me. I stayed around my hospital room for a couple of minutes. Then, there was an angel standing next to me, and he said it was time. We traveled upward out of the hospital. The feeling of peace was indescribable." He paused, remembering the euphoria of that experience. No pain. No suffering ….

"While I was going up, some other people were headed down. I felt afraid for them. Suddenly I was standing in front of a tall podium—like, really tall, maybe twenty feet—with a halo of emerald light all around it. I didn't see a face or the figure of a person, just heard a voice.

"When I approached, this booming voice asked, *Is your name written in the Lamb's Book of Life?* The voice was commanding, authoritative, and I knew it was impossible for me to tell anything but the truth. Without even thinking, I answered, 'Yes.' Then the voice asked, *How have you atoned for your sin?* The answer just kind of came out of me: 'By the Blood of the Lamb.' Then the voice said, *And so it is.*"

Jason shifted uncomfortably in his seat. He never liked attention, and Carrie's penetrating gaze made him uneasy. His knee bobbed slightly from anxiousness.

"The angel told me that the people taken away were not permitted into Heaven because their names were not in the Lamb's Book of Life. He said they were going to the dark place until the final judgment at the end of the age." Jason's eyes welled up with tears. "Can you imagine how awful that must be? They died, and their names weren't in the Book. No entrance to Heaven … ever."

Carrie couldn't help feeling the pain that Jason was experiencing for the people he thought were going to hell. *This guy really cares,* she thought. Then a startling question occurred to her: *Is hell real? What about me … where would I be carried off to?*

Jason stopped. He wanted to say only what God wanted him to say. When the Holy Spirit revealed her soul, he sensed no malice. Would she tell the story truthfully, or twist it? He really wanted to trust her, but he proceeded cautiously. Too much was at stake.

"What happened that day at your parents' house when the electronics fried and everyone was knocked to the ground?" Carrie asked, still a bit preoccupied by her own self-interrogation. *What would happen if I died?*

"Listen … uh … I don't determine when the Fire of Heaven pours out of me. It isn't something I own or control. I had no idea that was going to happen. I'm just a spigot that Jesus uses when He decides to. Trust me … it just happens."

Carrie jotted down a note, then continued: "So what is the Fire of Heaven?"

Jason didn't quite know how to answer. In truth, even after standing in the middle of the Fire, he still didn't fully understand it.

"I'm no theologian! I'm not completely sure myself. It's kind of like this place I went to once—a medical sterilization center where stuff was zapped with gamma rays to sterilize it. They took me into a room with five-foot-thick concrete walls, built like a maze. In the center of the maze was a room with a deep, square pool filled with water and pencil-sized rods of Cobalt-60. The rods gave off highly radioactive gamma rays, killing any bacteria within a nanosecond of exposure. Sealed boxes of hospital supplies moved along a conveyor belt when the rods were up out of the water."

While telling the story, Jason forgot he was talking to a reporter and the words flowed without effort. His knee stopped bobbing.

"A guy took me into the room to see the pool of water where the radioactive rods were kept. As long as the rods were under the water, I was completely safe. If the rods were pulled out of the water, I would be dead in the blink of an eye."

He continued the story with a boyish excitement. "The radiation was strong enough to make the concrete walls stay hot for hours after being exposed to the rods. The gamma rays were so damaging that the specially protected electrical wiring was replaced *once a month*. Those rods packed a lot of power."

Carrie listened, but didn't see the connection of the story to her question. She felt a little annoyed and lightly tapped her pen on the pad of paper. Jason saw the confusion on her face.

"Don't you see … the holiness of God is like the radioactive rods; the pool of water is like the Blood of Jesus. When the holiness of God comes, the Fire of Heaven radiates justice, exposing and judging sin. If you belong to Jesus, His Blood covers your sin so you're able to stand in God's full presence. If you don't have the Blood of Jesus, you're consumed like the radiation consumes the bacteria."

Whew! Carrie was used to taking in a ton of information as part of her job and never before had trouble understanding difficult concepts outside her area of expertise. At the moment, her brain felt numb. Information overload! This was a very different message from the one she'd heard as a youngster: God is love; God forgives; we all go to Heaven; hell doesn't exist. Jason was talking about seeing people escorted to hell. He explained that power from God shoots out of his body, exposing sin like gamma radiation kills germs. To Carrie, it felt like he was explaining a complex idea while speaking a foreign language from a different cultural reference. She needed time to process.

Jason could tell Carrie was preoccupied. She was relieved when Pat brought their food to the table. They both jumped in eating, neither of them talking much. Discussion was mostly limited to the good food and other small talk. After they polished off their sandwiches, Pat brought the cherry pie. Just as Jason had promised, the warmed pie with a large scoop of ice cream was a five-star experience. They dug in, grateful for the extension of time to complete their silent assessment of one another.

When they finished, Jason pushed back his plate, then asked Carrie, "So, tell me about yourself ... your family ... your upbringing."

Carrie was caught off guard. She was the one with the questions. Why would he ask about *her* background? Normally, she would redirect, keeping the interview focused on the interviewee. For some reason, that didn't happen this time.

"I was raised in a small bedroom community on the north side of Indianapolis," she began, a little surprised that she hadn't pushed back. "My dad worked for a pharmaceutical company in the marketing research area. He helped design the size, color, shape and name of each new drug they developed. Who knew there was a career in pill design?" she giggled nervously. "My mom stayed home, acting as chauffeur for my brother and myself. I belonged to the swim club and made the traveling team. My brother, Nick, played soccer and was the team captain his senior year in high school. We were always involved in some kind of activity."

"Why did you choose TV journalism?"

Carrie began to relax a little more. "My dad was a news junkie. My mom, not so much, but she liked writing. I guess you could say that I'm equal parts Dad and Mom. I love following breaking events and reporting them. I started off writing freelance articles for different news outlets, but I got my big break about two years ago. You know the old saying ... 'right place at the right time.' Working for WNN has been great. So far, management lets me report as I want to. I would love to be the one to tell America *your* story." She flashed a coquettish smile, silently congratulating herself on managing to turn the conversation back to the purpose of their meeting.

Jason leaned forward, searching Carrie's eyes and asked the question that was burning in his heart. "Who do you say Jesus is?"

The question completely blindsided Carrie. Jason's eye contact felt like he could see inside her, read the secrets of her heart. Sharing generic family stuff was no big deal, but this was getting way too personal. She leaned back in her chair in an attempt to escape the penetrating inquiry. She was supposed to be the one posing probing questions, but now she was the target of what felt like a piercing interrogation. She felt offended and defensive. *You just don't ask people that stuff,* she thought. She wasn't yet completely convinced of his experience ... and now this question made his persona annoying.

She took a deep breath and tried to think of an answer to this loaded question. She really wasn't sure, because she hadn't given it much thought. Playing defense, she asked a counter question. But he didn't bite, so it was a struggle to regain her composure.

Jason didn't break eye contact. This seemingly shy guy had turned into a bulldog. She focused on moving a leftover cherry around with a fork. Then she fidgeted with her ponytail, feeling the way she had felt when her dad caught her in a lie. She didn't like it ... not one bit. Now Jason's tone was soft and tender with genuine concern. "You're skirting my question, Carrie. Who do you think Jesus is? It's a question everyone has to answer."

Carrie's phone buzzed in her purse, a text from work. The interruption couldn't have been timed better. "I am so sorry to have to cut and run," she said, grateful for the reprieve. "My boss wants me back ASAP, some breaking story." She smiled, trying to appear in control. "Maybe we could finish this conversation later. Will you commit to an exclusive? You have my number ... just please let me know. Again, thanks for meeting me."

She hadn't gotten to many of the real questions she wanted to ask, but was happy to leave with her psyche intact, at least so far. She shook his hand, scooped up her pad and pen then headed toward the door. Even though she was leaving the Jesus question unanswered—at least to Jason—it nagged at her and she knew she still had to answer it for herself. If she landed another interview with him, he surely would ask uncomfortable questions again. Regardless, she did want that exclusive story in Jason Taylor—man back from the dead.

20

Ride Of A Lifetime

Sheila, Senator Taylor's office administrator, was busy fielding calls resulting from the prayer breakfast. She was surprised at the number of positive comments pouring in. Some fellow senators from the breakfast and others on the Hill who did not attend called or emailed their support. Many encouraging calls came from Dan's North Carolina constituents, who somehow got word of what had happened. Some who had been at the breakfast, came to the office, confused but looking for answers, while a few stopped in to say D.C. needed more of "whatever that was." Dan even got one invitation to pastor a church.

Those who took exception to Dan's story and what the Holy Spirit did to them that morning were mostly other elected or appointed government servants who cursed their displeasure in no uncertain terms. Outside of the constant profane language and personal insults, the phrase *separation of church and state* was the most prevalent expression communicated. Thankfully, those messages were via phone and email. No angry mobs at the door ... at least not yet.

Sheila Anderson was a loyal and tireless employee, having worked for Dan since his freshman year in the Senate. He liked her positive attitude, good sense of humor and her North Carolina accent, which made his working hours in the office more enjoyable than an all-business administrator. He mostly appreciated Sheila's integrity, knowing she could be trusted.

Sheila and Barb were longtime friends. As such, Sheila was treated as an extension of the Taylor family and was often invited to backyard barbecues. Even with the family closeness, however, Sheila always maintained professionalism in the office.

Through the years, Barb and Sheila had often prayed together that Dan would give his life to Christ. But they had never imagined that their prayers would be answered in such a dramatic way. Sheila sensed a profound change since Dan shared his story at the breakfast. God was moving ... and she wanted in.

Shortly after the breakfast, in a let-down-your-hair session, Dan had shared that he felt he was riding on top of a giant, two-bladed snowplow and Jesus was driving, easily cutting a clear path through banks of obstacles. Today, Sheila decided to ride with him, but she wondered how long it would last. Judgment would come ... but when and how severe would it be?

The sky quickly darkened as voluminous clouds rolled in the D.C. sky, creating a blanket of dark gray. Heavy raindrops buffeted the building, pinging against the glass as the wind drove the rain sideways. Sheila went to the window to watch the thunderstorm clouds turn in on themselves, thinking it a good picture of the spiritual atmosphere—dark and tumultuous.

D.C. needs a good washing, she thought. Standing at the window, she pictured America like the bloodied baby struggling to survive on the roadside, as described in Ezekiel. The Lord saw America's difficult birth, had compassion on her and declared her to live. He washed her and pledged Himself to her. He bestowed wealth and beauty upon her. He placed a crown on her head, making her queen among the nations. But because of her fame, she forgot what God had done for her and prostituted herself, turning away from Him. She bore children to Him, then delivered their children as food for idols, sacrificing their eternal future.

Sheila thought about the war for the hearts of America's leaders. The highest levels in the most powerful nation of the world foolishly recognized the conflict as only a selfish game of politics. The real war raged unseen—but would not remain unnoticed. America's future was riding on a choice, obedience or judgment. *Lord open their eyes to see the real battle*, she prayed and wondered which D.C. eyes could be opened.

The sound of the outer office door opening startled Sheila. She turned to see a man, rivulets of water dripping off his coat from the pouring rain. It was Gregor.

"Senator Taylor, Gregor Wallace is in the office and wants to meet with you. Do you have time, or should I reschedule?" asked Sheila.

"No, please send him in. No calls unless Jason or Barb is trying to reach me. Sheila, have I ever told you how much I really appreciate you?"

"Every time you get in over your head, Senator." She laughed softly, dropping her voice so their visitor could not overhear.

"You know me too well and that scares me!"

"I'll send him in right now, Senator."

As Gregor entered, Dan noticed the expressionless face of his new mentor and friend, his bedraggled appearance matching his countenance.

Dan had a growing sensation some major events were about to unfold on an unprecedented scale. Maybe Gregor sensed the same thing and that's what caused his friend's downcast demeanor. If anyone had insight into coming events, Gregor Wallace would.

"Senator Taylor, thanks for seeing me without an appointment."

"Gregor, call me Dan. Formalities with the guy who raised my son from the dead? C'mon. If that's the case, I should call you Apostle or Prophet Wallace!"

"No, don't give me any title," Gregor demanded. "I'm just a simple bondservant of Jesus Christ. No titles, ever! Your office seemed so … senatorial … I guess it just seemed right to call you 'Senator Taylor,' but I get the picture. It's Dan from now on."

"Deal. Have a seat."

Gregor pulled up a side chair, looked around, then leaned close, speaking in an undertone. "Is it safe to talk? We aren't bugged or something, right?"

"As Chair of the Intelligence Committee, I make sure my office is secure, even from other agencies who might want to listen in. I have cutting-edge jamming equipment stopping any listening devices from working if they were able to get by our sweeps.

"There are no microphones or cameras on any of my equipment, eliminating the possibility of them being turned on remotely. My windows have a special vibrating disruptor that prohibits someone from listening via remote sensors. Finally, I just unplug my land-line so potential eavesdroppers can't use the speaker phone. Pull the battery out of your cell phone, and we should be as secure as one can expect."

"Wow, all this cloak and dagger stuff to avoid our own government. Appears that the 'land of the free' is losing her freedoms." Gregor's tone became serious. "Dan, major destructive events will hit this nation in wave after wave in the coming months. There will be unprecedented natural disasters, terrorist attacks and economic hits to the banking industry."

There was an urgency in Gregor's voice that Dan had not noticed before. "On top of that, add out-of-control mobs who will cause unthinkable destruction in public places. Evil and lawlessness are coming, and we need to get the ministry center off the ground ASAP."

Dan had also realized they needed more people on board. Their small band of Jesus-seekers couldn't do it alone.

"Dan, we need to launch. The Awakening is going to take money, and we are lean on money, as in we have *none*. I know you have friends who are well off and might want to help if they catch wind of the vision."

Dan put his hands behind his head, leaned back in his well-worn, leather office chair. "Hmmm ... as a matter of fact ... I ... do." He sat straight up again, spinning around to face Gregor. "Word traveled fast about the events of Wednesday morning. Office staff is struggling to keep up with all the calls and emails. Sheila's tracked and tabulated supporters, and there *are* some deep pockets on the list."

Dan pressed an intercom button. "Sheila, bring that list."

Gregor pulled an additional chair next to Dan's desk as Sheila entered the room. "We need your help."

Dan presented a proposal to his longtime administrator. "Sheila, how would you like to add a part-time job to your already busy schedule? It'll have to be on the down-low in your off hours for now. God is launching a movement, and we need your administrative gifts. The pay's lousy, like zero, and hours could be long. Interested?"

Sheila smiled and almost let out a sigh of relief. "I was so hoping you would include me in on this. When I heard what happened at that prayer breakfast, I was grief-stricken that I missed it. I would've loved seeing God give the you-know- who's the you-know-what. You bet I want in! I've felt like the Dead Sea with no outlet. When do I start?"

With that, Sheila jumped up and started pacing the room. Her heart was stirring with something she had not felt in many years. She could tell this was God's appointment for her, and a profound sense of purpose flooded her spirit.

"Sheila, stop pacing. Sit," Dan commanded, pointing to her chair. "One lesson you've taught me over these years, Sheila: Prioritize first, execute later. So, first priority is money. Set up a meeting in the Grand Ballroom of the Downtown Capital Grand Hotel for this Sunday evening. Put it on my personal credit card. Go through your list of people who have expressed unwavering support. Tell them Barb and I are hosting a time sharing a vision for spiritual renewal for America ... something like that. If people say they want more of Jesus, invite them to come."

The wheels were turning as Dan continued in campaign mode. He turned to Gregor. "Talk to Tony and, of course, Jean. I'll reach out to Jason and get him up to speed, and he can contact Carlos and Diego. We need Holy Spirit-filled manpower and finances to get this off the ground. We're having a fundraiser."

Sheila paced again, hardly able to stay still. She asked Gregor to explain the ministry center concept. Gregor gave a short overview, then pulled a file from his backpack and handed it to her.

"Here, this will explain everything you need to know going forward. Jean is almost finished formatting it in a Power Point that can be used at the meeting."

"I can't wait to get started. Senator Taylor, permission to use some of my vacation time starting now?" Sheila asked as she jokingly saluted.

"Permission granted," Dan said, returning the salute. "We get one shot to nail this. Time is ticking. I sense the Lord is pushing this forward faster than we might like."

Now, Dan was pacing. "I think the Awakening is going to be short ... like Jesus' ministry on earth. No marathon, just a sprint to

166

the finish. Expect everything to accelerate at the speed of Light." Dan laughed.

Neither Sheila nor Gregor followed suit.

"You know, *Light* with a capital L, pun intended," explained Dan, waiting for Sheila and Gregor to get the joke. Still, no response. "Like He is the *Light* of the world … speed of *Light* …."

Sheila merely groaned. Gregor was too preoccupied to notice Dan's lame pun.

"Wow, am I that bad at Christian humor?"

"Yes, you are, and I would *not* quit your day job, Senator," commented Sheila as she left to arrange things for the Capital Grand Hotel.

Dan called Sheila back. "Oh, hey, one more thing. I emailed you the name and contact info of an intercessor friend of the Wallaces who has expanded our prayer network—Snow Peterson. She already knows most of the situation and can jump right in. Would you have time to bring her up to speed?"

"Absolutely! I'm going home to get started on my vacation," Sheila said putting air quotes around the word *vacation.*

"Gregor, Sunday's meeting is the most important one on my schedule all week … maybe of my entire life!" Dan was pumped, ready to jump into the game. Still, he was a bit puzzled as to why Gregor wasn't sharing in the excitement.

Dan's earlier comment that the Awakening was going to be short—like Jesus' ministry on earth—tugged at Gregor. He sensed it, too. "Well, if what you said is true, Dan, we only have a short time to get this wrapped up. Buckle up! We're about to take the ride of a lifetime."

21

"I Will Never Leave You"

Dan leaned back in his office chair, staring into space. He was processing his meeting with Gregor and Sheila. What struck him most was how Sheila had been waiting for this very moment, jumping in without hesitation. There had to be more like her—hidden, scattered everywhere, prepositioned and waiting to be activated.

Dan's new love for Jesus gave him a hunger for the Word. He dove into the Bible every chance he had time to read. From an earlier reading that day, the prophet Elisha was on his mind.

Elisha was plowing his field, doing what a farmer naturally does, working the land and planting crops. All the hard work was for one purpose—to bring in the harvest later in the year. One unexpected day, the prophet Elijah came to Elisha and threw his coat—a symbol of God-given authority—around Elisha's shoulders, passing on the prophet's call to leave all and follow the Lord. Elisha immediately stopped plowing, sacrificed his oxen—the means of his livelihood—and left all behind.

That day had probably started out like any other day for Elisha, the farmer. He woke up and went to work as usual, with no idea that in the time it took to throw a coat over his shoulders, everything would dramatically change. Nor did he know that he would go from plowing stony fields of dirt to plowing the stony hearts of men. Sheila was yearning for God's call just as Elisha had ....

* * *

As soon as Gregor reached his car, he pulled out his phone and hit speed dial number one. "Hey, it's me, hon. I just left Dan's office. Sheila, his assistant, is organizing a meeting at the Capital Grand Hotel for Sunday evening. She has a list of people who might share our vision. Could you finish up that Power Point by Sunday?"

"Wow ... Sunday evening. That early?"

"Yeah, I know. This is moving quickly. Could you and Barb head down to see Carlos and Diego about the building today? Take some pictures for the meeting. Jason will meet you there. What's ahead of us is way too big for our little team to handle. Make sure you call Carlos first so you'll have safe passage in that area of town."

"Sure, I'll call Carlos," replied Jean, her voice tinged with eager anticipation.

"I'll pick up some carryout so don't worry about dinner."

"Woo hoo! No cooking tonight."

"I knew you wouldn't object to that. Love you. Be safe and see you tonight."

"Love you, too. 'Bye."

Gregor headed to Frederick University to see Tony. He knew this brilliant man had been appointed to plow the harvest field of university souls, but Gregor also knew that Tony needed to hear from the Lord for himself. *Just like Dan at the prayer breakfast, Tony will learn with on-the-job training,* Gregor thought. *So much work and so few people.* With that, he took a deep breath as the Holy Spirit refreshed him, filling him with peace. Lingering worries of carrying a burden left—at least for now.

Gregor pulled up outside the bagel shop just around the corner from the Philosophy Department building. Tony was inside sipping an iced coffee. Gregor took a minute to study the man's features. He appeared to be enjoying his drink without a care in the world. Tony was smiling at no one in particular, and Gregor wondered if he was reliving the moments with Jesus and Andrea in Heaven.

"Hey, Tony, thanks for meeting me on such short notice. Let me grab a salt bagel and bottle of water and I'll be right back. Can I get you anything?"

"Nope, all good. I have my Mocha Frappuccino, and life couldn't be better."

Gregor quickly paid, gathered up his order and took the seat directly across from Tony at a small bistro table.

"Any more visits to Heaven?"

"I wish," replied Gregor. "Although, I'm still feeling the effects of that last visit. I can see you are, too."

"You know, bro, being in Heaven has done something to me that I can't explain. Things that were so important to me before have lost their significance. I sacrificed so much to get to the top of my profession ... including my marriage. And for what? Everything I thought was important is not important at all. I spent a lifetime in pursuit of a dream that I now see as worthless. I can't believe I was so blind."

Gregor couldn't help but smile. "Seeing Jesus face to face is definitely a reality check."

Tony set his empty cup on the table. "Where do I go from here? How do I stand up before all these students now, knowing what I have been teaching is a lie? To be honest with you Gregor, I really don't want to go back to my office, ever. I even drafted a resignation letter last night. I want something more meaningful, more Kingdom-related."

"Well, you need to see this from God's perspective. When people came to be baptized by John the Baptist, they had the same question. John didn't tell the Roman soldier to quit being a soldier. He told him to be a *faithful, honest* soldier, a witness to those who would never get a chance to hear the Good News any other way. God doesn't necessarily want you to leave what you're doing. He might be asking you to be a witness to those around you, just like the soldier."

Tony nodded, gazing off into the distance. "Hmmm ..."

"Remember the demoniac of the Gadarenes?" Gregor prompted.

"Yeah ... Jesus cast out a legion of demons, freeing the man to return to his right mind. He wanted to follow Jesus, but Jesus told him to go back home and tell everyone about the amazing thing God had done for him. So ... maybe I'm supposed to stay at Frederick and spread His message here?"

At Tony's realization of God's plan, the men felt the strong presence of the Lord. Gregor prophesied over Tony as the Holy Spirit spoke through him:

Tony, I called you out of darkness into light; now go and be light to those still in darkness. I can change the hardest of hearts. I will send the spirit of repentance to this campus.

Call a faculty meeting for your department. Share your story. Lay hands on these, the firstfruits of My work here. The Spirit of Elijah will rest upon you as it did with John the Baptist, calling hearts to repentance. If there is no repentance, there can be no Awakening. Go in the confidence of the power of the Holy Spirit dwelling in you.

Tony felt the Fire of Heaven energizing him for his mission. *So this is how it is to be,* he thought, his eyes downcast in reverence for the One who had spoken to him. His prayers would be answered, but not in the way he had expected. He wasn't being called *out* of his role as Professor of Philosophy, but *into* his professorship as an evangelist. A university founded on religious freedom had lost its way. Perhaps it was about to have a great Visitation that would forever redefine its charter.

Tony gave Gregor the usual man-hug. "Thanks, bro," he murmured as the two men parted.

* * *

From the coffee shop, Tony headed back to campus to organize an emergency meeting of the Philosophy Department faculty. As he sat down at his spacious desk, he felt an unusual warmth in his hands. Something had changed and he could physically feel it. He left his office and walked to the unit secretary's cubical.

"Maggie, can you call a quick meeting of the department staff? Let's say 4:30 today in the conference room. If anyone asks, tell them that this is a mandatory meeting."

"Not a problem, Dr. Robertson. Do you want me to arrange for refreshments?"

"Great idea! Better yet, tell them dinner will be provided. Order food from that catering place with the home cooking ... what's the name?"

"You mean Aunt Becky's Catering?"

"Yeah, that's it. That'll get them all to attend and be on time. When good food is provided, it seems to motivate in ways I can't. Oh, I want you to be there, too."

"Not a problem, Dr. Robertson."

"Don't charge it to the department. Put it on my credit card."

Tony peered at her over his reading glasses. For the first time, he saw Maggie as a person, not a robot, keeping things running smoothly in the department. "You know, Maggie, everyone in the department takes you for granted—I included, I'm afraid. I sincerely regret never having expressed my gratitude for all you do. You're the best, Maggie, and I really mean it."

Dr. Robertson never handed out compliments, making Maggie feel a little awkward. "Does this mean I'm getting a raise, too?" she joked nervously, thinking that would be the last thing he would ever do.

"Absolutely, it's long overdue. Draw up the request forms and give yourself a ten percent raise, no fifteen percent. Maggie, I want you to know how much you've really meant to this department. You're an amazing person, and I'm so grateful to have you here."

Maggie wondered what in the world had gotten into Dr. Robertson. She had never heard this kind of thing from him before. *I sure hope this change lasts long enough for me to get my raise,* she thought.

* * *

The tantalizing smells of delicious dishes from Aunt Becky's Catering wafted throughout the department. If anyone had forgotten about the meeting, this was an unmistakable reminder. Faculty trickled into the conference room and headed to the table laid out with made-from-scratch delicacies: fresh steamed vegetables, tossed salads with out-of-this-world French dressing, freshly baked rolls. There was roasted chicken with dressing, mashed potatoes and killer gravy. Great food was a surefire lure.

Tony called the meeting to order and went over the department's business items. The atmosphere in the room was cheery and calm as everyone discussed each topic while eating. Tony was a little uneasy knowing God's purpose for the meeting, but the previous words of encouragement strengthened him. His lips felt hot as if they had been touched with a hot coal. It was time to tell his colleagues his story.

"There is one final topic that is not on the typed agenda. Something happened to me a few days ago that shook my worldview. I believe it will change the direction of the university forever."

Focus suddenly shifted from the plates of food to Tony. Talk of major change struck panic. *Had the university been hit with a financial tsunami? Did they still have jobs? What was their colleague talking about?* If Tony wanted their full attention ... he got it.

Tony sensed the surrounding presence of God, while colleagues noticed moisture in his eyes—something they had never seen nor ever expected to see in him. They hadn't even seen him shed a tear at Andrea's funeral. Whatever he was about to say, they feared it was news of a cataclysmic nature.

In the next few minutes, Tony shared what happened the day Gregor knocked on his front door. All the encounters with Jesus, his visit to Heaven, the complete change in purpose and seeing the fruit of the Spirit begin to grow in his life. At first, Tony expected them to stand up, accuse him of losing his mind or becoming a religious nut and then walk out. However, his colleagues were too stunned to speak.

The presence of the Lord that Tony felt wrapped around each listener. He watched faces change from dazed disbelief to extreme sorrow. The pain of sin was felt so deeply, they cried out for Jesus' mercy. It was the sound of Godly sorrow that only comes when the arrow of repentance is driven deep into the soul. Their sin had become an unbearable weight, pressing them down, revealing their true state of separation from the love of God.

This was astounding! Instead of getting hit with bricks—or rotten eggs—for proclaiming his love and faith in Jesus Christ, Tony was struck with the awe of God at work among them. As he prayed for each person in the room, he realized that God was doing exactly what He said He would do.

Tony glanced out the conference room window and immediately took a second look. A mighty angel, garbed in glowing white linen, stood at the center of campus. Outside, the angel drew a ten-foot, golden sword out of its sheath, then thrust it deep into the ground as if striking the heart of the university, marking God's territory. Inside the conference room, Jesus marked hearts for His service to defend that territory and gain more for His Kingdom.

In the midst of the sounds of brokenness, Jesus quietly spoke to Tony. *Nurture and shepherd My flock. These that I send out will bear the light of My Fire, bringing it to other colleges and universities. I have put My sickle into your hand to harvest the field set before you. Whatever you ask in My name, I will give you.*

"Lord, I ask that I and my fellow workers in the Kingdom remain faithful," Tony humbly prayed. "Don't let us take a single step to the right, to the left, lag behind or get out ahead of you. Cause us to execute Your perfect will in humility, unity, love and purity to bring in Your merciful harvest."

You have asked wisely, My son. Since you have not asked for recognition, I will give you more. You will finish stronger at the end of this race than when you first started. You will not fail Me and I will never leave you.

The words *you will not fail Me* were worth more than all the recognition the world could offer. Tony had failed Andrea. He was determined not to make that mistake again in his relationship with God. But how could he fail? His loving Savior had also said, *I will never leave you.*

He lifted his arms toward Heaven and thanked the Lord for the first workers of the Final Awakening. The purpose for which he desperately yearned was right in front of him.

175

22

The Right Place

Jean was working on the Power Point for Sunday's meeting when she suddenly sensed the Lord calling her. Years ago, this routinely happened, but the long season of testing and refining made the thought of this close communion remote. Even after seeing Jesus sitting at her kitchen table, she was still cautious and didn't accept every thought as from the Lord.

She prayed a prayer to protect her thoughts. "In the name of Jesus of Nazareth who sits at the right hand of the Father, I command that all voices other than the voice of the Holy Spirit be silenced. Open my eyes to see what You, Lord, would have me see and open my ears to hear what You would have me hear. Fill my mouth with Your truth that I may pray according to Your will."

Jean, I tell you this: The evil one will attempt to sabotage what I am doing on the earth by posing as an angel of light, deceiving many. You must teach others to discern and not presume that all voices are Mine. The years of refining have taught you this valuable principle. Many who walk in the prophetic speak contradictory words for lack of testing and discerning.

"Lord, forgive me for complaining about the dark years of my life. I think I'm beginning to understand their purpose. Thank You for Your patience and lovingkindness toward me."

Many times, she had felt that she had disappointed the Lord in the moments of intense physical and emotional pain. He was longsuffering, merciful, and understood her limitations, yet she had longed for the day He would say, *Enough.* In this moment, all her feelings of failure washed away with a cleansing peace. She knew she had been forgiven!

The first ministry center in D.C. will be an example for others worldwide. At Sunday's meeting, you will reveal My plan. I will speedily do the work of the Final Awakening before the Great Tribulation begins.

Overcome by the tender, yet authoritative voice she had missed so much, she knelt on the den floor. "O Lord, I am Yours. Use me for Your purposes as long as there is breath in my body ...."

* * *

The doorbell rang, interrupting this surreal moment, and Jean rose to her feet, reluctant to leave the presence of her beloved Lord. Still, she knew He would be with her all day—and every day.

It was Barb at the door. Today, they were going to see the building that Carlos had suggested for the ministry center. Normally, neither would go near Carlos's notorious neighborhood under any circumstances whatsoever. But today they felt safer going to meet the leader of the Barrios on his home turf than making a trip to the corner coffee bar.

As they neared Baldwin Park, Jean called Carlos to let him know they were just about there. Carlos gave specific instructions as to what streets to use, then assured them he was sending word the two women were to be protected at all costs. Driving these streets, littered with refuse and the evidence of ungodly activity, was eerie. People stood on the sidewalks staring, but as Carlos had promised, no one approached them.

As Jean pulled around some abandoned warehouse buildings, she could see Diego in the distance, waving his arms to get her attention. She drove slowly through a narrow pathway between trash piles to where Diego signaled her to park.

"Welcome to my humble *casa,*" Diego said jokingly. "Carlos is inside. Jason with you?"

"He should be along shortly," said Barb.

As Jean and Barb exited the car, a wave of nauseating odors slapped them in the face. It took effort to control their gag reflex. They looked at each other, silently communicating their doubts about the location. Both wondered if the inside looked as bad as the outside. There were plenty of parking spaces, for sure, but the area had become a dumping ground for the neighborhood.

Rusted cars missing most of their parts, old furniture, beer and liquor bottles nestled among tall weeds growing in the crumbled concrete. Used hypodermic needles were sprinkled here and there among the piles of garbage and soiled diapers. A few addicts could be seen, huddling together getting their fix on a stained, torn mattress. Every building in sight was covered with graffiti, some not suitable for their eyes. All of the windows were broken or missing, mute testimony to the fact that these buildings had not been used in decades.

"Good morning, Diego." Jean and Barb smiled as they leaned in to give him a big hug.

A warm, infectious smile dimpled Diego's face as he gladly received the motherly hugs from the two women. No words could express his appreciation for the ability to do something as simple as walk. He now walked with a different purpose from most his age. He walked in the will of God.

"Because of my story, fifty-three of the Barrios now b'lieve in Jesus," Diego proudly announced. "Even two of my old teachers … they follow Him, too. They knew why I drop out of school—no legs. When you're dif'rent from ev'ryone else … well …" He shrugged, then grinned again. "But now, I just wanna to go outside and run all the time! All these new b'lievers ask about my church, but I don't have one. I tol' them there would be a place soon. They ask how they can help. Come … look inside."

Diego grabbed Jean and Barb by the hands as if they were beloved aunts and walked them into the largest warehouse.

Inside, the two women stopped in their tracks, taken aback by the contrast between the exterior and the interior of the building. Here, there was no trash, no broken glass or strung-out bodies lying around. The place looked like it had been gutted and scrubbed clean.

"Hey, Carlos, look who's here!" yelled Diego. Others scattered throughout the space stopped, turning to see what the commotion was all about.

Just as Jason pulled into the parking lot, he saw Jean, Barb and Diego open the door to the warehouse. He jumped out of his new Jeep and ran to catch up with them, stepped in between them and put his arms over their shoulders. Jean, Barb and Jason, dwarfed by the size of the expansive space, stood in the middle of the building, speechless at all Carlos and Diego had accomplished in such a short time.

Carlos put down a drill and wiped away the sweat from his brow. He motioned everyone to come close. "Hey, *a todos!*" he called out, motioning to about seventy-five others to gather around.

For the next hour, Carlos introduced former gang members and their families who had given their lives to Jesus. "These *hombres*— and *chicas*—use' to be drug addicts, dealers, alcoholics, adulterers,

179

prostitutes, thieves, murderers … now, they Jesus-people!" he said fondly.

As he called out sins like popcorn, several raised their hands. Each one was encouraged to give a brief testimony of how Jesus had delivered them. It was easy to see they had been in bondage but had experienced the freedom of the truth Christ offers in a way Jean, Barb and Jason would never really understand.

Hearts had changed, but the language of communicating their miraculous transformation had not caught up just yet. They were still rough around the edges. Neither of the women had ever heard the glories of God expressed in so many heart-felt expletives, but they rejoiced with them in their new life in Christ.

Feeling motherly about these fledgling believers, they were concerned for their new "children's" discipleship. These people were insatiably hungry for the truth of God. The old days of dragging people into a program were over. Entire families were already lining up, desiring to learn how to live the Christian life.

"When I walked into this building, I could feel the presence of God. I fall to my knees right here and had a vision." Carlos waved his arms around as if his vision for the building came into being from his fingertips. "I saw this place finish'. All the windows were fix', walls painted. This buildin' … it had lights, speakers, monitors so ev'rybody could see and hear what was goin' on. I saw a stage … *here.*"

Carlos ran to the right, pointed and spread his arms, trying to help the others envision what he saw. "Right here, classrooms filled with people learnin' 'bout God."

Then Carlos ran across the building to the left side, pointing and waving his arms to map out the space. "Over here, special room filled with people prayin'. Ya know … I think this place can fit around

10,000. I can' wait, so we all start cleanin' up. We found use' lumber in one buildin' and start makin' this platform."

A larger, young man wearing a red bandanna stepped forward from the crowd and walked toward Jason.

"Hey, no hard feelin's, man." He held out his hand to shake Jason's.

"Mateo?" asked Jason.

"Yeah, man, Hope your friend ain't mad at me."

"Mateo, so awesome to see you here!" Jason took Mateo's hand and pulled him in for a hug and a big pat on the back.

Jean's eyes welled up with tears as she looked at Jason and Barb, silently asking if this could really be happening. Barb took Jean and Jason's hands, and the rest of the group spontaneously did the same, forming a large circle in the empty warehouse. Jean asked Carlos if he would pray.

Carlos accepted with childlike faith. At his first utterance, a power went out of his hands into the person next to him and continued around the entire circle, shooting from one hand to another, much like electricity flows through copper wire. Adults and children alike experienced the impartation of the Holy Spirit, giving each person a gift.

As the sensation of the Spirit's power subsided, the silence was broken when a demure young woman named Maria asked, "What jus' happen?"

Jean pulled a small Bible out of her bag, quickly leafed through the pages to find the right spot and then read from Joel: "I will pour out my Spirit on all flesh; your sons and your daughters shall prophesy, your old men shall dream dreams, and your young men shall see visions."

Looking up from her open Bible, she continued, "You are part of what was prophesied thousands of years ago. Some of you will have prophetic dreams; others, prophetic visions. Still others will speak in a new language you've never learned. Many of you will heal the sick and perform signs and wonders."

Jason, Jean, Barb, Carlos and Diego burned with the Fire of Heaven. Others in the circle could see the unusual glow in their eyes and bowed on their knees, not to men, but to the holiness of God. It was clear—even to these new Christians—that He had established Himself in this place.

Jason saw an angel writing something on everyone's forehead. He knew a great Visitation of the Lord was coming, along with the fresh filling of the Fire of Heaven. He saw the future multitudes whose lives would be changed by entering this abandoned warehouse in a dangerous, forgotten part of town.

Maria felt a gentle hand lift her head. She opened her eyes and saw four magnificent angels, one standing in each corner of the building. Their shining robes lit up the entire warehouse with a brilliant, blue-white light. They looked out into the distance as if on patrol, protecting their charge.

She was confused and frightened. Four voices, like the sound of a waterfall crashing on rocks below, spoke in unison, saying, *Do not be afraid.* Strange and beautiful worship came like waves as the angels released songs of reverence to the Lord, their voices making music along with the words sung. She looked around the room to notice others' reactions to the heavenly beings, but all heads were still bowed.

Even though Maria had never heard the words or melody of the song, it was oddly familiar to her. Something within her sang the words that the angels were singing. Her voice started off faintly, but grew stronger with each word. She moved into the middle of the circle, lifted her hands to Heaven and sang, her voice pure and lovely.

Unafraid, she sang with her whole being. Newfound love for her

Jesus poured out as she joyfully sang with the angels. The resonating sound shook the building. The more she allowed the Holy Spirit to flow into and out of her, the more the ground shook, sending more and more powerful waves and lifting all in the warehouse to their feet by an unseen hand. Arms stretched to Heaven as all voices sang along with Maria and the angelic beings.

The four angels observed the group pouring out their hearts in deep, intimate worship. Overjoyed to see the number of souls sealed to the Holy One, the angels sang louder, sending shock waves of intense worship beyond the grouping of abandoned buildings.

Without hearing the sounds of the singing, those in buildings blocks away fell to their knees. All the wrongs committed against God played in front of each one—like a holographic movie. Conviction from the Holy Spirit came upon them, breaking off the blindness of their sin.

They wept and begged for mercy from a God they did not know. With each revelation of sin, more tears of repentance fell. Their eyes, opened to their lost and separated state, saw what awaited them in hell. They might as well have been swathed in concrete and thrown into the ocean. Each revealed sin pulled them deeper and deeper into the dark depths. Shedding the concrete blocks was their only hope. But how?

They were drowning, unable to help themselves rise out of the water. Each breath sucked in the salty water, burning their lungs. The descent grew faster as the darkness traveled upward now to meet them. The panic of eternal doom birthed a burning thirst to be loved and forgiven. Their desperation burst forth as one loud shout, calling out, *Forgive me, Jesus!*

In that instant, those falling into the dark waters heard the voices singing in the old warehouse. The sound grew louder within their spirits as they determined to get to the place where the heavenly sound originated. They knew it was there that the heaviness of their sin could be removed.

Quickly, groups of people from all directions sprang to their feet and ran to the place where Maria had opened her heart to sing. They came into the warehouse from any open space that could be found—doors, windows or holes in the walls. One after another poured into the large space and ran, falling on their faces.

The sound of the holy worship did not stop. The singers did not notice the multitudes of people, prostrate on the floor, weeping and crying out for mercy. God held the warehouse group of singers close to His bosom in intimate worship, releasing His strength and love, equipping them to minister to the new arrivals.

When the worship ended, the singers breathed in what felt like pure oxygen. Jean looked at her watch. It felt like they had been singing for only a few minutes, but it had actually been a couple of hours.

Barb quickly nudged Jean. There were about a thousand people on the floor, weeping and begging for mercy.

Jean was shocked. "Where did *they* come from?"

Then the Lord spoke to the team: *Worship Me first, and I will bring the people. Worship Me first, then minister to others. Remember this simple principle; it will serve you well.*

The thousand who had descended upon the warehouse stood to their feet. Carlos and Diego lifted Jean up onto the partially built platform.

"Listen, all of you!" Jean yelled to get the crowd's attention. "The Bible says that if you confess with your mouth that Jesus is Lord and believe in your heart that God raised Him from the dead, you will be saved."

As soon as the people heard the words, they shouted as one voice, *I believe.*

Jean asked the seventy-five worshippers who had cleaned the warehouse to lay hands on the crowd and pray for them. Many of the new arrivals collapsed under the power of God's love pouring over them like a cleansing waterfall. Perfect love, previously rejected, now lived within the new believers, laying the foundation for a deep relationship with their Creator.

Jean smiled at Carlos, ear to ear, as if to say, *You picked the right place!* She thought how the repurposing of this warehouse so perfectly mirrored the rejuvenation of lives in the love of Christ. Abandoned. Neglected. Useless. Now—like these fresh, new believers—restored, transformed, repurposed for His Glory.

23

Setting The Stage

Sheila arrived hours before the Capital Grand Hotel meeting was set to begin. After checking with the business office and the catering people, she felt comfortable about the details. The AV crew had been making sound checks and testing Power Point to make sure everything worked properly. But the entire crew had left.

In many ways, the setup appeared like one of the many hundreds of fundraisers she had planned over the years as Senator Taylor's employee. She respected Dan and his conservative efforts to keep the country on the right Constitutional track. However, for her, campaign fundraisers were a plug-and-chug, check-the-box type of event with little excitement about what would transpire. There were the greetings, eating and drinking, the rah-rah-go-team speech and hobnobbing with deep pockets—all things she could happily do without.

If this were a campaign fundraiser, she would have left for a break, but this meeting was different—more important than any other she had organized. This same room had held campaigners many times, but the atmosphere today was humbling with no place for self-importance. This was no elegant gala—no entertainment, no fancy centerpieces, no five-course dinner, no sequined gowns, no tuxedos. Tonight would be a simple come-as-you-are gathering of Jesus-seekers partnering in the Final Awakening.

She noticed that a couple of the hotel staff seemed to intuitively sense a holy presence, whispering when they returned to the ballroom to tend to last-minute details. *Hmmm ... this is a good sign,* she thought. From the podium, she looked out over the stillness of the room, hoping it would be filled with people sent by God. Right now, it was just Sheila, empty chairs and the Holy Spirit. She began to pray.

* * *

Cliff Duncan, the hotel manager, opened the large double doors leading into the ballroom. He and Sheila had worked together many times, making preparations for Taylor campaigns, through which they'd become friends.

"Hey, there's my girl," Cliff said softly, repeating it a couple of times before Sheila heard him.

"Oh, you startled me. I was just ..." Sheila stopped, mid-sentence.

Before Cliff made it to the podium, he suddenly grabbed the back of a chair to steady himself, falling into the seat behind him.

"Cliff, are you all right?" Sheila shouted from the stage, hopping down to hurry over to him.

He didn't answer, but bent over and buried his face in his hands.

"Cliff, are you sick? What's going on?" When he didn't answer right away, she plopped down in the chair next to him, grabbed her phone and pressed 9…1….

He put his hand over the phone. Surprised, Sheila gave him a questioning look.

Cliff spoke in a solemn tone. "All day, I've had flashing memories of my high school days when I first walked with Jesus. I had forgotten how much He changed my life. Did I ever tell you I was a youth leader back in the day?"

"No, you never mentioned it."

"I had a strong relationship with the Lord back then. Over time, I got side-tracked … career, family … you know." He threw out his hands in a helpless gesture. "Jesus got put on the back burner." He paused, not looking her in the eye. "When I started walking toward you just now, a weird feeling of heaviness came over me. My legs buckled under the pressure."

"Do you have chest pain?"

"No, just weak legs."

Sheila reached for her phone again to call 911, but when the image of a hand formed above Cliff, she put the phone down. The figure was pure, white light. She stretched out her hand. The radiant image engulfed her hand, guiding it to touch Cliff's chest over his heart.

At her touch, a flood of tears flowed from Cliff's eyes, his body tense and quivering as he wept. Sheila knew by the Holy Spirit that this was no physiological heart condition. As she prayed, his body relaxed.

"I need to pray." Cliff got up from his chair, went to a corner and laid himself prostrate on the floor, arms outstretched.

* * *

When Gregor and Jean entered the room, they immediately felt the Lord's presence. Not long after that, Dr. Tony Robertson burst in with his infectious, trademark grin. Carlos, Diego and Maria followed just a few steps behind.

Noting the early arrivals, Sheila wondered if she'd told people the wrong time. They had all agreed to pray beforehand, but not this early.

When Dan and Barb strolled in, she was sure she must have made some error ….

"I am so sorry for y'all comin' so early. I must've sent the wrong time in the last email. The meeting doesn't start for several hours."

Dan put his arm around Sheila to relieve her stress. "Sheila, you didn't make a mistake. I'd say this is a pre-meeting called by the Holy Spirit. Why is Cliff on the floor? Is he all right?" Dan asked as he started toward Cliff. Then Dan snapped his fingers as if he had just remembered something, before turning back to Sheila. "Wait … don't tell me. Cliff and the Lord are having a little meeting of their own."

"Should we be on the floor, too?" Diego asked in all innocence.

Tony's vibrant laughter echoed in the spacious room. Joyfulness was a welcome change from the seriousness of the last few days, and all joined Tony. The weight of their God-appointed roles in the Awakening lifted—a gift from the Lord.

Cliff got up from the floor, laughing along with the rest. His belly hurt and his eyes watered. He couldn't remember laughing like this— ever. It felt so refreshing that he kept drinking it in, even though still unaware of the joke. "What's so funny?" he managed to ask.

The group burst into laughter again as the stress of this life lifted.

Gregor wiped his eyes. "I don't know about you, but that laughter was inspiring. I was carrying a load I wasn't meant to carry. I have to keep reminding myself I am only responsible to obey."

The events of the past forty-eight hours became the topic of conversation. Tony shared what happened at Frederick University and how the faculty in his department met the real Jesus. "Professors are in the Lord's crosshairs. I also think students will come to Jesus by the thousands."

"Speaking of thousands …" Jean looked to Carlos, silently prompting him to share what happened at the warehouse.

"Yeah ... we were singin' and then all these people jus' show up outta nowhere! Must've been a thousand believe right then and there."

"Uh ... with that thought in mind, how many people are you expecting tonight?" Dan asked Sheila.

"I didn't get a lot of firm commitments. But, what I've been hearing from y'all, do you think we need to plan for more space?"

The group looked to Dan for guidance, since the rental fee *was* on him. "Hey, guys. Don't look at me."

Barb suggested the group pray. At the conclusion of the prayer, all agreed they should prepare for a larger group than expected.

"Cliff, at this late date ... any possibility?" Sheila asked him.

"Huh ... funny you should ask. Two groups canceled Friday." Cliff chuckled, marveling at how God had arranged it. "I'll have staff prepare the expansion spaces now. By the way, Dan, no cost for the rooms tonight, as well as the food." He shook Dan's hand. "For all you've done for this hotel and for me tonight, I'll consider it a tithe to the Lord."

Humbled by God's generosity, Dan gave Cliff a pat on the shoulder.

Diego smiled and leaned into Carlos. "Bro, we're ridin' the plow and nothin's gonna stop us now. That ministry center is gonna happen like you saw. And we need it like yesterday, man!"

Just as they were about to pray for the upcoming event, Jason popped open the service door. The hydraulically regulated door closer was broken and the loud slam startled everyone. Turning, they saw Jason sauntering into the room, munching on a chicken leg.

"Are you looking at me or this delicious piece of chicken?" asked Jason. "Best fried chicken in the area—at the Capital Grand Hotel, of all places. Who would've guessed?"

"Is Carrie with you?" asked Barb.

"She's coming later to *observe*. Don't worry, she's not bringing cameras. After a few conversations, I think she's searching for herself, not so much for a story."

Dan wasn't sure how he felt about Carrie being there at all, even without cameras. He straddled the line between trust and distrust. *If God doesn't want her here, then she won't come*, he thought, attempting to ease his suspicions. "We were just about to pray."

Jason took the last bite of chicken. "Hey, I had a vision. Do you want to hear it now ... or after we pray?"

Gregor thought he'd be too distracted to pray, wondering what the vision was. "Yeah ... what was it? What'd the Lord show you?"

"I saw all kinds of people—different ages, races and income levels. Each person carried a gift as they entered a room. The gifts were different sizes and looked like puzzle pieces. As people laid down their gifts, the pieces fit perfectly together. I was blown away when I saw the picture it made—workers in a wheat field, swinging sickles to bring in a harvest. But when one piece of the puzzle was missing, the entire image of the wheat field vanished."

"What's it mean?" asked Diego.

Jason looked at Gregor as if to say, *You take this one.*

"The size of the gifts is irrelevant, because all puzzle pieces are equal from God's perspective," Gregor began. "What matters the most is that each gift *was* given to complete the work. Just like the vision of the clock, each piece—big or small—is critical."

Diego gave his own interpretation, trying to understand. "OK, I get it. Like a car without a five-dollar battery cable. The engine costs way more than the cable, but the car won't run without that cable. So ... the least is equal to the greatest. Without one or the other, nothin's gonna happen."

Gregor smiled, thinking of Kyle, the early years' new believer with great wisdom. "You nailed it, Diego! You explained it better than I did."

Barb spoke thoughtfully, "Don't get distracted by *what* is given, but rather rejoice that it *is* given. In campaign fundraising, high-dollar donors are valued over the rest, being first in line for special treatment. Each gift brought tonight is an equal part of the puzzle, regardless of how many zeros come after the first number."

The group pulled some chairs together and prayed. Prayers absent of any self-seeking flowed as a pure aroma before God's throne. There were no powerful encounters this time. In childlike faith, they simply poured out their hearts and opened their ears, listening to the Holy Spirit's direction for the evening.

24

Come Back To Me!

Jesus smiled. In faith, these, His chosen vessels, humbly sought His will. "Storis, they are learning the foundational principles of the Kingdom. Their hearts are ready to delegate responsibility, raising up others to replace themselves. They will not seek to control nor take My Glory as their own."

To Storis, his human brothers were wrapped in mystery. Salvation was provided for man, but not for angels. His rebellious brethren, who had once lived in the glorious light of the Creator, were now banished to darkness. They had become his Master's enemy; therefore, making them his enemy.

Jesus rested His feet in the clear water as he sat on the banks of the River of Life. He looked beyond Storis as if lost in a past memory. "My disciples did not understand My words when I spoke in parables. How did I answer them?"

"Lord, You said, 'To you it has been given to know the secrets of the Kingdom of Heaven, but to them it has not been given.'"

Jesus patted the ground, inviting Storis to sit.

"To those who seek Me with earnest hearts, I give ears to hear and the mind of the Spirit to understand. To those who receive and practice My truth, I will give even more. Mysteries *are* written in My word, but are not revealed until the right time."

"Lord, will You reveal hidden things during the Final Awakening?"

"Yes, you know that I confide in those who fear Me and will give them the hidden riches of secret places and will validate those things in what is written. I will reveal My holiness and power."

"I rejoice, Lord, that the world will know You as You are!"

"Man continually puts Us in a neatly wrapped doctrinal box of his own fabrication. In this, he foolishly thinks We can be controlled." Jesus picked up a few rocks and skipped them across the water. "The lack of the Fear of the Lord produces irreverence, widening the door for pride and self-worship. In this, a man cheats himself of full knowledge."

"Lord, the ways of man are hard to grasp. Your Word records many examples from which man may learn, yet it seems the lessons go unheeded." Storis sighed, considering the foolishness of humans.

"Surely you know this: My Bride is easily deceived. She thinks she will not fall into her predecessors' failures. She has become dull-hearted. A worthless doctrine is a wooden idol, and she has fashioned many idols in her heart, placing them above Me." Jesus closed His eyes for a moment.

Storis sensed the grief of his Master's heart; His Church, His Betrothed, had turned her affections to others.

Opening His eyes again, Jesus gazed out upon the ripples of the water, ever flowing from the Throne of God. "My faithful servant Daniel lived, untouched, by the wealth and power of Babylon. He trusted and believed Me when all those around him spoke otherwise, never compromising the truth even at the peril of his own life."

A few more rocks effortlessly skipped across the gentle water, dancing their way to the other bank. "In Daniel's heart, his home was with Me, and for this, I showed him great mysteries, some of which are still hidden from man's understanding. John also saw great things of the Kingdom, some of which I forbade him to write. The Word is exceedingly deep."

Storis knew the majesty of his Master's words and works firsthand. He had shouted for joy when the Lord laid the earth's foundations. He had participated at the giving of the Law on Mt. Sinai. He had rejoiced at his Master's earthly birth. Then, years later, He had watched Him mocked, beaten, His Blood poured onto the ground, suffering separation from the Father.

Yes, Storis longed to look into the mystery of salvation, seeking to understand why the Son would change Himself forever to save His beloved man. He hung on every word that proceeded from Jesus' mouth to man, listening intently to understand the salvation plan. Even though he had heard His words numerous times, he never ceased to be amazed at the depths of His love and splendor. Every expression of Jesus' heart brought life; therefore, His words were never tiresome, flowing with freshness just as the revelation of His holiness was continually new.

Jesus turned, questioning Storis in frustration. "Would you not surrender something worthless for something priceless?"

"Of course, Lord! Only *You* are worthy of all honor, glory, power and praise. You alone are holy. I gladly submit to You, my Master, my Creator, and live to do Your will. Compared to You, Lord, all other things *are* worthless."

"You are a faithful servant, Storis. Until My Betrothed understands the value of My Kingdom, she will continue in her harlotry.

"I must call her to a deeper faith, for without faith, she will not survive the coming changes in the world. She must choose life in Me over a temporal world that is quickly perishing. I desire that each person understand that he or she is either for Me or against Me. There is no other alternative."

Birds sang in the tree above; a butterfly lit upon a flower; a fish nibbled at their toes. Storis noted the contrast between the peacefulness of Heaven and the concern in his Master's heart.

"The Church tends to relate to Us as three separate entities as if part of the Godhead had passed away at My coming to earth as a man. Dismissing the earlier Word is a grave mistake, leaving the Bride lacking the knowledge of My character. My Word is one as We are One. When I came to earth as a man, the heart of the Law burned in Me for I AM the Word from the beginning. To call upon the name of Jesus includes all of who We are—Father, Son and Spirit. Nothing of the Word never has nor ever shall pass away.

"Justice and judgment have not been eliminated. Yes, grace covers sin through repentance when one applies the Blood to his life and abides in Me." Jesus turned, looking into Storis's eyes. "I *must* execute My justice if the Blood is missing."

Storis knew these statements to be true, but also knew he would never fully understand through experience. As an elect angel, he never sinned, thus never needed forgiveness. That the Almighty's Blood covered a man's sin was perplexing, yet he accepted it as it was—a fact.

"My Church is weak, not teaching the true meat of the Word. Many listening to tickling philosophies believe they have received My gift of salvation, but they have not, for the word spoken in these places is not even the milk of a babe. They have not been born again into My Kingdom."

The presence of the Holy Spirit's seal clearly showed Storis who was born into the Kingdom. *How they deceive themselves, believing it possible to straddle the fence—one foot in the Kingdom and one foot in the world,* he thought. It puzzled him when those lacking the Lord's seal gathered to worship. But worship who? The testimony of Jesus did not dwell in them; therefore, their worship was not received.

Knowing Storis's thought, Jesus answered him. "The imagined jesus is one of many gods. It is like a man in India who places My image next to Brahma, Kali, Krishna or other pagan entities. He may call Me lord, but he also considers the others his gods. The western world does the same, yet in a different manner. Rather, things born of self are their idols, satisfying the lust of the eyes, the lust of the flesh and the pride of life.

"When things are lifted up as more important than a life abiding in Me, then another god has replaced Me. How does a man think, spend his money or spend his time? These things disclose his heart. The Church has created another gospel not of Me that excuses sin and worships self, entertainment, money and power. The people worship a false jesus of their own making, twisting Scripture to fit their ideologies—idolatry."

Jesus and Storis sat in silence, both grieved by the waywardness of the Church. Storis knew his Master's heart looked past her deficiencies and blemishes, knowing the potential of her beauty. She is His betrothed. Storis took comfort, knowing that the Bride *would* make herself ready. But at what cost?

Jesus broke the stillness of the moment. "If I AM her guide, ascending a dangerous mountain, I know the safest path of ascent and descent. When she charges ahead without seeking My will, she foolishly leaves the guided path only to find herself in trouble. I rescue her from the danger, and yet again, she abandons My knowledge and wisdom, risking the safety of others under her care. When the Great Deception of this age is released, how will she stand?"

He rose and leaned against the tree, resting his forehead on his arm. His voice was soft and pleading: "Oh, My Betrothed, seek Me. Forsake building empires; instead, gather souls to the Kingdom and make disciples. Humble yourself before Me and flee from the master of deception who schemes to blind you. Come out, My Bride, so that you will not share in the world's sins, bringing troubles upon yourself. Embrace My commandments over the ruler of a wicked world. Oh, My Beloved, you have wandered from the guided path and are walking toward great danger. Come back to Me …."

Jesus turned around to face Storis. "The Titanic, the great ship of man's technological achievements, was claimed to be unsinkable. Negligence toward the weeks-long fire burning within the bowels of the ship left the hull's metal vulnerable. The Church ignores that secret fire of destruction, making her disposed to disaster. She has not come to Me in humility seeking My heart, for if she did, she would not corrupt herself."

Suddenly, He put both His hands on Storis's shoulders, His tone urgent. "The Church believes she is unsinkable. The Final Awakening must remain clothed in humility. Arrogant wolves in sheep's clothing will appear to come with genuine motives, but unless Heaven intervenes, the powerful of the world will shipwreck this Awakening.

"Storis, you must form a wall of separation between My Church and this Awakening. The Final Awakening will first go to the highways and the hedges, compelling sinners to dine at My table. Eventually, the remnant of the old church model will merge with the new Awakening model, but for now, they must remain separate. I AM sending you to keep deceivers and dividers out. Lucifer has already asked for the small group under Gregor's tutelage. Keep the Awakening river separate from the Church river. Go … with all the resources of Heaven."

"Yes, Lord," Storis acknowledged with a deep bow, then hastened to return to his charges.

25

A Moment At The Capital Grand

Jason searched for Carrie among the throngs of people entering the Capital Grand Hotel Ballroom. He wondered if he should text her. Just then, he felt his phone buzz. He pulled it out of his pocket.

He felt a hollow feeling in his stomach. Carrie's name was above the text message: *on escalator... where are you?*

When her name appeared on his phone, his heart leapt. *What just happened?* he wondered. *I don't really know her. We've only spoken a few times. Stop it, Jason! You can't fall for her. She's just another poor lost soul who needs Jesus.*

Jason texted back: *right side as you come up escalator, meet you there.*

Jason's palms started sweating. It was déjà vu—the same feeling he'd had at Pat's Deli. The more he determined not to sweat, the more the perspiration rolled off his forehead. His pulse rate was increasing, and he knew it wasn't anticipation over the upcoming meeting. He realized he cared deeply for Carrie. No ... more than that—*loved* was the word. Yet, how could that be? He barely knew her!

"Carrie! Over here!" he yelled as he waved to get her attention.

His nervousness felt like a DEFCON 1 alert. Once again, seeing her expression as she turned in his direction, Jason saw the broken heart searching for what only Jesus could give.

"Hey ... no cameras, as promised." She pulled out a tissue from her purse and stuck it in his hand. She leaned in, whispering, "You might want to wipe off your face."

Jason didn't want to tell her the truth, so he fabricated an excuse for the bead of sweat he felt running down his temple. He attempted to laugh it off. "Been working all day on prepping for ... this," he said, gesturing toward the room, set up with dozens of round, skirted tables and chairs, ready to serve a crowd.

Then he wondered, as conviction slammed into his heart: *Did I just tell a lie and need to repent?* But he couldn't come right out and tell her, *You're beautiful, Carrie! I love you! Just being this close to you makes me so nervous, I'm sweating!*

Jason grabbed her hand, leading her through the crowd. As soon as their hands touched, Carrie felt a little light-headed. A surge of something jolted her body. It wasn't like the first time at the press briefing on the Taylors' front steps. No, this was different. *Behold your husband,* came a voice in her head. This sudden revelation stopped her mid-stride. She stood still, jerking Jason off balance. *Who said that?* Her heart hammered crazily.

He turned to make sure she was all right. Carrie smiled timidly and resumed walking beside him, her hand in his.

What are you even thinking, Carrie Summers? blasted through her thoughts. But she knew it wasn't *her* thought; it had come from somewhere else. Her entire body felt flushed. She worried that Jason would notice the tiny droplets of water forming on her upper lip.

As they drew near their table, she excused herself. "I had to run over here from work. If you don't mind, I'm going to freshen up," she said, making a beeline to the ladies' room.

Thoughts were flying through her head. *I'm losing my mind and hearing voices! Maybe something happened to my brain when I got zapped with electricity at the Taylors'. Is that what God's voice sounds like? Girl, pull yourself together! You're not only sitting with Jason but his parents, too! Oh, God, if you're really there, help me figure this out and don't let me sweat like a tropical rainforest!*

Carrie grabbed a paper towel and patted the beads of perspiration off her face, then powdered it. In all her career—interviewing celebrities, CEOs of Fortune-100 companies, and heads of state—she had never experienced anything like this before. She'd always managed to maintain a calm and steady demeanor. This unexpected anxiety was new turf.

She did a few relaxation exercises to slow her heart rate. A double-check in the mirror. *Whew, good to go. Now let's keep it that way.* She took a deep breath and left the restroom to join Jason at his parents' table.

Jason rose to greet her. "Mom, Dad, Sheila, I want you to meet Carrie ... Carrie Summers. She's promised to be an innocent observer and not a shrewd reporter tonight." Jason kept it light.

"It's a pleasure to meet you. I've followed your career for many years, Senator Taylor."

He stood up to shake her hand. "Please, call me Dan. I'm not a senator in front of these people, just a humble servant of Jesus Christ."

Barb took Carrie's hand, peering deeply into her green eyes. The penetrating stare startled Carrie. She wasn't sure how to react. Maybe something was wrong with Jason's mom that he hadn't mentioned. It was extremely awkward, feeling almost like a violation. Carrie glanced at Jason with a helpless look. When she turned her gaze back to Barb, it felt like Jason's mom had seen into her soul.

Barb finally released Carrie's hand and apologized. "Forgive me.

Guess I'm distracted. Excuse me. I need to make sure we're all set to begin."

"Oh, certainly. So nice to meet you ...." Carrie's voice trailed off as Barb was already out of earshot.

Wow, was that bizarre! thought Carrie. But what should she expect with the Taylors? Everything about them seemed extraordinary. Maybe more like ... weird.

Dan and Jason gave each other a questioning look. *What's up with that?* Dan frowned as if to suggest they drop it and move on, then left to greet many of the familiar faces in the crowd.

Jason and Carrie remained at the table. Both intentionally avoided eye contact, which actually generated more work than looking at each other. Not making conversation, he fidgeted with his napkin and tableware, while she checked for nonexistent text messages on her phone.

Finally, Jason broke the silence. "I know this could be a big story for you. Please keep an open mind as to what is really happening and why before you turn this over to your news desk."

Jason's plea for Carrie's consideration fell on deaf ears. Tonight, she wasn't Carrie Summers, top news correspondent for WNN News D.C. Bureau, but Carrie Summers, the woman who wanted to be his wife! *This cannot be happening,* she thought. She lifted her gaze from her phone to study Jason. *Who was he really?*

As their eyes met, Jason was struck with a wave of emotion he hadn't known was possible. A longing love for Carrie poured over him, warming and peaceful. At that moment, his spirit softly spoke, connecting to hers—a quiet knowing between them. No words, just silence that screamed the revelation over the background noise of the ballroom. There was no going back ... and they both knew it.

At that moment, Sheila came over to speak to Jason. "Y'all ready? The meeting's about to start now." She put her hand on Jason's forehead to check for a fever. "Are y'all right, hon? You look a little funny."

"Huh? Yeah, sure." Jason emerged from his stupor, looked at Sheila and asked, "What was the question?"

Carrie turned away in embarrassment.

Sheila stared at Carrie and then again at Jason. "I get the picture. Y'all don't have to say anything to me." She could see the flashing lights going off in both of them. *Oh, to be young again and in love,* she thought.

* * *

Dan and Barb made their way to the podium. *Where did all these people came from?* The list Sheila had used for her phone calls was about one-third this count. It was obvious to Dan that God's hand was on the meeting.

"Before we begin, I want to thank each of you for coming tonight on such short notice," he said after introducing himself and Barb. "To be perfectly honest, there are many faces I don't recognize. I'm curious as to how some of you heard about the meeting."

A voice from the back yelled out, "The Holy Spirit told me to come when I was praying this morning."

"I just knew I was supposed to come to the Capital Grand Hotel tonight," replied someone in the front.

Another spoke up, "God told me I would see the fulfillment of promises given twenty years ago."

Dan was awed. "Satisfy my curiosity. If you were not invited by a phone call, please stand."

More than two-thirds of the room stood. The crowd let out a loud gasp at the disclosure that so many had come without the Taylors' invitation, but at God's beckoning.

Dan introduced Gregor and Jean, giving a brief bio of their background, then stepped aside as Gregor came to the podium.

"Followers of our Lord Jesus Christ, we welcome you to the beginning of the Final Awakening of souls. We all have similar stories—ones laced with pain, isolation and confusion. You willingly lived through years of dying to self so Jesus could live in you in a greater way.

"Dying to self is a costly experience. I still pray that I continue to die to self every day so *my* self stays dead!" The crowd chuckled in agreement. "Even so, the cost paid was insignificant and not enough. The prison of affliction sculpted us, instructed us in humility and submission to Him, into vessels ready for His use."

Jean spoke next. "In God's mercy, He allowed afflictions to prevent us from a future sin, so that when the Holy Spirit is poured out in great measure, we will not fail Him. Many great men and woman of God have fallen, finishing weaker at the end of their lives. Jesus promised us our latter years would be stronger and more powerful than our former years.

"God creates the living water and He's the One controlling the flow, deciding when it is on or off. We are only faucets, just simple stewards of His mercy, love, healing and salvation. Our journeys required faith that forged unlimited trust and love, ready to flow to others at His direction."

Dan jumped in, saying, "We all come together to use our spiritual gifts, money, and time, placing the first stake in the ground while declaring the beginning of the Final Awakening. Join us in this mission ... only if God directs you to do so. Tonight, we want to share the vision as it was given to us."

Dan asked everyone to bow their heads. When he prayed, a holy fear fell upon the crowd. Some people removed their shoes as they felt they were standing on holy ground. Others knelt. All waited quietly, eager for the Lord's instructions. Hearts were ready for the vision.

Sheila started the Power Point slides as Gregor explained the concept of the ministry center. He told them about the dream, contrasting the bicycle wheel and the clock, then discussed the possible location of the first center and what was needed to get it off the ground as quickly as possible.

As photos of the decrepit warehouse appeared on the large screen, Carlos and Diego shared their personal transformations. They explained the new meaning of their red bandannas—how they had once announced the brutality and mercilessness of the Barrios, but now communicated hope, help, peace, protection and the salvation of Jesus through His Blood. They told of lives dramatically changed in one of the toughest neighborhoods of the nation's capital.

Behind Carlos, the image of a thousand smiling faces—the new believers from the warehouse—shone on the screen as he pleaded for help. "Diego, Maria and I are new believers and need help learnin' 'bout Jesus. So do all these people ... we all need ..." Carlos was cut off mid-sentence.

Without solicitation, a middle-aged man in the front stood to speak. "Ford Oliver Ashman's the name—high-rise construction contractor. A project like this is small potatoes for what I'm used to doin'. I'll take the job, no fee for my services."

Following Mr. Ashman's offer, a silver-haired, African-American gentleman in his seventies stood. "My name is Colonel John Parker, Marines, retired. Over the past forty years, I've mentored hundreds of young men and women in the Armed Forces."

Colonel Parker's authoritative tone sounded as if he was about to give a military briefing. "I love Jesus with all my heart, but don't go to church anymore. What happened to the meat of the Word? Just a bunch of empty ideas makin' people feel comfortable in false security. Jesus is not a 'love child' hippy savior. He is *the* Almighty King, Lord, Commander, deserving of all reverence."

Parker commandingly moved to the center of the room. "A soldier has to have his head and heart all in. Ya' gotta live smart ... fight smart. Sloppiness ... get ya' killed every time. God's love is immense, and outta worship for what He did for Me, I think I owe it to Him to love Him with all I got. Jesus told us to deny ourselves, *daily* ... take up the cross, *daily* ... and follow him, *daily*." He emphasized each *daily* by pounding one fist against his hand. He returned to his seat, waited a moment, nodded, and then sat. "What I'm sayin' is, I'll help with discipleship, if you'll have me."

An elegant, older woman stood. "Well, you younger ones are gettin' *shown up* by us old folks." There was a ripple of laughter from the crowd. "I'm Marjie Wegman. I've known the Taylors for well ... a long time. My husband and I were good friends with the senator's parents ... so now I've given away my age." Everyone chuckled along with her. "My late husband was a CEO at a top Wall Street firm. He taught me everything he knew about finances and banking. I'll take the role of financial administrator. If God is asking you to write the most outrageous check you've ever written, you better obey. He'll take it anyway."

A few *amens* sounded.

Marjie continued, "If you are of little means, don't give away your rent money. Give only what God is asking. Now for you with deep pockets—I see you sittin' here—you should know you can't take it with you anyway, so write the check like you were dying tomorrow. Dream big and live big is my motto. This is what most of us have been waiting for anyway—a harvest of souls—otherwise, you wouldn't be here. I'm writing a check right now."

When no one else stood, Barb closed with prayer, thanked everyone and dismissed them. The team didn't want to strong-arm or guilt people into giving time or money. This was the Lord's work. They trusted He would personally move hearts.

Maria leaned into Barb, speaking softly, "I think I'm s'pposed to sing."

"Oh, absolutely, honey. Please do."

Maria rose and, from where she had been sitting, sang purely, just as she had at the warehouse. Lovely and smooth, the petite woman's voice filled the ballroom with a heavenly atmosphere. The sound of song moved about the room like a velvety glove, caressing each person's heart. Tears of joy, hope and passionate worship flowed like living water as deeply driven spikes of despair and hopelessness were uprooted and washed away.

Thirty minutes passed. The singing stopped. No one spoke. No one moved. With eyes closed, each person prayed silently, having a personal vision of Jesus, all experiencing the same scene of their beloved Savior dying on a cross as it happened more than two thousand years ago.

The vision was not watched but vividly lived. Only two people existed in the vision—Jesus nailed high on the cross, arms outstretched—and each one of them, standing below His broken body.

The warmth of His Blood ran under their bare feet as the life of His body spilled onto dusty ground. Each heard His cry to the Father as He entrusted His eternal Spirit to Him who had been intently watching from Heaven. Jesus had done everything they could *never* do. He, the perfect sinless sacrifice, paid the price for their sins with His own Blood.

As they stared at Jesus' bloodied body, His eyes locked onto their eyes, saying, *Come up here.* Should they accept, it was understood the cross must be endured until it was finished. Agreed. Then, the broken figure nailed to the cross quickly morphed from Jesus to themselves.

Now *their* arms were outstretched, attached to a wooden beam, and *their* feet spiked to a post. He offered them the gift of dying to self. It was impossible for their physical body to grasp the gift—arms immobile, nailed to the cross—so their spirit man took the box, holding it close to their hearts, unaware of what awaited inside. The content of each box was personalized, designed for each self's path to death. Self hung there—beaten, bloody, nailed, unable to move, dying. One last breath. Self was dead.

Jesus affectionately and, with great care, removed each body from the cross, lay it on the ground and breathed His life into the lifeless form. There in the ballroom, believers momentarily lived a poetic expression of how fruitful the years of affliction had really been. The Spirit stood them upright in new strength, equipped and eager to follow their King into the conflict against Lucifer's vast army of darkness.

Their mission was to reclaim captive souls. The silent prayer ended as the vision faded.

* * *

With renewed purpose, groups spontaneously formed as people exchanged contact information. Worshipers gathered around Maria; those with the gift of evangelism, found Diego; and intercessors, Carlos.

Tony was taken aback when people came to him. He hadn't shared his story, but they sensed his calling to institutions like Frederick University. Those with prodigal children joined this group. Others complained that they had sent their children to Bible colleges, only to see them graduate as atheists. If they could prevent other parents this heartache, they wanted to help.

Carrie was speechless, keeping her eyes downcast.

Jason gently touched her hand. "You OK?"

Mascara-smeared eyes, wide and vulnerable, looked up at him. A solemn, introspective aura surrounded her as the weight of her eternal destination pressed heavily against her.

"Grab a coffee downstairs and talk a bit?" Jason asked as he gently held her hand, rubbing his thumb over the back of it.

Carrie nodded, *yes*. She had experienced the presence of the Creator of the Universe. *Jesus really existed. Jesus knew her. Jesus wanted her to be His.*

26

Preparing For War

Lucifer and the Prince of Europe strategized feverishly to move the pontiff's One World Order into place sooner. As usual, the dark warrior touted his accomplishment of breaking down nationalism, a critical component of Lucifer's plan.

"Implement my additional strategies ...," Lucifer stopped mid-sentence, grabbing his chest, as a sharp spike of pain thrust into his cold, dark heart.

He staggered, fell forward onto the war table, pushing maps to the stone floor. The Prince of Europe stepped back, knowing from past experience to stay away. He briefly entertained the idea of seizing this opportunity to overtake Lucifer and usurp his throne, but decided to wait. He silently watched his leader writhe.

Lucifer roared in agony. "Nazarene, my prisoners belong to me! Do you hear me? They belong to *me!*"

Lucifer steadied himself on the conference table, nearly breaking it in two as he gripped the edge in pain. With all his might, he gathered himself, finally standing as erect as possible. "Hermedes. Call an emergency meeting of the Council. Immediately!"

In little time, the great Council leaders gathered, keeping the mood subdued as they noted Lucifer's distress. Hermedes, who usually announced commencement of meetings with great fanfare, feared interrupting.

Lucifer seethed like a rabid dog, his pupils dilated, his mind disoriented, his weakness on display. Direct eye contact could be understood as a challenge to his authority, so the others avoided his maddened eyes, keeping their gaze downward while Lucifer paced at the head of the table.

He turned to address the Council. "Why no warning? Surely one of you saw something. I have given you the greatness of my kingdom. The world is ours. What do I get for all I bestow upon you? Absolutely nothing. Routed by the Nazarene! You, my comrades, have made me look weak." The last statement was spoken as a threat.

Lucifer's tone changed from anger to mocking hatred and disgust, speaking the name of Jesus disrespectfully while overly enunciating: "Jeee-susss of Naaa-za-reth, I will not tolerate this. No ... no ... no!" he bellowed, pounding his fist with each *no,* defying each member of the Godhead. "Anyone derelict in their mission will deeply regret it."

Hermedes finally spoke reassuringly. "We are your faithful servants and will not fail you, oh most high master. Messengers will return soon with the latest intelligence report. Those responsible for failing you will know not only your wrath but the wrath of the Council."

Lucifer dismissed Hermedes's statement as lying admiration and false devotion. There was a commotion, then a dark warrior marched into the room and handed Hermedes a book.

The high pontiff grabbed the book from Hermedes. He opened it and read: "Legions of Michael's warriors surround the Washington, D.C. area, providing protective covering for several followers of the Nazarene. Sightings of great manifestations of the Fire of Heaven are reported in multiple locations: Frederick University, Baldwin Park, and the Capital Grand Hotel."

Lucifer flung the book across the room. The listeners ducked, barely avoiding being struck in the head.

The messenger who delivered the book spoke up: "Another report, lord Lucifer, great dragon who deceives the whole world."

"Of course, there is." Lucifer's tone was filled with disgust. "Speak on."

"Intercessors have aligned themselves with the mind of Christ. Our distractions are to no avail as they are praying the Father's will in one accord. Lies are exposed and our deceptions collapse. Established high places are beginning to topple. We await your commands, oh great leader of the Council," the messenger concluded.

Aligned with the mind of Christ. Lies exposed. High places fallen. The words pierced Lucifer in the chest once again. A black slurry oozed from his wound as the crushing pain returned, along with his wrath.

"Who is responsible for this debacle," he calmly stated, revealing the depths of his anger.

The Council sat in fear as they watched Moldar, Lucifer's enforcer, drag the ruler of D.C. forward in chains and throw him at Lucifer's feet.

"No one fails me," Lucifer stated, maintaining an icy calmness. The shrill sound of his sword sliding against its sheath echoed throughout the cavern. The appearance of the dreadful weapon announced what was to come. With one mighty thrust, he pierced the guilty between the eyes, releasing a plume of dark yellow sulfur. The fallen angel shivered uncontrollably in a heap on the floor.

Fear gripped the Council members.

"Who has a plan to stop this intrusion?" demanded Lucifer.

A devious smile curled across Janis's face. "May I suggest, my king, grand prince of the power of the air, that we use their own religious brethren to condemn the works produced through the Fire of Heaven? It was successful at the first coming of the Nazarene; thus, why not repeat the process?"

"Go on."

"We will—with our subtle influences—convince the top religious leaders that this so-called Final Awakening will unseat their position of power, influence and wealth. They will discredit the harvesters with slanderous decrees from the pulpits, making the workers look like lunatics. Religious television and radio will attribute the wonders of God to you, my lord, as false signs and wonders. Mislead unbelieving religious leaders that this awakening is the great apostasy spoken of in the Word and that you are the author."

Lucifer's pain eased a bit as he pondered Janis's plan. "Yes ... excellent. Blaspheme the Holy Spirit. Go on."

"We influence the media to brand the true Nazarene followers as dangerous heretics who are intolerant of other religious ideas. Viewed as loveless in their doctrine, followers of the Nazarene will be flaunted as full of hate by their radical adamant stance that Jesus is the only way to Heaven."

"Brilliant, Janis. My thoughts entirely." Lucifer immediately lay claim to the concept, setting out additional elements of the blueprint. "Then, by their own law, the name of Jesus will be banned as we enlighten the human creatures that the Nazarene's teachings are contrary to being a good global citizen. So antagonistic, in fact, that His teachings and any followers must be eradicated to usher in the more highly enlightened view. Universities will demand obliteration of archaic religious beliefs and will ignorantly demand socialism over democracy." He let out an evil laugh, relishing in the fact that humans are so easily manipulated.

"Create an atmosphere in which speaking the Nazarene's words are hate speech. The world will terrorize and even kill them. First, we divide through violent revolution in each nation; then, we easily gather them as blinded animals to slaughter," Janis proudly finished the proposal.

Lucifer placed his hand on Janis's shoulder. "Our plan is excellent, my faithful servant. Stir up division, incite violence, implant jealousy, create confusion, instill fear in the hearts and minds of the abysmal creatures that God loves so much. Unfathomable that the Father sent the Holy Son to die for the ignorant, worthless things." He flicked away a wadded piece of paper. "Execute the plan, Janis, and you will be rewarded."

"I promise you this, I will not fail you, my king," Janis assured him.

Lucifer snarled. "Indeed, you will not fail … or you will join the others in disgrace. All of you are expendable and can easily be replaced."

* * *

In accepting the direction of the plan, Janis put himself at risk. *Failure is not an option,* he thought. He quickly called legions of demons, instructing the horde.

"All spirits of Pride and Jealousy, you are hereby dispatched to D.C. pastors, inducing a feeling of threat as Awakening laborers are trained and sent. Remind the religious leaders it is their godly calling to protect the flock from all deception. Just as at the Nazarene's first coming, the leaders will recoil at the works through the Fire of Heaven as heresy and a threat to the true nature of God. Block prayer through the usual distractions such as tragedy, sickness, financial problems, relationship issues, etcetera. Any method will do as long as I see results."

Janis tapped his fingers against his strategy book, then jotted down some notes.

"Reward them with money, fame, a larger flock and so forth to reinforce our twisted truth. The fools always equate blessings of this world as the Father's stamp of approval. Yes …"—once again, Janis paused to ponder the creatures' naïveté—"just keep them preoccupied with something, no matter what, as long as they do not focus their attention on Him.

"Increase infighting about doctrine and interpretation of Scripture. Confusion … yes, confusion through lies and division will do very nicely."

One demon spoke out: "What about Frederick?"

"Oh, yes, a ripe field for us. Cause students to riot and destroy property. They need no reason. Merely provoke them with some meaningless cause. You know the protocol, so I need not give further instruction on that. If the Nazarene is able to harvest there, prod financial donors to anger, encouraging them to withdraw funding unless the religiosity stops."

Janis turned to intelligence-gatherers. "Get a bio on each one from which the Fire of Heaven proceeds. The tiniest bit of information is not to be discounted. I want to know their weaknesses, struggles, fears, failures … information about their family and friends as a door to cause fear, shame, and confusion. You know the drill."

Legions of spirits stepped forward, standing at the ready before Janis—Affliction, Sickness, Pain, Death ….

"Afflict the Fire-starters." Janis ran his fingers over his written plan, thinking. "Unfortunately, we are still under the Holy One's authority and can do nothing outside His granted parameters. But … do take full advantage of our legal rights to oppress granted to us by their own sin. Also, put upon them any and all trials the Nazarene allows as their 'character-building lessons'.... ugh ...," Janis moaned at the nauseating thought that man could actually share in the Creator's Divine Nature, "... and let's see if the creatures will continue on their quest to follow the Nazarene when we push them through trials to the point of screaming out in anger to the God of love." He ended his order with a sarcastic tone.

All evil laborers disappeared to perform their designated mission. Janis sat back in his seat, picking at his nails, thinking it wouldn't take long. The human creatures were ready and ripe for the dark harvest of hell.

* * *

Some of the demonic agents returned with information, knowing the report would anger Janis. *Better to face Janis than lord Lucifer,* they thought.

"Janis, honored member of hell's great Council, we bring you news from the front lines," spoke Affliction.

"Report." Janis readied himself to record a victory in his strategy book.

Affliction stood silently, his eyes downcast.

Janis became agitated. He went to Affliction and pulled his chin upward to look into his eyes. "Quit staring at the floor and face me. Give me your report!" he demanded.

"My horde has tried everything that usually pulls humans far from the Nazarene." Affliction cowered, fearing punishment.

"What?! Impossible! Are you telling me that you cannot afflict them with any of your miseries? I will have your head for this!" shouted Janis.

"Wait, dark lord, please hear me out. The Nazarene has a

protective shield around the followers. Storis and his warriors stand guard over them."

Janis had been quite successful in the past with a similar blueprint. He fully expected to hear Job-like reports of distress. He hadn't anticipated such a strong move by the Son. He needed more detailed information before reporting to Lucifer. "Bring Datter and Gorfius now."

Two black, bat-like creatures flew to Janis, still healing from their recent escapade, ending in their self-inflicted wounds.

Janis barked an order, "Can this shield be penetrated? If we cannot directly manipulate their minds and lives, we will be limited to working through the unsealed souls around them. The Holy One's restrictions always come against us ...." He drifted away in thought, desperately searching his mind for a plan to avoid Lucifer's wrath. He finally commanded Datter and Gorfius, "Do not fail to find the weak link." He pushed them away, causing the two spies to knock heads.

The operatives flew off in the direction of the Wallaces' house. At first, spying was satisfying, perhaps even entertaining, if it were possible for a condemned creature to experience amusement. Lately, however, they had not pleased Lucifer and now feared his anger. Bad news meant more trouble.

"Let us take our time in returning to Janis," suggested Gorfius. "I think we need to recover from the last beating before the next round of pounding comes our way."

Datter just kept flying, but a slight smile appeared from his crooked, beak-like mouth. "Not a bad idea, my friend—not a bad idea!"

27

High Finances - High Hopes

Marjie Wegman—money guru for the warehouse renovation—prayed for wisdom. Executing the financials was a big responsibility and she wanted to get it right. The walnut-paneled study seemed more like a den for a pipe-smoking man, not a petite lady. The office had been her husband's, and she found comfort there.

Five years had passed, but the paneling still smelled sweet of his personal tobacco blend. It was her study now—a place to pray and think. Instead of mergers and high finance, the large mahogany desk would organize building of the first ministry center of the Final Awakening. Serious business.

Marjie knew that most people considered her a woman of strong opinion, yet no one could argue with her heart. Hers was the gift of giving. She and her husband, Byron, had had the privilege of blessing numerous shelters and missionaries through the years. But they had always preferred anonymity, shunning the spotlight whenever humanly possible. *It's better they not know,* she often thought. *It's better they thank God. After all, everything we have ever had has come from His hand.*

Sitting at his desk, she smiled as she reflected on the precious years with her husband. He was a gentle giant in the business world. Although coming from old money, he had worked hard for what he and Marjie had built together. With the new wealth added to the old, they were what most people would call "loaded." She chuckled softly.

Byron had founded one of the largest Wall Street banks and remained CEO before going home to be with the Lord. He'd had his hand on all sorts of business dealings, and God had prospered him.

She picked up the framed photograph she kept on the desk, thanking God once again for this man who had been her best friend, her lifelong love up until the day of his death. A point of pain for both was the inability to have children. So much to give and no one to give it to. They'd chosen not to be tested for infertility so that neither would bear the guilt and disappointment alone. Not knowing had allowed them to share this personal tragedy.

She frowned a bit, feeling a familiar pang. They had once started the process of making three orphaned siblings theirs. Soon after the decision to move forward, Marjie had become ill, and the adoption was put on hold.

Top doctors in the world couldn't explain or cure her condition. Years passed and, with the years, so did the prospect of having a house full of noisy kids. She'd learned to busy herself from home in philanthropic ventures as the Lord directed.

The long-protracted illness had stayed with her up until yesterday ... when she was set free at the Capital Grand. Feeling vibrant again, she longed for family to share the rambling estate. The silence of no children for decades and now the silence of no grandchildren reminded her of the void that Byron's passing had left.

Putting aside the photograph and reining in her memories, Marjie began counting the money given at the meeting—some checks and some cash. She entered each amount into a spreadsheet. A check for ten thousand dollars ... five ones ... one hundred... two hundred fifty thousand ... ten ... nine thousand, five hundred ... two dollars ... fifty-two cents. It took several hours of adding and rechecking before settling on a final tally—one hundred million, three hundred one dollars and fifty-two cents. A staggering sum considering the attendees at the event.

She knew there were many wealthy families in the group, but to collect that amount? Astonishing! The dollar bills and coins touched her the most. She stacked them neatly, admiring them for a few minutes. Those dollar bills and coins were given out of great sacrifice from those who had little. Marjie believed that kind of giving was worth more than the large checks. The sweetest gift of all was the fifty-two cents a little boy had lovingly shown her before sealing the change in an envelope and throwing it into one of the zippered banking bags.

Father, reward each one who gave, but more so to those who gave even in their own need, she silently prayed.

She placed her hands on the collection, bowed her head and thanked the Lord for His lavish provision. "I am in awe of Your great generosity that is beyond human comprehension. I asked You to use this old lady, and you are certainly doing that." She chuckled. "Show us how to use these funds to advance Your Kingdom, Father. I am a good business person, but I need Your divine direction."

Marjie felt the room grow warm against her skin, and a peace settled over her heart. It was if someone intimately familiar stood behind her, touching her shoulders. She clearly heard His voice. Was it audible? She didn't know and didn't care. She was just glad to hear it.

My beautiful child, Marjie. I have heard your prayer and grant you what you ask.

He spoke my name! she marveled. Her heart leapt. Life filled her.

Hearing her name spoken by Him was invigorating, yet humbling at the same time.

I see the deep hole of loneliness in your heart. Today brings change. Your home will continually be filled with My presence. To those who bear the seal of My Spirit, this house will echo with joy, laughter and refreshment. You will not be alone anymore.

At the building of the tabernacle in the wilderness, the people gave more than needed to the point that Moses asked them to stop giving. I can move any heart at any time to provide the means necessary for training disciples. I will guide you in administering funds for the birth of the ministry center.

Marjie let out a girlish giggle. A fresh joy touched the very spot loneliness had occupied. An unseen, inner healing was transpiring.

Suddenly her eyes were opened to a secret world of varying hues. The office came alive with brilliant streams of colored light, swirling in a choreographed dance set to a heavenly rhythm. Marjie watched the colorful ribbons of light spiral in graceful cascades of intertwining spectra. The ribbons curled around her body, tugging her gently to some withered plants underneath a window.

The dry, lifeless plants seemed a befitting representation of her brokenness since Byron's death as she was never able to keep them alive. She felt the constricting heartache of loneliness begin to fade.

The light streams danced around the plants, bringing life to every part—roots, stems and leaves. A stunning green ribbon caressed the dried leaves, changing them from greenish-brown to a healthy glowing succulence. Royal blue and lavender flashed gracefully, flowing through emerging buds. A crimson red rested upon the plants, caressing the buds, then whisked away to another part of the room, taking blue and lavender with it.

Marjie beheld the most spectacular white chrysanthemums and rose peonies blossom as if watching time-lapsed photography.

She witnessed the plants spring to life as a dramatic play portraying a growing garden—the characters Withered and Ugly forced out of the spotlight by Rebirth and Beauty. An unfamiliar fragrance, far sweeter than the flowers, grew stronger as more petals unfolded, replacing the sweet smell of Byron's tobacco. The whole house was awash in the heavenly aroma. Then, she heard her name a second time.

Marjie, prepare a celebration feast. Invite the little band of followers to dine with you tonight ....

* * *

Wasting no time in obeying, Marjie called her housekeeper, Yelizaveta. Byron had always had a hard time with her Russian name, so he'd dubbed her "Veeta" for short. She didn't seem to mind.

Byron was always so very kind and generous, Marjie recalled fondly. Room and board were provided for Veeta and her husband, Vincent, along with a generous salary for the responsibility of managing the household affairs. Their *room* was a 1500-square-foot apartment in the east wing, decorated in Veeta's favorite style—mid-century modern.

As a result, Vincent was more than a wealthy man's *man*. He'd become a trusted friend and sounding board for Byron while fishing, hunting or golfing. She knew that Vincent had studied and practiced to be well-informed on all the latest gear and techniques, helping Byron be a better sportsman. In fact, Vincent's godly character had inspired Byron to be a better person all the way around.

Veeta entered the study just as Marjie was making a phone call. Marjie held up her hand to caution her, not minding that she overheard the conversation. Veeta had been with the family thirty years and was a trusted employee. More than that, she was a trusted friend.

"Hello, Gregor, this is Marjie Wegman. We met last night at the Capital Grand Hotel and well ... have I got money on my desk! ... No, I am not telling you the total ... Nope. I'm putting you in charge of getting everyone together at my house tonight for dinner."

Marjie pointed to the chair in front of the desk. Veeta didn't sit; rather, she went over to examine the luscious flowers under the window. She was dumbfounded, wondering how they got there. The office smelled different, too. She couldn't put a name to the fragrance, but knew it did not belong to pipe tobacco or the flowers. She looked at Marjie, hands in the air, palms up, inquiring silently. Again, Marjie motioned her to sit.

"Oh, and Gregor, make sure those wonderful boys with bandannas and that little thing that sang like an angel get here ... Just come prepared for a feast. Dinner starts at 6:00 and the code to the gate is 2147. If you forget, think of Acts Chapter 2:1-47. See you tonight." The call ended.

Marjie hung up the phone, put both hands on the desk, and announced, "We're having a little informal celebration tonight, Veeta."

Veeta knew Marjie's definition of *informal celebration*. And it wasn't pizza and a few candy bars. "Who's cooking?"

Marjie thought for a minute. Veeta managed breakfast and lunch, or Marjie cooked herself. But this night was special. The cook came only a few times a week now that there were only three in the house, and tonight was his night off. Besides, she had something special in mind.

Another call. This time to Beau Randolph, the premier chief on the East Coast. He would cook the perfect meal. Beau owned several five-star restaurants and had personally cooked for some of Byron's largest merger deals hosted in their home. After a little arm-twisting,

Beau finally agreed to come—not any small miracle on such short notice.

With a few flowers in hand, Veeta was already halfway down the hall headed toward her own office to prepare for the evening's festivities.

"Thank you, Veeta. You're indispensable."

Da, da, echoed down the long hall.

Marjie thought, *There might be a pattern here.* Whatever God asked her to do, He would provide the means. Not just money, but people and places. A boldness welled up inside her. Nothing was going to slow the group down from launching the ministry center. She had another call to make.

"Elliott Schaeffer, please, it's Marjie Wegman ... Elliott, no time for pleasantries. Find out who owns the properties in the block of Ohio and Grant Street in Baldwin Park. Buy them and get back to me .... Yes, the entire block and any other surrounding properties that might be willing to sell. Shouldn't cost much since they've been abandoned for decades ... No, I am not going crazy ... I understand where they're located. Just make it happen within the next couple of days. Thank you, Elliott."

Marjie hit disconnect and entered another number. "Sheila, Marjie Wegman. Can you get me the construction guy's name and number ... Ford Ashman, yes that's the one ... Oh, you have his business card?... Perfect. Give me his cell number ... Got it. Thanks."

Marjie hit disconnect and entered another number. "Ford, this is Marjie Wegman from last night's meeting at the Capital Grand. First, thank you for your generous check. Are you available for the warehouse project within two days?... You can?... Good. Scout the building and start working up a project plan, along with materials and labor. I'll email some specifics ... You've already contacted

Carlos? ... Tomorrow morning? Perfect ... Looking forward to working with you, too. Thanks Ford, we'll talk soon."

Marjie hit disconnect, turning to the flowers under the window behind the desk. Her arthritic, wrinkled hands touched the soft petals, inspecting the blossoms. Byron never grew chrysanthemums and peonies. God Himself had planted these flowers for her. She took a deep breath, inhaling the fragrance of Heaven, grinned and finally let go. Byron was gone and that was all right. She would see him soon.

The light of Heaven danced for her, lifting her spirit high, severing the tethers of brokenness. With the winds of Heaven under her wings, she soared as never before. Flying felt good for a change.

But ... she had to get the house ready for the celebration dinner tonight. She would go to Veeta's office and the two of them would make plans. She no longer felt like a woman pushing seventy-eight. She felt youthful and vivacious, eagerly anticipating the promised new life for the old house.

28

The Summons

Tony opened the office door of the Philosophy Department with a new purpose this morning. He knew the Creator of the Universe—personally—and nothing else mattered.

As soon as he stepped inside, Maggie handed him a note. "Someone was waiting at the door this morning with *this*," she said, a little nervous. She hadn't read it, but she had a pretty good idea what was coming.

Tony took the envelope, recognizing the stationery. "Hmmm … it's from Hammond, I see. A little formal for a memo to a member of staff, don't you think?" He sighed. "Well, let's open it, Maggie."

This day was inevitable. God visiting Tony's faculty meeting was bound to reach the university president's ear. Tony believed God was in control of every step of his life now, but his stomach began to tie up in knots just the same. *If God is with me, who can be against me?* he reasoned, recalling a Scripture verse he had now read countless times. He braced himself, then opened the note.

To: Professor Tony Robertson
At 10:30 a.m., your presence is required at a mandatory
meeting in the President's office with President Francis Hammond
and Dean Patrick O'Conner, Dean Liberal Arts.

"Have you been summoned?" asked Maggie with a concerned look.

"I'm afraid so. Probably my employment termination. Pray for me."

Maggie didn't want to give Tony more bad news, but if she was walking into a hornet's nest, she would want some warning. "Dr. Robertson, uh … I know you don't like surprises …."

"Not particularly, but I guess I'd better get used to them. My life is one big surprise lately. Just say what's on your mind, Maggie."

"Well, there will be a large group of students in front of the Administration Building to greet you."

Tony could tell by her tone this would be no greeting of support. He turned his head slightly, eyebrows raised, which Maggie recognized as his *tell-me-more* face.

Maggie stood, walked around her desk and took a little hop to sit on the desktop. "It's a zoo out there!" she began, her voice rising. "A bunch of students demanding that Christian stuff be removed from university property. They don't care about any other religions—just stuff about Jesus. I bet there's at least two hundred ready to burn you alive."

Tony laughed.

"It's not funny, Dr. Robertson," Maggie said as she returned to her seat behind the desk, a little dejected he didn't share her same sense of indignation. "What if they fire you?" Her voice softened. "I don't want you to leave." With that, she lowered her head, too embarrassed to say those words straight to Tony's face. "You know your whole department is willing to go to bat for you. That has to mean something ....

"Uh ...." she paused, fumbling for a file folder in her desk drawer. "I looked up some stuff on how the university got started." She handed the folder to Tony. "Might be some useful information in there. With this intolerance movement in full swing, you need facts to counter their absurd thinking. Why emotion trumps facts, I'll never understand."

"Thanks, but I'm fully aware of the university's history. I ought to. I bashed it enough ... worked hard to erase its religious affiliation. I *was* a leader of the intolerant. This isn't a battle between ideas, but a battle between darkness and Light, Maggie."

He rose, dropped the folder on her desk, and began to pace. "I can empathize with Peter and John when they stood before the Sanhedrin on charges of preaching the gospel of Jesus. God gave us a spirit not of fear but of power and love and self-control. I'm ready, let's do this, Maggie." He gave her a high five and left the office.

* * *

Walking across the neatly groomed campus without a care in the world, Tony texted Snow Peterson to rally her intercessors. Armed with an inner peace and righteous anger, he was not going down without a fight.

He spotted some pebbles in the landscaping, stooped down and grabbed five of them, putting them in his pocket as a reminder that David had prepared for his fight against Goliath with five stones. *A giant fell with one small stone to the head*, he thought. He knew personally that the battle was for the mind. If the mind is filled with lies, it cannot operate in the truth.

As Tony neared the Admin Building, he saw the students gathered in the grassy commons area just outside. They displayed the usual protest behaviors—marching in a circle while carrying signs and chanting their cause.

Now that he understood the fight between good and evil, he wasn't surprised at how quickly word had spread across campus, inciting student emotionalism. He suspected that the students were prodded by Lucifer's dark messengers.

Tony passed the protesters, unnoticed, as none had ever been enrolled in his classes. Along the way, he stopped to ask a student what the protest was about.

The young woman couldn't define the cause other than, "Some radical faculty guy is cramming religion down students' throats, harassing them with emails and stuff, and flunking them if they don't believe in Jesus ... or something like that."

She shrugged. "I'm not actually a student at Frederick. A friend called and invited me ... free pizza for lunch, she told me. Couldn't turn it down!" She laughed, then added, "Hey, ya wanna join the march? We need some older guys ... mature, ya know."

Oh, did he want to accept. *How ironic to march against oneself, hidden amongst those who hate you,* he thought. He had to get to the meeting, so he politely declined.

Tony thanked her and hurried on.

* * *

Inside President Hammond's outer office, it was apparent that he had already informed his receptionist that Tony was top priority. Her cold, impersonal manner tipped him off as to the purpose of the meeting. No surprise there. He took a seat.

While he waited, he encouraged himself, knowing that Andrea would be proud of him today, fighting to proclaim the name of Jesus at a university founded on that very mission. Reliving Heaven and his visit with Jesus, Tony recalled his Savior's overwhelming love. He pictured again the immense power of the throne room in Heaven, the glorious brightness of Truth and tenderness in the midst of that lightning and thunder. It didn't matter what Hammond said or did, it was God who ordered Tony's steps.

"Dr. Robertson, you can go in now," the receptionist said, interrupting his reverie. "President Hammond and Dean O'Connor are waiting."

He walked in and shook each man's hand, exchanging greetings before getting down to business.

"Tony, I'm sure you see the obvious nature of this meeting," Dean O'Connor began.

"No, I do not. What are we here to discuss, gentlemen?"

Tony's apparent lack of awareness confused Hammond and O'Conner for a second. They had been sure he would come like a dog with its tail between its legs, begging to keep his job and promising never to force the name of Jesus on anyone at the university again.

Tony had actually done nothing against written university policy. Frederick University's charter—which had never been altered since its founding two hundred years ago—clearly stated that the school's purpose was "to train messengers for the work of spreading the gospel of Jesus Christ." Before his awakening to the real Truth, Tony had fought to change the wording of the charter, eliminating the religious nature of its mission; the seminary had folded decades ago. Pressing Hammond and O'Conner to define their objection was the Holy Spirit's wisdom. Advantage Tony.

"C'mon, Tony. You must know why," replied President Hammond impatiently.

"No, I don't know what you're referring to."

President Hammond scooted his chair as close to the desk as

possible and leaned so far forward, his upper torso almost covered the surface of the desk. But this attempt to intimidate Tony failed. Tony didn't back away; he leaned forward, too, his face about two feet from Hammond's.

Tony's action threw Hammond off. He pulled away and, leaning back in his chair, crossed his arms. "OK, you can drop the appearance of ignorance, Tony. Are you researching religious social behaviors for a new book? If so, I wish you had let us in on it." Hammond seemed somewhat relieved at what he deemed this unexpected epiphany.

"As a matter of fact, I'm not researching."

"Oh, you're not …." He paused, tilting back in his chair again. "Well then, I've heard reports of some crazy things happening at your last departmental meeting. Care to explain?" asked Hammond, swiveling around and tapping his pen on a pad of paper.

"Define *crazy* for me, please. I'm still trying to figure out what you're referencing."

Hammond raised his voice in frustration. "I'm talking about you calling a mandatory department meeting to talk about sin and Jesus, for cryin' out loud." He got up from his seat, walked around the desk and leaned against it. "And then to top it off, staff falling to the ground in an act of contrition to God? Come on, Tony, what the hell happened?"

"Oh, that! It was great! I sincerely wish you could've been there. If only I had known, I would have invited you."

"Very funny. This is no joke. I don't think you get it, Tony. The university cannot tolerate mandatory meetings, preaching Jesus with weird, emotional manifestations of whatever the hell that was. Do I make myself clear?"

"Why not?" Tony couldn't help but flash his big smile at the humor of the situation.

Hammond walked back around the desk to his chair and sat down. He removed his glasses and pinched the bridge of his nose between his forefinger and thumb. There was no easy way out. Tony was not researching for a new book, nor was he willing to admit any wrongdoing.

"You're serious! What happened to Tony Robertson, the nation's number-one advocate against religion? Tony, of all the faculty here, I never expected this from you. If I remember correctly, it was you who ripped students to shreds in any discussion about Jesus. I never once reprimanded you. You want to know why?"

Hammond's tone changed. He talked calmly now, almost as if he were reading from a script. "Because we are a world-class national research and teaching institution. We seek to foster an environment where students can develop their unique gifts and insights through reflection, service and intellectual inquiry. Frederick's identity today is binding members of the community across diverse backgrounds— all faiths, cultures and traditions. There are more than fifty different religious services taking place across our campus—Catholic Masses, Muslim prayer, Orthodox Christian, Jewish, and Protestant."

The ugliness of hypocrisy rang loudly at Tony, worse than the sound of a dentist's drill inside his head. *How could forbidding thought be enlightening?* he thought. *Hammond's blind like I was blind. Why should I expect anything different from the enemy's manipulation?*

Hammond continued, "Don't you see? We have people from all faiths come here. We want them to feel comfortable and accepted. We must be sensitive and tolerant of other people's views. I'm sure you can agree with me on this point."

"Frederick is about helping others find spiritual enlightenment," O'Conner, Dean of Liberal Arts, chimed in. "The idea that Jesus is the only way crosses the boundary. Who are you to say that one religion is truth and another is false? Are you blind? Didn't you see the mob demonstrating out front? They don't like you forcing Jesus down their throats."

Tony silently laughed at the question, *Are you blind?* And, the fact was, he had not forced Jesus down anyone's throat; plus, none of the students demonstrating were at the faculty meeting. Tony merely smiled and said nothing, hoping this would make both inquisitors feel profoundly uncomfortable. After a minute or two of painful silence, Tony got up to stretch, going over to the window. On the way, he prayed, asking how he should respond. It was then he noticed something unusual outside.

"Gentlemen, please look out the window."

Hammond and O'Conner expected to see the demonstrators still circling like buzzards, waiting for Tony's termination. Typically, one would see students walking to class, sitting on the benches or throwing a Frisbee in the commons area on a blue-sky, fall day like today. The two hundred protesting students was not common, but certainly within the realm of student behavior.

The scene outside the window both bewildered and alarmed the interrogators. Students lay face down in a circle, protest signs on the ground beside them. In the center of the circle, stood two people.

Hammond spoke with indignation. "What's going on out there and who are those two people? They look too old to be students. Are they faculty?"

Tony's laughter caught them off guard. It boomed through the room as if he were speaking into a microphone. Both Hammond and O'Conner turned to him, angry at this outburst.

"Do you have something to do with this stunt? You're crossing the line here, Robertson, and I will not tolerate it. Stop it now or …!" yelled President Hammond as he pressed the intercom button to instruct his secretary to alert security to break it up.

"Or ... what?" Tony calmly asked. "You want to fight God? Go ahead and have at it. This isn't about me, gentlemen. Turn around and look at the cross etched in that stone wall behind you. Jesus is responsible for what you see outside the window. As He built this university two centuries ago, He is coming back to claim what is rightfully His. Make no mistake, you are either with Jesus or against Him. What side of that fight do you want to be on?"

A look of dread came over the two men's faces, but the fright quickly faded when antagonism for the name of Jesus overshadowed rational thought.

Shut it down! The idea filled their beings. Datter, who had been waiting in Hammond's office for Tony's arrival, seized his opportunity and whispered a suggestion into O'Conner's ear: *Appear open-minded. Schedule a debate. Bring your most influential thought leaders into this, and let's expose this sham for what it is. Science will show this is not a supernatural event, but rather a very skilled con artist, playing on the emotions of young, impressionable students. Act quickly so it will not spiral out of control. Urgent, urgent, urgent!*

Dean O'Connor jumped in with the urgency Datter had suggested. "I propose an intellectual debate this Friday in the spirit of this great university known for openness and enlightenment. Let's assemble a panel of top thought leaders from various departments to debate Tony on the origin of these phenomena. Tony, you put together your own team to discuss the merits of your point of view. If we reveal that this is a sham ... or ... uh, I mean not of God, then you will put an end to this nonsense now. Agreed?"

"Agreed," replied Tony. "If God proves Himself, you will get out of His way and allow Him to finish what He's started. Agreed?" He took a stone from his pocket and placed it on Hammond's desk.

Neither man would answer the question. Instead, they showed Tony the door. As he looked back, Hammond and O'Conner were already on the phone, notifying the best and brightest faculty members to argue against him

Tony was not fazed. "No way are they going to win this debate, absolutely no way in Heaven!" It felt good to stand for truth. And already, he knew that Gregor, Jean and the Holy Spirit would carry his team.

* * *

Striding briskly down the hall outside the president's office, Tony exited the building and made his way to the circle of students he had seen outside Hammond's window. When he got close enough, he recognized Gregor and Jean, holding their hands high in deep worship in the middle of the circle.

He walked over and touched Gregor's shoulder. Gregor opened his eyes and saw Tony beaming with delight.

"How did you know to come here today at this time?" Tony asked, then chuckled. "Wait, I shouldn't have asked that question. I should have known *He* sent you. Thanks for your obedience. Your presence, I mean the Holy Spirit's presence, made a huge difference. Let's head over to the bagel shop and grab some lunch—my treat. I'll fill you guys in on what's going on."

Before leaving, Gregor, Jean and Tony prayed with the students lying on the ground. One by one, they got up as if they had been raised from the dead. No longer bound by the powers and influence of darkness, they were alive with a new heart, yearning to love God and follow His commandments. Most of these new believers didn't know what those commandments were, but that didn't matter. The Holy Spirit would show them the way. All two hundred students heartily agreed to attend the debate!

"Hmmm … Elijah's challenge to the prophets of Baal … only, Hammond and O'Conner threw down the gauntlet, not me …," mused Tony on the walk to the bagel shop.

"Yeah … the Fire of Heaven," Jean contemplated.

* * *

Datter watched from a safe distance in the bell tower while the Nazarene's angels ministered to the newly gathered souls, protecting them from Blindness, Deafness, Doubt, Lies and Unbelief. Unable to get near their victims, the spirits that would steal the seed of truth joined Datter. Gorfius drifted over from his perch in a nearby tree.

Datter tapped his fingertips together, speaking with excitement. "We are going to have a showdown here, my dear old friend— a showdown, for sure. And at my suggestion." He let out an evil cackle. "The followers of the Nazarene against the powers of science, intellectualism and religious tolerance, empowered by Lucifer himself."

Gorfius answered Datter's tidbit of information with consternation: "We are too insignificant. I am most certain this battle will be directed by the great princes themselves. You will have made a grave mistake if Lucifer loses this battle, Datter. If we lose, I fear there will be no stopping the momentum of the Awakening. I, for one, am not getting caught in the crosshairs."

Datter's attitude changed from puffed pride to cowering fear. No doubt pushing O'Conner toward confrontation could prove catastrophic. "My sentiments exactly, Gorfius, my sentiments exactly," he backtracked. "Let us not mention it was my idea. Let upper management take the fall for this one. The farther away from this, the better. Yes, we must stay far away, my friend."

29

Dinner at Grandhaven

Gregor wandered around the house, searching for something to relieve his fidgetiness. Peeking into the bathroom, he paused. *Hmmm ... that shower corner might need some caulk,* he thought. He stepped in, then knelt to examine the spot.

Just then, Jean, passing by the bathroom, saw him on his knees. "You know, Gregor, there are more comfortable places to pray."

"Ha, ha, funny." He turned around. "I think this might need re-caulking."

"You're looking for a project while Rome burns?"

"Huh ... you're right." He sighed. "Something's stirring in me."

Jean detected a familiar restlessness in his voice.

"Remember when we'd get those feelings like we were supposed to do something, but didn't know *what?*"

"Hmmm ... I've been getting that same vibe." Jean stepped into the room and perched on the edge of the tub.

"No job, no income ... so, what's next?" Gregor sat next to her and simply pleaded, "Jesus, what are we supposed to do?"

They expected days or even weeks to go by before getting an inkling of an answer. On the way out the door, Gregor took Jean's hand and said, "Hey, wait a minute."

Jean turned around. "Yeah, I heard that."

They stopped to listen to the Holy Spirit's voice speaking plainly:

Place an ad in the local newspaper to sell your house and belongings: For Sale by Owner. Put no sign in front and tell no one. A buyer will pay full market value. Divide the profit among your children as their inheritance. Take nothing except your clothes and personal items. Do not let pride steal this gift. Learn to receive.

A couple minutes passed in silence, then Jean commented, "Well, that was weird. What kind of gift is being penniless and homeless?"

"Huh ... yeah," Gregor replied, wondering what the Lord was up to this time.

As unsettling as the prospect was, they rested in the fact that there is safety in obedience. Besides, they were no strangers to the Lord's mysterious requests and had been through similar situations before. Nothing this drastic, however.

Nevertheless, without wasting another minute, Gregor called the newspaper and placed the For Sale by Owner ad.

* * *

Around 5:15 p.m., Tony pulled into the Wallaces' drive and tapped a soft *beep beep* on his horn. Gregor and Jean hurried out of their house, got in the SUV and the threesome headed to Grandhaven, the Wegman Estate. As they approached the security gate, Tony rolled down the window and entered the code for that day—2147. The massive gate swung open, and Tony drove along a winding cobblestone driveway leading to an imposing, stone French Tudor estate.

He stopped a few hundred yards from the house and exited the vehicle to get a better look. Gregor and Jean did the same, taking in the splendor. *Wow!* they spoke in unison under their breath.

Three stories of sandstone with hundreds of windows, lined by gray-blue shutters. A slate roof the same color as the shutters topped the house. There was a large central section with wings on either side. A symmetrical garden adorned the front entrance with a fountain in the inner part of the circular driveway.

Approaching the entrance, they stepped up huge slabs of granite leading to the ten-foot-tall double doors of hand-crafted solid walnut. Searching for a doorbell, they could find nothing. No door knockers, no bells—nothing to announce their arrival.

"How do you let someone inside know we are outside, wanting in?" Tony laughed.

"Yeah ... I wonder if there's a butler in uniform," Jean whispered.

Just then, the doors opened and Marjie's voice came over some speakers. "Come on in and go to the drawing room to your left. Can't come to the door ... in the kitchen right now. Gadgets were Byron's hobby. Electronic doors will automatically close. Eliminates the need for full-time butler."

They passed through the stately doorway and stood in the foyer. Just as Marjie had promised, the doors closed silently behind them.

"Wow, this is somethin' else!" Tony whispered as he turned to take it all in.

Fresh, white chrysanthemums and rose peonies adorned a central round table with a sparkling chandelier above. Two stairways flanked the table, curving gracefully to meet on the second floor. A few fluffily padded loveseats and chairs gave the entry a little less formal feel. Obviously expensive but not pretentious—honest, direct, like Marjie herself.

"I'll bet one of those paintings is worth more than ours and Tony's houses put together," Jean surmised, noting the gorgeous art pieces adorning the soaring walls in the foyer.

They made their way through a large archway into the drawing room. The architecture was classic with vaulted ceilings and tall windows. A warming fire flickering in the fireplace, along with updated furnishings, dressed the space, creating a cozy and welcoming air.

After a few minutes, Marjie, wrapped in a white apron that showed some wear and tear, greeted them. "This get-together is a little last-minute and the chef needs extra hands, so I'll be in the kitchen for a few more minutes. In the meantime, give yourselves a tour." Marjie whisked herself away as fast as she had appeared.

Gregor got a weird feeling at the sudden revelation that he was well acquainted with this estate. All was familiar—the drawing room, the paintings, the grand entry, the tree-lined driveway. Even Marjie, whom he had only met once before, seemed like a longtime friend.

"Gregor, you're pale ... you all right?" Jean asked, concerned for him.

"No ... I mean, yeah ... I feel fine, but ... something tells me I know this house."

Surely he would have told me about visiting such a spectacular home, she thought.

"Follow me for a guided tour." Color returned to Gregor's face, along with a spring in his step.

Jean and Tony looked at each other with wide eyes. They both shrugged and followed Gregor up the elegant staircase. From room to room, Gregor announced interesting tidbits, much like a docent in a museum. Jean and Tony listened through a total of three rooms before stopping Gregor to demand an explanation. "OK, what gives?" asked Jean, suspicious of Gregor's knowledge of this splendid house.

"I've been here before. Well, not physically, but in a dream ... twenty-five years ago." He turned away from admiring an antique dresser to direct his comment to Jean. "You remember ... I told you the house had something to do with the Lord's commissioning us. I forgot there was an older lady in the dream. This is *that* house! I think we're going to live here."

"So, you're just going to walk up to Marjie and say, *Hi, there! Meet your new roommates?*" Tony commented.

"No need. She already knows ...." Gregor's voice trailed off to a whisper. "The impossible has become the ordinary ...."

Jean could have been knocked over with a gentle puff of air. It was too much to comprehend.

Keeping this tidbit under wraps, the threesome returned to the drawing room, greeting new arrivals as Marjie was still fussing in the kitchen. First, Dan and Barb; then, shortly afterward, Jason, Carlos, Diego and Maria, with Sheila trailing a couple minutes behind.

Dan leaned into Barb and asked, "Why the emergency meeting? What's Marjie up to?"

Barb shrugged her shoulders. She didn't know what the urgent meeting was about, but when Marjie caught the bug for something, it was full steam ahead. Nothing could dampen her enthusiasm.

Dan and Barb had been in the house before and had felt its overwhelming grandeur, just as the first-time visitors were experiencing now. But something was different. A reverent atmosphere surrounded the guests as it had when they were in Heaven—love, forgiveness, peace and an expectation of the extraordinary.

Veeta then appeared, directing the group to the dining room, where she served some beverages. "Sorry for Mrs. Wegman's delay. She should be here shortly. Now excuse me, please, while I return to the kitchen."

The dinner party was much smaller than the eighteen-foot table could seat. The breakfast room would have easily accommodated the dozen diners, but this was a special occasion, and Marjie wanted them to be surrounded by the stateliness of the dining room.

White plates with royal blue and genuine gold bands lined the table like soldiers on parade—perfectly spaced from each other, with one at the head. The space between place-settings was graced with striking arrangements of the same flowers in the foyer—white chrysanthemums and rose peonies. Three silver candelabras with lit candles shone their light on the glimmering settings of silverware. Three crystal chandeliers above the table sparkled like diamonds. The entire scene was reminiscent of a set from the zenith of Hollywood movies.

It was a grand setting, befitting royalty, yet no one had dressed for such a formal occasion, making everyone feel uncomfortable. Marjie finally emerged from the kitchen, minus the apron. The fact that she, too, was dressed casually somewhat eased their discomfort. However, as they sat there, awaiting her instructions, Carlos, Diego and Maria still looked a little anxious, as if something prickly was underneath their clothes.

Finally, Diego broke the silence. "Miz Wegman, 'scuse me, but I don' know what all these forks and knives are for ... an' there are ... like five glasses and five plates here. I don' use but one fork, one glass and one plate. An' sometimes"—he ducked his head in embarrassment— "I jus' use a paper towel for a plate."

Everyone chuckled, because they occasionally did the same thing. Diego may have seemed a little shy about the table setting, but his honesty was endearing.

"Diego, I insist you call me Marjie. I feel younger tonight and don't want to be reminded that I'm an old lady." Marjie's earthy warmth contrasted with the elegant formality of the surroundings. She had a knack for making people feel at home, banishing the awkwardness. "Don't worry about all the silverware. Use what you want, when you want. The only rule at this table is to have fun and enjoy the meal. I promise you no one will grade your etiquette."

Diego smiled, but didn't understand. He leaned into Carlos, whispering, "What, 'zactly, is etty-cut?"

Marjie answered before Carlos could get a word out. "It means how we conduct ourselves at the table tonight—our manners. I expect you to be yourself and bring your love of Christ to this meal. As Jesus told the Pharisees, it's not what's on the outside that's important; it's what's in the inside that really counts."

The house was majestic, suited for crowned heads, but there was nothing ceremonial about Marjie. Diego appreciated her directness and began to warm up to her. He read Marjie as a *what-you-see-is-what-you-get* kind of person. He liked that … very much.

"It's true, that we all come from different backgrounds, income levels, education and the amount of time we have lived with Jesus. We're not to judge with those scales. What's measured by God in His Kingdom is whether we have learned to love. Love Him, love other believers, and yes, love your enemies. All here are graced with His immeasurable love." Her statement was from the heart.

"In the same light, please don't measure me by my wealth. I'm just a simple follower of Jesus. All this stuff"—she gestured around the room with a sweep of her hand—"doesn't define who I am, just as your surroundings should not define who you are."

She reached over, taking Diego's hand in hers. "My dear child, you are precious in my sight, and I am so honored you came to sit at my table. Relax and let the celebration begin."

Marjie thanked the Lord for provision and for those who had come to share it, then on cue, Veeta and Vincent entered the room with trays of food—the meal of a lifetime—and then sat joining the group.

With every taste sensation, there was the sound of enjoyment from the grateful partakers, which thoroughly delighted Marjie. People she was falling in love with shared her home, which tonight, was filled with laughter, lively conversation and friendship. To Marjie, the people were the feast, not the food. Fellowship with this unlikely group was a gift given by her Heavenly Father.

When all the guests had finished the last morsel, Marjie stood, picked up a knife and clinked it against a crystal goblet. "Everyone, I have some announcements to make. First, I deposited one hundred million, three hundred one dollars and fifty-two cents into the ministry center account."

Jaws dropped. Eyes opened wide in disbelief. Others gasped, unable to comprehend that amount of money in one place.

Dan choked on his drink, thinking he surely had misheard her, then managed to say, "Marjie, would you run that by me again?"

"One hundred million, three hundred one dollars and fifty-two cents." Marjie continued speaking, unfazed by the group's reaction. "Second, I am in the process of purchasing the land where Carlos and Diego believe the ministry center should be established."

Yep, Marjie is in the zone, Barb thought as a big grin grew across her face. It took effort not to laugh as she silently rejoiced at God's moving hand.

"Third, Ford Ashman, the general contractor from Sunday's meeting, agreed to work up a project plan. Gregor and Jean, coordinate with Ford to determine what's needed on the design side of things. Carlos, Ford will meet you tomorrow to survey the property. Take Diego and Maria with you. I know your hearts want to stay in that area, ministering to your neighborhood ... so some residential housing needs to be incorporated into the plans. You three take charge of that end of things."

Marjie was moving so quickly, there was little time left in between announcements to absorb it all. In the middle of considering one statement, she had already moved on to something new.

Marjie turned to Jean and Gregor. "Now before you say no, hear me out. With great certainty, Jesus told me that you are to move to Grandhaven. I have more rooms than I will ever use in five lifetimes. Please receive this gift, not just for your sakes, but for mine. Well, there it is. A little bossy maybe, but that's the way I see it." She sat down. Tears filled her eyes as she thought, *Byron would have loved to be here.* In a way he was; he had prepared the way through his wealth.

Marjie's generosity and efficiency dumbfounded everyone as they glimpsed into the heart of this amazing woman. She gave it her all. Bossy, yes. Marjie even admitted it herself, although she would describe it as "efficiency." Through her unwavering love, faith and talents, the massive project would be completed.

Tony got to his feet. "There is one point of business that needs prayer." For the next few minutes, he explained the scene of aimless protesters, Hammond and O'Conner's disdain for Jesus and the big debate, hurriedly scheduled with the university talking heads. "The veil covering darkness may be pulled back soon."

At the conclusion of his summary, all agreed to end the evening in prayer. What loomed ahead required the wisdom and intervention of the Father Himself!

30

Preparing For Showdown

The day of the debate had come—Frederick University versus Dr. Tony Robertson. More accurately, the kingdom of darkness against the Kingdom of Light.

All of the team members arrived at Marjie's by mid-morning, shutting themselves in the library with one purpose—to pray for evil to be uprooted and for stony hearts to be softened. They knew there was no reason to be anxious about tonight's debate because the outcome was the Lord's. Even so, the uneasiness of the unknown was difficult to tame.

Holding hands, they formed a tight circle. Songs of worship jump-started their spiritual circulation. Each humbled himself, inviting the Holy Spirit to search the inward man. Any sin He brought to mind was confessed. The process was an intense stretching exercise, much like an athlete's warm-up prior to a peak performance.

A great sense of holiness pressed on them as they knelt, bowing their heads. Several minutes passed silently as they waited with no expectation of any physical expression of the Lord's presence.

Sometimes, He chose to reveal Himself; other times, He did not. The only desire of every heart was to know and do His will.

Lift your heads. Open your eyes.

Jesus stood in the middle of the circle, smiling, pleased with their humble hearts. He thanked His Father for giving these faithful disciples to Him. He ached for the day when His children would live without the evil one's influence as He had designed life in the beginning.

Have eyes to see and ears to hear, dear ones. As I AM one with the Father, you are one with Me. Drink deeply of My love for you; it is the conduit of My power. Those who come against you are not the enemy. They are merely Lucifer's pawns, carrying out his evil plans. Look at the opposition with My compassion. Direct your righteous anger toward the powers of darkness, which enslaves people in deception.

The sound of His voice was reassuring. Confidence replaced uncertainty. Their Coach had a strategy to defeat the opposing team.

Lucifer and his princes are seeking to destroy you, but I will protect you. Darkness believes it can stop the Awakening by turning the hearts of the students and faculty against your message. Tonight, what you see and hear in the physical will mirror what is happening in the unseen realm. Do not let the storm distract you. Those prophets of Baal—who are ignorantly influenced by darkness—will speak against who I AM. Do not worry about what to say or do, for I AM with you.

Jesus then turned to each of the debate team and gave specific instructions. Tony would explain what happened with his department faculty members a few days ago. Jean would talk about the people saved at the warehouse. Gregor was commanded to merely listen and obey. Instructions complete. Jesus disappeared before their eyes.

* * *

As word about the debate spread, the university had taken on life as a living organism, vibrating with expectation. Something mysterious was happening.

So much interest had been generated that the administration was forced to move the venue to a larger facility. The auditorium they had originally planned to use would seat only a few hundred, while the Hammond Center—a basketball arena—was able to seat over five thousand.

The team arrived and walked together toward the Center.

Barb leaned into Dan. "Things are really charged around here. Do you sense the tension?"

"Yeah, but it's not my own anxiety anymore. Feels more like a force pressing against me."

"Hmmm ... yeah, kind of like being jabbed on the outside while remaining peaceful on the inside."

He nodded in agreement. "Feels a lot like it did at the prayer breakfast, when evil rushed in, hoping to take the upper hand."

Jason, who had been walking slightly behind them, interrupted their conversation with a cheerful exclamation. "Don't you love days like this? Clear blue sky... warm sunshine ... colorful leaves ... just soakin' in God's beautiful creation!"

Dan whispered to Barb, "What's up with Jason?"

She shrugged.

As the group drew closer to the Hammond Center, they noticed the WNN News trucks parked near the entrance. Jason's heart began to race as thoughts of Carrie flooded his mind. It had been just a few days since he'd told her he was falling in love. As he walked, he relived their first kiss and again felt the earth shift beneath his feet.

"Do you think Carrie's over there?" Barb asked her son.

"Hope so ... uh ... might be," Jason said in a failed attempt to appear disinterested.

Dan's gaze met Barb's, and she knew he was silently asking: *Hey, what's going on? Does Jason have a thing for Carrie?* Barb merely shrugged again.

* * *

Life had been so hectic the last few days for both Jason and Carrie, they hadn't had a chance to say two words to each other. Anxious to see her again, Jason picked up his pace, breaking ahead of the group.

Do not allow distractions, the Holy Spirit spoke unmistakably, reminding Jason that he was on a mission for the Lord. *There will be time for Carrie later.*

Jason spun around, headed in the opposite direction of the WNN trucks. "I'm gonna' go this way. See ya later." Following the Holy Spirit's lead, he took a longer path to avoid any chance of an encounter with his sweetheart.

Dan gave Barb another puzzled look. She shrugged it off for the third time leaving Dan a bit confused. His wife usually had *something* to say in matters regarding their son. He knew something was up, but what?

As Jason entered the vast arena, he contemplated the empty seats and wondered about the lives that would fill them. His eyes were drawn to one particular area, and he knew that he was being led to sit there. Sliding into the seat, he began to pray.

Gregor, Jean and Tony took their places on stage. Carlos, Diego, Maria, Veeta, Vincent and Marjie found seats halfway back, center section. Dan, Barb and Sheila sat behind Marjie's group. All the protesting students who had encountered the Holy Spirit the day before split into groups of a hundred, taking seats on both sides. The Philosophy Department came in full support of Tony, sitting front and center.

Anticipation was high as the arena filled with lost souls—a convergence of darkness and Light—with the Hammond Center as the point of contact. An invasion from both kingdoms would soon take place. They all knew that the Lord would win the war, but had Jesus planned for *this* battle to be victorious?

31

Day Of Reckoning

Unexpectedly, the skies darkened. Distant thunder sounded, quickly growing louder as a strong storm front rolled over the campus. Cracking, jagged bursts of brightness lit the sky as the wind tossed dust, leaves and small branches, swirling them in the air. The tempest quickly transformed into straight-line winds, bending trees near the ground. The last of the debate attendees rushed for shelter, creating a human logjam at the Hammond Center doors.

Inside, the brilliant flashes radiated through the upper windows of the center, giving a strobe effect. The full force of the turbulent storm covered the campus with heavy clouds, lightning, thunder and rain. An imminent second storm brewed, not outside, but inside the Hammond Center.

The speed at which the storm approached and intensified created an atmosphere of uneasiness among the spectators and the university's select debate panel. Even inside the safety of the stone coliseum, the sound of pounding rain on the roof, the nearness of lightning and the bone-rattling rumble of thunder made for a nervous crowd. Attendees murmured about the eerie sensation.

As Jason watched the thunderstorm rage, he remembered what Jesus had said: *Tonight, what you see and hear in the physical mirrors what is happening in the unseen realm.* No doubt, the battle between darkness and Light had begun.

* * *

With no prompting from Jason, Carrie felt she should be at the debate with a camera crew. It took some convincing and shrewd negotiating on her part. Her superiors didn't deem a small discussion of religious philosophies newsworthy until she mentioned that Senator Taylor and his son would be there. Her boss's expression of annoyed disinterest suddenly changed to one of rapt attention. Carrie mentioned, too, that this could be an exclusive for WNN since no other news had likely gotten wind of the scheduled debate, certainly not that the Taylors would be attending.

Carrie didn't know what might happen, but Jason's presence raised the probability of a charged showdown between philosophical sides. This time, she wasn't so much interested in an exclusive for WNN as she was in recording a possible miraculous event. *Things just happen when the Taylors are around*, she thought.

WNN News cameras were in place. Carrie watched from just off the platform. Her eyes darted back and forth, searching the coliseum for Jason. She would rather be with him than behind the camera right now. She spotted Senator Taylor and Barb but didn't greet them; she still wasn't quite sure how they felt about her. The strange moment with Barb at the Capital Grand Hotel had given Carrie cause to keep her distance.

* * *

Entering the arena from a side door, President Hammond scanned the crowd, noticing a prominent university donor sitting a number of rows back. He squeezed through the packed audience to greet her. "Well, hello Ms. Wegman. So glad to see you here supporting the university, as you faithfully do." His patronizing tone annoyed Marjie no end. "We do so appreciate your continued support through your generous gifts, endowments and scholarships."

"Yes, President Hammond ... I don't think you understand how *very* glad I am to be here," Marjie shot back, knowing she and Hammond were polar opposites. She had come for Jesus, not the university.

What Hammond didn't know was that, before he became president, her husband Byron had anonymously funded the building of a large library—the campus's main library now—which was sustained by a trust fund. Payments were received yearly under one condition—the university would not censor Christian materials and the library would be open to the public. The latter was actually Vincent's idea—one that Byron liked very much.

Byron could have easily insisted that the library be named the Byron C. Wegman Library, but he cared nothing for notoriety. *Don't let the right hand know what the left hand is doing, or is it the left from the right?* he would ask with a chuckle. He could never remember exactly how Jesus said it, but he shared the sentiment.

Hammond noticed Carlos and Diego sitting on either side of Marjie. Although Carlos's and Diego's inner man had been completely transformed, the two brothers still bore the look of hardened gang members with their tattoos and red bandannas. Hammond was alarmed that such an important supply of university funds as Mrs. Byron C. Wegman was forced to sit next to such riff-raff. Hammond was so focused on Mrs. Wegman, the donor, that he completely overlooked Dan Taylor, the senator, sitting right behind her.

"Ms. Wegman, there's a better seat up here nearer the front," Hammond said as he reached to help her up.

"Thank you, President Hammond. There are nine seats?"

"Oh, you have other guests coming?"

"No, we're all here. Come on, guys, let's move up closer to the front," Marjie directed.

All nine stood—Carlos, Diego, Maria, Marjie, Veeta, Vincent, Dan, Barb, and Sheila. Finally noticing Senator Taylor, Hammond was rattled. He knew of the resurrection claim and the senator's religious outbursts from news reports. All the blood drained from President Hammond's head, making him look rather bleached.

He finally found his voice. "Oh ... you're all ... together ... ah ...," Hammond said as he slowly ran his finger through the air, drawing a circle around the group. "I ... uh ... don't know if there are that many seats up front ... I can see if ...."

At his hesitation, Marjie interrupted, "We're just fine where we are, but thank you anyway."

She thoroughly enjoyed putting Hammond on the spot. The first time she'd met him, she had seen right through his snaky hide. The only thing he liked about her was her money. *He deserves what's coming tonight*, she thought, then wondered if she needed to repent.

Flustered, President Hammond walked up the steps and made his way to the microphone at the center stage. He looked across the packed arena and then at the WNN cameras. As he began to address the crowd, an unnerving feeling came over him. His confidence deteriorated with each word. When Carrie had contacted him about televising the debate, he was thrilled with the idea of media coverage ... but not now. Thoughts raced through his mind in rapid succession. *Something doesn't feel right. Did I make a mistake? Why did I let O'Conner push me into this mess?*

"Fellow colleagues, faculty, students and guests. As president of this great university, I welcome you. As you know, Frederick prides itself on its high academic achievement, world-class research and its openness to spiritual enlightenment. So tonight, we all have the honor of joining this esteemed panel in considering the facts of … the facts around … uh…" Hammond stammered, losing his train of thought.

"Openness to spiritual enlightenment?" Not so much, Hammond, thought Carrie. *Nice job tilting the debate in a backhanded way. I hope he chokes on his own words.*

Hammond coughed and asked for a glass of water. Carrie covered her mouth to stifle a giggle.

Noticing Tony's entire department sitting in the front row center, Hammond convinced himself that the man had conned his colleagues to follow him into religious insanity. The WNN cameras pointed at Hammond's face suddenly felt like an invasion. *The world could be watching … and for what? It was just one crazy meeting and a few students lying face down in the grass,* he thought. *Students do bizarre things all the time. Why was this time any different?*

He felt panicked and acutely aware that possibly millions might watch a broadcast of the event. *How did this become such a big issue so quickly?*

Regaining a modicum of composure, he launched into his introductory remarks. "We are here to debate a logical conclusion based on factual information to explain some unusual phenomena that recently happened on our campus. I promise you that, by the time you leave tonight, you will have come to the same supposition as our brilliant university guest panel. I really don't want to persuade you, but facts are facts."

Hammond finally introduced the university dream team debate panel. "Sitting on my left is our top academic scholars. Representing the Psychology Department is Dr. Doris Jenkins, PhD., Psychology and PhD., Social Sciences; from the School of Medicine is Dr. Ajay Patel, M.D. and PhD., Neuroscience. Finally, from the School of Religious Studies is Dr. Ellen Morton, PhD., Theology and PhD., Anthropology.

A polite round of applause went up from the crowd as each panel member smiled and nodded in acknowledgment. President Hammond turned to his right toward the undersized table provided for Tony's team.

"On my right, we have with us Professor Tony Robertson from our Philosophy Department." Hammond's terse introduction excluded any mention of Tony's accomplishments and ignored Gregor and Jean altogether.

Saboteur! Not even introducing Gregor and Jean. There's a weird smugness about this guy. What's he up to? wondered Carrie.

Tony's department, the two hundred protesters and about a thousand people in the middle block of the seating stood to their feet, giving a boisterous ovation in support of Tony, Gregor and Jean. An obvious uneasiness parked itself on the faces of the now perplexed university talking heads. This also momentarily shocked President Hammond and once again he lost track of his thoughts.

He suddenly noticed that the thousand cheering spectators in the midsection looked strangely out of place on the campus—definitely not students from this prestigious institution. Covered in tattoos and piercings, they looked like hardened criminals and drug addicts. Some of the women wearing heavy makeup and unnatural hair colors of green, blue and purple were scantily dressed. More like street-walkers. Extremely worried about the impression this display would have on the viewing public, Hammond had a desperate urge to flee, but restrained himself. After all, O'Conner had assured him earlier that the university panel would clearly take down Robertson and his religious zealots. Somewhat bolstered by this thought, Hammond called Tony to the podium.

As he approached, Hammond covered the microphone with his hand. "What the hell are you doing busing in fake supporters. Thugs and drug addicts don't belong here. I thought better of you than this, Robertson, but I can see my confidence in you as an educator at this university was falsely grounded. Mark my words, *you* are going down."

No one else on the team knew that Carlos and Diego had organized transportation for the thousand lost souls who had been saved at the warehouse. Tony searched for the two brothers in the crowd, made eye contact and tapped his chest with his fist to say, *Thank you.*

Tony bowed his head and took a deep breath. He started with his own story. "Not long ago, feeling depressed and hopeless after my wife's death, I planned to take my own life. But this gentleman"—he turned and nodded toward Gregor—"was sent by God to make sure I didn't carry it out. How else could he have known …?" Choking up, Tony came to a halt before continuing. "I tell you, Jesus is real! I saw Him with my own eyes. Not only did He save me, but when I shared my experience with my department at our faculty meeting, all I can say is that the Kingdom of Heaven invaded that room! No pressure from me, no coercion. All I did was tell them what Jesus had done for me."

As Tony took his seat, Gregor clapped him on the shoulder, then rose to address the crowd. "You've already heard the account of Jason Taylor's resurrection from death as certified by the doctors at St. Vincent Hospital. It has been widely covered in the media … although I think the reporters missed the point." Gregor smiled, thinking of the "insanity slant" they had given the story. "Let me warn you," he said, striking a more serious tone, "there is no sitting on the fence here. Either you are with Jesus and the Kingdom of God, or you are with Lucifer and his kingdom of darkness. No in-between. The choice is yours. But time is short. Choose well."

Grimaces and murmuring amongst the university panel clearly communicated their disdain for Gregor's statements. The crowd didn't miss the rolling of the panelists' eyes and their smirks of contempt on the large screens when a camera focused on them at Carrie's request.

The obvious opinions of the university panel confirmed the crowd's thoughts, giving them boldness to make their feelings known. Some stood, waving their arms while booing and hissing at the account of Jason's miraculous healing. "Hoax, hoax, resurrection joke!" some chanted. All those who confessed Christ remained seated and silent.

Jean took her turn at the microphone, but the crowd was too unruly for her to be heard. Storis signaled the order for his warriors to quiet the rowdy crowd. Within seconds, no sound was heard except Jean's voice.

She told the story of Carlos's and Diego's conversion and how Jesus had restored Diego's missing legs.

Again, the audience erupted in jeers. Storis allowed the outcry for a moment longer to reveal the hearts of those opposed to the wondrous works of his Lord and King. Then he signaled for order and the crowd quieted.

"We are excited about another phase of ministry—the building of an equipping center—to train new believers to go out and tell others about Jesus," Jean continued. "Soon after Diego was healed, a thousand people in the neighborhood fell to their knees under the conviction of the Holy Spirit, surrendering their lives to Jesus. Each person was either healed of some sickness or set free from addictions.

But an even greater healing took place in that abandoned warehouse—the healing of a thousand broken hearts."

At that statement, the thousand people who had met Jesus that day silently stood as a reverent statement of gratitude to the Living Word.

Seeing those unsightly people rise to their feet hit the hecklers hard. The presence of the Lord upon the newly saved believers silenced the militant Jesus-haters.

This irritated President Hammond, and his hatred toward religious fanatics erupted. He stood at the podium, motioning to the huge group to sit down. They did so without contest.

Hammond looked to his panel of academic scholars, hoping they would crush Tony's team. "Yes, well, we have just heard that the questioned occurrences are not limited to this campus and are quite interesting, to say the least. Now, let's hear from the leading academic minds of today about the real origin of these unusual phenomena. Dr. Jenkins, please enlighten us."

Dr. Doris Jenkins led off. "Thank you, President Hammond, for allowing me to be part of this debate. I have to be honest with you when I say I am extremely troubled. No person has the right to influence these young developing minds with ideas of supernatural events. Simply put, they do not exist.

"From what I have observed so far, I would have to say that Professor Robertson and his guests suffer from what is known as mass psychogenic illness, much like the Tanzanian laughing epidemic in 1962, which affected around one thousand people. Psychogenic illness is not as uncommon as one may think and often presents in times of sudden traumatic stress. Psychogenic illness can manifest in various ways such as laughing, flu-like illnesses, self-mutilation or even supernatural apparitions, to name a few. It is obvious that my colleague, Professor Robertson, and the others involved in such unusual behaviors suffer from such an outbreak."

Jenkins was one hundred percent convinced she had correctly diagnosed the Philosophy Department's condition. "Belief in the paranormal begins when our mind forms some kind of defensive shield. This can be directly attributed to a person's inability to deal with challenging truths that arise in this very complicated and changing world. The awareness is formed when something unexpected happens—an untimely death, tragic event, or perhaps even when one is fired from a job. The brain scrambles for answers, looking for order in the raging disorder. The mind finds itself in an indifferent state; if it cannot achieve control objectively, it will create objectivity by observing more unseen structures while, in reality, they do not exist.

"What is really needed is intense counseling to open the brain's pathways. We have achieved amazing breakthroughs from our new clinical trials being conducted at our psychiatric center."

Hammond, O'Conner, the university panel and most of the audience nodded in agreement.

"May I add that one must consider group psychology or, as it is commonly termed, 'mob mentality.' In a tightly knit group such as the faculty in Professor Robertson's meeting, people can often lose their individuality, viewing the group as one unit. In their desire to maintain harmony within the group, they may capitulate to ideas or actions, even if they seem extreme and are not necessarily their own private desires. In other words, sometimes people do things in a group that they normally would not do alone. I strongly recommend that faculty and students overtaken by such actions attend the free-of-charge meetings organized with our top psychologists after learning that some of our own dear university colleagues exhibited these disturbing behaviors."

Dr. Ajay Patel approached the podium to speak next. "I concur with Dr. Jenkins. MRI results back up her findings. Certain parts of the brain experience extraordinary neuro-electric responses when faced with unexpected difficulties that overwhelm a person's emotional state. We have studied these events in real time."

There was more nodding from university supporters.

"Also, as a neurosurgeon, I have stimulated certain parts of a patient's brain while performing surgery. The patient will claim to have seen departed family members speaking to them right there in the operating room. Remember, my patients are not in a sleep-like state, as they would be under general anesthesia during … say … an appendectomy. My patients are fully awake and aware of what is going on around them. I can testify that no deceased person has ever stood in any operating room speaking to any of my patients."

The audience roared.

Dr. Patel continued, "One more thing I would like to share. Chemical imbalances in the body have proven to produce bizarre and unnatural behaviors. A clinical study from the University of Studengrad was presented at the last World Health Congress Summit, which I attended. Dr. Hans Wolfson showed that a group of people living near a former pharmaceutical company began to see ghosts walking the streets in broad daylight. After running a battery of tests, it was discovered that each person's body registered a dangerous level of the drug noroprozine in their blood. The pharmaceutical company near the village manufactured noroprozine and the drug had made its way into the ground water and eventually leached into the village water supply."

Murmurs of agreement with Dr. Patel's theory circulated through the crowd.

"My point is that there are many ways to explain these experiences, which are definitely not supernatural in nature. Trust me, I am a medical doctor and have observed behavior like this before. There is a scientific explanation for these events. If the symptoms persist, a full physical examination could reveal the cause. The patient could then be treated and restored to normalcy."

Up next was Dr. Ellen Morton from the School of Religious Studies, whom Hammond felt sure would pound the final nail into Tony's coffin.

32

Delivered

Two speakers down, one to go, Hammond thought. He scanned the crowd, noting with satisfaction the number of nodding heads, expressing agreement with the opinions of Dr. Jenkins and Dr. Patel. *We've already won.*

Dr. Morton stood at the podium. "First, I want to say that I concur with my two colleagues, but I would like to add a theological perspective.

"I've spent over thirty years studying every major religion. With great deliberation, I've read each religion's holy books and teachings, taking part in their traditions and rituals. In order to understand the underlying immutability of humanity's battle with its own nature, one must explore beyond the limitations each religion imposes."

Hammond's heart leapt as Dr. Morton spoke.

"No one religion has a corner on the truth. Combining all religions allows for the full discernment of all revelation given to man. In order to achieve true enlightenment, we must broaden our minds, souls and spirits to become one with the universe. Only when all religions are brought together can we attain a higher level of human consciousness."

Wow! I believed the same poison when I was in college, but I never noticed how absurd it was until now, Carrie thought. She scanned the audience once again, but instead of looking for Jason, she studied the faces of the students. *What if death came today? Where would they go?*

Dr. Morton beamed with pride at her opening statement. If her smug look was a weapon, she meant it to be a sword, piercing Tony, Gregor and Jean right through the heart.

How much of this nonsense are they going to spew? Jean thought as she shifted in her seat.

Gregor noticed, patted her hand and whispered, "Hang on, just wait."

Dr. Morton continued, "You may have heard reports of Jason Taylor's so-called resurrection. For those in the audience unfamiliar with the definition of 'resurrection,' it is the raising of a dead body to make it live again."

Her remark was directed at the thousand ruffians in the center section of the arena. Her words were so painfully condescending that even her supporters seemed annoyed. However, fans quickly brushed it off, knowing the brainless "Jesus people" might need a definition, even though the crux of their faith depended on His resurrection.

"I have investigated many near-death experiences. Some tell of a tunnel of light or a peacefulness; some have even reported seeing religious figures. However, I can most assuredly tell you dying is nothing more than one's spirit merging into the universe, back to its origin. As a modern, educated, scientific people—not dependent upon fables to explain life—we need to recognize this one truth and not deny it: There is no heaven and there is no hell. We exist in universal consciousness, the merging of all minds into one stream of thought."

Righteous anger surged within one spectator, mounting to an energy that could no longer be contained. His eyes glowed brightly with a fiery light. That same fire surrounded his body. When he lifted his head, the roof of the building faded, revealing the spiritual battle between Lucifer and the Host of Heaven being fought above the people below. The glowing figure raised his hands to Heaven and cried out in a loud, thunderous voice. "The Lord Jesus rebuke you, Lucifer! Be gone!"

The voice boomed throughout the arena. Most dismissed it as thunder from the storm, but Carrie caught the words and directed the camera crew, "Find the source and get cameras on it."

Immediately, multiple strikes of lightning cracked against the arena. A deafening roar blasted as the swirling winds of the Holy Fire of Heaven descended from the Father's throne, striking Lucifer and his army above the arena.

A horrifying scream pierced the heavens. It sprang forth with such volatile anger that the unearthly sound broke through the realm of angels to earth, freezing the audience in fear.

Suddenly, the crowd's attention was diverted from the unsettling frequency to the giant media screens. They saw the image of a figure, glowing with the brightness of Holy Fire. A different kind of fear fell upon the onlookers—the Fear of the Lord. No one spoke. No one moved, only the glowing man making his way down from an upper row. As the figure passed, people dropped to the floor under the pressing holiness of the Fire of Heaven.

Screams of terror, then moans, coughing and gagging occurred as the presence of God passed by, and the demonic fled. One row after another, down like dominoes, then back up again—one section bowing and then rising, like the wave at a sporting event.

The figure moved with intense focus, straight for the stage. The spectacle was both terrifying and hypnotizing. No one could look away.

C'mon, Tony, what kind of stunt are you pulling now? A glowing man? was Hammond's first thought. He didn't believe it was from God, because in his mind, no omnipotent creator existed who ruled over all men. As the figure stepped onstage, even in his unbelief, Hammond trembled in fear.

The burning brightness spoke with Heaven's authority, "Lies, lies and more lies! You cling to lies that send you to eternal torment. You say there is no one god, but I tell you there is only one true Savior and His name is Jesus. There is no other god in Heaven, on earth or in your imaginary universal consciousness other than the Creator, Jesus the Christ, sent from the Father. You deceived and unbelieving people, how long will this generation accept the lies of the evil one? What will it take for you to believe? Do you ask for a sign?"

Dean O'Conner, empowered by rage, jumped from his seat and ran backstage. He emerged from behind the curtain, pushing a gurney. "Get out of my way! Let me through! I have the test to see if your god is God!" Stepping to the microphone, he bellowed, "*Here* is your challenge!"

The gurney was now center front stage, the view captured on each of the giant arena monitors. The irate dean unzipped the large, plastic bag, letting it flap open to expose an anatomy class cadaver. "No god can restore *this* to life!" He let out an unsettling cackle.

Hammond was unaware that O'Conner had planned this experiment. Though he himself was no friend of religiosity, this was going too far! He hurried to his long-time friend, shaking him to get his attention. O'Conner's eyes were bloodshot and his face contorted. His voice was low and throaty as he shouted over and over, "Raise this body from the dead!"

Hammond quickly dropped his hands, backing away in shock. *What had pushed him to this level of crudeness? He's insane!*

Feeling lucky to still be standing upright, Hammond found himself swimming in a stupor of confusion, disgust and embarrassment—for O'Conner and for the university. What was supposed to be a small debate, squelching the religious commotion in a faculty meeting, had spiraled into a national event in less than four days. Hammond's world nosedived out of control.

Taunting voices could be heard from various locations in the arena, shouting, "Yeah, raise the cadaver ... if you can!"

Prompted by the Holy Spirit, Gregor stepped forward, accepting O'Conner's challenge. Just earlier that morning, Jesus had commanded him to listen and obey. But Gregor never imagined that he would be asked to raise a body that looked like a dissected frog! Despite a momentary hesitancy, he pushed out every inkling of doubt.

This was not about proving Tony's point correct. This was about saving souls from eternal separation from God—unending torment in hell. Gregor prayed, *Lord, give me the faith to obey and ... give me Your love for these people so that the Fire of Heaven will flow through me to them for Your name's sake.*

Jean and Tony gasped, standing to get a better look.

"How long has this person been dead?" Gregor asked O'Connor.

The crazed dean rudely shoved Gregor aside, causing him to stumble into the gurney. Then the demented scholar shouted into the microphone, making sure the audience heard: "This, my friends, is a John Doe—dead for six months—and donated to the medical school by the county morgue. I can assure you he is *quite* dead, because this body is full of embalming fluid and has been dissected many times over. Go at it, Jeeeee---suuuuusss-man," he sneered, letting out a creepy laugh.

Waves of laughter rolled through most of the crowd.

Gregor stood by the body with the glowing figure behind him. He placed his hands on the cold, lifeless mass of flesh, more nearly resembling spoiled meat than what had once been a living human being. The glowing man lifted his arms to Heaven as Gregor assessed the butchered body, skin flapped to the sides, exposing nerves, vessels, muscles and missing organs. *Lord, Jason was dead ... but this ...*

Just obey, the reassuring voice of the Spirit prompted.

Gregor glanced out at the crowd, then looked upward toward Heaven in a moment of silent petition to the Father. As he started to speak, a news crew member rushed to put a second microphone in front of him. Unfazed, Gregor spoke to the audience, "I did not come tonight to offer persuasive words of wisdom, but to demonstrate the power of the Holy Spirit." Then, in a commanding voice, he turned to address the corpse: "In Jesus' mighty name, arise and walk!"

While most of the audience laughed again, the thousand believers from the warehouse fervently prayed. The team watched closely. Carrie stared breathlessly.

The stage began to quiver, then shook like an earthquake was erupting underfoot. Lights popped and bits of glass crashed to the floor, hitting some in the audience on the way down. The sound system issued a screeching howl at the surge of power. People covered their ears, but mesmerized, never broke their gaze from the cadaver, displayed larger than life on the arena monitors.

The body—stone-cold dead, with no possible hope of life— began to shake uncontrollably. The crowd gulped, trying to look away from the gruesome image, but the extraordinary sight was spellbinding.

Severed blood vessels and nerves reconnected. Absent organs quickly grew. Missing muscles reformed. Limbs stretched and cracked as the joints aligned themselves. The seams, where skin had been cut, gently faded into nonexistence, changing from a grayish beige to a healthy, tannish brown.

The crowd watched in silent awe. Joy rose in the believers, who wanted to shout to the heavens, but they remained quiet in this holy moment.

A faint gurgling sound leaked from the cadaver's mouth. Hair sprang forth from the head. The cheeks filled out, and it was apparent that the body was a male. Next, a loud gasp, his lungs filled with air, and the cadaver abruptly sat up.

The crowd made varying sounds of shock. Some fainted. Tony's faculty, the thousand believers from the warehouse, the two hundred protesters, along with Marjie and her group, jumped to their feet and cheered, shouting praises to the Lord. Jean and Tony embraced each other, spun around and praised God, joining in the celebration. Gregor, greatly relieved, grabbed a tablecloth to cover the man's nakedness.

Carrie and her crew stood by silently, cameras recording the scene. As the light faded from the glowing man, she squinted, barely making out a face.

"Jason!" she cried as she recognized him, his name escaping her lips with a breathy sound.

The light of the Fire of Heaven continued to burn in Jason's eyes. He put out his arm to shake the man's hand. "Welcome back."

"What is this place?" the man asked, gripping Jason's hand with a force that caused him to wince.

"Frederick University."

Astounded, the man peered into Jason's eyes, weeping while still squeezing his hand. "Don't make me go back there," he begged. "Please! Don't make me go back!"

From this statement, Jason assumed the man meant hell. *If he had come from Heaven, he would be begging to return!*

"You don't have to go back," Jason assured him. "You can go to Heaven if you confess with your mouth and believe in your heart that Jesus is Lord. He loves you and died for your sins, so you don't ever have to return to torment if you surrender your life to Him."

"I believe," whispered the man. He suddenly jumped from the gurney and bounced around the stage, shouting, "I believe! I believe!" So absorbed was he in this moment of jubilation, he forgot to cover himself with the tablecloth. Then he fell to his knees, bowed prostrate and worshiped Jesus.

Joyful over this man's physical and spiritual transformation, Jason laughed and picked up the tablecloth to cover him again.

The university panel of Morton, Patel, and Jenkins slipped away while everyone's attention was on the risen body. Hammond stood motionless, his lower jaw dropped in astonishment.

With unnatural speed, O'Conner rushed the cadaver man, his eyes wild with hatred, arms flailing. "You are not alive! This is a trick!"

Before Gregor and Jason could stop him, O'Conner locked his hands around the man's neck, attempting to strangle him. It took both men to pull O'Conner away. The resurrected man choked, working to catch his breath.

Gregor grabbed O'Conner by the shoulders while Jason held his head, forcing him to look into his fiery eyes. "I will not! I will not look into the light of the Nazarene!" O'Conner screamed, trying to turn his head away.

Jason commanded O'Conner to behold the Light. The dean's eyes opened wide as, reluctantly, he looked into the Fire of Heaven. But he quickly closed his eyes and moved his head side to side, shouting profanities.

Storis—unseen by onlookers—forced O'Conner's head to remain still. His eyelids looked like they were held open with an ophthalmologist's tool as he stared directly into the Fire in Jason's eyes. With one last bizarre scream, O'Conner collapsed.

Carrie rushed to the stage, stopping about fifteen feet from Jason. He smiled at her, wondering what she must be thinking after watching him light up like a hundred thousand volts. Slowly, she walked closer, looking into his glowing eyes. When she still hesitated, Jason reached for her hand, guiding her the rest of the way into his arms.

What manner of man this is, I do not know. I only know I love him with all my heart, she thought, nestling comfortably in his embrace.

* * *

The reality of God's truth shot through the crowd like a blazing arrow, consuming layers of sin and deception. Those in bondage were set free in the power and truth of Jesus Christ. Many wept, while some shouted joyfully, reveling in the newfound sensation of freedom.

The new believers were organized into groups and matched with the team, Tony's faculty, the warehouse thousand and the protesters for prayer. With this pairing accomplished, Jean motioned to Maria to sing.

Fresh waves of godly sorrow continued to fill the people as Maria's sweet voice was joined by an unseen angelic choir. Imprisoned souls, freed from bondage, celebrated their new life in Christ. The Fire of Heaven had mightily invaded hell's territory, emerging victoriously. This night, four thousand souls—plus one John Doe—were delivered from Lucifer's evil grip.

33

Better Than Sacrifice

It was late by the time everyone left the Hammond Center. Tony, Jean and Gregor walked leisurely toward Tony's car. He pressed the open button on the key fob. On command, the car beeped and the doors unlocked. Jean slid into the front passenger seat while Gregor headed for his spot in the back.

Tony started the car, but instead of revving the engine, he let it idle. Gregor and Jean didn't notice as they, too, reflected silently on the night's events.

Finally, Tony broke the silence. "I just saw Jason glow like Jesus at the transfiguration on the mount, a cut-up cadaver brought back to life and four thousand people exchange their old lives for new lives in Christ. So … why do I feel as if this is just the end of another day and I'm heading back home for dinner and bed?" he said, a little perplexed at his lack of excitement.

Gregor and Jean looked at each other and laughed. "Tell him, Jean," said Gregor.

"When we first learned to hear the voice of the Lord, He told us that when amazing events begin to happen, like tonight, we would simply shrug it off and act like it was just a normal day," she explained. "The emotional highs and lows would be removed. We're not unhappy about the outcome—quite the contrary! It's just that we are to expect it and go about the Father's business, not allowing emotion to carry us away in the moment."

Gregor leaned forward, inserting himself between the two front seats. "Jesus explained to us that many past moves failed because leaders didn't understand how to handle being flooded by His presence as they ministered. Consequently, they added a lot of man-made hype, show-boated, acted drunk—making me doubt it was truly the Holy Spirit in the first place. And if it was God, pride and error crept into the move, causing it to fall apart. Desiring an experience more than accomplishing God's will overshadowed the Holy Spirit's moving in miraculous ways. Remember, if Lucifer can't keep you away from the mark, he will push you right through it and beyond."

"Yeah, I know what you're saying. I watched some videos of people 'ministering' like that while researching for my book." Tony sighed. *That book,* he thought. *Wish I could retrieve every copy and burn 'em all. Oh, Jesus forgive me.*

"If we stay focused on merely obeying and let God do what He wants, we'll simply walk in it as the new normal. The experience is not what we're seeking. God is Who we seek. We're bondservants to Jesus, not masters of the Spirit. As He goes, we follow. He owns it, we don't," Gregor finished.

Tony thought for a long moment and then asked, "OK, I can see that. Are you ever afraid you might make assumptions you shouldn't and get ahead of the Lord?"

"Yes, but fearing getting off target is a good thing," Jean replied, picking up the conversation once more.

"In the book of first Samuel, God—through the prophet Samuel—had ordered King Saul to utterly destroy the Amalekites. Nothing was to be saved; he was commanded to kill all the people and animals. But Saul disobeyed the Lord and spared the Amalekite king. He also saved the best of the sheep, oxen and cattle, thinking it a good idea to sacrifice them to the Lord.

"Saul disobeyed God's direct command, presuming in his own wisdom that his plan of action was better than the Lord's; however, God didn't care about the animal sacrifices. He wanted Saul to obey. Samuel rebuked Saul, saying that listening and obeying is what pleases God, not burnt offerings. In other words, obedience is better than sacrifice.

"The prophet continued telling Saul that rebellion is as the sin of divination—seeking the truth from fortune-tellers or witches—and presumption is as iniquity and idolatry—the sin of worshipping false gods. That's a serious rebuke! Plain and simple: Presumption is sin. Because Saul vetoed God's plan and went with his own plan, God rejected him as king over His people. We tend to grade our disobedience by levels of 'badness.' But to God, sin is sin, and disobedience on any level is serious business."

"There's plenty of examples to learn from," Gregor interjected. "In the Book of Joshua, a band of foreign ambassadors came to meet with Israel's leaders saying their king had heard of the amazing acts of Israel's God that had instilled fear throughout the nations. The travelers stated that they had been sent to negotiate a peace treaty. The foreigners wore tattered clothing, worn-out sandals and carried stale, moldy food. The evidence seemed to match with the ambassadors' statement that they had traveled a great distance."

"But ..." Jean interrupted, "God had commanded Israel not to make any treaties with people inside the boundaries of the Promised Land; in fact, He ordered that these pagan nations be utterly destroyed. However, a treaty with the travelers seemed reasonable since they had obviously come from well outside those boundaries.

"There was only one problem. The ambassadors had lied, deceiving the Israelites. They were really Gibeonites, living inside the borders, disguised to trick Joshua and the elders. The treaty was binding forever, and the Gibeonites became an ongoing thorn to Israel. One seemingly harmless assumption created a perpetual open door to evil." Jean paused, dropping her voice. "The evil one will most assuredly pull this tactic of deception out of his playbook soon. I'm expecting it," she finished.

Tony pondered all he had heard. Like any college professor, he wanted to know more. "Tell me then, how do we spot deceivers trying to do the same thing today? How can we prevent a tragic mistake like this from happening to us?"

"Prayer," replied Gregor. "Listening in prayer and then obeying what we hear. Pray for discernment so we don't make 'treaties with lying foreigners.'"

Tony was silent for a few moments as he processed this information. "So ... what else should I know about our enemy? Will he try to deceive us into doing something we shouldn't do?"

"Count on it. Go ahead, Jean, tell him about the old man and the prophet," urged Gregor.

"Oh, right. In first Kings, God sent a young prophet to warn the ruler of Israel about a future event. Understand that the young prophet has been given strict orders by the Lord not to eat bread or drink water or return by the way he came. He manages to deliver the prophecy and, after some of what was prophesied happens before the king's eyes, the king realizes the young man is a true prophet. He asks him to pray for him and then invites the young man to come home with him and share a meal. He even offers the young prophet a gift. Remember, this is the *king* who is making this request.

"The young prophet holds true to the Lord's command and refuses the king's offer. Pretty good so far, right? But as the young prophet heads home a different way, just like the Lord commanded, he runs into another, much older prophet, who also invites him to his place for dinner. Again, the young prophet refuses ... at least, at first.

"Now the older prophet tells him that an angel, sent by the Lord, has issued the invitation to return and eat with him. So ... what should he do? The young prophet has no reason to doubt the other prophet. After all, he is older, more experienced. So, the young prophet believes him and follows him home. But the older prophet lied! Suddenly the older prophet warns the younger of doom awaiting him because of his disobedience. So, while the younger prophet is on his way home, he is mauled by a lion and dies."

Tony put the car in drive and slowly moved out of the parking lot. "For one mistake, the guy's eaten by a lion?"

"I know, right?" Gregor acknowledged Tony's objection. "But once again, a bad assumption was made. The young prophet assumed that the old prophet was telling the truth. Not seeking the counsel of the Lord cost the young prophet his life. The lesson for us is that we can't just listen to some big-time ministry leader in the Body of Christ and assume what they are telling us is of God. They may claim they had a vision, a dream, whatever ... and Jesus says He wants you to speak at their church or conference."

"How do you handle a situation like that?"

"We should respond to this type of request by thanking the person for sharing what they believe is of God and go home and pray. We must test what was spoken against what the Lord is commanding us to do."

"Whew!" Tony let out another deep sigh. "I've read those stories, of course, but if you hadn't pointed this out, I'm sure I would have eventually found myself in a predicament. There's so much I need to learn. I'm glad I'm partnering with you guys."

"Tony, we need you just as much as you need us," Jean assured. "Any of us can fall into traps. We need to be working together, challenging each other, looking out for each other and praying for each other. It's written that a cord of three strands cannot be easily broken, meaning a rope is stronger than a single strand. When you take all the individual strands and twist them together, the result is a much stronger cord."

At this, Gregor jumped in. "We all know a great time of judgment is coming upon this nation as well as the world. We are at the foothills of the Great Tribulation told in the Book of the Revelation of Jesus Christ. Before those judgments come, God in His mercy, is sending a move of the Holy Spirit. By His nature, He has to exact justice, but sometimes He will delay the judgment, giving people a chance to turn away from sin and be restored to Him.

"There are plenty of examples of this in history, but a favorite of mine surrounds the account of an eight-year-old boy. Some Old Testament kings were good rulers and some were extremely wicked, doing unspeakable things. Israel's participation in sinful acts, like idol worship, created a people worse than the surrounding pagan nations.

"Once, right before a time of judgment, God sent revival through Josiah, who became king of Judah when he was only eight years old. Josiah actually read a prophecy about himself that was written around three hundred years before his birth. God had appointed him to bring the people to a right relationship with Him before judgment. Hilkiah, a faithful high priest, trained Josiah in the ways of the Lord, equipping him to do amazing things that no other king had ever done. Josiah ordered that the pagan altars on the mountaintops be destroyed. Believe it or not, parents sacrificed their children to pagan gods at this time through fire, but Josiah put an end to that!"

"Kinda sounds like good ol' America, doesn't it?" interjected Tony on a somber note as he considered the horrific stats on abortion.

"Exactly my point. The Israelites' moral compass was pointing in the wrong direction and God was very angry. He sent prophets to warn the king, religious leaders and people, but they rejected each one—killed or imprisoned most of them—for calling them out in their sin. Anyway, God had had enough. When Josiah's reign ended, God permitted Babylon and the Assyrians to kill, rape and murder the Israelites. Repentance of Josiah's time couldn't stop God from executing judgment. God *is* justice and His justice cannot be wiped away, only deferred."

"So … you're saying today is that Josiah generation?"

"Yep … the greatest revival took place just before the dispersion of Jews and the destruction of their nation. God gave a short season to turn back to Him before His judgments came. He is giving us the very same thing. He's raising up a generation, giving the nations an opportunity to throw down their altars of evil," Gregor concluded.

"What Gregor is saying," Jean began in summary, "is that when judgment hits a nation, the new believers in Christ will be dispersed into other nations. This makes them missionaries, carrying the gospel to the places God wants His Kingdom to reach. Don't let the concept slip by you. Just like Josiah had Hilkiah to train him, we're called as Hilkiahs to the younger generation."

Tony only nodded as he pulled into the Wallaces' driveway. *So much, so fast and when will it slow down?* he wondered.

"Let's all meet at Marjie's tomorrow afternoon," Gregor began. "We need to figure out what we're going to do with four thousand new believers. Add the warehouse thousand and the two hundred protesters, and we have our hands full!"

"Goodnight, Tony, see you tomorrow," called Jean as she got out of the car. "Get some sleep, you look like you need it, my friend!"

34

The Adara Center

Ever since Tony began teaching at Frederick, driven by the need to succeed, he had spent his Saturday mornings catching up on grading papers and meeting with students in his campus office. After seeing a cadaver come to life the night before, going to the office seemed pointless since he would likely be canned any moment now. Nevertheless, feeling restless, his usual routine got him out of the house.

In fact, he expected to find his personal items heaped outside a locked office door, leaving him with an obsolete key in his pocket. *How did last night affect the campus atmosphere?* he thought. *If I tried to guess what would happen today, I'm sure I'd be wrong anyway. Unpredictability is the new predictability.*

The ride to campus was peaceful enough, but as he approached his office, he could see that campus security was preventing hundreds of students from entering the building. To avoid the mob, he drove around to the back service entrance.

Tony was surprised that even this seldom-used entrance was guarded. "What's going on, Mike?"

"Don't know, sir. Just told to keep students out."

Wow! Even on fall break, they want to lynch me, he thought.

Inside the halls, his footsteps echoed in the usual Saturday stillness. Tony breathed a sigh of relief until he noticed the Philosophy Department door was ajar. He gingerly pushed it a bit, peeking through the sliver of an opening. To his surprise, Maggie was at her desk on a Saturday—a notable anomaly.

She was staring at her computer screen, sipping a steaming drink, a morning rite she had faithfully performed for the past ten years. The familiar smell of cinnamon tea wafted through the crack in the door. He could see her favorite mug which read: *You may speak when the cup is empty.* Tony thought it best to quietly slip by, allowing her to finish her tea before asking about the campus scuttlebutt.

Without turning to face Tony, Maggie asked over her shoulder, "And where do you think you're heading off to without first speaking to me?"

Surprised, Tony turned back toward her desk.

"You trained me not to talk to you until you've finished your morning tea. Remember, *boss*?"

"That rule is temporarily suspended." Maggie spun the chair around. "I have the inside scoop and you're not going to believe what I'm about to tell you."

"Yeah … I noticed something was up. I'm afraid to ask why security is barricading hundreds of students from entering the building. It's fall break. Why aren't they all in Florida?"

"First things first. Get this … President Hammond extended fall break by an extra week! And … Dean O'Connor is leaving the school. Claims he needs time off to deal with some personal issues. Yeah, like he didn't come across as a complete moron last night? Good riddance! He was always a weasel, brown-nosing his way up the ladder. That man never had a good idea in his life other than to leave Frederick."

"Why, Maggie … a weasel?"

"Yes, and you know it! Finally, people want you to answer questions about last night." Several lines lit up on the office phone, but Maggie didn't pick up.

"Answer questions? I thought they were here to hang me!"

"Oh, and get this … Dr. Ellen Morton in Religious Studies wants to talk to you as well. She's left multiple voicemail messages, emails and called three times this morning. Last night must have rattled that woman's cage."

"Really!"

"I hope all that thick mush she tried to peddle last night made her as sick as the rest of us. You will meet with her?"

Tony noticed more lights on the office phone. "Shouldn't we answer?"

"Let it go to voicemail. Probably more students from last night, or angry parents demanding an explanation."

Maggie displayed an openness Tony had not seen before. She was excited, bursting to tell him all the news.

"You'll have to tell me how your meeting with Professor Wacko turns out. Promise?"

"I promise." Tony chuckled at Maggie's energetic mood and her word choices. "Since it's fall break, the lecture hall at Gunderson should be available. I could have a gathering to answer questions there. Could you check on its availability?"

"Did one of those lightning bolts zap your brain? I'm not talking about a few hundred requesting audience with you. Try over five thousand students and faculty—not including all the others who don't go to school here—who got wind of cadaver-man. Who's going to feed the hungry newbies?"

"Options, Maggie … what do you propose?"

"I'm past proposing, Professor. I am in the executing phase." She handed him some papers. "Here's your assignment. Mr. Wallace didn't call you?"

"No, I haven't spoken to anyone but you this morning."

"He gave me topics for new believers. Every student will have access to the dates, times and locations via various social media, directing them to the new website. I booked the lecture halls and rooms, now you book the teachers. There's just so much I can do." She went to the small break area to warm her tea in the microwave.

"Dates? Times? When, exactly?"

"Tuesday morning. You'd better hurry. Clock's ticking. Send me the info and I'll post it."

"Wait … what new website?"

"A student in communications and marketing started it … Mark somebody. You're running a little slow here, Doc. You gotta catch up with what's happening." The microwave beeped. Tony's cue to exit.

"Thanks." Maggie's language wasn't polished, but she got things done. He felt there was too much to do and not enough time to keep up with the Lord's fast pace.

He stopped mid-stride, partway to his desk and poked his head through the doorway. "Maggie, did you tell me earlier that Hammond *extended* fall break?"

"Yep, he sure did."

"Wow, I'm speechless. All right then … I'll get working on those teachers."

He sat at his desk for a moment, wondering if Hammond had had a change of heart, then called Gregor. "Hey, this is Tony. Things are in warp speed here at the university…."

"Oh, I called you, but it went to voicemail."

"Sorry, I missed it, but Maggie explained. She said we need material to post on a website?"

"Colonel Parker gave me his studies from the past thirty years. I've been going through them since the Capital Grand meeting. It's solid Biblical material."

"OK, send that to my email. Maggie has access and will post everything."

"Just clicked the send button. Meeting at Marjie's for lunch, one o'clock."

"*Lunch*? Wow, Maggie's right. I *am* moving slow ... I'll explain later. See you soon."

* * *

Marjie had ordered Aunt Becky's Catering for the team's working luncheon. The familiar smell of the meal took Tony's thoughts back to the faculty meeting that jump-started the previous night's events. The group was unusually quiet, but he appreciated the short break from the turmoil of the last few days.

After a light dessert and prayer for direction, Marjie called the meeting to order. She was perfect for the job—smart, articulate and able to move quickly through a laundry list of "to do" items. Organization and implementation were her indispensable talents. She expected each one to do his or her part, no excuses. Time did not permit hem-hawing around.

"We've thousands of new believers and we are few. We need to add to our numbers. After screening, we'll pray to see which prospective candidates the Holy Spirit has selected."

All agreed. Gregor would schedule times, and available team members would come for the interviews.

Dan interrupted. "I'm dying to know ... who was the dead guy on the gurney last night?"

"Yeah, I tried to find him afterward, but he was gone," Jason put in. "I was hoping one of you got his info."

A moment of silence passed as all hoped somebody would speak up with the man's name, history and location.

"Where does a naked man—raised from the dead—run to?" Jean wanted to know.

Carlos tentatively shared a bit of information. "Hey ... you guys not gonna b'lieve this. I think I've seen that guy before." He turned to his brother. "Diego, isn't he the wino dude hangin' 'round the liquor store?"

"No way, man. Yeah ... that's the guy. Always passed out by the dumpster. He was loco." Diego put his head down, feeling compassion for the outcast. "Man, if I'da known Jesus back then, I'da helped him."

Maria raised her hand to speak.

"Put your hand down, Maria. Just jump in and don't worry about stepping on someone's toes," Barb gently instructed.

"What he say when he come back, you know, from bein' dead?"

"Maria, he was in hell," Jason was quick to reply. "He was terrified that he might have to go back—squeezed hard enough to hurt my hand and wouldn't let go. His story is the epitome of all second chances. We need to find this guy! I've *got* to hear his story."

Carlos spoke with confidence this time. "I can find the guy. I know people who know people." Carlos winked.

"This conversation is important; however, you'll have to save it for later," Marjie redirected. "There are items on the agenda that still need to be addressed."

She was right. Everyone gave her their attention.

"My lawyer called this morning. We own the warehouse and the surrounding buildings. Apparently, the corporation that owned the land was in a dire position and was looking to dump it. We got it for 1.9 million. A bargain—or should I say a gift—at that price. Also, negotiations are in process for properties in the surrounding city blocks.

"Ford Ashman is presenting to the city planners Monday. His contact in city government assured him that with such large-scale improvements to a bad part of town, it will be fast-tracked. Civil government had been after the previous owner for years because the abandoned buildings were a haven for gangs." She turned to Carlos and Diego and smiled. "No offense, boys."

"Hey, that's my turf. Only reason I knew 'bout that warehouse." Carlos spread his hands through the air as if making a statement with graffiti. "Gang Leader Contributes to Kingdom of God." He chuckled at his own joke. "As Barb likes to say, '*The Lord works in mysterious ways.*'"

There was a ripple of laughter around the table.

Marjie continued. "Ford broke down the construction into three phases. Phase one consists of the main warehouse build-out. It will include a multipurpose main area that will seat about 10,000 pretty comfortably. Restrooms, a kitchen, a dedicated prayer area, offices and classrooms are included. Parking lot repaved and security lights installed. Ford pulled in some favors, and subcontractors agreed to work twenty-four/seven. He thinks the time line to complete this project is six weeks. In construction terms, that's nothing short of a full-fledged miracle.

"The main meeting area could be completed in four weeks and can be used while the rest is still being finished. Phase two: The abandoned mental hospital will be renovated to a fifty-room dormitory. It will be used to temporarily house other leaders coming for training and Carlos, Diego and Maria, your apartments. Time line for full completion is three months."

Jean leaned into Barb and whispered, "Is she always like this?"

"Yeah ... a little like a bulldozer that makes things happen. I don't know how she does it—creates and executes a plan in the same breath."

"The other large central building will eventually be a community center," Marjie went on. "The remaining buildings will be meeting rooms, offices, auditorium and more classrooms. The aim is to have vocational type classrooms teaching practical living skills like reading, writing, how to cook, how to bathe, vocational skills and such. Getting people saved is just one side of the coin. They need real-life training on how to live. Remember, God is turning around drug addicts, prostitutes, gang members, the mentally ill, and homeless people who have lived on the streets. The *lost* of the lost are coming our way, people, and we need to be there for them in every area of life, not just the spiritual side. However, the spiritual side must come first. Without God's mighty hand of deliverance and healing, we will never get them ready in time to be harvest workers."

In short order, the awakening movement transformed from a handful of directionless believers to a well-oiled machine by this petite widow.

"By the way, Gregor, a realtor specializing in out-of-state relocations has a buyer for your house—computer guy from Seattle. He wants all the furniture and is willing to pay full price with cash at closing on Friday."

Before Gregor could agree to the deal, Marjie instructed him to see her lawyer. "Elliott is drawing up the paperwork now. Make sure you sign them later today."

Marjie's whirlwind rundown completed.

Everyone was stunned. How did this little old woman move like lightning? They were all getting a glimpse into the supernatural or "God natural" world that just a few weeks ago had seemed impossible.

Tony had some papers in hand ready to pass around. "Over five thousand have contacted my office wanting answers. Hammond extended fall break so university property is available to us at no charge. My Admin booked lecture halls and classrooms; we just need to arrange for teachers. Here's a list of rooms and how many they accommodate."

Barb grabbed the papers before Marjie could look at them. "Stand down, Marjie. You've got to let us do some of the heavy lifting. Sheila and I will take this one."

"Count me in," Jean volunteered. "Maria, would you like to help?"

"Oh, yes!" She beamed at the idea of being useful.

Barb turned to Carlos. "Have some of your associates reach out to those who got saved last week. I'll have buses ready to transport them to the classes."

"Hmmm … we'll need some Spanish-speaking teachers or interpreters. Maybe y'all could put feelers out," Sheila suggested.

Jason raised his hand. "I'll build a social media presence for the ministry center—best way to move info fast. Also, I was thinking of a name for the place. How does The Adara Center sound? It's a girl's name in Hebrew, meaning 'fire.'"

Name agreed upon unanimously. The Fire of Heaven was leading them like it led the Israelites in the wilderness—a clearly lit path through darkness to the promises of God. A place of training workers for the Final Awakening of souls was birthed.

Meeting adjourned in record time.

35

Back To Basics

Facing the Host of Heaven head to head had ended in humiliating defeat. Anger and hatred toward the Holy One had pushed the princes of darkness and the demonic army to go throughout the earth, randomly afflicting any human as sport.

Lucifer sat in the quietude of his private chamber, whispering to himself, "I should have known better than to make a frontal assault upon Michael and his band of holy warriors. My hatred momentarily confused my judgment."

He paced the cavern floor, wringing his hands, then suddenly stopped, lifting his arms into the air in defiance of the Holy One's omnipotence. "You cheated, Nazarene—as you always do—otherwise, I would have triumphed."

He paced again, reviewing all strategies. *I will return to the basics,* Lucifer thought. *Fight the battle in the mind. Yes, win the mind, own the heart.* Suddenly he shouted, breaking the solemn mood, "Hermedes, call a Council meeting!"

* * *

The princes had returned from their sorties, somewhat invigorated. Pouring anger and hatred upon their selected human victims preserved the illusion of absolute power, deluding themselves that victory was won.

"Read from the book, Hermedes," Lucifer commanded with a toss of his hand from his throne at the head of the Council table.

Hermedes read names of souls condemned to hell. The evil princes were already sentenced to the lake of fire by their willful choice to believe Lucifer's lies. They gloated that multitudes of human creatures were also condemned by rejecting the Truth. Confidence returned. The Council was focused on the prize once again.

"My faithful followers," Lucifer began, "as encouraging as the increased tally is in the book, we must assure the numbers increase. As long as there is life in the body, the creatures have opportunity to pledge their allegiance to the Nazarene. My comrades, we must guarantee the fate of those who have not yet made a choice, tipping the balance completely to our side."

Lucifer stood for an important announcement. "I bear good news, my friends. The Holy One has released to me greater authority over the earth."

A great shout echoed throughout the cavern.

"Let us concentrate on those who lack the seal of the Nazarene. Lead them deeper into the sewer. Pervert their minds and bodies with addictions to sex, drugs, alcohol, video games, entertainment, sports, gambling, power, wealth, false religions, etcetera. I want extremism in everything.

"Inspire discord. I want kingdom against kingdom, nation against nation. I want total chaos, division down to the smallest member of a family group. Divide friends, families, co-workers, teams, politicians, religious leaders, races. Anywhere division can be achieved, make it happen with no hope of reconciliation. Stir up pandemonium to press man to search for a savior. I will be their savior and they will revere me as god."

Applause sounded from the horde. Lucifer continued to stand, asserting his stance against the Holy One, relishing in this moment of exaltation.

"With the release of more authority over the earth—an exciting development indeed—we can multiply our efforts exponentially." He strolled amidst the listening princes as he reminded them of basic strategies. "Work diligently to prevent genuine prayer to the Holy One. Convince the creatures we do not exist nor seek to oppress, thus eliminating the need to test the spirits against the Truth. If they do not test, we have an open door to deceive."

A low tone of mumbling agreement swept through the attentive group.

"Even if believers have broken free, constantly remind them of their past sins. Encourage reattachment to the chains that bound them before being sealed to the Nazarene. They can choose to put the shackles back on again. It is well within their rights." Lucifer's sarcasm mocked the Holy One's decision to give his beloved man the power of choice.

"Go after ones already seeking leadership as a plant seeks sunlight, bending and twisting to attain what it craves. These are easily overcome with pride and the perpetual need to dominate subordinate followers. So then ..." he returned to his throne, turned and smiled, "we will give them what they want—thousands upon thousands of followers."

Lucifer's confidence in his newly given authority incited restlessness in the evil princes. Yet, on the other hand, the release of rights over the earth also signaled nearness to the end. Regardless, the lure of showering pain, despair, sickness and all evil upon the inhabitants of the earth was all-consuming, pushing the thought of the lake of fire from their minds.

"Prevent Bible reading. Distract the people with busyness even in their supposed service to the Holy One. Less reading the Word, less hearing the Word, less studying the Word and less prayer equates more opportunity for fraud. Simply include a bit of the Nazarene's truth with your lies, and the ignorant of the Word will never notice. It only takes one gray strand in the white chord of truth to promote a false jesus." Lucifer threw back his head and laughed. "Why does the Nazarene bother with such feebleminded creatures? The truth is laid out before them—contained in one convenient volume—and they are too lazy to pick it up and study it. Indeed, the sluggard buries his hand in the dish and will not even bring it back to his mouth."

He rubbed his chin, thinking for a moment. Abruptly, he flung his arm out, pointing to a prince near the front.

"Prince of Hollywood, push the boundaries beyond man's imagination with widespread perversion so that what is evil becomes natural, normal, accepted. Produce movies with extreme graphic depiction of violence and sexual immorality. Cause those films to yield immense profits for investors. In their greed, they will ignore the horrid nature of these productions convincing themselves it is just business. The love of money, which is worth less than a fleck of dust, moves people to do the most unimaginable things."

Lucifer laughed again, but the princes listened attentively.

"Many minds have been owned through pornography with the advent of twenty-four seven access. Make the obscene more violent and push it to mainstream television. We have been successful in attacking the male of the species, now assail the female. Wait ..." he stood in a moment of brilliance. "Why limit this strategy to adults? Why not expose the flower of youth to such filth, also? Fill movies, cartoons and educational curricula with abominations, swaying young minds to falsely believe that the lifestyle is good and acceptable—even expected."

A round of applause resulted. Lucifer reveled in his followers' admiration of his cleverness.

"On the thought of violence, send Fear, Violence, Lust and Addiction with any other associates to those watching such movies and engaging in such video games. Make the participants play out their violent fantasies with action, not just thought. The goal here is to shut down any social barriers still in place. Convince them they have the right to infringe upon others with their vile speech and actions, because their true freedom is at stake. Those coming against the 'absolute freedom without consequences' philosophy must be labeled religious, narrow-minded zealots, something to be eradicated from an enlightened age."

Lucifer faced the wall, admiring a mural memorializing one of his victories. He ran his fingers over the painting, then turned to the princes, obviously pleased with his speech reviewing basic strategies with some small additions.

"Prince of Vegas, expand gambling into every city in America. Make communities dependent upon the income generated from this insidious industry. Add additional venues for gambling to make it commonplace without stigma. Filled with greed and covetousness, the creatures will gamble themselves into poverty, a strategic condition opening the door to my one-world government.

"Prince of Pharmakeia, I commend you in your success, especially for your new advances against the young. A pill for everything. One to sleep, one to eat, one for sex, one for stress, one for pain, one for focus, etcetera, etcetera." Lucifer seemed almost giddy at the prospect of greater authority over the earth and its inhabitants.

"Yes, my prince, continue with addiction. Alter their minds, making them emotionless, unresponsive creatures. Their dependence on anything other than the Holy One is to our great advantage. In a drugged stupor, they will be too tired, too confused, or too disinterested to seek the Nazarene."

Lucifer addressed the entire Council. "Utilize every portion of our new rights. Just get your foot in the door. Persistence, comrades, wears them down.

"Understand this, we will not win this fight head on. That strategy failed in Egypt when my servant Pharaoh went out to kill the people of God at the Red Sea. With that plan, Elijah disgraced us on Mount Carmel. And now, we have been defeated at Frederick. So, my friends, steal their faith with fear, for without faith, they will turn away from the Holy One and revert to sin.

"My excellent outline will take back what *you* have lost. I have studied the nature of man since his creation. I know the creatures better than they know themselves. These things take time, but I am confident we will have great success."

At Lucifer's last words, the princes fled, going throughout the earth to implement the plan, only this time with greater impact.

Datter and Gorfius quietly ensured their obscurity by staying still in a dark corner until all had left.

"So, any thoughts on Lord Lucifer's new plan?" whispered Gorfius.

"Our leader is at his best when he remains in the background," Datter replied. "Yes, hidden is best. However, the pontiff's pride overrides logic, and he foolishly makes a public display."

The room was vacant now and Gorfius stood. "We all know the end of this game. Lord Lucifer cannot stop the plans of the Nazarene. The best he can accomplish is a delay."

"His hatred for the Nazarene is immeasurable. Truly incalculable, Gorfius." Datter impulsively grabbed his companion, whispering in his ear, "A certain intelligence sortie revealed a tidbit, which we will withhold to our advantage. You are bound to the agreement, Gorfius. Bound. One day, we may use this information to save us from Lucifer's wrath."

"I will keep silent about ..." Datter smacked Gorfius hard across the chest, making a strange hollow sound.

Lucifer returned. "Datter, Gorfius, do you have something to report?"

"No, my Lord Lucifer, there is no report at this time," the two spies said simultaneously.

"Then leave me!" Lucifer's tone held a hint of suspicion.

Datter and Gorfius swiftly slipped away before the pontiff changed his mind.

Mistrust was constant amongst all the evil horde, but Lucifer dismissed his feelings. After all, Datter and Gorfius *were* incapable of conspiring a mutiny; however, might they withhold information critical to the cause? His thoughts seemed so absurd, he burst into laughter.

36

The Interview

So far, WNN knew nothing about Carrie's relationship with Jason. One of two outcomes was inevitable, she figured. *Either my career at WNN News dies, or my relationship with Jason does,* she thought. *The two can't co-exist.*

Carrie anxiously waited in an outer office while WNN's upper management wrestled with the fate of the exclusive footage from the Frederick University debate. She pointed out earlier that the network had been out-hustled by social media, with clips immediately going viral. The Internet was aflame, demanding WNN air the debate; thus, intense public interest assured high ratings. The world would be watching Sunday evening.

* * *

Carrie sat beside Shane Sanders at the anchor desk. Her heart was racing—only one minute before the ON AIR sign lit up. Bzzzz. She glanced at her phone. It was a reassuring text from Jason: *All at Marjie's watching, praying ...you've got this ... love you.* Jason had included several heart emojis at the end of the message, making her smile despite her jitters.

No time for a return text. Studio lights on. Cameras in position. Shane checked his computer and tested the teleprompters. A make-up assistant rushed to do one last touch-up, then quickly jumped off the stage. "Three, two, one ... the director pointed.

"Good evening, America. This is a WNN News Special Report. I'm Shane Sanders and joining me is Carrie Summers. Many of you have been following the strange events happening in the D.C. area. We aired a story a few weeks ago on the mysterious circumstances surrounding the rapid recovery of Jason Taylor, the son of the North Carolina Senator Dan Taylor."

Photos of the Taylors' home and the family standing on their porch were shown.

"As you may recall, Jason was involved in a severe car accident, then claimed to have been raised from the dead. When attempting to interview Jason at his parents' home, an unexpected electrical overload short-circuited the electronic equipment. First-hand account of that event was reported by Carrie Summers here on WNN."

Oh, man, he really toned down what actually happened, thought Carrie. *Although, I would, too, if I hadn't seen it and felt it myself.*

Shane turned looking into the left camera. "After the event at the Taylors' residence, more unusual occurrences were reported at the Senate Prayer Breakfast, where Senator Taylor was the keynote speaker. Many claim to have encountered a deep religious experience while being mysteriously held to the floor for over thirty minutes by an unseen force. We had no camera crews there, but some managed to record a bit with their phones."

The director nodded and the prayer breakfast montage was broadcast.

"These phenomena also manifested at Frederick University in the faculty meeting of the Philosophy Department when Dr. Tony Robertson addressed his staff."

Tony's picture appeared on-screen.

"Then again, students on campus encountered a similar experience on the grassy commons area. The university's president, Francis Hammond, looked into the matter and became gravely concerned that mass hysteria was negatively influencing students and faculty. A debate of two opposing viewpoints was set for this past Friday evening at the Hammond Center. In the spirit of intellectual freedom, the debate encouraged listening to facts and allowing *us* to determine for ourselves the source of the extraordinary events. Supposedly, at this debate, a cadaver was brought to life—all highly suspect since the man has not been found. WNN has decided to play the entire debate, unedited. You decide."

The director signaled a tech to start the video. The staff in the control room were glued to the monitors as they played a clip of the glowing man in the top row. They had seen it before while preparing for the broadcast, but the sight was captivating even a third time.

O'Conner's sinister demeanor as he rolled out the gurney made everyone uneasy. He conveyed the impression of an actor portraying a crazed man full of evil—only this was real, not an act. The participants debated whether the cadaver was actually even a human body. But when Gregor called for the mass of flesh to rise, the power in the prayer was felt in the production studio. The crew concluded something mystical had, indeed, happened that night. This wasn't any sci-fi movie!

When the video clip ended, the television screen was again filled with the images of Carrie and Shane, sitting behind the news desk. Seeing Jason's glowing figure again brought back all the thoughts and feelings of that night, ruffling Carrie enough that she had to work hard to keep her composure.

298

Shane Sanders, a seasoned, veteran newscaster, who thought he'd seen it all, also experienced some overwhelming sensations foreign to him. He felt confused. In his mind, God did not exist and an empirical scientific approach explained everything. Yet, he felt twisted, torn in two directions. His logic said God was fiction, yet his heart pulled him toward belief.

At the urging of certain governmental officials, Shane had agreed to slip in comments from various experts, discrediting the video and explaining away the experience of thousands as the influence of mass psychosis. Shane was so internally disturbed by the disorienting conviction, however, that he completely forgot his scripted agenda.

A weight of sin was felt by all—camera, sound, make-up and production crews alike. Keeping their reactions to God's presence private was easy as their faces weren't viewed by millions via television.

On the other hand, Carrie's and Shane's reactions were in plain sight, with nowhere to hide. A long silence elapsed, although it was evident someone should say something. The cameras continued rolling without a commercial break, which would have been the usual protocol. Under normal conditions, the WNN crews could have done this Special Report in their sleep, but the Lord's presence threw everyone off kilter.

It was Carrie who finally broke the awkward silence. "Some of you may think what you've witnessed is an elaborate deception, created with special effects. As an eyewitness, I can assure you it is not a hoax. The university validated that the cadaver had been in their possession for almost six months. Vital organs were removed by surgical residents during instructional teaching sessions. There is no logical way to explain how this man was raised from the dead."

The camera panned to two upholstered chairs to the right of the desk. A man was sitting in one chair, waiting for Carrie to join him.

Shane had thought it a nice touch to conclude the program by interviewing an eyewitness—hopefully to put all the mysticism to rest.

Carrie took the seat opposite the guest and greeted him. "Hello, Kevin, thank you for being here tonight."

"Good to be here … uh … in ways you cannot understand."

Carrie looked directly into the camera. "America, this is Kevin Jefferson, the 'cadaver' who, as you can plainly see, is alive and well."

Gasps filled the studio. Shane's stunned reaction was audibly heard, even though he was off camera. Everyone had assumed the man to be interviewed was an eyewitness, not *the corpse*. But there he was, cadaver-man, very much alive.

"Kevin, tell us a little about yourself."

"My name is Kevin Jefferson. I'm thirty-three years old, born in Pittsburgh to a typical middle-class family. Loved sports as a kid and excelled in baseball, but not much of a student. I played college baseball and was drafted into a minor league team. It was during my time with the Richmond Tornadoes that I was diagnosed with paranoia schizophrenia. Looking back, I can honestly say that I struggled with it my entire life. My psychiatrist tried multiple medications to control my symptoms, but nothing worked."

"How did you end up homeless on the D.C. streets?"

Kevin shifted in his seat. He felt uncomfortable talking about himself, but knew his story needed to be heard. "Side effects of the meds made me dizzy, interfering with my ability to play baseball, so I quit taking them. I played around recreationally with street drugs … got hooked on cocaine. Got arrested a few times for bar fights. My stats dropped quickly, and I was cut from the team.

"Each day got worse. I found myself sucked into a life I didn't want. The schizophrenia took over, engulfing me in a world of

300

confusion, paranoia, voices in my head. I drank or drugged myself until I blacked out. It was the only way I could escape."

"Do you know your cause of death?"

"Nope … probably an overdose."

"What's your last memory?"

"My last memory …" He shifted again and gazed out into the distance as he relived the vivid scene. "Well, I thought I was asleep, dreaming behind a restaurant dumpster, but it wasn't a dream. I was dead. I remember a large, bright being taking me away. Within a few seconds, I realized we were in Heaven. I couldn't believe it.… Heaven was real and I'd made it! My mind was clear for the first time. I felt so alive that my entire time on earth was like a living death." Kevin paused, gazing out into the distance as he reflected. "Funny feeling … discovering that death has more life than living."

Carrie took a deep breath, absorbing the profound statement, then in a virtual whisper, she asked, "What happened next?"

Kevin's attention snapped back to Carrie. "I was standing in front of a tall podium with a big book on it. The book opened and beautiful jewel-like colors shone all around the book and stand. An authoritative voice asked, *What is your name?* I answered, *Kevin Jefferson.* The voice asked, *Is your name written in the Lamb's Book of Life?*

"I thought, *I don't know, is it?* Just as I opened my mouth to say *yes*, I heard myself crying out, 'No!' I desperately wanted to say yes, but I spoke the truth against my will. Then, I was handed a different book. Everything I had ever thought, said or done was written on the pages. The voice commanded me to open the book and asked, *Are your sins—written on the pages—blotted out by the Blood of the Lamb?* I looked at the pages and there was only black and white. Not one spot was red. I couldn't answer the question because I had no way to pay for my wrongdoing.

"Every bad choice, every sinful deed I had ever done was right there in front of my eyes. Couldn't deny it or make up excuses. As bad as the regret was, one scene got to me most of all. Jim Gates, a guy on the baseball team, often told me about his relationship with Jesus, eternal destiny, Heaven and hell and stuff. The guys on the team, me included, gave Jim a hard time about it.

"So ... I told him I didn't need a crutch. Ha! What a joke coming from a drug addict. I brushed him off every time. It wasn't 'til I was cut by the team that I finally said the prayer. I thought I had my ticket to Heaven in my back pocket. You know, only pull it out when ya need it. And that was that. I didn't take it seriously.

"Religion didn't matter. Life after death and Heaven and hell weren't real anyway. I thought when I died, that was the end, but just in case, I had that insurance policy ready to cash in. But man, standing in Heaven, I was required to give an answer. When I heard that voice, I realized I'd blown it! I had the opportunity and I snubbed—no more like *trampled on*—the greatest gift ever offered me ... or anyone else, for that matter."

It was apparent from Kevin's demeanor that his experience had deeply affected him. He pulled himself together and continued. "The voice said, *It is as you say. Your name is not written in My Book. Depart from Me, for I never knew you.*

"I knew I didn't belong in Heaven; I belonged in hell!" Kevin sat on the edge of his seat, adamant about his next point. "I *knew* the truth that *God* was *not* sending me to hell. I *chose* to send myself there while I was alive on this earth. I rejected Jesus!"

Kevin's words suspended in the air as a lingering summons, tugging at the hearts of millions of listeners.

"What happened next?"

"Immediately, the angel took me away. Panic and fear crushed my heart like vice grips. I pleaded for mercy, but I knew it was no use.

I'd already made my choice earlier. We sped away from Heaven's light under a force a million times the gravity of earth. Within seconds, the angel stopped and set me down.

"A frightening hand that looked more like talons grabbed me by the neck. I begged the angel to take me back with him, but as soon as he let go, I was instantly in a black hole. Nothing good there—only the deepest darkness and death. Well, my body was dead, but my spirit was alive—forever! At that moment, I got it ... I mean, the real scoop about hell. Hell is not simply going to sleep and never waking up. And it isn't complete annihilation, either. It-it is never-ending torment. Sharp, burning pain and agony and terror like I never knew existed ...."

Kevin couldn't hold back the tears any longer as he relived the torture. The flood ran down his cheeks, dripping off his chin. Carrie handed him a tissue. He wiped his face before continuing, his sentences broken between tears.

"We all ... groaned and gnashed our teeth ... the heat was blistering—a million times hotter than a steam bath ..." He reached for another tissue. "But that wasn't even the worst part ... it was seeing that parade of every evil thing we had ever done or thought ... made us all vomit ...."

Carrie waited while Kevin regained some control.

"The sound of my screaming was ear-piercing ... and if I wasn't shrieking, others around me were. People cursed Jesus ... begged for mercy, but nothing stopped the torture. I often heard others crying out, 'Don't you know who I am? I'm an important person. I don't belong here!'"

Carrie shuddered as Kevin described the pain, suffering and hopelessness. *Hell isn't a place of joyfully engaging in sin and perversion like many people joke about,* she thought.

"Tell us what it was like returning to your body."

Kevin's eyes changed from hopeless pain to sparkling love and hope. He smiled at the memory of being called away from torment. "All hell froze at something unexpected. A massive hand blazing with white fire came out of nowhere.

"The creatures torturing us seemed confused, and they howled in sheer terror. The fire that burned on the hand ... well, it was full of life and love—opposite of hell's fire, full of death and hatred.

"The hand stopped in front of me. A loud voice like a rushing sound said, *I implored you to come to Me, yet you resisted My many promptings. Gird yourself. Prepare to stand before Me, for it is a frightening thing to be summoned before the Lord without the covering of the Blood.*

"I stepped into the hand and just like that, I was immediately taken out of that horrific place. Next thing I knew, I was looking down at a body, disfigured like a dissected pig. I saw two men—one normal-looking guy and another one that glowed with the same fire as the hand. There were thousands of people watching.

"The voice said to me, *Pray for yourself, Kevin Jefferson, that your name be written in the Book of Life. Condemnation awaits you a second time unless your name is in the Book. Be sober. Be vigilant. Seek Me with all your being for your life is weighed in the balance. Blessings of Heaven await. If you come to Me, I will raise you up as a deliverer to set others free from oppression. I will rebuild you on a sure foundation if only you will open your eyes and see the way of life I have set before you. Warn the multitudes who think saying a simple prayer without acting upon it spares them eternal torment. You will be a sign and a wonder if you choose wisely.*

The studio was silent. Only the faint buzzing of the lights was noticeable. There was no mumbling, no rolling of the eyes at the religious, fanatical, schizophrenic lunatic. Listeners remained keenly absorbed in Kevin's account. The break for a commercial was either ignored or forgotten.

"Who do you think was talking to you?"

"It was His voice. *Jesus* was speaking to me."

"Go on."

"Suddenly, I realized that it was me lying on that gurney. When the Lord's hand put me back into my body, I felt an impact like a collision. I desperately tried to fill my lungs with air and panicked when I couldn't breathe. I tried to scream for help, but no words came out."

Again, tears rolled over his cheeks. A flood of emotions hit him in wave after wave. He bowed his head, covered his face with his hands and quietly sobbed, whispering, "Thank You, Jesus. Thank You."

Carrie reached out and touched his hand. "Kevin, are you, all right? Do you need a break?"

"No ... I'm good." Resolute, he took several deep breaths, lifting his head. "I felt like I was going to suffocate, trapped in my own body. I didn't want to go back. I *couldn't* go back there. I was desperate to live just long enough to make the right decision this time.

"I felt pressure in my chest as my lungs filled with air. At first, I thought it was the man standing over my body performing CPR. Then, I suddenly realized it wasn't a man; it was Jesus, breathing life into my lungs! Every cell in my body felt like it was exploding ... but I wasn't being ripped apart this time. I was being healed! I felt blood flowing through my veins ... and every cell in my body gulping in oxygen. With every beat of my heart, more life flowed into me. Muscle tissue and organs grew back! I was strong and alive! I gasped as I took the first breath on my own ...." Kevin paused, took a deep breath as if reliving that moment, then exclaimed, "I came back to life through the power and love of Jesus the Christ, the Holy One of God!"

His last statement, spoken with authority, left Carrie breathless as the magnitude of Kevin's account touched her soul. She was reliving what she had witnessed, only this time, from Kevin's very personal perspective.

"Do you have any lingering problems?"

"No … I feel like a new creature. I see life so differently. It's not about here; it's about *there!* Sounds crazy, but I look forward to death now. I've made my choice and that's to surrender what life I have left to the One who took me out of hell."

Kevin looked into the camera. More gasps filled the studio as his eyes changed from brown to orange. The view zoomed in on his orange, fiery eyes as the glow changed from orange to bright white. Then the cameras backed away to reveal the glow forming around his body. Shane dashed from the set in fear, but Carrie stayed put. She had seen the same Fire in Jason's eyes and the same white light on his body.

"My name is Kevin Jefferson, the cadaver-man brought back to life. Don't put your decision off for later, because you don't know when you're going to die. Accept Jesus' offer of life *now*. As evil presses in, the time is coming when it will be harder to pull away from this world and believe on the only One who can save you. My testimony is a sign and wonder of God and I was sent by God for only one thing—to tell you that it's all true—Heaven, hell, God and His Son Jesus. *Now* is your time to choose Him. You will not get a second chance."

37

Deep State Stalkers

Wendy Galloway was the Block Watch Captain for the Taylors' street. She lived for this assignment like one driven to achieve a long-studied career. She took great pride in being up to date on the neighborhood happenings just as a watch dog protects his master—at least, that's how she justified her nosiness. On several occasions, she had actually halted a few instances of adolescent mischief and two burglaries, fueling her fervor all the more.

One of the neighbors Wendy liked most was Barb Taylor, who was such a kind lady that she just drew folks to her. Barb even organized meals for people who were recovering from surgery or a death in the family. In fact, she had done that very thing for Wendy after her husband died.

Not that they had a super-deep friendship or anything. The Taylors were so busy that she and Barb hadn't done much more than exchange a little chit chat here and there or wave at each other from across the street. But Wendy liked the Taylors—and that was that. She was sympathetic to the invasion of their privacy and felt it her civic duty to protect them from meddlesome gawkers, one of which she was definitely *not*.

When the news crews descended on the Taylors' front lawn, Wendy boldly walked across the street and demanded an answer from one of the reporters, offering her services for possible interviews, of course. To her disappointment, no reporter ever called.

By this time, the media's only interest in Senator Taylor was to disparage him as a religious dogmatist unfit for office. Things had mostly died down from the day Jason's resurrection was reported. Fortunately, Jason was not publicly identified as the "glowing man" of the debate, keeping things status quo. Today, only a scattered presence of three obscure media crews dotted the Taylor's street hoping to scoop the big players with evidence of Dan's lunacy.

Wendy paid little attention to the marked trucks with logos plastered on their sides. She did, however, take note of something most people would have completely overlooked—two men in an unmarked SUV. Binoculars revealed an open car window with something resting on it. *I bet it's a listening device*, she thought, ever on the lookout for a conspiracy.

The vehicle had parked under a large oak tree in an unsuccessful attempt to be less conspicuous. *At least they should have disguised themselves as repairmen of some sort,* Wendy theorized. She happily called the Bethesda police as she watched safely from her front porch.

* * *

About the same time, Dan did his routine check on the media truck count for the day. *Hmmm ... only three today.* A sip of coffee. *Hopefully they're losing interest,* he thought. But then he noticed the SUV with the camera and the long-distance listening device, barely resting on the edge of the car's open window. Dan casually walked away, purposely leaving the curtains open to hide the fact he had spotted them.

He turned on the TV, pressing the volume a bit higher than normal. Barb hurried into the room. He motioned her over and he drew her close, making it look like a loving smooch, then whispered in her ear, "Take a gander down the street to the left. Have you seen that SUV parked around here before?"

Barb returned the kiss and left for her sneak peek. They convened in the kitchen. "No … no one on this street owns a black SUV that I know of. Who are they?"

"I think the government's watching us. Deep State fears what happened at the prayer breakfast. Likely our presence at the Frederick debate earned us a spot smack dab in the middle of their radar. Thousands of converts scare them because they can't be controlled. If I'm right, we need to stay alert. They take people out of their way— plant fake evidence or …" He hesitated. Didn't want to frighten Barb.

"Or murder?" she finished his thought.

"Yeah … too many convenient coincidences right before court testimonies that could take them down. Discredit or eradicate us, and the message goes away."

Barb shrugged and topped off her coffee. Her unfazed reaction surprised Dan. "I wish I had your faith, hon. He filled his cup and walked out onto the front porch. Taking his cue, she followed.

The two of them acted as if they were enjoying a warm fall morning in the porch rocking chairs, but Dan's motive wasn't relaxation. He wanted the guys in the SUV to know they had been spotted. All it took was one friendly wave.

Flustered that they had been found out, one of the men in the vehicle pushed the ignition button, but instead of starting the engine, the alarm system blared. The vehicles lights flashed and the doors instantly locked.

Cameras rolled. The bored, obscure media just got a story—albeit not the one they had come to film.

Barb's phone rang. It was the Bethesda Police Department inquiring if the Taylors had a security detail parked near their home.

The officer told her a neighbor had called about a suspicious SUV parked on the street. *Probably Wendy,* Barb thought.

She assured the officer they had no connection with the SUV. He informed her that a patrol car was already on its way. Just then, as promised, a Bethesda police car pulled around the corner and flashed its lights while giving a quick *whoop whoop* of the siren.

In a few minutes there were five police cars, lights flashing, surrounding the SUV. The added backup signaled to Dan that the unwelcome observers had weapons.

As Dan and Barb stood to get a better view, an officer jogged over to them. It was Captain Pete Kowalski of the Bethesda P.D. "Better go back inside 'til we I.D. these guys. Could be a threat, Senator."

Barb calmly changed topics, asking Pete about the new baby. "How's Michelle doing? Is the baby sleeping through the night yet?"

"No, but we don't care. After trying for so many years to start a family, lack of sleep is no big deal. I actually don't mind getting up at night and holding her. I dreamed of this for so long that I cherish each time I'm able to look at that innocent face." Pete beamed.

"Speaking of 'innocent,'" Dan jumped in, "I'm not so sure these guys *are*. I'd say they're up to no good with their telephoto lens and listening devices pointed at my house. A timely glitch set off their alarm."

"Have you received any threats?" Pete wanted to know.

"No, just some stuff on the back porch got moved around. I thought it was reporters or kids, but it was probably these guys."

Police pulled weapons and pointed them at the SUV. The doors opened and the two men exited the vehicle, arms behind their heads and humiliation on their faces. If these guys were professional surveillance agents, this kind of thing should never happen—*ever*.

Police officers quickly pushed them to the ground. The men's weapons were confiscated and handcuffs slapped on their wrists while their arms were awkwardly bent behind their backs.

"Pete, can you give me the skinny on who they are?"

"I'll see what I can find out, Senator. Wait here." Pete winked.

He returned with news that the trunk contained an item labeled *Property of Slater Defense & Security, Inc.*, a well-known subcontractor to the NSA and CIA. They often did the dirty—highly illegal—work of spying on American citizens for underhanded government purposes. It was a back-door scam to protect both the NSA and CIA, enabling them to claim innocence from any involvement in directly violating civil liberties.

"Thanks." Dan leaned in closer to Pete to have a private word. "Any way I can get a look at what's on that camera and hear what's on that recording?"

"Might be possible." Pete nodded. He knew he shouldn't, but he liked Dan. In all the commotion, it was likely no one would notice.

Pete went to the SUV and volunteered to mark the devices as evidence. He took them to his squad car and motioned to Dan. Dan slipped into the car's backseat, where the camera was located, while Pete stood watch.

Scrolling through the photos, Dan found shots of his house from all angles—Jason coming and going, Barb leaving and returning, the mail carrier, the FedEx guy, the lawn crew—all activity from morning 'til night. *Huh… I was right … They were fishing for dirt,* he thought.

Pete poked his head into the car. "Better wrap it up."

Dan got out of the car and quietly thanked Pete. Nothing incriminating was on the recording, just Dan and Barb talking about what to have for dinner. There was nothing usable on the camera, either, but the Deep State was collecting data for a reason.

"What's goin' on, Senator?" Pete whispered. "Is this a national security issue?"

Dan didn't answer the question. "Do me a big favor," he said. "Detain them in your lock-up, but be careful. These guys are probably former Special Forces. If they escape—and they will try—all this could disappear as if it never happened. Get my meaning?"

"Yeah, I gotcha," Pete said as he stuck out his chin and rubbed it. He looked at Dan with a knowing look in his eyes and a slight nod of his head.

"Do what you can to prevent them from making a phone call for as long as possible," Dan continued. "Don't question them and don't let them lawyer up. I'll get some FBI agents to come take them off your hands as soon as I can. Let me take a picture of their I.D.s and faces to run against facial recognition software ... and send me a copy of their fingerprints. Names on the I.D.s are fake, guaranteed."

Pete agreed and popped the camera and audio recording in the trunk. He had his officers put the two men in the back of his car. Then he motioned to a rookie—his nephew—whom he could trust. "Cal, I've got an undercover assignment for ya'... sort of off the books ... get my drift?"

Cal nodded.

"I wanna know who comes lookin' for this SUV. Report to me and *only* me. Do not approach. Got it?"

Cal was overly eager to please. He saluted. "Yes sir, yes sir."

"Cal, just do the job. No salutin'. Undercover, got it?"

"Yeah, sure."

Pete informed Dan that he would leave the SUV in place. An undercover officer would watch, then report to Pete as to who retrieved it. After the SUV was picked up, Pete would increase patrols on the street.

Dan shook his friend's hand. Barb gave Pete a hug goodbye and sent her love to Michelle and the baby.

As soon as the police officers drove off with their detainees, Wendy ran to the Taylors' to get the scuttlebutt. Dan and Barb chatted with Wendy a bit, telling her just enough to satisfy her curiosity, but withholding certain details. Wendy said she would increase her watch patrols and inform the neighbors to be on the alert for burglars. She volunteered to do a door-to-door sweep, encouraging neighbors to sign up for the MyNeighbor App, a social network for the neighborhood that would enable instant alerts for any unusual activity. With her mission clear, she promised to be on it.

Barb took Dan's hand as they walked. "The alarm and locked doors were no accident."

Dan could only shake his head "You must be right, because I've never known of *any* Slater guys ever being in a spot like *that*! Pretty ironic ... arrested by local police." Dan laughed.

As soon as they were back inside the house, Dan hugged Barb. "Thanks, sweetie, for believing in me all these years. Your faith sure paid off.

"I need to call a friend in the Bureau ... someone I can trust. Deep State has tentacles in all agencies. I've got a guy in mind. He knows Slater's a slime outfit and hates them as much as I do. Someone high up always gets them off the hook. I want that source exposed."

"Now *that* would take an act of God."

"I hope Pete can hold them off long enough to make them think they're not getting bailed out. There was a picture of one of the guys with his family in a wallet—a real rookie mistake. He'll want to get home for Thanksgiving. He just might cough up the right person."

"If they're after us, will they be after Gregor and Jean, too?" Barb asked. "Maybe we'd better tell them to be on the alert for ... this sounds ridiculous ... but be looking out for spies. We don't know when, where and how all the attacks will come, but we have to expect it now."

Dan pulled out a burner phone and signaled Gregor to call him back on another burner, according to Diego's plan. The word went to all team members: Keep your guard up. This was definitely a shot in the war against them. This time, though, it had been divinely diverted.

Barb grabbed Dan's hand. "Oh ... hey ... before you call your FBI friend ... uh..."

"What? What is it?"

"Remember when we first met Carrie Summers at the Capital Grand Hotel meeting?"

"Yeah ... but can this wait?"

"No, I've been meaning to tell you since that night. Do you remember when I stared at her for a long time?"

"Who doesn't? It made everyone really uncomfortable. What was that about anyway?"

"She's the one."

"She's the one ... what?" Dan's dazed expression revealed that he was clueless.

"You know ... *the one* ... Our son is going to marry her. I don't know how I can explain this other than ... I just know."

Dan lifted one eyebrow. *Why do women have to share things at weirdly inappropriate times?* "Uh ... OK ... so you tellin' him?"

"Absolutely not! I think the Lord just wants us to know so we're not shocked. Jason and Carrie have to make that decision for themselves. We'll not mention this until the day they announce their engagement. Then, I'll share it and *only* then. Agreed?" demanded Barb.

"Agreed. Am I excused?"

"Oh you ...."

Dan smiled, gave Barb a peck on the cheek and left to make the phone call.

38

"Professor" Jean

The Frederick campus was abuzz. Faculty, students, and former ruffians, along with visiting teachers, arrived and made their way to their assignments. Lecture halls and classrooms were quickly filling with eager students, even though no university classes had been scheduled for the week.

Jean welcomed people as they filed into her small lecture hall. A lingering excitement filled the air from the miraculous manifestation of God's power during the debate. Some jubilantly marched into the room, elated in their newfound freedom from whatever sin, addiction or past hurts had controlled them. However, she sensed a couple of people who were not triumphant, at least not yet.

Silence fell as Jean asked everyone to bow their heads. As she prayed, a portal joining earth with Heaven seemed to open above the campus. Truth rushed like a boundless waterfall, ready to give life.

After a chorus of *amens,* she began her lecture with a simple question. "What was Jesus' purpose in coming to us as a man?"

A long pause as her students searched their meager knowledge of the Bible to find an answer.

"As an example to be a good person?" someone ventured. "Like … do unto others as you want them to do to you?"

"He healed the sick!" yelled a man who had been healed of a lifelong, painful condition the night of the debate.

One joyful college student stood on his chair, unable to contain his excitement. "To take me to Heaven, cuz I'm goin' there now!" He shouted a war whoop of victory with both hands held high. "Woo hoo!"

The room erupted in grateful agreement, as so many were now relishing the hope of a life following Jesus. Jean, knowing full well the enemy's *modus operandi*—to steal their joy and diminish their faith—prayed, *Lord, don't ever let them leave their first love.* In a minute, the room quieted. There was soft murmuring about which answer was correct.

She walked toward the tall windows, stared out for a moment and then turned to her students. "Jesus said, 'I must preach the good news of the Kingdom of God to the other towns as well; for I was sent for this purpose.' He came to tell us about His Kingdom, His government.

"There are two realms. One we are very familiar with because we experience it with our five senses—the kingdom of this world which Lucifer rules over. The other realm can only be experienced when the Holy Spirit dwells in us—the Kingdom of God. Every soul belongs to one of the two."

A young college student raised her hand. "Hi, I'm Lisa. That makes it sound like people who don't go to church are worshipping the devil. Aren't they just kind of in between … like on the fence? Like isn't earth a waiting place?"

"That's what Lucifer would like you to believe, but that philosophy is not God's truth; it's a lie. Jesus said, 'Whoever is not with Me is against Me, and whoever does not gather with Me scatters.' Only two states; there is no third option. If you are not born into God's Kingdom, then by default, you remain under Lucifer's rule."

Lisa still objected. "But kind people go to Heaven. You know, like people serving in humanitarian projects ... like ... well, those who help the homeless and stuff."

"No, I'm sorry, sweetie, that's just not what the Bible says. Let me ask this: Why do we need a Savior in the first place?"

From the back of the room, someone shouted, "Adam and Eve sinned in the Garden!"

"OK, good. Let's define sin. Sin is missing the mark of perfect obedience to God's will. The first two people lived in perfect relationship with God as citizens under His rulership until they disobeyed when they ate the fruit from the Tree of the Knowledge of Good and Evil. God explicitly told them not to eat that fruit, because if they did, they would surely die. Lucifer—who sinned against God and was cast out of Heaven—suggested to Eve that's not *really* what God meant. He suggested to Eve, 'You will not surely die.'

"Eve believed Lucifer. Note that she couldn't claim ignorance because she reiterated to Lucifer exactly what God said. No, she blatantly disobeyed God's clear directive. Her sin caused a cataclysmic event because man was designed to be ruled by the Creator—by Him and only Him."

Dr. Jacobs, mathematics professor, made a point. "But they didn't really die ... well, at least, not for a long time."

"No, their bodies didn't instantly drop dead, but their sin caused immediate spiritual death, severing their perfect communion with God. Souls are eternal. If their souls were no longer ruled by God, what realm ruled them?"

The professor spoke tentatively as this was a new perspective to him. "So, if sin cut them off from God's rule ... they are governed by the ruler of this world ... under Lucifer's dominion."

"Right. And if their souls are under Lucifer's rulership, where will their souls continue to exist when their bodies die?"

"Uh ... well ... they would be sentenced to hell." His face turned white as this truth hit him hard. "Everyone ... is condemned unless ... God is the ruler of their life."

"Yes, that's the hard, cold fact of life. We all deserve hell because we all fall short of God's perfect will; we all sin. But His love made a way. God temporarily covered Adam and Eve's sin through animal sacrifice, making clothes from skins. Physical nakedness, however, was not the problem. Covering their naked bodies was only a picture of what was happening in the spiritual realm. Their disobedience exposed them to the world of evil. Their nature was corrupted, resulting in lost relationship with the Creator."

At that moment, the same young man who had stood on his chair had an epiphany. "So that's why people sacrificed animals! I mean, it's weird, but I get it now. What changed? Like ... no one sacrifices *animals* anymore!"

"Jesus—wholly God and wholly man—*lived* his life and *gave* his life as the perfect sinless blood sacrifice once and for all, making a way for you to restore relationship with God. His Blood acquits your sin if you believe and continue in actively choosing to do His will.

"Lucifer is the ruler of this world. His government: pure evil. His goal: separating you from God. If you are not a disciple of Jesus, Lucifer already holds your soul captive. But Jesus paid the ransom, which can free you from the rule of sin and Lucifer's grip. Jesus' sinless life and shed Blood opens the door for anyone to belong to God and live in His Heavenly Kingdom forever. The door is open, but you must walk through it."

Brenda, another Frederick student, commented. "But I said a prayer a long time ago. Haven't I been saved since then?"

"Well, maybe, maybe not. Saying a onetime prayer doesn't guarantee salvation. Jesus said, 'If you love Me, you will keep My commandments.' Following His Words makes you more like Him in character, which is fruit. Jesus said that the branch in Him—a believer attached to Him—that doesn't produce fruit is cut off. In a parable, Jesus called a servant who failed to bring increase on his master's investment a slothful, worthless servant, fit only to be cast out into outer darkness. And, the Parable of the Sower says that all four types of people heard and received the seed in their hearts—the Word of salvation—but only one produced lasting fruit. Which of the four abided—endured, persevered—in Jesus?"

"The one who kept producing fruit?"

"Right," Jean affirmed. "Jesus expects us to produce fruit with what He has given."

"But if I have the Holy Spirit, isn't fruitfulness guaranteed?"

"If producing fruit was automatic, Peter wouldn't have urged us to be diligent, making *every effort* to continue growing in godly character. It takes cultivation—effort to study the Word, effort to resist sin, effort to obey, effort to pray, effort to serve … sometimes effort to love. Yielding to the Holy Spirit while doing these things, nurtures your heart in Christ keeping it tender toward Him. Have you cultivated Christ-like character through prayer, obedience and studying His Word? Have you matured in the fruit of the Spirit?"

Brenda hung her head. "Honestly … no … I hardly read the Bible and, I have to admit, most of my prayers are token … like before a meal or an exam." She suddenly lifted her head. "But what about grace? If Jesus paid for sin, then aren't we all forgiven anyway? It's not like I'm a murderer or anything like that."

"Don't misunderstand. No one can *earn* salvation by doing things, but faith without spiritual disciplines is dead. If you really belong to Jesus, your actions will show it," Jean corrected. "Everyone's sins are not automatically forgiven, but grace and forgiveness are always granted to a genuinely repentant heart. A flippant attitude toward sin is wrong. We must hate sin as much as God hates it. The more you set out to *purposefully* do God's will, the more He is able to sculpt you into a closer resemblance to the character of Christ.

"Jesus knew no sin—didn't sin even once—yet He became sin for our sakes so that we could partake in His right standing before the Father. It cost Jesus everything to give the gift of salvation, but to receive that gift costs us nothing; it is given by grace through believing faith. However, to walk out that salvation costs you everything. Jesus said, 'For whoever would save his life will lose it, but whoever loses his life for My sake will find it.' You cannot omit Jesus' Lordship from the salvation package."

An older gentleman stood. "I grew up in the Church, still go. My granddaughter dragged me to the debate, and boy, am I glad I went! My church focuses on social issues—being kind, forgiving others, giving to charity, speaking positivity into your own life and others' lives, and having community. Reading self-help books seems more popular than reading the Bible. Never once did I hear a sermon about sin, repentance, the Kingdom of God or hell. I don't even know if my pastor believes hell exists.

"I watched Kevin Jefferson's interview. All those years I sat in church … I really didn't have a clue." The man's eyes teared up and his voice cracked. "I thought I *was* a Christian … if I had died before Friday, I would have …" his voice trailed off as he sighed and sat down.

"Hmmm … the message of repentance is unpopular," Jean said, nodding sympathetically. "Don't rely on someone else to feed you. In the end, it's your responsibility to know His truth. We live in a hostile world where Lucifer schemes to kill and destroy—believers and non-believers alike—and he's successful by watering down the true message or creating an entirely different one. It's not enough to simply *believe* that Jesus died for your sin. James reminds us that even demons believe and shudder but what good does mere belief do for them?

"Jesus commanded that we make disciples not believers. We must become students of His Word, steadfastly living by it, and testing what we hear against Scripture. The only way to protect ourselves against Lucifer's false doctrines is to know Truth as it is written in all of Scripture—both Old and New Testaments. Obedience to God's Word is not legalistic with extra-biblical 'rules' nor does a slip-up send you to hell. But faith should be an outward manifestation of our inward man's state of mind. As we mature, we should bear fruit from our characteristic tendency to obey out of love for our Savior to do what pleases Him.

"If our lifestyle doesn't matter, why does God's Word admonish us to stop doing things He hates? Is sinning loving God?"

She waited a moment but no one responded.

"An emphatic *no!* Yes, Jesus conquered sin through the work of the cross, but we have to exercise His victory by putting it to use in our lives. Choosing sin rejects His triumph over Lucifer leaving it dormant." Jean took a deep breath hoping she was getting through to them—not just their minds but their hearts.

"Paul again makes the point that there are only two options: You are either a slave to sin leading to death—meaning hell—or a slave to God leading to eternal life—meaning Heaven. You cannot separate the person of Jesus from His Word. It is impossible to love Jesus and ignore His Word because He *is* the Word. Loving Jesus is an action of the will, not a feeling. In your obedience, He gives you the power of His Spirit so that you may share in His divine nature."

It was beginning to click with Jean's listeners that a simple one-time prayer of salvation wasn't the gospel's message. It goes deeper than that, demanding commitment and continued growth.

"The Bible is clear; we fight an enemy. God provides armor and weaponry, but you must put on that armor and take up your weapons, because the enemy is relentless. Obeying Jesus is *the* most potent weapon against the powers and principalities of darkness. His commandments are for your survival; there is safety in obedience. It's not complicated! If you do what He says, you can't help but bear fruit, and the more of Him that is in you, the less influence Lucifer has over you.

"Each person is commanded to love the Lord with all his heart, soul, mind and strength, making God priority, giving Him every part of his life. Ask Him to write His Word on your heart. Picture it as if He was carving His character into your bones so that all you do originates from the abundance of the Holy Spirit dwelling in you. This is His will for you."

"OK, so what happens now?" a student asked.

"Right now, is the time of the Final Awakening, the Lord's mercy poured out to open our eyes. Paul said we must present our bodies as a living sacrifice, holy and acceptable to God, which is our spiritual worship. Lucifer will press you to conform to the ideologies of this world. Don't accept compromise in your life. The more you grow in Jesus' nature, more of His power is able to flow through you to help other people. You have been set free; now, introduce that freedom to others."

A man toward the back stood to speak. Some huffed in distrust and turned away.

"When I was younger, I wanted to believe, but never crossed from this realm to God's realm. I finally quit trying to understand. But after the events of Friday night … well … why does faith seem so easy for others and hard for me? Why does God seem impossible to understand ... and well ...?" He gave up in frustration, hung his head and took his seat.

To Jean's surprise, it was President Hammond, the man who was so opposed to them at the debate. *Hmmm ... was he here to harass or is he one of the two I sensed was struggling?* she thought.

Hammond's comment was prompted by memories as a seminary dropout. Never finding satisfaction in the professors' pat answers, he had left seminary, disappointed, confused and empty. If Scripture was truth, why didn't he experience the things written in it?

His professors had seen him as a troublemaker, asking searching questions they definitely were not interested in attempting to answer. Their message was to do the work on the syllabus, don't ruffle any feathers, get your seminary degree and preach the same dry, meaningless clichés from the seminary lecture halls. To Hammond, his professors were academic fools who neither loved God nor lived what they preached.

There had to be more, but he had never been able to tap into the missing power, so he'd walked away, suppressing his inner conflict. He'd left it all behind, sure that religion was a crutch for weak fools who didn't have the intelligence or fortitude to deal with life's issues. He had proudly lived under that philosophy ... until now.

"Yeah, I get what you're saying, President Hammond," Jean offered kindly. "Sometimes I feel like I'm trying to play checkers while God is playing multidimensional chess. We are all equally loved, but not all set on identical paths. Some people will have greater challenges to overcome while others will have lesser. We each play a role, but most often, we don't understand because of our limited perspective. God's position is all-seeing, all-knowing and all-powerful. From His vantage point, it all makes sense. He sees the beginning and the end simultaneously. The future is history to God."

A girl with her hair covered in a hijab raised her hand. "My name is Rajah and my family is Muslim. Friday night, I gave my life to Jesus."

The room erupted in spontaneous cheers.

Once the listeners quieted, Rajah continued, "I tried to get them to watch the debate on TV, but they refused and demanded that I leave." Tears rolled off her cheeks. "I am dead to them, to my friends, to my community. My whole life was taken from me, but I just can't turn back ... not knowing what I know now. I don't understand why I must go through this pain for doing what is right."

"Oh, honey, I'm so sorry." Jean handed a student a box of tissues that was passed back to the broken-hearted girl. "Jesus said He didn't come to bring peace, but a sword, setting one against another— mother against daughter, father against son. When you live under God's rule, those under Lucifer's rule will hate you. Jesus said, 'The gate is narrow and the way is hard that leads to life.'

"As a believer, each of you is required to live in His spiritual realm, submitting to His will. Trust Him innocently and completely, like a child, even when what happens in this world makes no sense. I'm learning to just live the day, obey to the best of my understanding and leave it at that."

"I'm afraid for them," Rajah stated with a tender pleading in her tone. "They're lost to God and, from what you said earlier, they have condemned themselves."

"God wishes that none should perish, but that all should reach repentance," Jean said gently. "Pray that the enemy's hold on them be destroyed and their hearts open to receive the Truth. Even though their words and actions show hatred toward you, love them as Jesus commands. God is not out of control. Believe He has a plan."

Jean redirected her thoughts from the courageous young woman to address the entire group. "All of history is like a great symphony.

There are different chords, notes and timing. Some people have prominent roles and will be seen by the masses, while others remain unseen. What makes the music of the symphony so great is that each is under the Conductor's leading. Each person must perform his part with all of his heart.

"This symphony of God's children working in the great power of the Holy Spirit as one under His direct supervision is the sound of Heaven filling the earth. New music is produced as His people faithfully play their roles to the fullest, carefully watching the divine Maestro, each playing at the right time with gifts He has imparted. The sound of Heaven for the Final Awakening will be heard across the planet."

The girl sighed. "Maybe my community will believe in this Final Awakening."

"I understand your angst over your family, Rajah. I pray they will," Jean empathized, then again spoke to the group. "As harvesters, you will be the conduit of the Holy Spirit's love and healing power. See people as God sees them, a beloved lost child He desires to come home to Him."

Jean looked at Hammond and heard the Holy Spirit speak, *Ask him if he believes.* "President Hammond, do you believe?"

"I saw a cadaver raised to life and speak of Heaven and hell. I *want* to believe."

"May I pray for you?"

"Please," Hammond replied as he bowed his head.

The room was silent and still. The only sound heard was Jean's soft footsteps as she moved to stand behind him, gently resting her hands on his shoulders. She felt his body relax and saw a picture of his heart encrusted in unbelief. As she prayed, the hard encasement melted away like wax as the Holy Spirit began His work.

She prayed for one man, but it was a prayer for every person in the room. The presence of God was undeniable and inescapable, swaddling each soul like a newborn baby. The stone pillars of hurt and bondage fractured and crumbled to the ground, exposing tender hearts. Any lingering toll of sin was pulverized into a fine dust and lay in a pile at their feet.

Then it came. A familiar wind of warmth and freedom swept throughout the room, brushing over each soul as it blew away the powdery heaps from past lives—a new beginning, ransom activated, born anew and set free with claimed citizenship in the Kingdom of God.

39

Benediction

The week of intense teaching was over. The Lord had fed even the youngest of believers the meat of His truth. Tonight, all gathered at the Hammond Center for a commissioning before taking the Lord's message to the community.

The arena was at full capacity since more had been added to the number of believers during the week. The atmosphere was bittersweet. A mild sadness hovered at the separation of new friends, bonded as brothers and sisters, countered by the expectation of what was to come.

As Gregor walked to center stage, the buzz of conversation stopped. Every eye focused on him. He scanned the faces, marveling at their number, and thought, *This is the fulfillment of things spoken thirty years ago. Thank You, Lord, for all these added to Your Kingdom.*

"My brothers and sisters in Christ, I am overwhelmed by God's mercy and lovingkindness. When I came here a week ago for the debate, you were a divided and confused bunch. I honestly thought a brawl might break out."

The crowd agreed with some soft chuckles.

"We witnessed the demonstration of the Creator's power through Kevin Jefferson's resurrection. God Almighty touched your hearts, filling you with hope to live in the truth and life of Jesus our Savior. What a change!"

The crowd cheered in celebration of their citizenship in Heaven. After several seconds, Gregor lifted his hands to quiet the group. It was right for them to express joy in their new lives, but the weightiness in his heart had to be heard.

"Well, it's been an amazing time together of teaching, healing and deliverance, and you are right to celebrate. We've seen miracles and experienced His glorious presence and His power to transform lives. Right now, you feel unstoppable as your hearts are filled with overwhelming joy and love for your Savior and victory over the enemy. The Final Awakening *has* begun with power, signs and wonders, but I warn you, there is a cost. Jesus gave you everything, and He expects you to give Him everything.

"God desires that all come to the knowledge of the Truth. I believe multitudes of souls will be saved from hell's torment during this Final Awakening; however, evil will fight you every step of the way."

Gregor wished he had a more uplifting message for tonight, not one of dire warning.

"Even though Jesus is moving mightily, do not be surprised when the world hates you on account of His name. You learned this week that Lucifer is the ruler of this world and hates everything God loves. Tolerance for the name of Jesus will disappear as Lucifer is given greater authority. Other religious messages will be acceptable, even endorsed, but the name of Jesus and the gospel of His truth will become repulsive and illegal. In this world, you will be abandoned, ridiculed, harassed, beaten, slandered, falsely accused and possibly jailed. Even loved ones will betray you.

"It seems an unlikely source, but expect opposition from the Church. Some will accuse you of preaching apostasy and portray you as a lunatic cultist."

He stepped from behind the podium, desiring to talk with each one as a loving father, not a stranger preaching at them.

"Even so, don't be afraid. Fortify yourself in His truth and in prayer. Whatever troubles you endure, they're only for a moment. Maintain a Kingdom perspective by honoring His commandments. Keep your eye on the prize—eternal life in Heaven—and remind yourself that this life is temporary. 'Let us hold resolutely to the hope we profess.'

"Therefore, boldly stand against the schemes of evil in the confidence of the Lord's protection. God has the last word, not him who will be mocked at the end when he is thrown into the lake of fire."

Gregor paused. A wave of love rushed through him as he felt the Lord's heart for these disciples.

"I plead with you to guard your relationship with Jesus, as it is your most valuable asset. Abiding in Him does not rest on a foundation of emotion; love is an act of the will. Beware you don't run after encounters because they never supersede the Word. Everything you need to know about God is in the Bible; you need nothing else. Even though we have seen and will again see mighty works of God in signs and wonders, the Pearl of Great Price is *not* the experience; the priceless treasure is Jesus and Him alone."

Gregor's heart ached that none fall away like a seed snatched by the enemy before it took root in Christ. His father's heart for these new believers pleaded with them to stay the course—growing, enduring, and overcoming to run after Jesus so that they might receive the prize.

"To love Him is to do His will—grand or mundane—so if the

feelings you have today fade or even disappear, don't abandon your first love in weariness. Love for Jesus is not only a strong weapon and shield against the enemy, it is the greatest gift you will ever receive and the greatest gift you can give. He will impart to you the ability to love others as He loves.

"Jesus said when you host a banquet, invite the poor, the crippled, the lame, and the blind, and you will be blessed. His love seeks the impoverished, the despised and the forgotten. Your reward awaits you after you have completed His will for you here on earth."

He pulled a chair to center stage and sat to tell a story.

"Years ago, in a vision, I saw my wife and myself in a Middle Eastern country. A man stood over us as we were on our knees, with our hands tied behind us and heads covered with black hoods. He held a large sword above, ready to decapitate us. I asked if I could speak before my death. Surprisingly, he agreed.

"I stood and he removed the hood, uncovering my face. I looked into the eyes of the swordsman and spoke to him with the love of Jesus, saying, 'I forgive you. One day, my God will appear to you. As a mighty soldier for Jesus, *you* will bring many into His kingdom. You'll look back at this day and be filled with deep regret and sorrow. But I rejoice in my death because I will see God and live in His presence forever. May Jesus' peace come quickly to you. I will greet you, my friend, when you arrive in Heaven, and we will have much to share.'

"Many of you in this room now will die as martyrs for His name's sake. If you belong to Christ, there is no fear in death; it is your reward. Think of Stephen, the first martyr, who saw Jesus standing at the right hand of the Father while he was being stoned. Scriptures often refer to Jesus as *sitting* at the right hand of the Father. At Stephen's death, Jesus *stood* to honor him. How awesome that our

God would rise from His throne for just one—a profoundly great and humbling honor. Therefore, run the race to the finish line."

Gregor stood and returned to the podium. When he bowed his head, tears dripped onto his open Bible. The arena was silent for over five minutes as he waited for the Holy Spirit's direction. Jean, who was sitting with the team in the front row, took Maria by the hand and led her up the stage stairs.

Gregor reached out, putting his arms around each of the women. Maria began to sing, so personally and intimately to Jesus that only Gregor and Jean could hear. However, her barely audible voice moved something in the spiritual realm, causing the ground under the campus to shake.

An atmosphere of surrender filled the arena. As one body, the crowd of thousands was immersed in a profound desire for Jesus to take absolute control of their lives. With arms outstretched as if trying to reach Heaven, they cried out that His perfect love would flow through them to the lost.

A sweet aroma went up as the Fire of Heaven consumed the thousands of lives willingly laid on the golden altar before the throne. Heaven opened as if the roof of the building was lifted away. There, visible to all inside, was One seated high on a throne and Jesus seated to His right. The voices of thousands upon thousands of angelic singers rang from Heaven:

You are worthy, O Lord our God,
To receive glory and honor and power,
For You were before the beginning,
And all things were made by You and for You.
Jesus, the Lamb of God, is the Life and Light of men.
The Light shines in the darkness,
and the darkness will not overcome it.

Lightning flashed and thunder rumbled. The swirling, white Fire of Heaven in the midst of the throne suddenly spiraled downward to inscribe the Fear of the Lord upon each heart.

Outside, a large cloud hovered over the brick building. It darkened the sky and then dropped to the earth like a thick blanket of pure white fog, completely covering the arena.

Abruptly, the sound of a roaring fire sounded. White hot flames shot upward from the roof hundreds of feet into the sky, causing the cloud to glow with the brightness of the sun. Horrified that thousands of people were trapped in the building, phones lit up as bystanders pressed 911 into keypads.

Unknown to the people inside, fire trucks and ambulances arrived. As emergency personnel attempted to enter, the cloud pulled them in and onto their knees.

A dispatcher called for her administrator. "Sir, listen. What is that?"

A few seconds passed. "Sounds like wind. Is that singing? Why doesn't the fire crew respond?"

"Unknown, sir, but there's an event tonight. Arena's packed."

"Oh, hell, can it get worse? I'll call neighboring departments."

At first, it was reported that the Hammond Center at Frederick University—filled to capacity for a religious service—was a blazing inferno. Unusual circumstances categorized it as a possible terror attack. The cloud that descended was thought to have been a disabling gas because no one attempted to leave the burning building. Fire and police lost communication with their crews who had entered. The worst was feared; thousands could be burned alive.

Towering flames gave the appearance of sure disaster; however, a cameraman noticed that nothing was actually being consumed. "Something's off. A fire of this magnitude and this hot should be demolishing the building, but nothing's changed. This building is burning ... but it's not!"

Inside, Gregor watched as the heavens began to close and the Fire of Heaven retracted to its place before God. Once again, the view above his head was the plain ceiling of a large building.

Outside, onlookers saw the cloud lift as quickly as it had descended. The flames that had engulfed the arena swirled in a tornado-like whirlwind of white fire and disappeared into the sky with the deafening roar of a jet engine.

What can I say? Gregor thought. *He has said it all.* He gave a short salutation. "You are sealed in Him. Go with the Father's heart."

Just as he concluded, President Hammond hurriedly skipped steps up to the stage and jogged over to Gregor.

"Wait, ... I ... I have an important announcement to make." Hammond was breathless with astonishment.

Gregor peered into Hammond's eyes. When he saw the Fire of Heaven in the man's pupils, Gregor handed him the microphone headset.

"We ... we have been in the midst of the holy presence of God ... the Creator of the Universe!" President Hammond stood for a moment, his mental faculties overwhelmed. "The university facilities *must* be available to continue seeking Him. I propose we continue times of gathering for the next four to six weeks. Scheduled classes are canceled and tuition money will be refunded at your request."

The crowd erupted with a loud cheer to the Lord's Glory. Storis and his fellow angels shouted for joy, also. The victorious rumble of voices—human and angelic alike—rattled the chests of bystanders outside the building. Then, the angels sang, allowing their voices to be heard by all present.

The crowd gathered outside was captivated by the heavenly worship. They experienced a sense of frightening confusion, but the sound was so gripping, they stayed and listened in awe. The words of the songs were not of any earthly language, yet all believers sang along with the angels, expressing their devotion to the King of Love in words they had never heard before ....

40

Sent Out

During the following weeks of teaching and training, some stood out as mature believers, equipped to minister to the community. They were eager to reach the lost and came together to seek the Holy Spirit's direction. Teams were organized into groups of people with different but complementary gifts—evangelism, healing, prophecy, mercy, wisdom and teaching.

The first to hit the streets that day called themselves Team Alpha, only because they were the first to leave. Tim Hunter and Vicki Morrison headed the group. Both—in their mid-twenties—loved God with all their heart, soul, mind and strength, even when it was difficult and isolating. They were faithful from their teens to live a life pleasing to the Lord, following His commandments without compromise. After weeks of powerful polishing at Frederick, they had gained the necessary tools to lead this unit into the heart of a dangerous city.

Team Alpha's first mission was in Baldwin Park, where gangs, prostitution and drugs flowed as a homogenized mixture. Their assigned street was lined with abandoned houses by the dozens, but one drew Tim's attention—boarded windows with people coming and going.

Hmmm ... a trap house with an ample assortment of drugs for addicts to get their fix, Tim thought.

The group huddled for prayer as they battled against the powers of darkness, controlling the lives inside the death trap. Several demonic beings rushed out of the house in terror. Then, one hideous creature came forward, dripping with the life blood of the people inside. The evil spirit let out a loud scream, cursing the name of Jesus. As the powerful demon drew his sword, it burned hot in his hand. He dropped it as the team continued to fight with the truth of God's Word.

"Who are you to come to my territory and demand I leave?" questioned the being. "I have a right to be here! These souls have forfeited their salvation so now Lucifer owns them. Leave us alone!"

Vicki raised her hand. "The Lord Jesus rebuke you. Now go quietly." With her hand still raised, the Fire of Heaven shot out of her fingertips like white lightning, engulfing the demon. Now instead of defiant anger, the creature's face betrayed sheer terror as the light of Jesus swirled around him. He screamed and convulsed violently, then dropped to the ground powerless, enabling the team to walk past into the dilapidated house.

An odd mixture of odors hit the team even before entering. Tim swung the door open, and the pungent smell of urine and feces was enough to make some in the group choke. Addicts lay on old mattresses, smoking crack and meth, filling the air with a chemical smell like burnt plastic.

An unconscious woman lay on the floor. One of the team members, Claudia, knelt and scooped up the limp body. The girl's skin was covered in scabby, bleeding lesions and her hair was so matted and dirty, it appeared to be alive as a habitat for various parasites. As Claudia's own tears hit the cheek of the comatose woman, the woman's eyes opened.

It seemed as if Jesus—not Claudia—was holding the frail body in His arms of compassion. His love did a work without words. The woman's eyes opened and she grinned, her smile revealing the years of abuse. Most of her teeth were missing, and her breath smelled like rotting flesh. Claudia didn't see the woman's natural state of decay; instead, she saw the renewal of her mind and soul as Jesus spoke to the addict's heart.

Her words came out as a throaty whisper, "Are they gone? Am I free?"

"You can be free, but you must give your life to Jesus and turn away from your lifestyle."

"I want to be free. Show me how."

Another woman, appearing to be in her early thirties, spoke with a labored voice, "Jesus … is … is … that You? Have You … come for me?"

Her name was Tisha. Patty, a team member, looked into her eyes as she held the bony shell of a woman in her arms. Tisha's eyes were bloodshot and hollow, like her hollow life, deeply hidden in the darkness of her addiction. "My name's Patty. Jesus says to you, 'Arise, be free from your bondage.'"

Tisha shook several times and coughed hard. When she opened her eyes, they were no longer bloodshot, but a clear, deep golden-brown, bursting with life. Strength returned to her malnourished body as she sat up. Spiritual blindness fell from her eyes as if scales had closed them and then flaked off.

Alex, who had the gift of healing, laid his hands on Tisha's shoulders. "In Jesus' name, be restored."

Within a few seconds, Tisha's muscles gained strength and tone. The track marks and bruises from countless injections, along with sores from habitual scratching, gradually faded away. Smooth, deep dark skin emerged. She squealed with excitement as she felt and observed the rapid transformation.

Tisha hated herself for the choices she had made and the consequences that had come as a result of those choices. One night, pressured to be accepted, one stupid act of disobedience—one injection of heroin—had landed her here in this hell trap. But now, at the touch of God, her right mind was restored, and she wept bitterly, mourning the three babies she had aborted. Tears flowed over the hurt she'd dumped onto her family, but the worst of it was knowing she had willfully left the path she knew was right.

Tim, who had the gift of evangelism, took her hands, now soft and tender with new skin. "Look at me, Tisha. Do you want a new life?"

Her gaze met Tim's and she felt a surge of hope. "I knew Him once. Please help me."

"Do you *want* to be a follower of Jesus?"

"Yes, I want to follow Him. I don't want to live like this. I want to help others escape this hellish prison. Oh, Jesus, I want You more than life itself!" Tisha sobbed and fell into Tim's arms.

One by one, the team heard similar stories. Using all the gifts together, they watched God do the unimaginable—retrieve every person in the house from the gates of hell. The team prayed for their new brothers and sisters, then Claudia walked them to the Adara Center.

* * *

The day was young with plenty of time to go somewhere else. The team grouped together and prayed, asking the Lord to show them if, where and when to go. The Lord instructed them to go to the community park several blocks away.

When they arrived, they waited for the Lord to reveal His heart. Vicki noticed a man in a wheelchair. He was wearing an old, tattered army jacket. A group of teenagers were harassing him, wheeling him around in circles. The man cried out, demanding the teens leave him alone, but his pleas did nothing to dissuade the pack of boys. Others in the park chose to avoid the commotion, pretending not to see. Vicki knew this was the one.

As the team approached the man, the teens looked them over as if the boys were lions and the team, their prey.

The pack leader, Jaylen, boldly took a stance inches away from Tim's face. "Whadda *you* want? You ain't from 'round here. You better get yo butt outta here before somethin' bad happen to you."

"My name is Tim and I came to tell you about Jesus. He is willing to save you."

"Say what? Save me from who?" Jaylen laughed. He turned and addressed the other teens. "Hey look, this skinny guy gonna *save* me ... oooooo." He shook his hands mockingly as if he were shaking from fear. "I ain't afraida you or yo band a pitiful followers. You need *me* ..." Jaylen confidently pointed to himself with both hands, "... to save *you*, lil' man. My boys might just beat you to a pulp 'less I sayz otherwise." Jaylen pushed Tim, making him stumble backwards a bit. When Jaylen laughed, the other teens joined him.

Tim regained his balance and prayed aloud. "Lord Jesus, open their eyes to the battle for their souls."

Suddenly, Jaylen and his friends saw demons swirling around them, whispering into their ears, while others militantly clung to the boys' backs, repeatedly sticking daggers of evil thoughts into their heads. Other demonic beings snagged them with chains, binding the boys to darkness.

A demon called Violence yelled, directing the other demons to kill Tim and his team. Jaylen and his friends covered their eyes and shrieked in terror. "Stop, man, stop 'em now! We're gonna die!"

Tim raised his hand and bound the demons in Jesus' name. The boys watched as the horrible creatures temporarily stopped their torment. In an instant, the frightening beings were once again unseen, which somewhat calmed the rattled teens.

Jaylen lifted his hands from his eyes and straightened up. "Who *are* you? What da hell was that?"

"I'm a follower of Jesus Christ. Those were the demons that have the right to torment you," Tim stated as a matter of fact.

God had opened the boys' eyes and Loraine—with the gift of evangelism—shared the gospel. The boys listened intently. When she was about finished, Allen, gifted with healing, went to the man in the wheelchair who had witnessed all in the natural and spiritual. "What's your name?"

"Malik."

"Do you want to be healed?"

"My legs are messed up from an IED in Iraq. One is missin' and the other hasn't moved since 2006. I ain't never gettin' outta this chair."

Malik hadn't answered his question, so Allen asked again. "Do you *want* to be healed?"

The Fear of the Lord fell upon all present. Allen's eyes began to burn with the Fire of Heaven, making Malik's heart pound with terror. He wanted to look away, but the Fire had locked onto his eyes, drawing Him to Jesus.

Malik began to weep softly. As the Fire of Heaven grew brighter in Allen's eyes, Malik cried out. "Yes! I want to be healed!" He clutched at Allen's collar and begged him, "But don't stop at my legs. Heal all of me, my mind and heart, too! I'm really messed up, man."

Allen placed his hands on top of Malik's greasy, matted hair. Instantly, the Fire of Heaven completely engulfed both of the men in its raging blaze. Mesmerized, the teens watched in silence, mouths agape in disbelief. They instinctively stepped back and huddled together, not wanting to get caught up in the inferno.

Slowly, the Fire subsided. There stood two men on their feet with bodies intact and no trace of the wheelchair. The image of Malik was confounding. He was standing tall, staring at his feet and bending over to touch them repeatedly. He took a few tentative steps. A few more steps, then shot off at full speed toward the playground, pivoted and returned.

"I'm free, I'm free, oh man, I am so free!" He dropped to his knees and sobbed. He had carried a spiritual backpack of heavy rocks for years. Each year another weighty rock of pain and anguish. His body was made whole, his mind cleared of darkness and his heart awash in hope. "How can I ever thank you? How can I pay you back?"

"You owe us nothing, but you owe Jesus everything. Commit your life to following Him and find the joy you have been searching for. Love and obey Him. Sin no more."

Loraine went to Jaylen and his friends. "Today you witnessed the great love of the Lord Jesus. Who do you want to belong to? Lucifer, who wants only to hurt you and make you his slaves … or Jesus, who wants to heal you and set you free? I warn you, if you do not choose Jesus, the demons will remain with you, and if you continue to reject God's salvation, you leave yourself open to even more oppression— possibly fiercer than before."

Most of boys looked to Jaylen and waited for him to respond. But before the gang leader could speak, one boy unhesitatingly stepped out of the pack. "I want Jesus," he spoke, his tone definitive.

Jaylen's eyes were watery and his lower lip quivered. "Yeah, me too. I want Jesus. I don't ever want those creatures messin' wit' me again. But there ain't no church 'round here that does that stuff."

One by one, the other boys came forward with desperation in their eyes, wanting to follow Jesus, but not knowing how. Vicki described the Adara Center and how they would be welcomed and embraced there.

The boys and Malik fired questions about what they had witnessed. The team members with the gift of teaching answered each inquiry. For the next two hours, they explained the Kingdom of God and how the new converts could live a life committed to their Savior. It was enough to get them started in the right direction. Each of them promised to attend the upcoming free classes at the Adara Center and receive a free Bible.

Team Alpha headed back to the Center—Malik and the teens following—for a debriefing, anxious to share with the other teams what God had done. All had tasted of the Lord's goodness that day, witnessing a first step out of many to win the city for Christ.

41

Final Instructions

Soon, the Adara Center would be publicly dedicated to the Lord. Three months earlier, nothing had existed in this location except the condemned warehouse and surrounding blocks of abandoned industrial buildings. No team member had ever dreamed that they would be thrust headfirst into a world-changing ministry, especially Gregor and Jean.

Gregor reflected on the group he had addressed a few days ago at the Hammond Center—young, old, black, brown and white. They were one in Jesus. Diverse backgrounds drawn closer to each other than their own flesh and blood; each person so dedicated to Christ, they would give their lives for one another.

The world around them was splitting apart. Race against race, nation against nation, religion against religion. A revolution of discontent was sweeping the planet, an uprising birthed in the heart of evil, Lucifer himself.

But God had declared a counter-revolution of unity in Him, sparked in the center of the nation's capital, where political parties foolishly sparred with each other as a serious sport. The country was fragmented, and D.C. would become the epicenter of the great divide.

Jesus would show the world that the door was open to all willing to surrender to His great love. Shortly the door would close just as the door of the ark had closed by God's own hand. The end of the age was near. Those without the oil of the Holy Spirit burning within them would suffer the judgment of the seven-year tribulation.

The groups sent out earlier joined the rest of the team who had gathered in the room, which was solely dedicated to one purpose—prayer. A holy presence surrounded everyone, and all knelt in reverence remaining quiet, waiting. Time was suspended here, and every thought not born of the Spirit vanished. There were no distractions, no pressing engagements, projects to complete, or hurts to heal—only rest in the abiding presence of God.

With eyes closed to keep the world out, there seemed no need to speak. The room suddenly filled with a familiar fragrance. Jean recognized it immediately and opened her eyes to a different world, lush and alive with His love.

Just over a small hill down by a flowing river sat a figure under the most remarkable tree which emanated life. The large tree was full of deep green leaves; multicolored, ripe fruit dangled from its branches, causing them to drape in beautiful curves. She ran as fast as she could to Him, her beloved Jesus. He stood with His arms wide, inviting her into His embrace.

Laughing and shouting erupted as all raced toward the tree. Marjie couldn't believe her old legs were carrying her as if she floated on air. She marveled that her previously aged, wrinkled hands were now covered in supple, youthful skin. She felt at home, filled with perfect love and peace. *It won't be long now,* she thought.

The group caught up with Jean and surrounded Jesus. He laughed, enjoying their loving devotion as much as they were drinking in His returned affection.

"Come ... sit."

Everyone sat as Jesus leaned against the Tree of Life. He gazed into the eyes of His faithful disciples, His workmanship. He smiled. Then, it was down to business.

"Always equip others to replace you, no matter your role, whether a well-known teacher or an unseen administrator. Cell replication brings life. A new cell is created when one cell divides. In the Kingdom of God, division brings multiplication.

"I will establish Myself in the Adara Center. There will be no doubt who I AM. Many places like the Center will equip harvesters, and those will instruct even more. When workers are ready, they will go into communities, ministering My love, healing, deliverance and salvation. As small bodies grow large enough, they will divide, reproducing again and again."

He reached up, pulled a cluster of fruit from a branch. He sat, crossed his legs and divided it among the group.

"When I return to earth, will I find faith? I seek those alive through obedience to the governance of My Kingdom, which if followed, guarantees fruitfulness. The message is simple: Love Me and do as My word says.

"Faith without fruit is dead, and obedience to My commandments without faith is also dead. Faith and the fruitfulness of My commandments are like a coin—both sides are of equal value only when they exist together on the same coin. One side without the other renders the coin worthless. Faith and fruitfulness through obedience are inseparable."

Jesus shifted and leaned into the group, his heart heavy with the dividedness of His Church.

"The Church—with its individual church plants—is fractured. She has become many kings ruling manmade realms with passive subjects. My true Church is not united under Me, the True King. The members—subjects—rely on their earthly king and do not search My Word, even though I AM clearly presented in the Scriptures. I AM the Alpha and the Omega, the First and the Last, the Beginning and the End. Every page of My written Word reveals some attribute of who I AM, for I AM the Word.

"The current church model produces atrophied believers who are weak from lack of exercise. Gifts must be exercised and faith practiced to build spiritual strength. Yet, how can one exercise truth if Truth is not known and understood?

"Because the true precepts of My Word are not always taught, and the subjects' slothfulness to act upon My Word, the Awakening river must flow separately from the Church river for a time before the rivers are united once again. The flow of the Awakening river necessitates that each believer be active, practicing faith and exercising gifts. When the gatherings become too large, the group must divide to maintain strength and become even stronger.

"I tell you now, the equipping centers will pass away. One day, they will no longer be needed. At the end of the Awakening, I will send leaders from all the nations to Jerusalem. Just as My Word was sent out from Jerusalem, it will return there.

The listeners remained alert, clinging to His words as He deposited them into their hearts. Jesus reached for another cluster of fruit and passed it around.

"Faithful servants, empowered in the Fire of Heaven, will be sent to places of darkness to preach the good news of My salvation. As they obey this mission, many will die as martyrs. I will send them, for I do not leave souls without a choice. There will always be at least one voice of True Light proclaiming My Kingdom."

Man, why would anyone choose darkness? Diego wondered. He had lived in the darkness of this world and in darkness of spirit. Now that he had been released from evil's grip, he couldn't understand why somebody would pick a life apart from Jesus ... on purpose!

Jesus, knowing the young disciple's mind, lovingly answered, "The place of blessing is the obvious choice, Diego. The sad truth is that man's heart is wicked and will choose the place that best meets his deepest desires. Many choose anger, hatred and bitterness, falsely believing it gives them purpose. Others believe that ignoring My commandments to live as they please gives them freedom; however, My commandments *are* freedom. Still others have sold their souls to Lucifer and do not want to leave their master. They like the power he has given them and do not want to part from it.

"I lived among men as a man, enduring all temptations, yet without sin. I overcame evil; likewise, each believer must become an overcomer. Strength to resist evil comes from above. Often forgoing the needs of my natural body, I purposed to fellowship with my Father in prayer, gaining strength from Him. I saw what the Father wanted me to do, and I committed Myself to do His will; therefore, evil has no place in Me.

"Never sacrifice prayer on the altar of ministry. If you do, the enemy will deceive and direct you down a path leading farther from My will. Many great leaders failed when prayer became secondary to service. If you pray, I will meet you as My Father met with Me. Make this the core of who you are, so those coming behind you will see your life dedicated to prayer and will follow in fruitfulness.

"Again, I say, do not be deceived. The true gospel always points to Me, My Word, the Holy Spirit and the completed work through the cross. If it takes away from these things or adds to them, then it is a false gospel of Lucifer."

Jesus stood and the group followed His lead. They walked together toward the small hill from where they had first spotted Him.

"Finally, let love rule over all—not the love of this world that is infused with emotion, but Divine Love as an act of your will. Love Me sacrificially first in order to love those around you. When your heart belongs to Me, I will pour My heart out of you. This Final Awakening will be marked by My love and the Fear of the Lord. Where My love abides, liberty abounds."

When they had reached the top of the hill, He stopped and turned to face them. "It won't be long before you are called Home to live with Me and the Father forever. I have prepared a place for each of you. Let My Kingdom be your true home in your heart. Declare it so, My children."

Just as suddenly as they had been in Heaven under the Tree of Life, they returned to the prayer room. Torn between the desire to remain with Him and complete the task commissioned to them, they found comfort in His promises and His warnings. The unexpected visit energized them for the dedication tomorrow, pressing on to finish well.

42

Big News

See you guys tonight." Jason gave his dad a pat on the back as he left the Adara Center without lingering to chat. *Another visit with Jesus! How can things keep getting more awesome?* he wondered.

"Yeah, see you later." *Hmmm ... what's his hurry?* Dan thought.

Tony, too, noticed Jason's speedy departure. "Huh, where's *he* off to? He usually sticks around to debrief after a face to face with Jesus."

Dan shrugged. "I'm looking forward to the celebration dinner at Marjie's tonight. Might be the last calm get-together before the rush."

Barb slipped her hand into Dan's. "You're right. We're on the Lord's train now. Things are going to accelerate."

"Hmmm ... my thoughts exactly," Tony agreed.

"It's exhilarating on one hand and exhausting on the other." Gregor sighed. "We're going to have to stick to the plan of multiplication by division to keep the train from derailing."

* * *

The team relaxed in Marjie's living room, waiting for Jason to arrive. To their surprise, he brought a guest, Carrie Summers. The others were not only stunned but also suspicious. *Why would Jason bring a reporter to this intimate dinner?*

Jason and Carrie were holding hands. At first, the group didn't know what to make of this, except for Sheila, Barb, and Marjie. At the couple's entrance, Sheila realized that her observations of the starry-eyed looks between Jason and Carrie at the Capital Grand were indeed accurate. The Lord had already told Barb about the romance. Marjie suspected for other reasons. Upon second glance, it was perfectly obvious. Jason and Carrie's glowing smiles and the glittering rock on her finger gave away what was coming.

Marjie was the first to greet them. "Welcome Jason, dear ... and Carrie, so glad to see you again." Marjie gave them both a grandmotherly squeeze, knowing the inside scoop.

Carrie had an uneasy feeling about Marjie—like she knew things that people might rather she not know.

While Carrie was surrounded with joyful congratulations from the rest of the group, Jason approached his parents with a quirky expression on his face. "Mom, Dad, I wanted to tell you first, but things kind of moved faster than planned ...."

"We know, hon." Barb smiled, happy for her son.

"You know? How? I never talked about her. The only time you've ever seen us together was at the Capital Grand Ballroom. Wait ... wait that's what the weird stare was all about. You knew back then?"

"I knew she was the one as soon I touched her hand. I told your father shortly after that, didn't I, Dan?" Barb lovingly nudged Dan. He smiled and nodded.

"Man, is that a relief!" Jason sighed. "I thought you might think I was making a mistake. I struggled with how to tell you. Your confirmation, Mom, assures me this is the right time and the right girl.

These past few months have flipped the way I see things. I feel like I'm living the impossible."

Barb and Dan hugged their son in a tight embrace. God was answering years of prayers for him. It was just a short time ago, they thought death had taken their only child, but now he was vibrantly alive ... serving God and, soon, getting married.

"Attention, everyone. Barb and I have an announcement to make. Carrie." Dan gestured for her to stand next to Jason.

Barb put her arm around Carrie and whispered, "I've known since that awkward meeting at the hotel. I'm happy for both of you."

Carrie turned and looked at Barb with surprise. Barb just shrugged and pulled her closer. Everyone already knew what Dan was going to say, but they didn't want to rob him of this fatherly moment.

"Tonight is truly a night of celebration. We're hitting two birds with one stone. Not only are we celebrating the dedication tomorrow, but I would like to announce the engagement of our son Jason Taylor to Carrie Summers." He walked over to Carrie and gave her a hug. "Welcome to your new extended family in Christ."

More congratulations with hugs, pats on the back and ogling over the ring. Then, Marjie led everyone into the stately dining room where the table was set for a formal dinner, but the love between them made it feel more like a family Thanksgiving feast. Everyone knew how much this night meant to Marjie. She was no longer alone, but they, too, felt bound together, related by the Blood of Christ.

The engaged couple sat at the end of the table near Marjie. These had become more than friends to her; she loved each one of them as they filled a void in her heart. Adding to her joy, Jason and Carrie's engagement reminded her of Byron, and she was comforted, knowing she would see him soon.

That same five-carat, crystal-clear diamond, set with pale rose stones all around—now on Carrie's hand—had been placed on

Marjie's finger over fifty years ago. On her wedding day, she carried a bouquet of white chrysanthemums and rose peonies that matched her ring. When the Lord brought life to the planter garden with those same flowers, He was reminding her that *He* was her groom. When she gave the ring to Jason, she was merely obeying the Lord's command, thus, her suspicions that an engagement was coming shortly, although she never suspected it would be Carrie.

When Jason had proposed just an hour before arriving at Grandhaven, Carrie wondered how he could afford such an expensive ring. But as he slipped it on her finger, the thought completely left her mind. She sensed the ring was consecrated to the Lord somehow. It seemed right to wear it. She felt the sacredness of marriage and the mystery of two becoming one.

In that moment of popping the question, Jason was so relieved when Carrie cried and flung her arms around him—which he assumed meant "yes"—he forgot to explain about the ring. He leaned over to Carrie now and whispered. "Marjie gave me the ring. I'll tell you more later."

Carrie thought, *Barb and Marjie knew all along. I'll never have any secrets with this family.*

Marjie took Carrie's hand to admire the ring that once united her to her beloved Byron. "Do you like the white chrysanthemums and rose peonies on the table."

"Yes, they're gorgeous!"

And they were, with every petal and every leaf perfectly formed and blooms full and magnificent by the touch of the Creator's hand. "Oh, then let me provide the flowers for your wedding, dear."

"I would like that." Carrie smiled and Marjie gave her a kiss on the cheek, then called her guests to attention.

"We must pray," she said. "Father, we come to you in Jesus' wonderful name. We give You great honor and thanks because Your generous gifts are overwhelming. I especially thank You for my new family and for uniting Jason and Carrie as one. May Your presence always be in the Adara Center to the glory of Your Kingdom. Make us faithful and true to Your Word. Pour Your love out of our hearts and into the lost souls seeking Your help. In Jesus' name, amen."

After a few bites of food, Jean asked the question on everyone's mind: "Carrie, do you think your marriage to Jason Taylor will make you too controversial for WNN?"

Carrie's eyes misted a little. "I've thought the same thing. I love my work, but I know marrying Jason means I'm no longer in the TV news business." She laughed. She knew she had to accept the fact that everything was different now, not because of Jason, but because she belonged to Jesus. "I plan to submit my resignation on Monday."

"Any thoughts on what's next?" Tony asked.

"I have no clue. I guess I just need to take one step at a time. I've watched all of you put everything on the altar and walk away. From my perspective, you came away with a lot more than you left. I believe the same will happen to me ... I mean *us.*" She reached out and held onto Jason's hand under the table.

Carrie's resignation was Marjie's missing puzzle piece. In that moment, the Lord had revealed how Carrie would fit into the plan. Marjie was so excited, she shot up from her seat, stood behind Carrie and planted her hands firmly on her shoulders. "Young lady, you did not lose a job, you just changed employers! I thought about buying WNN, but the Lord has something else in mind. That model's dying anyway. We're building a news and information channel to broadcast online all over the world."

All at the table were speechless. Marjie hadn't given any indication of such an endeavor, nor had it entered anyone else's mind.

"I can assure you that the mainstream media will not report what's going on in this Awakening. If they do, it will be portrayed as a cult or just plain kooky. Who's going to show the world the truth? When this is all said and done, this channel will pull more viewers than any TV news conglomerate.

"Elliot, my lawyer, has been putting together all the legalities and I've been reaching out to people I know who have the experience we need—top-notch talents who want to serve God. They're ready to leave their current employer and work for us. Carrie, you will be the face of ADARA News Services."

Eyes around the table opened wide and mouths dropped open.

"No freeloading. You'll pull your weight just like everyone else." Marjie laughed giving Carrie a little hug around her neck.

Gregor found his voice. "Wow, I didn't see *that* coming!"

The group was learning that with Marjie, surprises were the norm. The Lord told her what He wanted done and she made it happen. She had engineered the completion of the Adara Center in record time. She may look like a little old woman, but she was sharp, savvy and smart. The perfect administrator.

Dan marveled. "If you were president, this nation would explode with prosperity while balancing its budgets at the same time." From Dan's political imagery, he implied that Marjie seemed to make the impossible happen. "Man, are we lucky to have you out front of us. Marjie, thank you!" Dan lifted his glass of Pellegrino to Marjie and all at the table joined in the toast.

Marjie accepted their compliments with humble grace. She knew the real power that fueled her was not Marjie Wegman's, but the power of the Holy Spirit dwelling in her. Later that evening, she would be on her knees, returning all the praise to Jesus.

* * *

After a five-course meal and plenty of seconds, the team retired to the spacious living room. Marjie's house was large and formal in architecture, but nothing inside felt stiff and regimented. The promised peace and love of God resting in the house was a powerful unifying and relaxing force. The room was furnished with comfortable couches and chairs on which no one hesitated to lounge.

Now, the most important time of the evening came—time to pray. As much fun as they had enjoyed already, this was the crowning jewel of the evening. Fellowshipping was good; listening to Jesus was great.

All that had happened over the past few months was awe-inspiring. No words could relay the depths of simultaneous joy and the serious nature and eternal significance of their mission.

As they prayed, often pausing to listen for the Lord's sweet voice, the soft sound of perfect harmony swirled around the room like silken fabric, settling peacefully in each person's heart as He showed them a shared vision. Each saw an impressive angel carrying a golden sickle with the words GLORY UNTO THE LORD engraved on the long, curved blade. One enormous swipe of the blade gathered thousands of believers. As that angel stepped aside, another equally impressive angelic spirit appeared, swiping the earth with his golden sickle and gathering thousands more. Again and again, mighty angels with golden sickles moved across the earth bringing souls into the Lord's house.

No invitations had been sent nor any schedule of events laid out for the dedication since the Lord had not directed them to do so. Now, expectations rose and hopes were high the Adara Center would be filled with those who needed to hear the message of Jesus' love and salvation.

43

Special Guest

The Adara Center sat in the middle of the city in what was the capital's most notorious neighborhood. The grouping of previously dilapidated buildings was no longer littered with trash nor plagued with crime. Peace and safety had replaced fear. The area, composed of several blocks, had the cleanly landscaped appearance of a downtown renewal with an atmosphere of kindness and charity. In addition, the newly converted Barrios gang had taken it upon themselves to self-police their new neighborhood—a notable wonder.

Today—sunny and unusually warm for this late in December—was scheduled for the dedication of the Center. The air smelled like spring, fresh with new life. Carlos, Diego and Maria strolled among the buildings. So much had changed in such a short period of time. They had never imagined something so wonderful could happen to them. How could the God they once cursed love them so much?

"This is awesome, man! Can you b'lieve we live here now?" asked Diego.

"Lil' bro, it's beyond awesome!" Carlos countered. "If Jesus can turn our messed-up lives into somethin' good for His Kingdom, the *world* is about to be changed."

Usually quiet, Maria was even quieter today. She strained to see what she sensed. She closed her natural eyes, hoping it would help open her spiritual eyes. And so it did.

Angels with instruments sang as they worshipped. Others carried scrolls with decrees from the throne to restore bodies and heal disease. Those nearest the outer perimeter of the complex carried burning swords inscribed with the word TRUTH. Maria walked the entire time with her eyes closed, yet she saw clearly. The angels knew and nodded at their fellow servant as they passed each other.

The threesome had just returned to the main building when a tall, slender woman in her early seventies walked through the front doors. The joy radiating from her drew the three near.

"Hi, I'm Snow Peterson, one of your remote intercessors. I just flew in from Nashville. Is Gregor or Jean here?" She fumbled with some bags, freeing one hand and extending it to Carlos.

"My name is Carlos," he introduced himself as he shook her hand, "and this is Maria and Diego. We know 'bout you."

"Yeah, you're the lady that prays a lot," Diego added.

"Well, I'm thrilled to meet you. Gregor told me so many wonderful things about the Lord's work in your lives."

Surprisingly, Maria offered to show their guest around. "Follow me," she invited.

"Absolutely, I would love to see everything! Oh, I just know Heaven is coming, and there will be no mistaking who Jesus is. This is glorious!" In a sweeping glance, Snow took in the large auditorium. "By the way, have you noticed all the angels? Never seen anything like it."

"You see them, too?" Maria asked excitedly.

"Oh, yes, I recognize they are not ordinary angels ... they seem to be high-ranking angels with great authority."

Carlos and Diego looked at each other and shrugged. They didn't see any angels, but took Snow and Maria's word for it and proceeded to tag along for the visitor's tour.

Afterward, Snow asked if she could be alone in the prayer room. This room could easily accommodate about 200 people with plenty of space to spare. Chairs circled the outer edge of the room, with a few padded mats in the center for those who were called to intercede on their knees or to lie prostrate.

"Oh, they've thought of everything." Snow commented. "Warfare can get pretty intense, you know. As for me, I rarely stay still when fighting against the rulers, authorities, and powers of this dark world and spiritual forces of evil."

The three left Snow alone and closed the door behind them. She primed her heart with prayers of thanksgiving. One after another, she cried out with acknowledgments of God's great blessings—His shed Blood, His forgiveness and salvation. Her love and gratitude burned hotter with each proclamation.

Knowing that sin was a barrier that needed to be addressed before entering into the Father's presence, she knelt, praying Psalm 51 and confessing any sin His Spirit brought to mind. A door in Heaven seemed to swing open wider.

Zealous to enter deeper into His presence, Snow stood and walked around the room. Each step increased in speed as she prayed for protection. As she prayed against evil, asking that blind eyes and deaf ears be opened to God's truth, the Fire of Heaven shone through the skylight as a pure white light. It grew in intensity, and all in the building—including angels—sensed the holy presence so strongly they knelt in reverence.

Snow stood in the midst of the light shining on her face, lifting her arms fully stretched toward Heaven. The light flowed through the small gap under the door like water. It worked its way throughout the building and exploded into the main auditorium, permeating stone, steel and glass and finally circling back to the heavens through the roof as multiple lightning strikes. The strikes occurred in such rapid succession that they merged into one steady beam.

Snow prayed aloud with all her heart, mind and soul. "Lord Jesus, be glorified in this place tonight and always. Equip workers for Your harvest. In Your great love and mercy, restore what the evil one has stolen. Heal broken hearts, broken bodies and crushed spirits. Father, I pray that the Fire of Heaven would burn within us and that the Fear of the Lord be strong in our hearts."

A loud voice thundered like a sonic boom, rattling all the windows. *I have not forgotten your prayers nor your tears upon My feet. I will reveal Myself. Look among the nations and see; wonder and be astounded. For I am doing a work in your days that you would not believe if told you. Even in your wildest imagination, you could never envision what I AM about to do. Tell the people I AM coming.*

Snow stayed in His presence until the light faded away. She lay face down with her arms out to her sides in the middle of the padded floor, resting in the Glory still radiating from her body.

Gregor and Jean had just arrived when the light beam bolted out of the building's roof. "What's that?" Gregor rushed in. "Is everyone alright?"

Carlos pointed to the prayer room and said, "Snow's in there."

Gregor cracked the door open and peeked in to see Snow getting up off the floor. She turned around and a blast of bright light caused Gregor to close his eyes and turn away. "Snow? You OK?"

Overwhelmed by the holiness of His presence, she remained speechless. She stared past Gregor as if she were in another world. While shielding their eyes, Gregor and Carlos each took one of her arms and led her down the hall. They gently placed her on a couch in the conference room. Her eyes and her body glowed with the Fire of Heaven.

As other team members arrived, Diego steered them to the conference room. When they opened the door, the light stopped them dead in their tracks.

"Whoa!" Dan gasped, covering his eyes.

Gregor pointed to Snow. "Everyone, I want to introduce you to Snow Peterson."

Dan had an "aha" moment as he connected Snow with the laser beam of light above the building. As Chair of the Intelligence Committee, his phone had already alerted him that there was a national emergency—a miles-high, white swirling pillar of energy pouring from space, pinpointing a building somewhere in D.C. "Guys, the government picked this up and went into lockdown. Airports are closed. The Secret Service is escorting the President and other key personnel to safety, believing D.C. may be under attack."

From his phone, he read: *Energy's origin undeterminable ... military has confidence source is not from earth. Remain DEFCON 1.* "Guys," Dan said, glancing at the group gathered around the conference table, "America's on high alert until someone can give a satisfactory, rational explanation of what that light is. I *know* its source, but how do I make *them* understand?"

He leaned back in his chair and stared at the ceiling, his hands locked behind his head. Barb and Sheila recognized the familiar position. "I'm already a nut case." He sat up and chuckled. "Get this. I got a box of Cocoa Puffs with a note: *I'm cuckoo for Cocoa Puffs.* I certainly have an undeniable presence on the Hill." He shook his head. "They are *never* going to believe me, unless …."

"Unless what?" asked Barb.

A calculating expression flashed across Dan's face. "Unless … I convince key people to come for the dedication. Let them see for themselves. They're on their way here anyway, guaranteed. Let them join the cuckoo club, if you know what I mean. Yeah, that's it. Excuse me."

Dan stepped out and quickly notified his contacts in Military Intelligence as well as Homeland Security, telling them he had intel on the origins of the mysterious energy beam and where to meet him as he was already at the location.

When he returned to the conference room, he seemed relieved. "All taken care of. We'll be ready by the time the military surrounds us. I don't want them shutting this place down out of ignorant fear."

"Hmmm," Jean pondered aloud. "If Jesus is showing signs in the heavens, you can bet the evil one will stage his demonstration shortly. I think our new normal just got newer. The battle has raised a notch."

Snow shifted, then sat up. Barb made a makeshift veil from a napkin. Jason put on his sunglasses while Carrie clung to his arm, overwhelmed at the light's sacred nature. The rest just looked at the floor, averting their eyes from Snow's face.

Snow grabbed Gregor's arm, pulling him down onto the couch. "Oh, Gregor, you are so right when you said this place has a direct window to Heaven. I was just praying for tonight and then it happened ... I saw Him, Gregor ... I saw *Him.*"

"You saw Jesus?"

"No ... well yes ... I mean I saw all of them, all three at once in a way ... oh my, I think I saw the Glory of the Godhead—the Father, Son, and Spirit! I didn't see the Father's face, but I saw His figure on His throne and Jesus sitting at His right hand with the full presence of the Holy Spirit in their midst."

She covered her face, taking a moment. She was overcome, humbled, knowing she didn't deserve His great measure of love, mercy and grace. "He held me in His hands, Gregor. God held me in

His hands! Beauty beyond words! Glory unutterable! Oh … and the love! How can I express the depths of His love?"

She seemed frustrated, but Gregor didn't quite know what to say. "Wow, that's awesome, Snow."

Squeezing Gregor's arm tighter, attempting to make him understand, she removed the napkin veil, causing him to squint and turn away. "Oh, Gregor … you're not getting it … this dedication is beyond our comprehension … it's epic!"

44

Song Of Angels

Some physical strength had returned to Snow's body. The light still shining from her face brought Heaven's fragrance, recalling for the team memories of sitting with Jesus under the Tree of Life. She wanted to be with the other intercessors during the dedication, so Gregor walked with her to the prayer room.

"Snow, I cannot express my appreciation … well, all involved with the Adara Center are grateful for you and your camel-kneed friends. Thank you."

"Oh, bless you, Gregor! Prayer warriors are not often recognized as an essential ministry tool. Some of the others have told me that they are purposely kept hidden. Their church leaders don't feel comfortable with … well, with those who pray against rulers, authorities and powers of this world's darkness. They even consider us weird." She chuckled a little. "I've been reprimanded for scaring people."

"Hmmm … yeah, seems the focus is on the physical realm, and the devil's attacks only happened in 'Bible times' … as if Lucifer had retired. *If-you-can't-see-it,-it-doesn't-exist* maxim seems to have been adopted. It's tragic so many have fallen for Lucifer's ploy. The Word is clear; we fight against an evil enemy. I think the Church's decline started when leaders omitted prayer to combat the darkness."

"Exactly! They don't distinguish the two kingdoms—one Truth and one lies—and try to live somewhere in between to make everyone comfortable."

They stood at the prayer room door. Snow turned to Gregor, forgetting that he couldn't look at her. The light forced him to divert his eyes downward. Her voice revealed the pain in being misunderstood. "You know, Gregor, those battling the devil's schemes have been ruined for the ordinary. Our eyes have been opened to the war and we cannot *un-see* what we've already seen. And we cannot choose to ignore what we've understood."

Gregor captured Snow's hand in his own. "I know, Snow, I know. You and other intercessors have endured ridicule from believers. You've been attacked in your bodies, relationships and finances, yet you've pressed onward in your passion to serve Jesus. Your selfless, tear-stained prayers have advanced His Kingdom."

Her eyes filled with tears and when she blinked, they ran down her cheeks. She hugged Gregor and joined her fellow prayer warriors.

* * *

Marjie marveled at the numbers already seated inside without any marketing campaign. "This is truly the Lord's doing!"

Barb, Jason, Carrie, and Tony accompanied Marjie, greeting people as they entered the main auditorium. Some were dressed in expensive designer outfits. Others wore thrift store finds. Some were neatly groomed, while others seemed to need a good scrubbing. Whites, Asians, Latinos and African-Americans walked side by side—a melting pot of D.C., searching for something beyond themselves.

Word about the miraculous had obviously spread as those needing physical healing streamed into the Center. Carlos, Diego, Veeta and Vincent ushered gurneys and wheelchairs to the space at the foot of the stage.

Dan and Sheila waited outside, watching for the expected convoy. The Homeland Security Director's SUV came to a screeching stop. He jumped out, along with his armed escorts, and rushed toward the senator. More vehicles streamed in behind, quickly creating a perimeter around the Adara Center complex.

"Gentlemen, please, there's no emergency here," Dan assured them. "I guarantee the light is not a threat to America or anyone nearby." Miraculously, the men listened. "The light is from Heaven."

"From Heaven?" Alex McDonald, Homeland Security Director, rolled his eyes. "As in 'from *God*'?"

"Yes, and if you'll just come inside ...."

"C'mon Taylor ... you're embarrassing yourself!" McDonald sighed, saddened that this once respected senator had been reduced to this—an unstable religious fanatic unfit for office. "So you're seriously claiming the light from outer space is from God?"

"Yes."

"You belong in a padded room. Our sources say the light could be from a super nova or meteor. If it's shining on your church building, it's *absolute* coincidence. It is not, and I repeat, it is *not* the glory of God!"

"It's not a church ... inside, gentlemen, please," Dan appealed.

McDonald turned to address a technician. "Radiation levels?"

"Normal, sir." His voice revealed an obvious attempt to control the urge to laugh.

"All right, inside. We'll need to take a look around anyway."

The governmental entourage was surprised to see veterans in full dress uniform. Colonel Parker—after honoring their service with a salute—seated the brave men and women in the front middle section.

Various disabilities exposed the scars of war—some with prosthetics and others with burns. Parker understood firsthand that some of the country's defenders also suffered unseen wounds in the mind and heart.

* * *

"Where're they all comin' from?" Sheila whispered to Dan as they escorted Director McDonald and the accompanying military through the building. "We're gonna need every inch of this place."

"Yeah, I noticed people going into the classrooms. Full capacity is around 10,000, and it looks like it's getting close. I just hope these guys don't shut us down before things get started."

"Oh, Senator, you should know by now *no one*—not even the United States Armed Forces—shuts down God!" Sheila unknowingly flashed that look when she caught Dan in an error and knew she was right.

"Duly noted."

Satisfied with the tour, McDonald et al took the seats that had been reserved for them.

* * *

Gregor squeezed Jean's hand. "It's time."

They soberly stepped up to the sparsely furnished stage. No oversized chairs—or "thrones," as Gregor called them—would ever occupy this platform. Today was a simple dedication. Nothing had been rehearsed. There was no band, no fancy lighting. Large monitors were placed around the auditorium, ensuring everyone a good view. Jean didn't like the fact that the setup resembled that of mega-ministries, but logistics were logistics.

Standing together, hand in hand, they faced the people. The

auditorium fell silent and Gregor addressed the crowd. "Hello, my name is Gregor Wallace and this is my wife, Jean. We hadn't anticipated thousands since we didn't advertise the date of the dedication. We're astonished at what God has done! With glad hearts, we welcome you to the Adara Center.

"These buildings are committed to serve the Lord Jesus Christ. But understand, this is not a church; there will be no Sunday services here. The Center's purpose is to equip believers to go into communities to tell the good news of Jesus Christ and His salvation. Once God deems the Center's work is done, this place will return to its former state— emptiness and ruin."

His statement confused his listeners. *Why take the trouble to build such a complex, then let it go to shambles?* they wondered.

Director McDonald and his colleagues rolled their eyes, bemoaning the fact that they were sitting in a zealot's religious meeting, yet something more than duty compelled them to stay.

"In His mercy, God is making Himself known through the Visitation of the Fire of Heaven in the Final Awakening. This awakening is not what many call the rapture—when Jesus meets his Bride in the clouds—although this harvest is preparation for that day.

"The Final Awakening is an open door, much like the door on Noah's Ark, which remained open for seven days before the rains of judgment came. Sadly, the Bible records that no others were added to the eight people that made up Noah's family. I urge you to walk through the door today while it is easily entered."

Homeland Security officials kept a watchful eye for suspicious characters, remaining in contact with operatives via ear-coms. All reported to the Director that the audience was focused on Gregor, as everyone seemed to be ignoring the government's intrusion. So far, there had been no persons spotted with intent to harm.

"Today is the day of salvation," Jean finished. "You could die sitting here and never have another opportunity to secure citizenship in Heaven. If you do not pledge your life to Jesus, giving Him full authority, you've already allied yourself with Lucifer. There are no sidelines. The Scriptures tell us if we are not for Jesus, we are against Him."

People testified of Jesus' miraculous touch. Jason briefly recounted his resurrection, as did Kevin Jefferson. Francis Hammond, Frederick University's president, explained what happened during the weeks dedicated to Bible teaching. Carlos described the amazing changes in his neighborhood now that the infamous Barrios gang had been transformed by Jesus' love, forgiveness and deliverance.

People were visibly affected by the stories as they continued to listen with attentive ears, hearts and minds fixed on the testifiers' words. The accounts birthed hope in the crowd as if they had experienced the miracles firsthand. Diego's healing sprouted hope in a disabled veteran's heart. Carlos's break from crime and drugs became another's desire for freedom. Kevin Jefferson's miraculous resurrection created possibilities where there was only despair. Doubt and hesitation were overturned by belief and surety.

The one thousand people touched by God's power at the abandoned warehouse—now the Adara Center—stood in place at their seats as a spokesman told how they had been drawn by a heavenly conviction. He explained they were delivered from addictions and diseases and that every adult, teen and child numbered in the thousand had committed their lives to Him that day.

No heart was left untouched at the revelation that God was present to change lives. A sweeping hunger engulfed the crowd, an aching to know their Creator, a need for a sure eternal connection.

During the testimonies, Gregor had noticed three figures quietly entering through the main doors. They had slipped in sideways and were standing against the back wall. No one else seemed to notice them.

Each wore a bright white robe with a hood pulled over his head, almost covering his eyes. The hoods and the distance made it nearly impossible to identify them. Two were tall and stood on either side of a shorter figure. Gregor had an idea as to who they might be, but he couldn't be sure—at least, not yet.

It was time to enter into the Lord's presence through worship. Gregor and Jean left the stage, and Maria stepped to the microphone. She stood under five feet tall, but her heart for Jesus gave her great stature in the Kingdom. Her song would not be directed to the sea of people listening, but rather her voice would be lifted up to the King who had captured her heart.

Maria bowed her head and silently asked her Lord to sing through her by the Holy Spirit. Before the first note, she raised her head and opened her eyes. Magnified a hundred times on the large monitors, her usually glistening, dark brown eyes shone with a fiery, white glow, the Fire of Heaven. Those who had never seen this manifestation were taken aback including Dan's VIP guests who now watched intently.

Alarmed, Director McDonald leaned into Dan. "What is this?"

"Prepare yourself."

Maria's voice was powerful, not in decibels, but in purity. Projected by her devotion to Jesus, her song saturated the Center with a heavenly sound filled with potential energy which suddenly erupted in powerful worship. The extraordinary seemed imminent as angels—heard by all—joined her.

Then, the sweet sound of a child's voice captured the crowd's attention. A little boy's pure, celestial resonance was heard above Maria's and the angels' voices. Everyone searched for its source, only to discover it came from a frail, Asian boy about six years old, lying on a stretcher. He seemed to have endured several chemotherapy rounds as evidenced by his hairless head.

369

The longer the boy sang, the stronger his body became, causing him to sing even more exuberantly. A grin stretched across his face for the first time in months. Color returned to his skin and his chalky eyes twinkled with brightness. Plumpness filled out his frame and strength revived his muscles. He removed the straps that had held him to his bed, swung his legs around and hopped off the gurney. He spun and glided with a partner only he and Maria could see, an angelic fellow worshipper.

Jumping and giggling, the boy ran to others who had been brought on beds. With innocence, he peered into each person's eyes and, when he touched them, the life that had filled him seemed to pour into their bodies, also. The gurney-ers—as someone in the crowd had dubbed them—danced in the aisles, rejoicing, singing the angels' song.

Elated, those who had just been healed and freed from their beds ran to people in wheelchairs, releasing them from disabilities and sicknesses. Thankfulness overflowed, and those no longer bound to a wheelchair also rejoiced, embracing one another, jumping for joy.

Next, the blind began to sing along with the angels. One by one, their eyes were opened in the natural and the spiritual to see the angelic host positioned around the auditorium. Overwhelmed with their new sight, they, too, whirled with angelic partners.

Military personnel in the center section suddenly shot up from their seats, awash in the Holy Spirit's healing power. Gone was physical pain caused by IEDs and bullets that had ripped their bodies. Those with burns observed baby-like tissue forming over previously ravaged skin. All with PTSD felt their minds and emotions becoming stable and whole—the horrific sounds, smells and scenes of war erased.

Hundreds in the Adara Center were freed from pain, anguish, and mental illness. A penetrating surge of hope and expectancy flowed throughout the crowd. Then, the three figures Gregor had spotted earlier left their place of silence against the back wall and began the walk down the main aisle toward the stage.

45

The Visitation

As the three figures began to move toward the stage, a self-initiated stillness abruptly commanded the audience. Noticing that the angelic choir had ceased singing, Maria slipped off the stage and took a seat with the team. Those who had been healed also quieted down. The three dressed in odd, monk-like clothing ignited curiosity, sending hushed murmurs through the crowd.

The Wallaces returned to the stage for a better vantage point. Jean studied the figures as they approached. "Is that ...?"

"Not ... sure ...."

At least a minute passed before the three strangers stood at the foot of the stage stairs. Recognizing them, Gregor and Jean lay prostrate on the platform. Their action was so sudden that some in the crowd postulated they had been shot. Director McDonald's instinct to take command of the situation, however, was momentarily suspended, and he remained speechless, frozen in his seat.

The three robed figures ascended the steps and stood with their backs to the audience. The two taller ones on either side of the third figure touched Gregor and Jean on the shoulders and pulled them to their feet. Before the Wallaces exited the stage, the middle figure stopped them and spoke, but the crowd could not hear the words.

Now, only the three mysterious characters in white robes stood center stage. They turned and faced the crowd. The two on either side of the middle man pushed back their hoods. Immediately, a glorious beauty radiated from their faces, and their robes glowed with the brightness of holiness.

The audience gasped in awe. One blazed as a reflection of his Master's love, uncovering his strength as a warrior, yet with perfect loyalty to his heavenly Commander. The other gleamed also, exuding the manifest value of God's Word and the eloquence of Truth.

The two mighty angels—Michael and Gabriel—now turned, bowing to the middle figure, whose robe looked as if it had been dipped in blood. That One lifted His head and gently pushed back the hood. As the fabric fell around his shoulders, a flash of intense, white light—far greater than the angels'—pierced the observers' hearts, invoking both dread and reverence.

The two archangels and the angelic choir cried out, "Holy, holy, holy is the Lord Almighty; the whole earth is full of His Glory." At the sound of their voices, the doorposts, windows and roof beams shook as the building filled with the sweet-smelling smoke of an unknown incense.

Non-citizens of Heaven, unprotected by the Blood of the Lamb, collapsed under the full weight of their sin as nothing was hidden in the midst of Truth standing before them. Terrified, they cried, "Woe to us! We are uncovered. We have seen the Lord of Heaven's armies, Jesus, the King of kings, and Lord of lords. Who is worthy to stand in the Risen Lamb's awesome presence?"

Those belonging to Him, sealed by His Spirit, worshipped in reverence and thankfulness for His gift of salvation.

The Son of God's face was unveiled—his hair of the purest white,

His eyes burning with fire, His face as bright as the sun and His robe glowing in holiness. He was fearful to behold. His voice was like the sound of golden trumpets announcing His Kingship, the call to war against evil and the judgment of His return.

Still, His words—and the tone He used—carried love, compassion, forgiveness and adoption. He embraced the crowd with the heart of a father, watching and waiting for his prodigal child to return home. Even the warning to heed His Word, declared the invitation of Love.

Open your eyes to see and your ears to hear and understand. Time is short. The Great Darkness is about to be released. Lucifer, the father of lies in whom there is no truth, that great enemy of God, will deceive the whole world.

Put away all things of this world that ensnare you, for blessed are those who abide in Me with a pure heart. The one who is victorious over the seduction of this world will be dressed in white, and I will never blot his name from the Book of Life, but I will confess his name before My Father and before His angels. Only those who walk in Spirit and Truth by doing the will of My Father will enter My Kingdom.

Jesus' words pierced the hearts of many, and they softly wept. Dan glanced at Director McDonald, trying to get a read on him. So far, there was no indication that his stony heart had cracked.

Now, Jesus encouraged the ones who had already answered the call to gather souls in the Final Awakening.

My gift of love is the greatest of all the gifts, greater than prophecy or signs and wonders. Give sight to those who are blind to Truth and proclaim liberty to those chained in darkness. My mercy and compassion will bring comfort to those broken and grieving in the gutters of this world.

Know you will be reviled and persecuted on My account. Take courage and do not grow weary. Rejoice and be glad, for your reward is great in Heaven, for so they persecuted My messengers who went before you.

Life is in reproduction, not stagnation; therefore, reproduce, making disciples. Never attempt to bottle My power. If you try to contain the treasures of My Kingdom, My power will not rest with you. I give to you freely, now freely give. I love you, My children. Take the Good News to the world, and we will rejoice together at the wedding feast.

Jesus looked up, stretched his arms out to his sides and cried with a loud voice, *Father, just as You are in Me and I AM in You, may these also live in Me so that the world may believe that You have sent Me.*

For the second time that day, the bright laser-like beam penetrated the roof of the Adara Center, this time focusing on the platform just behind Jesus. A heavenly fog surrounded the light.

Michael and Gabriel stood to the left and right of the radiant holiness. Jesus took several steps back into the beam and He and the brightness were One as He is the Light. Then, the Son of God spoke, admonishing all to run to Him before directing Gabriel, *Take a horn and fill it with water.*

Gabriel held a golden ram's horn, as water from the cloud of splendor filled it to the brim. Then, the faithful messenger of God stretched out his arm and held the horn high in the air as his Master spoke.

This is the cleansing water of My Blood, washing the Bride and making her ready to receive her Groom. Pour it out. Wash her clean.

Gabriel tipped the horn and the water slowly poured from the golden shofar. Now, Jesus' voice was like the roar of rushing water and, as He spoke, crackling lightning and loud claps of thunder erupted.

Those who do not run to this cleansing water will be left to endure trials and tribulations as never seen upon the earth. Worse than Sodom and Gomorrah, worse than Noah's time, wickedness will abound without measure. Woe to you who do not run to the water.

This mercy awakening will flow liberally only once as the horn will not be refilled. Run to the cleansing water while it freely flows before the Restrainer leaves the earth, for then the end begins.

The harvest is Mine and Lucifer will not have it, yet you must choose. Make no mistake; I do not sit passively upon My throne, waiting for souls to come back to Me. I actively pursue all people; thus, you are without excuse. All who choose to reject Me must endure an eternity apart from Me, never to know a morsel of My presence as they had enjoyed on earth, even in their sin.

Gabriel obediently stood holding the golden shofar. As the water cascaded from the horn, more of the Lord's majesty was revealed and the brilliance of the cloud intensified.

Those who reject Me will never see Light again. They have sown sin and will reap sin's reward. Stubborn and unrepentant hearts live in total darkness, but surrendered and repentant hearts dwell in the Holy City where the pure Light of Heaven shines.

I AM the First and the Last, and the Living One. I died, and behold I AM alive forevermore, and I have the keys of Death and Hades. To you who overcome, I will grant to sit with Me on My throne, as I also overcame and sat down with My Father on His throne.

Within the mist, crackling power produced jutting lightning bolts, followed by deep thunderous rumbles—an atmosphere so frightening, many covered their heads in terror.

Those who dared to look saw four heavenly creatures appear underneath the radiance of His Glory. The creatures had wings and eyes all around, and their countenance glowed like red-hot coals. Their outstretched wings covered the breadth of the platform and beyond, through the building's walls. Lightning of every color of the rainbow flashed and spiked throughout the Adara Center, followed by deep, rolling thunders. From within the brilliance, another booming voice spoke, shaking the complex and the earth beneath.

Listen to My Son. He paid a great price to redeem you from darkness. As you live out Our Truth and believe in the Son who died and rose again, you are eternally changed from sinfulness to holiness and through His Blood, you are blessed in Our presence forevermore. We have hidden no good thing from you. We have not given Our Word as burdensome commandments, but as a clear revelation of the reality of truth and lies, life and death.

Yes, you fight against an enemy, yet if We are with you, who can be victorious over you? Stay close to Our bosom in prayer. Listen to the Son and obey Him, for He is the Word, the embodiment of Love and Truth.

The crowd cowered in fear as the holiness and magnificence of the God of the Universe seemed as if it would consume them all. Once again, multiple blades of crackling lightning burst forth, extending out of the Lord's splendor and through the building.

The loud sound of metal ripping above them drew the crowd's attention upward. The ceiling of the auditorium appeared to peel open. The manifestation of God's Glory suddenly retracted, curling upward toward Heaven and leaving behind a faint mist of holiness.

As the four living creatures began moving their wings, the mist gusted throughout the Center. Another thrust of the mighty wings against the air caused a rushing wind, and the sweeping movement lifted them upward toward their heavenly home. Before the very eyes of the watchful crowd, the Father, the Light, the cloud and the creatures vanished.

There was silence. Thousands in the Adara Center were bathed in the lingering remnants of the cloud of brilliance. The creation instinctively thirsted for the Creator's life as it had been given in the beginning. Only His holy presence could satisfy the inherent longing for oneness with the Life-Giver, the Eternal God who had paid the unimaginable price of redeeming creatures not worthy of His salvation.

Minutes passed in quietness, giving those who wanted intimacy with Jesus time to commune. When the mist faded, the time needed had passed.

Despite their visits to Heaven and talking with Jesus face to face, the team was just as stunned as the other witnesses. In their hearts, they knew that even after this phenomenal encounter, there would remain those among the 10,000 whose eyes would persist in blindness. However, attuned to the Father's great heart of mercy, they knew that as long as these had breath, there was hope for their redemption.

The team looked to Gregor, asking wordlessly, *What now?* He merely shrugged, then stood and walked up the stage steps. Most of the audience remained silent, waiting for Gregor's instructions, but some murmured, filled with anger and disbelief. It took a moment for him to find his voice as it was overwhelming, standing in the same spot where the presence of the Lord had been.

Gregor had stepped to the microphone to dismiss the people when the main entrance doors at the back were flung open. The sound of the heavy metal hitting the hard, brick walls magnified in the quietness.

Everyone turned to see the source of the commotion. A young man was yelling and running down the center aisle toward the front platform. He stopped for a second, realizing he had abruptly interrupted, then sprinted for the stage.

He shouted breathlessly, but his words couldn't be understood. Gregor motioned for him to come to the microphone. Skipping steps, the young man bolted up to the platform. It was Diego.

"You're not gonna b'lieve this!" He could barely speak through his panting—half from excitement and half from running. He bent over as he caught his breath. "There's a ... a giant cross of fire ... it's above the Center ... gotta be a thousand feet tall!"

* * *

Lucifer sat with his head between his hands, taking in the crushing blow. The knowledge of his ultimate destiny erupted in multiple lesions, hatred oozing from the gashes. This heavy defeat, heaped upon other recent losses would have pressed him even deeper into darkness, if that were possible. He dug in with resolve to add to *his* book as many souls as possible. He falsely hoped that adding names would ease his torment before the Holy One threw him into the lake of fire. The Council came to order as Lucifer addressed his cohorts.

"Using every inch of our newly granted latitude, we will answer the Holy One's signs and wonders with our own! Our strategy ... nothing new ... deceives multitudes." He let out an evil cackle.

Grunts of agreement circulated amongst Council members.

"Need I speak the words? But I must ... I detest the Nazarene ... I abhor the Father ... I loathe the Fire of Heaven who dwells in man!" Each pronouncement of hatred perversely refreshed him in his own lie. He paced.

"The Holy One knows my capabilities, but the world has not yet seen my full fury. We will never extinguish that damnable blazing symbol of His sacrifice and resurrection that now burns over D.C., but we can snuff little firebrands in the hearts of the creatures He loves so much! Search the planet and snatch any seed of the Fire's kindling across the earth before it can take root. This is *my* kingdom! Go! Destroy ... and let the fires of hell extinguish the Fire of Heaven!"

COMING SOON
The Fiery Unveiling
Book Two in the Fiery Awakening Series

The Holy One's Visitation to the Adara Center in the heart of D.C. had officially propelled the Final Awakening to the forefront of the nation. The towering cross over the capital remains as a blazing reminder that the Fire of Heaven has come to war for lost souls and prepare the Bride for her Groom. Lucifer and the Council of Darkness are not about to let Heaven's last demonstration of the God's power go unanswered without counterfeit signs of their own.

In fear of losing control of the U.S. government, Lucifer schemes to maintain his power over America, a notable obstacle in his plan to dominate the nations. Senator Dan Taylor fights evil head-on. His colleagues on the Hill press hard against him, along with the clandestine Deep State. From their perspective, the menacing Final Awakening message engulfs the ignorant masses with intolerant dogma and conservative morals, creating a looming threat to their agenda—birthed by the Council of Darkness.

Even so, the Adara Center is in full swing true to its heavenly charter, equipping laborers for the harvest of souls. In extra measure, Lucifer utilizes yet another groomed organization to quench the Fire—the United Alliance of Religious Leadership that officially views the Final Awakening as the Final Apostasy. While Lucifer assumes all is back on track, unbeknownst to him, God has planned another unveiling. Ground zero: Nashville.

Devoted to their Savior, Jesus, and steadfast to complete their assignment, harvesters will endure persecution and some will give their lives while taking the Final Awakening across America.